RORY'S BOYS

Alan Clark was educated in Scotland, where he wrote his first children's novel at the age of twelve. He dropped out of King's College London and landed in the advertising business in which, as a copywriter and creative director, he has won several international awards. In recent times he has digressed into travel journalism, specialising in the western Mediterranean, and has also compiled a quiverful of celebrity profiles, ranging from film stars and theatrical knights to bishops and duchesses. He finally got around to writing this novel when Sue Townsend bluntly informed him that he had wasted his life so far.

RORY'S BOYS

Alan Clark

Arcadia Books Ltd
15–16 Nassau Street
London w1w 7ab

www.arcadiabooks.co.uk

First published in the United Kingdom by Bliss Books,
an imprint of Arcadia Books, 2011
Copyright © Alan Clark 2011

Alan Clark has asserted his moral right to be identified as the author of this work in accordance with the Copyright, Designs and Patents Act, 1988.

A catalogue record for this book is available from the British Library

ISBN 978-1-906413-88-0

Edited, designed and typeset by Discript Limited, London wc2n 4bn
Printed in Scotland by Bell & Bain Limited

Arcadia Books supports English PEN, the fellowship of writers who work together to promote literature and its understanding. English PEN upholds writers' freedoms in Britain and around the world, challenging political and cultural limits on free expression. To find out more, visit www.englishpen.org or contact
English PEN, 6–8 Amwell Street, London ec1r 1uq

Arcadia Books distributors are as follows:

in the UK and elsewhere in Europe:
Turnaround Publishers Services
Unit 3, Olympia Trading Estate
Coburg Road
London n22 6tz

in the USA and Canada:
Dufour Editions Inc.
PO Box 7
Chester Springs, PA 19425

in Australia/New Zealand:
The GHR Press
PO Box 7109,
McMahons Point
Sydney 2060

in South Africa:
Jacana Media (Pty) Ltd.
PO Box 291784
Melville 2109
Johannesburg

Arcadia Books is the *Sunday Times* Small Publisher of the Year

For Robert and Sue, without whom...

ONE

I suppose I've never quite dealt with the fact that I owe my existence to a pimple. A spot, a zit or, as they call it in my native Scotland, a plook.

It's a cautionary tale. The plook had popped inwards, you see, that was the trouble. My father's first bride, on radiant honeymoon in Kenya, couldn't cope with the horror of a blemish and had simply squeezed too soon. Blood poisoning had sneaked in and, before anyone realized she was ill, she'd slithered down the side of an elephant and been stiff as a board by the time they'd got her to Nairobi. Thanks to this bizarre death, my eager mother had sprinted down the aisle to become the second Mrs Blaine and receive some of the most socially prestigious seed north of Hadrian's Wall. Then, hey presto, there I was.

'Let that be a wee lesson,' Miss Elspeth Wishart had warned, when my teenage face began turning into the sebum repository of Perthshire. Miss Wishart, the school matron from whom I had few secrets, had repaid my confidence by regularly thrusting the tragic bride at me in the same way she delivered my weekly dose of syrup of figs. But the guys in my dorm took a different view.

'For Christ's sake Blaine, why don't you just splat them like everybody else?' they'd groaned during my nightly ritual with the Clearasil. 'They're like fucking fried eggs.'

Yet I never had. Perhaps I'd felt that, in the circumstances, the least I could do was to give some of them a home. But it's not a very edifying reason for existence, is it? Of course the act of conception is often a matter of luck: the car marooned in the snowdrift, the Babycham too many, the one feisty sperm that can swim like Esther Williams. But how can it be that the creation of Rory Blaine, gorgeous and gifted, was not part of some great celestial plan but merely the by-product of a blocked pore? As a reason for entering therapy, it's got to be right up there with Hamlet and his dad or Oedipus and his mum. So I have.

My therapist is a big fat chick in expensive shoes; I call her Ms Prada. The shoes imply that I, or rather BUPA, is paying her far too much and I kind of feel that people in the caring professions should look just a wee bit threadbare. But once a week I go to a room with eau-de-nil walls and a droopy azalea where she dribbles my psyche around on her shiny toe-caps. It seems I'm both clinically narcissistic and suffering from low self-esteem. This paradox appears to be very common which pissed me off because I'd assumed I'd be a pretty interesting case; a response which Ms Prada said merely proved her diagnosis. She has this weird high-pitched voice which makes you wonder if her vast shape could be due to helium ingestion and not chocolate éclairs. This week she declared that one way of dealing with emotional pain is by metabolizing it into art. So every day from now on, I'm supposed to write my thoughts onto this PC. It's to be strictly stream-of-consciousness stuff.

'Expect plenty of rocks and whirlpools,' squeaked Ms Prada, who's never shy of an obvious metaphor, 'but there will also be stretches of cool translucent water which will help carry you towards the self-cognition you seek.'

Well babe, today there was a real whopper to metabolize. Today was my forty-fifth birthday. So now I'm well and truly middle-aged, though frankly I don't yet see that concept as a goer. Rory Blaine, middle-aged? I don't think so, do you? Too many adjustments would be necessary, none of which I feel prepared to make. I believe in sticking to what I'm good at and I'll be shite at getting older.

Anyway, extensive research suggests that no such image-repositioning is yet called for. I'm still a product with a satisfied public. The whiff of Issey Miyake wafting off my dick this morning proved it. Luckily its source had done a bunk in the wee small hours, cooing something about being slotted for the first flight to Malaga. I'd met him online. He was five feet six, built like Selfridges and a stranger to the polysyllable. In short, Perfection. But Perfection had turned out to be a trolley dolly who lived in East Acton with his mum and a whippet called Bruce. He was devoted to his mum; she always put condoms in his pocket when he went out on a date. I'd opened a bottle of Chablis Premier Cru to impress him.

'Ooh, it's a bit tart,' he'd giggled into his glass. 'Just like me.'

Christ, another fake. I'd binned the empty bottle along with the Post-It note with his mobile number inside the outline of a heart. This is where you'll expect me to write how empty I felt after another disappointing and meaningless encounter. But I didn't. Not any more. Now, it had become a bit like when the cleaning lady appeared. I was quite pleased to have the company for three hours but then, with the job done and the necessary materials put back in the cupboard, I was more than happy to see the front door close again.

Today as usual I'd looked in *The Times* birthday column. I'm not there of course, which depresses me. Every year, I visualize myself in that élitist wee paragraph, sandwiched between the TV gardener and the transgender activist but sometimes a new name has shouldered its way in, someone much younger than me, which depresses me even more. I wonder how I might have been described. 'Rory Blaine, advertising executive, 45.' Not quite worth a fanfare on the nation's breakfast tables, I suppose. Once, I'd dreamed that some day it might say, 'Rory Blaine, writer', but I'd long ago dumped my childhood sweetheart and let myself be seduced by the tawdry old slapper of advertising; all fur coat and no knickers. Now here I was, under therapist's orders, trying to write my way towards some sort of contentment. Maybe if I'd stayed faithful way back then, it wouldn't have been necessary.

Oh shite, lighten up Rory. This just isn't like you. Most people who know you would wet themselves.

'You're like the fucking Andrex puppy aren't you?' my secretary had once slurred at our Christmas party. 'Nose into everything, demanding attention, doing cute little tricks. Adorable in your way, but such a relief when you trot back to your basket.'

I waited a decent interval and down-sized her.

So Ms Prada is my dirty wee secret and will remain so. Of course it was a bit more than the blocked pimple in my pedigree which had led me to the eau-de-nil room with the droopy azalea. As Will The Quill once wrote, lately I have, yet wherefore I know not, lost all my mirth. Well not quite all, but I'd certainly been getting more 'Miltons' than usual. That's my word for feeling low, in tribute to Milton Keynes, the most miserable place on earth; endless, rain-soaked boulevards from which it seems impossible to escape. So I reckoned that maybe I needed to pull myself apart a bit, check out the inner workings, spring-clean the cogs and wheels. I'd never taken medication for it, never would; the only chemical I'd ever allow to mess with my mind came from Waitrose in pretty dark green bottles. Probably I just needed someone to talk to, which I couldn't imagine doing with anybody I knew. Not really talk, you know? When I visualize my buddies, they've got a glass in one hand and a Blackberry in the other. I couldn't really see them doing tea and sympathy. Rory Blaine and the blues? A most unlikely couple, they'd say.

But Rory Blaine and charm would be a much more recognizable pairing. Old biddies queue up for me to help them cross the road. Bull-dyke traffic wardens nearly weep at the sad explanation of why my meter's overrun. I've worked hard on the charm because I couldn't, to be painfully honest here, be called handsome. My features are makeshift at best, as if God had arranged them quickly when He wanted to get to the golf course.

But then I discovered the power of the facelift that comes from within. I long since decided I wasn't going to be plain and so I'm not. Besides, I've got the hair, Rory's famous golden mane. I wear it unfashionably long but instead of feminizing me it has, as I calculated, the opposite effect; underpinning the rugged masculinity of the complete package. Through a world of Roundheads, I stride like a Cavalier. The rest of the body's holding up too; stomach flat as Norfolk, arse still like two new-blown balloons. No sign yet of the dreaded swagging effect that makes it look like an Austrian blind. The gym is boring, but it works. What would have happened to a generation of gay men if the fitness revolution hadn't come along? There's a Ph.D. in that for someone.

Today was Saturday, thank God, and I didn't have to go into Blaine Rampling. The rockier economy was committing GBH on our profit margin, clients were cutting budgets, I'd had to let people go, good people. I'd even wondered about re-mortgaging the flat. I'd been the main man for nearly twenty years, but now I could feel the kids at my neck, their breath stinking of ambition, more aggressive than I ever was. Thatcher's children. Not a pretty sight. Last week, my junior partners had slammed a document on my desk; what they called a strategy for survival. They say we're not so cool anymore and in this business that's death. Quite often these days, they'd explain something to me, as if they didn't expect me to still be on their planet. I didn't like that. Smug wee shites.

I never hung around the flat much at weekends. It'd been designed by this uber-chic Brazilian queen, everything from the tinted windows to the bog-roll holder, so that it almost felt like his place rather than mine. Before Devonshire Street, there had been a loft in Soho, a studio in Chelsea and a penthouse in St Katherine's Dock, I think it was. Not sure; I've moved around a lot and they've all sort of blurred into one image of stripped-back brick and recessed light switches you can never find when you're pissed. The image is furnished by various faces, a few of whom I'd even allowed to park their toothbrushes for a while. Usually it'd just been for a few weeks or months; though one time a strange brush had nestled against mine in the tumbler for a whole summer. It'd never quite looked right to me though.

I pulled on a black T-shirt and my Versace jeans; waist thirty-two and holding. I put the sheets on the boil-wash programme and fed the cat. I couldn't remember if I'd last done it yesterday or the day before. The cat rubbed against my ankles when it sensed I was going out again. I felt guilty about the cat. I'd stumbled into Harrods pet shop after too good a lunch and my judgement was impaired. Sod's law dictated it was the one cat in a million searching for commitment, which I didn't feel able to give right now. It'd just have to butch-up. There was only one card on the mat. Miss Elspeth Wishart, bless her. Nobody I know sends cards these days. No doubt my email box would be as crammed as a Primark sale, but I decided to check it later. Out in Devonshire Street, the sun pierced into the hangover like a lance. A horn tooted, a hand waved.

'How's the plumbing?' yelled a small man in a big Maserati.

It was my genito-urinary doctor. His name is Rod. Honestly. The other day he'd shoved steel rods down my cock to widen my urethral stricture. It needs doing about twice a year and it's not pleasant; but Rod distracts me with gossip about his celebrity patients. Apparently the worst case of haemorrhoids ever seen resides in the arsehole of the most viciously homophobic columnist in the tabloid press. To understand is to forgive, Rod says.

Don't laugh, but I really moved to Marylebone to be handy for my specialists. Over the years I've built up a whole team so I've now got one for every part of my anatomy. I call them my mechanics and their job is to keep me in racing condition. I once read about the importance of listening to your body and now I've got the hearing of the blind. The slightest creak, gurgle or rattle and I pull myself over into the relevant consulting room to be tinkered with. So Rod looks after my stricture, my recurrent anal fissure and what he calls my 'recreational collateral-damage'. Other mechanics have responsibility for, *inter alia*, my mitral valve murmur, deviated septum, gastric reflux, grumpy back and a genetic tendency towards hernias. Whilst, on the outside, my body suggests low mileage and one careful owner, it probably wouldn't pass much of an independent inspection. It's travelled to too many places it shouldn't have gone. Luckily, in my world, it's only the chassis that matters.

I had a croissant and a decaf latte in Staff of Life, currently the coolest organic bakery on Marylebone High Street. I chatted up the cute Latino waiter I'd been cruising for weeks and flicked through the papers. War, famine, unemployment, some bimbo's breast implants that went wrong and left her looking like Ann Widdecombe. Depressing news about depressing people. Don't know why I bother. You've got to keep your distance from all that shite, create your own wee world and have one hell of a time in it. Unless of course it's something that directly affects you; then you've got to gallop out over your drawbridge and give the bastards hell.

I wondered how to fill the hours before my party tonight. I was taking a few of the gang to The Ivy. I couldn't really afford it, but it wouldn't have been wise to let them know that. Unfortunately, the usual time-killing notion now broke in, squatted and couldn't be shifted. I told myself I shouldn't, then reminded myself it was my birthday after all. Half an hour later my Merc was parked by a row of seedy railway arches in east London. A sign depicted two thonged gladiators locked in sweaty combat. *Lose yourself in The Catacombs* it suggested; advice which I confess to taking at least once a week. I'd confessed it to Ms Prada in fact and she'd suggested I might consider adding the sex addiction module to our therapy structure. It would cost extra of course.

In the steam room I cast myself out along the tiled bench and waited for a nibble. Though it was a bit early, there was a steady traffic moving between the steam, the sauna, and the jacuzzis. Some of the regulars were in. The furtive, pot-bellied ones were often married and would be safely back in Pinner by tea-time. I always gave them a wide berth or you'd find yourself trapped in a conversation about decking. I avoided the screamers too, who tended to be rent or silly shop-girls. I looked for the relaxed, blokeish sort, the ones who didn't need to be defined by their sexuality. The sort I consider myself to be.

I was on nodding terms with several of today's selection; in fact I'd had a few of them. The young black barrister was in; the one with the cock like an ebony table leg who'd started shouting 'Fuck me Your Honour' at our climactic moment. I was half-wondering about a second round, something I usually steered clear of, when I saw him disappear with a John Prescott lookalike. I always felt a bit miffed when an 'ex' went off with a real minger; it somehow sullied what we'd had together, however brief that might have been.

You can't see very clearly in the steam room. A forty-watt bulb struggles like a candle in a fog. When the door opens, you can maybe judge somebody's age and condition by their silhouette against the brighter light outside. If the steam thins out, you might get sharper definition, a bit more detail. But facial features usually stay as smudgy as an Impressionist; which of course doesn't always matter, depending on what you have in mind. The door opened now and a Saggy came in. I cursed myself for getting here too early. The younger guys mostly came in the late afternoon; till then their granddads colonized the place. Tits to their knees, bellies like concertinas but libidos tragically unimpaired. I'd sworn to myself that I'd never be a Saggy. At some point in the dim and distant, I'd know when to walk away from all this. I'd know when I'd become like milk on the turn and I'd deal with it, no problem. The Saggy leaned on a stick, flopped down near me and started to play with himself. I reeled in my body and closed my eyes. The stick tapped on the tiles as he abandoned hope and hobbled out.

When I looked again there was a new presence in the vacated spot. Well-built, hairy. Mediterranean or Arabic maybe. I stretched out along the bench again, letting one leg dangle onto the floor. In a few seconds, other toes brushed mine. I twitched them in reply. A hand reached out and pinched one of my nipples.

'Great nips, mate,' said an estuary voice, young, unabashed. I'd tried dropping my own glottal stops for a while but it doesn't really work with a Scottish accent.

'Like them?' I asked. 'Go for it then.'

Soft lips started moving expertly across my chest. The breath was sweet but the skin smelt of fucking Issey Miyake yet again. I let out a slow sigh. This was what I came here for, to this grubby armpit of London, to this clinical place. The young guy nuzzled my ear and stroked my hair but even this close the face remained featureless. Three or four intruders had drifted in.

ALAN CLARK

'You wanna go play downstairs?' he said.

I hesitated. The Catacombs is a fast-sex establishment where you can either eat in or take-away. I always prefer the latter, on the same snobbish basis that I'd never actually sit down in a McDonalds. But I had the party tonight.

'No problem,' I said. 'I'm a bit tight for time though.'

'I'm a bit tight too,' purred the brazen voice, rising from the bench. 'See you down there, stud.'

I took a long slow shower then headed to the top of the staircase leading to the basement floor. They were steep, slippery stairs, as if designed to make you think twice. This was the moment when my gastric reflux problem usually kicked in. Down below, in stygian gloom, were your actual catacombs, a maze of corridors lined with ironically-dubbed 'rest rooms'. Some doors were firmly shut; from behind them came cries and whispers, shouts and exhortations. Others rooms, though occupied, had doors left open at varying angles of provocation. Some sat with hands clasped, knees together, eyes lowered, demure as a wall-flower at a dance. Others displayed themselves sensuously, lewdly even, their positions indicating what sort of pleasures they were willing to provide. The catacombs were a stuffy place, heavy with sweat and amyl nitrate, a sort of perverse catwalk where approval was gained by your lack of clothing; your audience lined up along the walls or peering out from the wee rooms. I'd learnt not to be daunted by an impassive reception. Only the old or the ugly, who had nothing to lose, took the risk of revealing admiration. But it wasn't until I caught an eye whose brow was raised in a question mark, when I noticed a spine straighten or felt a hand brush against my passing thigh that I could be sure today's appearance had wowed the punters yet again and my intestines would finish their salsa and leave the floor. Today though, at forty-five no less, I strolled along the catwalk with the carefree arrogance of a man who can still pull a real cutie. A dark-skinned arm waved at me from a few doors along. Today there was no need to feel lonely.

Ms Prada has asked me to examine the possibility that casual sexual encounters are, as she puts it, speed-bumps on the road to full emotional maturity. But as I surrendered to the furry, perfumed embrace, I reminded myself what crap that was. This was not an addiction. It was not demeaning, it was life-enhancing. Okay, so maybe you didn't know, or care, what his name was,

8

what his dreams were. Maybe it could be a bit mechanical, embarrassing even; but that was usually just before and after. During those central exhilarating minutes it could be ecstatic. There were no barriers or betrayals, no expectations or let-downs. I would be refuelled with confidence in myself and in the essential beauty of mankind. And I always offered to buy them a cup of coffee afterwards, even if praying they'd refuse. But during that short glorious fusion it would seem like the most potent communication I'd ever experienced. Yeah, yeah, Ms Prada, honesty on these pages, right? Yes, there were times, the bad days, when I did it for comfort, like some people buy Cadbury's Creme Eggs. And yes I'd known other, deeper forms, a couple of times anyway, but they'd never worked out for me, so why hurt myself again? This would do.

And God, did this guy know what he was about. Though he'd dimmed the light in the tiny room I could see him properly at last. Arab. A bit older than I'd thought. Twenty-five even. Bit too athletic; all thrashing limbs and a running commentary. In loud porno-speak, he enunciated both the services he had to offer and those he hoped to receive. I felt obliged to answer, but I'm oddly inhibited with all that stuff. The rooms were separated by partitions, thin as Rolf Harris's wobble-board, which didn't even reach to the ceiling. I could clearly hear the progress of neighbouring encounters and presumably vice-versa. So when the Arab barked a demand that I give it to him doggy-style on the floor, I snapped 'on all fours, bitch' as quietly as possible without sacrificing the necessary authority. Nevertheless a familiar voice vaulted over the partition.

'Rory Blaine, is that you in there?'

'Jeremy?'

'I thought it was you, you randy old sod. Listen, love, don't you even think about that movement or you'll be screaming on my table by Monday.'

Jeremy is the mechanic responsible for my bad-tempered back.

'Oh, right then, Jeremy,' was all I could think of to reply.

'Lie flat out and let him get on top. He's not too heavy is he?'

I looked down at the Arab who had shrunk back into a corner and did indeed look smaller than he had a minute ago.

'Don't think so.'

'Remember, love, you might pass for thirty-something in this light, but your spine's forty-five today. Hope you got my e-card.'

I turned back to the Arab, raised my eyebrows and scratched my head like Stan Laurel. The Arab gave a nervous smile, then reached out and turned the dimmer switch full up, flooding me in a pool of sickly yellowish light. The smile flinched. There was a long pause before he spoke.

'Er, listen mate... look, gonna leave it.'

'Leave it?

'Yeah. Put it on hold for tonight.' said the Arab. Another pause. I could hear his brain working. 'Started feeling a bit shivery. Tickle in me throat too. Might be going down with the flu. Best not to pass it on, right?'

'No big deal,' I said. 'Want to give me your mobile?'

'Sorry mate. Got nicked yesterday. Bastards.' By now, his fingers were on the door handle and his towel wrapped round him, tight as a second skin. 'Maybe check you out in here again sometime.'

'Sure,' I said.

'See you later.'

The Arab closed the door behind him. For a moment I stood still in my spotlight, then flicked the room back to near-darkness and sat down on the bench on which Issey Miyake still lingered. A new emotion had landed on my plate. I began toying with it but realized it was going to be too hard to swallow.

After a few minutes, I fled the sweaty cell and turned back towards the staircase. I wanted to grab somebody, anybody. But the corridors were deserted. Sweat and amyl still hung in the air, but it was like the *Marie Celeste*. I knew this maze like I knew the thread veins round my nostrils, but I suddenly lost all sense of direction. One turning was a dead end; another led me to a fire exit. I retraced my steps trying to find the staircase. I pushed at the half-open doors of cubicles, one after another. Empty. Empty. Empty. I started to feel a wee bit sick. I was half-running round a corner when I crashed into Jeremy, the osteopath.

'Good time then, you old ram?' said Jeremy with the usual shifty grin that made him look like a timeshare tout in Benidorm.

'Where the hell is everyone?' I said, trying to calm my breathing.

'Upstairs for the new afternoon cabaret,' said Jeremy. 'Who'd have thought the post-Millennium gay community would still be dazzled by the sight of sequins? Drag or shag, it's no contest. I just came back down for my tit clamps. You coming up, love?'

'You lead on,' I said, searching for my smile so I could graft it back on. But upstairs I turned for the locker room and got dressed. The old Chinese queen on the front desk wished me a nice evening on behalf of the management.

Outside, the April sunshine had given way to drizzle. I got into the Merc, and sat for a while watching the raindrops stipple the windscreen. Then I drove slowly west towards civilization. As I waited by the lights at Clerkenwell, I saw the Arab, mobile clamped to ear, heading into a gay bar. The numbness inside my head was dispelled by a red raw anger.

'Fuck you!' I yelled out of the window. The Arab turned, confused for a moment, then gave me a cheery two fingers.

'Hey, what did you do in the war, Daddy?' he shouted back.

Cars behind me were tooting. I wrenched the Merc half onto the pavement, leapt out and grabbed him by the lapels.

'Listen to me, you wee shite. This Daddy was in a war once. About twenty-five years ago, when I was even younger than you. There weren't many on our side at first; maybe just a few hundred here and there who stood up to be counted. And there were millions against us. David and Goliath. So we were really bloody brave, don't you think? Some of us actually got killed too; beaten up, left in gutters to die. Others only lost their jobs, had their kids taken away or got chucked out by their loving families. So why do you think we went through all that? You going to tell me?'

The Arab shook his head, the sweat beading his brow along with the raindrops.

'Because we wanted to know what it felt like to stand tall, not be cowed or scared any more. But it was also to make sure that kids like you wouldn't have to go through the same crap one day.'

The Arab found his voice, though it was a bit strangulated as his feet were half off the ground.

'So I'm supposed to build you a fuckin' statue in Trafalgar Square?'

'No, I don't expect gratitude. Not from your self-centred wee generation. But if it hadn't been for the likes of me, this bar wouldn't exist, or that sauna or your financial advisers with their pretty pink mortgages. So I'll live without your thanks, but I'm sure as hell not going to take any shite from a piece of gay-ghetto trash like you.'

The Arab looked me hard in the eye, curling one of the fat lips I'd been enjoying on my nipples only an hour ago.

'That's history, mate. It's our time now. You've had yours. Get over it.'

I put him down before I killed him. This wasn't completely beyond the bounds of possibility; Ms Prada had also urged me to attach her anger management module to our therapy structure but I'd turned it down. I'd been controlling my lousy temper all my life and I did so now. I twisted the car back onto the road and roared off. Then, for the second time that afternoon, I lost my bearings. I tore down unrecognized streets and got trapped in cul-de-sacs until I found myself on the Embankment.

It was raining quite hard now and blowing a gale, but I pulled in. I needed some fresh air. The odours of the Arab and of the room where he'd walked out on me were still in my nostrils. I walked along the river, trying to breathe deeply, trying to fumigate from my memory his expression as he'd turned up the light. But the dear old gastric reflux began to go into overdrive again, gnawing at my diaphragm in its familiar way. By Cleopatra's Needle, I flung myself against the river wall and projected the contents of my stomach over the side. A shout came from far below. Still retching, I looked down and saw a wino sprawled on the steps that led to the water's edge. There was vomit all down his front.

'Christ, I'm sorry,' I croaked. 'I'll buy you a new shirt.'

'No worries man,' said the wino, 'that's mine. Yours is there; all over Jonathan Livingston Seagull.'

Among the soggy flotsam of plastic coffee cups and take-away chicken boxes, a frantic bird was trying to flap its wings.

'Chill, man,' said the wino. 'I'll piss on it in a minute. That'll do the trick. Uric acid has a hundred applications. It's what they use in Sketchley's.'

'Thank heavens, I thought I'd...'

'Well, there you go man,' smiled the wino. 'Nothing's ever as lousy as it seems, is it? However shitty your day, some little thing comes along to restore your faith in an essentially benevolent Providence.'

By the time I got back to Devonshire Street, it was getting dark.

The flat was silent, apart from the delighted squeak of the cat as it wrapped itself pathetically around my ankles. I picked it up and sat with it on the sofa. It thought Christmas had come early, nuzzling its furry chin against mine. I really must get round to giving it a name.

I sat for a while in the dusk, watching the lights in the street come on, listening to the traffic and the fragments of other lives that floated up through the window; shouts, laughter, obscenities. In another hour or two, I'd step out there again, all dressed-up, and join the quite nice people I'd invited to The Ivy. I would kiss the cheeks, slap the backs, tell the jokes as they expected me to. Later, we'd all go up in the glass lift to the private members' club for coffee and liqueurs. I called them my friends and they, I guess, called me theirs. It's what we all do, isn't it? Except I wasn't really sure what it was supposed to mean, just how far it was supposed to go. Never been great at working that one out. Ms Prada says relationships are a major area I need to work on. Big news babe.

Today I'd become forty-five years old and been sexually rejected for the first time in my life. I felt fairly close to a major 'Milton' and I couldn't let that happen, not tonight, not at The Ivy's prices. But Ms Prada wasn't the only therapy I was concealing from the world in which I moved. I, Rory Blaine, am a closet folk-singer of traditional Scottish songs. I didn't claim that great a voice but I liked to think that what it lacked in finesse it made up for in feeling. I went and dragged my old guitar from its hiding place under the bed. The cat lolled on the arm of the sofa and patiently sat through *Annie Laurie*, *Ae Fond Kiss* and *The Skye Boat Song*. As I sang, I looked across at Miss Elspeth Wishart's card, a predictably cheesy view of lochs and mountains. And somehow, after that, I felt a bit better.

It was almost dark in the flat now; only the distant wink of the washing machine reminding me that last night's sheets were now cleansed from sin. I switched on my mobile and left a message for Ms Prada, asking if she could squeeze me in on Monday. Then I checked my voicemails, and lo the prophecy of the wino on the Embankment came to pass. There were ten of them. The first nine were birthday greetings of a coarse or consolatory nature. But the tenth was about to change everything.

TWO

Today I went to dig up Granny. It's thirty years now since I buried the old bitch alive, way down deep with a stake through the heart. So it was with a certain queasiness that I found myself going to open the tomb armed only with a box of Belgian chocolates

Not that her Ladyship had exactly rested in peace. From time to time over the years, she'd reared up at me in the papers or on the box, each time more barking, each time more mocked. I'd always turn the page quickly or grab the remote but she'd still thrash around my consciousness for days. Sometimes I'd even go off my food, turn down invitations, stay in the flat, drink a bit too much. Then gradually she'd sink back into the oblivion to which I'd struggled to consign her and I'd be all right again. I'd sometimes wondered if my image ever materialized to her, but I doubted it. Her annihilation of me had been complete. Granny had never done anything by halves. She was infamous for it.

And now they said she might be dying for real; at ninety-five, a second stroke, a month after the first and a lot more severe. The nursing home had somehow tracked me down; I'm still next of kin, after all. I was quite sure the patient wouldn't know I was coming. I could see a perfectly-pencilled eyebrow arch as if to say 'what on earth for?' As I drove through the gates, I asked myself the same question.

It was a Victorian toad of a house, crouching on the outskirts of Beaconsfield. How she must hate it after the beauty of Mount Royal. I felt a tickle of pleasure at the thought; amazing how long venom can stay in the blood. But as the ugly brick portico began to fill the windscreen, I fought the urge to turn the wheel and run. No, fuck it. Rory Blaine doesn't run. Not this Rory Blaine anyway, the one my grandmother had never encountered and I realized I wanted her to meet that man, even just once. I accelerated towards the front door then braked pretentiously, sending a cloud of gravel-dust over a bed of plebeian geraniums. Faces appeared at a couple of windows. That's right. Wake up. I'm here. I took the stone steps two at a time.

The lobby was deserted, sickly with the smell of lilacs and beeswax. I slammed a bell on a table. From here, I could see into a cavernous lounge with tall windows overlooking the garden. Around its perimeter were twenty or so identical winged chairs, positioned at snooty intervals from each other, facing into the centre of the room. They were occupied by wisps of people, most in tweeds or twinsets, but some in dressing-gowns and attached to drips on metal poles that stood behind them like flunkeys. Nobody was talking. You could almost hear the pulses, faint and feeble though they were.

A surly Welsh nurse appeared, smelling of the cigarette I'd clearly interrupted. She summoned my grandmother's doctor, a youngish guy with a tired smile and a clipboard.

'She's quite a girl, isn't she?' he grinned. 'That last attack would have finished most folk her age, but Sibyl's still in the ring.'

'But I thought she was at death's door?' I said.

'Only for a day or two,' he replied, swallowing a yawn. 'Maybe she wasn't sure of the welcome she'd receive. I never imagined that one day I'd be trying to save Lady Sibyl Blaine. I'm a good *Guardian* reader, you see.'

In some distant swampy corner of my brain, a primeval loyalty stirred and I stared him out till his cheeks flushed.

'Sorry, no offence,' he said, burying the blush in his notes. 'Anyway, another attack would almost certainly see the Grim Reaper win the bout. Her Alzheimer's has accelerated quite rapidly too. She may or may not know you. When did you last see her?'

'Thirty years ago,' I said

'Gosh. Shame her speech is so badly affected then,' he replied with a wee grimace of fake empathy, 'I guess you've got a lot to talk about.'

He led me down a long corridor of identical doorways till we reached one bearing a wee card with 'Sibyl' hand-written in ornate script. God help them if she ever clocked that. He gave me a limp-lettuce handshake and scurried away.

Centuries ago, I'd so often stood outside my grandmother's rooms at Mount Royal, waiting for the 'come' without which it had been strictly forbidden to enter. The word had been a reliable weather forecast; usually bright and breezy but sometimes, for no accountable reason, heavy with a likelihood of thunder later. Now, as I raised my hand to knock, three decades shrank into seconds and I began to feel Rory Blaine haemorrhaging away into the pretty pink carpet. But today, there was no answer. The Welsh nurse zooming past barked to go right in and flung the door wide for me. Oh fuck.

It was sepulchral in the big room, as if she were already dead. The curtains were drawn against the daylight and the atmosphere was clammy with decay. As my eyes adjusted to the gloom, the ghost-white hospital bed materialized like a ship in the night, a Flying Dutchman of tubing and monitors.

Ms Prada had instructed me to write down here what I was experiencing. She knew all about Granny. I'd called this morning and told her I'd been summoned. She'd given a wee gasp of satisfaction, like you do when you finally crack the last clue in the crossword. We'd booked an extra session for tomorrow.

I shuffled towards the bed a few steps at a time. No need to rush after all these years. Jesus, what a tiny creature she'd become; harmless now, innocent even. Safe inside the railings, she was a grotesque parody of a baby in a cot; the fuzz of hair still gold, the powder-white skin, the lips painted in a rosy bow. But the mouth was toothless and twisted sharply to one side. Her prosthetic leg was propped beside the bed, absurdly, as if she might suddenly fancy a stroll. Her hands lay on the sheet, brown and shrivelled as two dead leaves. My own gripped the side of the bed, knuckles white as the railings. Sorry, Ms Prada, I'm not sure I can write down what I felt. I didn't know what it was. I still don't really. Probably some messy mixture of pity and pain, of love and loathing. Whatever. Maybe some perspective might crash in later, apologizing for its late arrival. But it hasn't got here yet.

Then as I peered down at the mummified thing, the eyelids shot open. I leapt back before she grabbed my throat like in fucking *Carrie*. The eyes were unchanged, still the same blazing blue that could either make your day or freeze you like a dentist's needle. Inside the body of the ancient child, the woman I used to know was instantly there again.

'Hello Granny,' I said, unable to expel more than a whisper.

The twisted mouth tried to produce some words, but all that came out were a string of drool and an incomprehensible high-pitched squeak, like the Weed in *Bill and Ben, The Flowerpot Men*. I realized she'd not be up for my Belgian chocolates. Then the eyelids fell shut again.

From a dark corner came a sudden gargling snore. I'd not even noticed the fat old man dozing in an armchair; mouth lolling open, a magazine splayed across his belly. He'd woken himself up and looked a bit dazed.

'Hey, we got company,' he said after a moment, his wide face flooding with a smile. In an expensive cream suit, pink shirt and matching tie, he looked a bit overdressed for the occasion. A stick was hooked over the arm of the chair.

'Give us a hand up, will you, toots?' he said. 'Got a dodgy leg, or mobility issues as they say in this shithole.'

It was an odd accent, pitched somewhere between Bermondsey and Broadway. I pulled him to his feet, but he kept hold of my hand and pumped it greedily which sent a thick wave of white hair tumbling down across his forehead like snow sliding off a roof.

'The grandson, I presume?' he said 'I'm Vic d'Orsay. You might have heard of me.'

'Don't think so, sorry.'

'Fuck you then,' he laughed. The smile never seemed to entirely disappear; it just went up and down as if on a dimmer. 'Doesn't Sibyl look nice? I make her face up every day. I just know it cheers her up.'

As he admired his handiwork, there was a long wretched moan followed by an overwhelming smell.

'Oh Sibyl, honey, I told you before,' said the old man, going over and patting her arm. 'Never trust a fart once you've turned sixty. But chill Sibyl, chill. We'll soon have that old pussy smelling like Harvey Nicks.'

He pointed to a chest of drawers.

'There are clean sheets in there. Would you get them for me?'

'Aren't you going to call someone?'

'No need, toots,' said Vic d'Orsay. 'We can do it ourselves. I'm supposed to take a little light exercise every day now. You'd be amazed how many calories wiping an ass consumes. Nothing like it for increasing the pulse-rate.'

He took off his jacket, folded it neatly over a chair, removed a pair of cufflinks the size of gobstoppers and rolled up his sleeves. When he pulled back the bedding the stench swamped the room. The taste of the bacon roll I'd bought on the motorway returned to my mouth. Vic d'Orsay threw the window wide open and directed me to a conservatory next door. As instructed, I returned with a big bowl of pink and white flowers.

'Nothing like brompton stock to obliterate the smell of shit. It's a horticultural SAS,' he said, whipping off my grandmother's nightgown like he was skinning a rabbit. She can't have weighed more than a few stones now. The old woman started to cry a little; he leaned down and kissed her forehead.

'Air-freshener's no goddam good in places like this. All the pee and poo; the walls soak it in and breathe it out again like halitosis.'

He went into the adjacent bathroom, returning with a bowl of warm soapy water and a flannel. I had to look away.

'Stargazer lilies are pretty effective too,' said Vic, wittering on as he worked. 'And hyacinths of course, but they're so Victorian now. Luckily the gardener here knows the score. Look out of that window.'

Sure enough, from the blustery April garden, endless rows of pink and white flowers waved back at me like hankies on a dockside.

'Right. I need you to hold her now while I put the clean sheets on,' said Vic. I walked up to the bed and hesitated.

'Come on toots, move your ass,' he ordered. 'Just roll her over gently while I slide the sheet onto one side of the bed, then same again other side.'

I looked down at my grandmother. Her eyes had closed again; full of drugs no doubt. But I still couldn't believe they might close forever, it was too against the grain. Amazingly, beneath the scent of the flowers and the reek of the shite, I could still just detect the smell she'd always had; the one I'd known since I'd arrived at Mount Royal that day long ago when, like the house itself, her arms, now shrivelled and useless, had wrapped themselves around me and felt so strong and sheltering.

That summer when I was seven, my father, half-pissed as usual, had put his Rolls into reverse and shot backwards off the ferry to Skye, drowning himself, my mother and a pair of lesbian hitch-hikers in Mallaig harbour. That was when my English grand-mother, till then just a distant, half-drawn figure, had exploded into my existence like shrapnel. I knew quite well there were pieces of her still in me, though I'd tried so hard to pick them out. I also knew that, for the years we'd spent together, we'd saved each other's lives. And then, in one terrible instant, it had all gone wrong and we'd both been left to fend for ourselves. For neither of us had it gone particularly well.

Now this fat smiley old guy wanted me to touch her, to hold her again. Christ, how many times along the years had I imagined doing that? In touching, slow-motion scenes of reconciliation, accompanied by the strings of Mantovani.

'I'm sorry, but I just can't do this. I need to go.' I said, striding to the door. 'I'll send a nurse in to help you.'

'Ok toots,' said Vic, the smile dimming a bit. 'Go grab two chairs in the lounge and order coffee. I'll be there in ten.'

There was another moan from the bed. My grandmother was looking straight at me. She tried to raise herself on her pillows, the scrawny shoulders trembling. She was struggling to say something. The old guy put his ear to her mouth; he seemed able to understand her.

'I think she's asking if you're Archie,' he said.

I forced myself back over to the end of the bed.

'No Granny, it's Rory.' I said, 'Rory, your grandson.'

The blue eyes peered, widened for a moment, then screwed tight shut against me. The skull under the dyed golden frizz began to thrash from side to side on the pillow, so violently that I thought it must splinter.

'Go, Rory Blaine,' said Vic. 'Go now.'

*

Vic d'Orsay limped into the lounge, his belly preceding him like the page-boy of some Oriental potentate. Coffee was brought by a teenage girl with bad skin. Vic was irritated by the scruffy layout of the tray.

'You'd think this was some goddam Little Chef rather than an extremely expensive nursing home,' he said. 'Bet she knows how to lay out a line of coke though. Apparently the staff-room here's like something out of William Burroughs. And this is fucking Beaconsfield.'

I found myself a tad shocked by this old guy using expletives and wondered at exactly what age I'd have to stop swearing in order not to distress the younger generation.

When I'd entered the lounge, I'd pulled two of the winged chairs together by a window, causing heads to turn.

'Good afternoon,' I'd said politely to the nearest tweedy waxwork, but it had turned away again.

In his flashy clothes, Vic looked like a peacock in a chicken coop. A middle-aged woman, visiting one of the winged chairs, crept over and asked for his autograph. Her husband had proposed while Vic was singing *Moonlight In Amalfi* on the car radio, they now had four children, a golden retriever and an apartment in Croatia. Vic said he was honoured to be 'a figure on her landscape of love'. He signed a paper napkin, kissed her on both cheeks and patted her bum as she turned to go. She was thrilled.

'You've never heard of me, have you, toots?' he asked, pouring the coffee.

I lied and said that I thought his name was coming back to me.

'Vic d'Orsay, also known as The King of Croon. Five Top Ten singles, three gold albums, one platinum. Second in the Eurovision Song Contest, six Royal Variety Performances. There might have been a seventh but I flashed my dick at the Singing Nun and was never asked again. Oh yeah and an honorary degree from Lowestoft Poly, now called the University of the Fens.'

He put down his cup and peered at me with blatant curiousity.

'You all right now?'

'Oh yeah, sure.' I lied again, but I don't think he was fooled this time.

'Well, well, the grandson,' he said.

'I'm surprised anyone here knew she had one.'

'Oh I did,' said Vic. 'I knew Sibyl slightly many years ago, though she doesn't remember me at all now. It was me who tracked you down. Not difficult in these Googling times. I knew you were estranged but I thought it was right.'

'I nearly didn't come.'

'So why did you then?' he asked, cutting us both more Madeira cake. I bit into mine, shuffled a pack of answers in my head and, to my surprise, heard myself dealing the honest one.

'I wanted to find out if there was anyone to visit.'

'And is there?'

'Not on today's evidence,' I said.

'She's ill, confused, easily upset,' said Vic. 'Give it another go. You might not have much time to fix whatever it was that broke.'

That last sentence was spoken in an odd shifty way, as if he already possessed the information. But I couldn't imagine Granny ever unlocking her skeletons, even when faced with the imminent prospect of turning into one herself.

'Hey look, it wasn't the loot, my coming. I knew I'd have been dumped decades ago,' I said. 'Anyway who *is* the heir to Mount Royal these days? Battersea Dogs Home or that crowd of loonies she hangs out with?'

'The loonies, I'd guess. It's not right. Not the way things should be.'

For the first time, Vic d'Orsay's smile completely disappeared. He looked quite different without it. I almost felt I should turn away, like I was seeing him undressed. He twisted in his chair, spilling crumbs onto the pink silk tie.

'Forgive me, but am I right in thinking you're Jewish?' I asked.

'Well Barbra called my agent about *Yentl* but the part just wasn't me.'

'So how come a Jew is wiping the arse of a notorious fascist and anti-Semite?'

Vic put down his cup and brushed the cake crumbs from his tie, creating a yellowy smudge. The tie was ruined. He shrugged.

'Because all of us reach a stage in our lives where everything can be, has to be, forgiven. Everything. Even the very worst things.'

'I don't think I'm quite there yet,' I said.

'You will be. At least I hope you will,' he replied. 'Anyway, I just felt sad for her when I found her here in this state. I thought she needed a friend. There didn't seem to be many others.'

'How long have you been here, Sir?'

'Jeez, call me Vic or you'll make me feel as old as Max Bygraves,' he replied. 'Two endless, fucking months. Just a minor stroke, nothing like as bad as Sibyl's. Leg still a bit screwed, that's all. But I needed looking after for a while, so I had to come here.'

He leaned in closer.

'No little woman at home, you see,' he said. Bright pink indicator lights flashed onto his cheeks and two untamed eyebrows did a wee jig. It was said.

I looked around the soulless room. The silence was broken only by dozy breathing and soft, scattered sighs.

'Why does nobody here speak?'

'Nothing much left to say. We know all about each other's lives, or as much as each of us chooses to weave tales from.'

'What tales do *you* tell then, Vic?' I asked.

'Only the ones which make it easier to fit in.'

'And do you?'

'Well it's either this place or another like it,' said Vic. 'Anyway, I can play the part. I learned the lines a long time ago and I've been speaking them ever since. The King of Croon, arch-celebrant of heterosexual love. In lots of ways, I've become the part, as they say. And I'm not the only one. There are two or three other men and women in this place who I strongly suspect are playing it too. Mind you, poor old Dickie over there is so ga-ga now he can't keep up the performance any more. That makes life here a bit hard for him.'

An emaciated, daddy-long-legs of a man was snoozing over by the door; his chair at a distance from the others, bony fingers clawing at his chest as if sleep brought him no peace.

'But I'm lucky,' Vic went on. 'I'm only here on remand till proved well enough to leave. Most of these folk are sentenced to life, to use a very inappropriate noun.'

Despite his leg, Vic insisted on walking me out to the Merc. As we passed the daddy-long-legs, a hand shot out and grabbed my arm.

'I was fucked by The Master,' The voice was wheezy, androgynous, but the eyes begged me to believe him. 'I was fucked by The Master.'

'Which school were you at then, Sir?' I grinned.

'Hush now Dickie,' said Vic gently. 'He means Noël Coward. Dickie was a chorus-boy in his day.'

'Well I can see that,' I said 'You've still got the legs for it, Sir.'

Dickie gurgled with pleasure. As we went out of the door, the sexless voice called after us.

'I was fucked by The Master.'

'Be quiet, you disgusting old man!' shouted a woman in a champagne-coloured wig. 'It's intolerable to have to live with people like you. I served in the ATS.'

'And Dickie served in the Royal Marines, Mrs Parker-Brown,' Vic replied, 'where he won the DSM.'

'For buggery, no doubt,' the woman snapped, before returning to her copy of *The Lady*.

'I hope that by the time you ever need a place like this, things will be different,' said Vic as we reached the lobby. 'But I'm ashamed to say a lot of my generation would still shove Oscar in Reading Gaol with a much longer sentence and no hope of parole.'

Outside, the sky had darkened and the Merc was sequinned with raindrops. Vic was much taken with it. He'd had one himself long ago, bought from Tom Jones. There'd been a pair of panties still in the glove-box.

'Well, if I come again, maybe we could go for a spin to the nearest pub.' I said, realizing that I actually meant it. I often say things I don't mean; it's an occupational hazard in advertising. But was I going to come again? It hadn't exactly been a success. Vic d'Orsay seemed to have read my thoughts.

'Listen toots, I know this has been rough,' he said. 'But try again. Just be here. Words don't always matter.'

I reached out to shake his hand, then, on an impulse, gave him a swift manly hug. I felt him flinch for a second but, when we broke apart, the smile was back at full blast.

'Sorry, shouldn't have done that,' I said, glancing back at the windows of the lounge. 'I hope nobody was watching.'

'Thanks anyway' said Vic. 'That'll keep me going for weeks.'

When I was turning round the gravel circle towards the head of the drive, I saw Vic watching from the lounge. As the car rolled past the window I stabbed the horn, but he'd already turned away and been swallowed up by the room.

*

I'd walked across to the pretty middle-aged lady with the diamonds on her head, handed her the bouquet and bowed. Granny and I had been rehearsing it for weeks. The Queen had asked if I'd travelled far. Only from Hampstead, I'd replied, though I went to school in Scotland. She'd thought that was very interesting and thanked me for coming. I'd told her it was okay, I'd not been doing anything else that night anyway. She'd said I had lovely golden hair. I'd said hers was nice too.

Granny hadn't been able to curtsey of course, not with her leg. The film première had been in aid of her disabled charities. Afterwards at the Savoy, we'd hobbled round the dance floor together, the brave aristocrat and the sweet orphaned grandson. There had been a pic in the posh magazines. 'Lady Sibyl Blaine and Master Rory Blaine,' the captions always read as Granny trotted her miniature escort round the social circuit. We'd become quite a celebrated pair, smiling out at unknown readers in dentists' waiting-rooms.

Not long afterwards, she'd announced that we'd both go up to Scotland a week before the autumn term started at Glenlyon. I must have been about ten by then. There was something we ought to do she'd said. This was strange because Granny never went to Scotland. She'd often declared that three years of it had been enough to last a lifetime. But having made the decision, she'd seemed determined to make it a great treat, as was her way. And so we'd been chauffeured round the Lake District, the great abbeys and houses of the Borders and then to Edinburgh; St Giles Cathedral, the National Gallery, Holyroodhouse. I'd tried to play guide; history was one of the few things I was good at. I'd wanted to show her my country wasn't the backward puddle of a place she mocked before her important guests at Mount Royal. On a chilly late August evening, we'd huddled under a blanket on the Castle Esplanade as the pipes and drums skirled and strutted past us. Granny had given me a wee nip from her flask. A man on her other side said he worked in childcare and that he'd report her. She'd laughed so much he'd moved his seat. I'd laughed too of course. I was never shy with Granny. I was a different person when we were together.

And then we'd taken the road to the isles. On a crisp clear morning, we'd stood together on the pier that jutted out into the blue-grey waters of Mallaig harbour. The air was sharp with the smell of the sea and the coming of autumn. Each of us had carried a bunch of white lilies.

'I rather thought we should both come here, even if just the once.' she'd said. 'I felt you were ready now, my darling. I do hope I wasn't wrong.'

She'd turned and gazed at me intently. She'd seemed to be searching my eyes for something, just as I'd been discreetly searching hers. After all, it was her only child whose bloated body had been pulled from the bottom of the harbour three years before. But I'd seen nothing unusual there, only a sudden shiver underneath the suit of peach-coloured linen which had turned the heads of the drab women in the village. We'd taken turns throwing a lily out onto the water until they'd all been carried away on the early tide towards the distant mass of Skye.

'Well that's done,' Granny had said. 'Shall we have an ice-cream?'

And we had. Then she'd decided we deserved another one. She'd put her arm tightly round my shoulders and we'd licked our way back to the car.

'Joined at the hip, aren't we, my darling?' she'd laughed, tapping the top of her false leg. 'Joined at the hip.'

THREE

At Battersea Dogs' Home, there will be a barking and a gnashing of teeth. In leafy suburban avenues, fascist loonies will be stuffing shite into envelopes with my name on it. The fickle finger of fate has poked down through the clouds and tickled me under the chin. I have inherited Mount Royal and all that goes with it. I have no idea how or why.

She went in the middle of the night. They'd found her in the morning. Another massive stroke. It would have been quick and without pain, they'd said. But how the hell did they know that if nobody had been with her? I didn't like to think she'd been frightened.

They'd asked if they could keep her false leg; 'to maximize the life-style quality of a future mobility-challenged resident.' Can you believe that? At their rates, they could have supplied prosthetics to half the casualties of the Somme. At first I'd told them to fuck off, but then they'd pointed out that it wouldn't burn anyway, so I gave in on condition it was only attached to a needy Jew or homosexual.

She'd wanted a service in the chapel at Mount Royal but its crumbling condition had thrown up health and safety issues which, her solicitor decreed, could rebound on the estate in the event of injury. So a week later, there was the usual fast-track disposal in the red-brick caverns of Golders Green, attended by myself, Vic d'Orsay and a pick 'n' mix bunch of weirdos; desiccated nobility with cracked lips and bad breath; creepy middle-aged types in cheap suits, even a few shaven-headed young bruisers.

Vic d'Orsay had just been sprung from the nursing home and was back in his flat off Sloane Street. After our first encounter, we'd met two or three more times over the following weeks as my grandmother had slithered downhill. I'd actually, as promised, taken him out to lunch at a country pub. He'd managed to top me in the telling of filthy jokes; there had been one about clitoral farts even I'd have baulked at. I'd liked him, I'd felt sorry for him, though I'd made no plans to fertilize the acquaintance. But when Granny died he'd called me up and offered his help in organizing the funeral. Totally clueless, I'd been only too grateful. Mind you, Granny had left fairly precise instructions. It was just to be a few of her favourite hymns and Bible readings croaked in monotone by shuffling relics of a long lost age. She'd ruled against any sort of eulogy but as the vicar stood up for final prayers, Vic hissed in my ear.

'Jeez, somebody has to say *something*'.

He went over to the coffin He addressed not the congregation but the corpse, leaning towards Granny just as I'd seen him do when he tried to understand what she was struggling to say. He talked about journeys and paths chosen, about the crosses we carry, about the loneliness of it all and the comforts we sometimes turn to, rightly or wrongly. He talked about forgiveness too, as he'd done with me on that first day I'd gone to see her. And then, tears on his podgy cheeks, he kissed the coffin.

But I didn't cry. I don't now. Haven't for a very long time. Ms Prada doesn't approve. But I'm all cried out, as the fat lady once sang. However the gastric reflux was going at full blast and for days I'd been in a 'Milton' that just wouldn't shift. I stared at my wreath on the coffin, so white and fragile against the harsh mahogany, the same lilies we'd thrown into Mallaig harbour. Then the flowers and Granny slid silently away to wherever they were going.

The weirdos started gathering their hats and coats and shuffling towards the exit. Suddenly, the piercing scream of a woman came from the mysterious spaces into which the coffin had disappeared. Everybody froze. I thought Vic might have a second stroke. We found out later that a trainee disposal operative had caught her finger in the machinery that rolled the box towards the ovens. The finger had come clean off. Good old Granny. Fucking-up people's lives till the last possible second.

*

The obituaries had been extensive but not very charming.

Lady Sibyl Constancia Blaine. Born Mount Royal, London, 1913. Only child of the Earl of Ashridge (earldom now extinct). Married Sir Archibald Blaine, Scottish shipbuilder 1932. Divorced 1935. One son, Hector Rufus (predeceased). Socialite. Member of Edward VIII's circle. Loses leg when crushed by horse; 1968. Personally shoots horse before being taken to hospital. Prominent figure in right-wing politics from late-1970s. Creates neo-fascist salon. National Front candidate in elections of 1979 and 1987. Imprisoned in Holloway for incitement to racial hatred; 1989.

Becomes *Spitting Image* puppet; 1994. Attacks Michael Foot with walking-stick on Hampstead Heath; 1997. No charges pressed. The *Guardian* called her 'a sad corruption of *noblesse oblige*'. The *Daily Telegraph* mourned 'a misguided woman whose excesses obscured her sometimes valid arguments'. *Pete 'n' Denise* blogged that 'she spoke for us all', while *Ollyboy* felt 'she was a fuckin nutter, may she rot in hell.' The last word however went, as it should, to *The Times*. 'She is survived by a grandson.' Well, sort of.

A few days later, I'd taken delivery of the ashes. I'd hidden the urn in a distant cupboard with my folk CDs till I figured out what to do with them. And I'd assumed that would be that. But then there was a summons to a posh office in the Temple. Her Ladyship had scribbled a codicil to her will a few days before she died. Bingo.

I, Rory Blaine, am one of the few gay men in London who can honestly tell you I've never been to Hampstead Heath since reaching the age of consent. Thirty years ago, I'd thrown a self-imposed cordon around NW3 which, until this very day, I'd never once crossed. NW3 is where Mount Royal stands.

It was quite bizarre of course, when I returned from Oz and started living a couple of miles away. Tricky too sometimes. If friends living there invited me to dinner, I'd always suggest a West End restaurant. If a business meeting called, I'd plead illness or send somebody else. If I were flying in from the east, I'd never look down in case I glimpsed the cupola. But over the years, it somehow worked. I'd created a black hole in the landscape of the Borough of Camden. A place that no longer existed. Dreamscapes however were another matter. They were less amenable to annihilation. In dreams, I went there constantly.

Once upon a time, you see, I'd been a Blaine of Mount Royal, an insurance policy in bricks and mortar against the worst vicissitudes of existence, guaranteeing a life-long payout of respect and deference. Then suddenly I'd no longer been covered. But now, through some fluke of fortune, it had come back to me and I didn't quite know how to handle it. Ms Prada was really excited, saying that a physical return to my childhood could represent a major milestone on my road to total mind-management. She also felt I should increase the frequency of our sessions. There were some brochures for the Maldives on her desk.

With two more exceptions, I decided not to tell anyone else, at least not yet. The first of these was Vic d'Orsay who answered my email with just four words: 'Justice has been done'. The other was Miss Elspeth Wishart, my old matron from Glenlyon. She replied, by second-class post, with a warning about rich men, camels and eyes of needles and an enquiry as to how punitive the Council Tax might be.

Granny's will was still in probate. But one morning the final papers on the house were signed. Among the reams of legal guff, I was handed a yellow Post-It note with a scribbled security code for the gates of Mount Royal. With six wee numbers, I became the owner of one of the greatest mansions in England. Shite, what did I do now?

I went back to the flat, made some cheese on toast and watched a TV programme about a semi-literate Bradford couple struggling to set up a B&B in a derelict farmhouse near Avignon. I put out the rubbish and tried to remove a wine stain from the carpet I'd been living with for months. In this way I managed to delay for three whole hours. Eventually I swore at myself and grabbed the car keys. I suddenly wished I had somebody to go with me so I asked the cat if it fancied a jaunt and it squeaked that it did.

The journey back across thirty years took about twenty minutes. As I drove up the leafy tunnel of Fitzjohn's Avenue into Hampstead village, it felt like I'd never been away. Though pockmarked now by the usual chain stores, it still oozed its effortless conceit with the Mary Poppins lamp-posts, cobbled alleys and wee bow-fronted bookshops bulging like hernias. A nice middle-class sun, not too hot, not too cold, shone down on the glossy ladies with the well-groomed dogs taking coffee at the pavement tables. A dishevelled man was selling *The Big Issue* outside Maison Blanc but none of them seemed to see him.

The Merc climbed up to Whitestone Pond on the breezy brow of London. A few hundred yards along Spaniards Road, I swung across the traffic and onto an overgrown path, hemmed in by towering oaks, which ended below a high wall and dark-green metal gates. I punched the numbers on the yellow Post-It note onto a keypad. The gates hesitated before creaking open. Maybe they weren't glad to see me; I could hardly blame them for that. Driving through, I was blinded by fierce summer sunlight. The trees had given way to a vast clearing where everything was sky and space again. And there, against the water-colour backdrop of the city, was Mount Royal.

With the sun on my retinas, its image was hazy, as it had sometimes been in my dreamer's eye. The geometric perfection of its walls and windows was diffused; its outline seemed to sway a little, like the oaks that guarded its entrance. But then I angled the car into some shade and all such fragility vanished. The walls reared up like a honey-coloured cliff, arrogance in every stone.

As the cat and I got out of the car I had a frantic urge to piss. I often do. Rod, my genito-urinary mechanic, says it's not prostate, just another manifestation of tension. I did it into an urn of half-dead geraniums, guiltily, till I remembered they were now my urn and my geraniums. Back up in the oaks, as they'd always done, the rooks were gossiping loudly, no doubt about me. A scruffy caravan parked inside the gates disgorged a fat, sixtyish man in an unkempt security guard's uniform.

'It'll be Mr Blaine?' he asked in a fierce Irish accent, attempting a half-baked salute. 'Welcome, Sir, welcome.'

He handed me a chubby bunch of keys, each one neatly labelled. Did I need him to accompany me? He was clearly glad when I declined. A Bruce Willis film was about to start on TV and he never liked to miss one. You never knew when a *Die Hard* scenario might arise in today's security environment.

'A very fine house, Sir,' he said, contemplating his charge. 'But the heart's gone out of it. Still, not my place to say so. Shout if you need me.'

The gravelled carriage circle enclosed a roundel of shabby grass. At its centre was a marble plinth with the figure of Father Thyme. We were old buddies. I used to dress him up in sunglasses, a string vest, a bra stolen from a maid, anything I'd thought might make Granny laugh. I leaned against him and stared at the place which, despite my best endeavours, I'd never stopped thinking of as home.

'Well look at you,' I said.

Christ, it was a stonker of a house. They said that Wren had doodled it on an envelope then handed it to a minion while he got on with St Paul's. Money had been no object; the first Earl of Ashridge had gone into exile with Charles II and been rewarded with baubles, bangles and job opportunities. Artists, sculptors and woodcarvers had crammed Mount Royal with treasures. Nell

Gwynn, Mrs Fitzherbert, Lily Langtry had strolled in its gardens, Walpole, Pitt, Disraeli had nattered in its rooms. For three hundred years, it had stood as evidence of what civilized people could achieve when they weren't beating the crap out of each other.

But Bruce Willis hadn't been wrong. Her Ladyship had neglected her legacy. The stone was pitted with pollution and the shining slate I remembered was scabbed-over with bird-shite. Pediments had crumbled and window-frames cracked, gutters were broken and loose drainpipes reeled off the walls like drunks. And though time had been merciless, the hands on the Clock Tower had, paradoxically, long stopped ticking. But despite the ravages, the beauty was imperishable. The sunlight still glanced off the panes of the cupola that crowned the roof, the lions were still rampant around the portico. Maybe Bruce Willis had written it off too soon. Perhaps there was still the possibility of rejuvenation, with Rory Blaine as its saviour of course. But that was a fantasy. Granny's solicitor had made it pretty clear that inheritance tax meant the Chancellor was the real new owner of Mount Royal. Sooner or later, it would be raped by developers, drawn and quartered into yuppie apartments or sold off to become some fat Arab's harem.

The cat had already climbed the wide shallow steps to the front doors. I wondered if it might be experiencing agoraphobia never having been further than my teeny roof terrace, though no doubt a cat from Harrods can handle anything. But I wasn't quite ready to go inside yet. Instead I went through the gate in one of the wrought-iron screens that framed the north front and began to circle the house, warily, as if something might leap out at me.

On three sides Mount Royal was simple, austere almost. As if it were totally sure of itself, not needing to dress up and show off. Only on the south front, which overlooked the gardens and the city, did it show a splash of flamboyance, like an accountant in a blue suit. Here the wings of the letter 'H' flung themselves further out, the pediments were more ornate and, just below the roofline hung the huge stone shield with the Ashridge coat of arms and its Latin motto which basically translated as 'fuck everyone but us'.

Below the terrace, a horseshoe staircase curved down into the Italian Garden with the Great Fountain, the statues, the giant urns and, at the furthest point of the axis, the Orangery. But the paths I remembered were long gone, buried somewhere under

thigh-high grass and years of indifference. Here and there, chorus lines of ancient dahlias, blowsy in scarlet and purple, bra-
zened their way up through the chaos. But the tall glass doors of
the Orangery were chained now, the latticed panes crusty with
dirt. The dry fountain basin was clogged with long-dead leaves,
a ripped bag of compost and a pair of mouldy wellingtons. As I
pushed my way onwards, my shoes crunched on the skeletons of
rooks and squirrels.

I sat down on a mucky stone bench and gazed up at the house.
Where did I start with all this? I felt a bit detached, as if it weren't
me going through the experience. With its rows of shuttered windows, the house looked fast asleep but I felt sure it was watching
me. Okay, that sounds bonkers but you don't know it like I do.

'You've been in deep shite for a while, haven't you?' I said. 'Me
too.'

Back round on the north front, violent mayhem was blast-
ing out of Bruce Willis's caravan. Shouts of 'Die, motherfucker!'
weren't the background music I'd imagined to putting my key in
the lock of Mount Royal, but life's a funny thing.

The high double doors, the wood fissured and filthy, didn't
want to budge. Perhaps, like the gates, they felt some token reluc-
tance was appropriate. I stepped back, unsure what to do. Then a
cry of 'Take that, asshole' exploded from the caravan and inspired
my left foot. Thirty years after being kicked out of Mount Royal, I
kicked my way back in.

It was almost pitch black inside, the air thick as unstirred porridge. I threw the doors wide and prised open the shutters, letting
air and light puncture the gloom. The chandeliers tinkled inside
their shrouds. Wow. Mount Royal wasn't a wall-flower that made
you wait for its charms, it delivered right away. The Gilded Hall
was the grandest room in the house, rising two storeys high to a
wild Verrio ceiling. At ground level it was dominated by a pair of
marble chimneypieces, cavernous enough to park a Mini. On the
white panelled walls were endless Ashridge portraits, some the
size of billiard tables. Twin staircases flew up its opposing walls
and linked arms at the top. On three sides of the first floor, open
galleries led to the rooms in the east and west wings. But though
the gilding was flaking and the chequered marble floor had been
hidden by bargain-basement rugs, the sheer nerve of it still hit
you between the eyes.

The cat and I went for a prowl; the Saloon, the Library, the Music Room, the State Dining-Room, the Chapel. Some rooms were still in their original Caroline clothing; masculine, dark-panelled, rooms with no fat on them. Others had been remod-elled by Wyatville in the early nineteenth century, flibbertigibbets in plaster, silk and damask, girly by comparison. The huge spaces shrunk you like Alice. Even now, damp and grubby, the furniture under dust-sheets, they still did the business. As much as Glenlyon, these had been my school-rooms. I'd taught myself about everything in them, the chairs and tables, the silver, the china, the carvings. The pictures on the walls were old acquaintances; the swan-necked ladies and their complacent lords, the ribboned girls on swings with sad, attendant blackamoors, the dishy nobleman with curls like Marc Bolan. Sometimes I even knew their names and stories; the frail countess who'd died in childbirth, the younger son who'd been lost in a shipwreck. Long dead, they had still breathed for me. Along with Granny and the servants, they'd been palpable presences. We had all lived together, a world in a house. They will be your charges one day, Granny had said. I'd not forgotten a single one of them.

But it was tiny things that carried the shock of familiarity; the same tongues of cold air darting out round the same corners, the beefy doorknob that had squeaked forever, the unchanged touch of a satinwood banister. The smell hadn't altered either; something given off by the wood, the fabrics, even the stone of the walls, a strange fusion of opulence and decay. What wasn't familiar was the silence that enveloped the house, as if Mount Royal were holding its breath, waiting to see what was going to happen now. When a distant door banged somewhere, the cat and I jumped together.

At the foot of one branch of the staircase, one of the portraits had been covered over. I didn't need to guess whose it was. I tugged at the dust-sheet. With a slow hiss it crumpled to the floor and my grandmother stared down at me. She can't have been more than twenty or so; in an ice-blue gown that matched her eyes, sapphires threaded through her hair. But it was the expression de Laszlo had captured in her youth which struck you. Hard to articulate exactly what it was. Not just a rich kid's arrogance, but something in the blood perhaps, the utter certainty that things would go the way she wanted them. But they hadn't. That was for sure. And yet that look had never entirely left her, not even after the strokes had twisted her features. It was probably on her face inside the mahogany box they burnt at Golders Green.

My heels echoed on the uncarpeted wood of the staircase. At the top, I faced the suite of rooms which had been hers, but I wasn't going in there. In time maybe, but not today. Instead I headed for the corner of the east wing which, for eight years of my life, had been mine. Here the door was locked, which was odd as all the others had opened. But the lock was ancient and anyway it was my lock now. I reprised my heroics. Jesus Christ. The room was empty. Totally. No furniture, no carpets, no curtains. The light fittings had gone, the wall-sockets torn out. It had been laid waste and left to rot. I'd been vaporized.

With an instantly recognizable groan, a floorboard sagged under my weight. Bloody hell, could they still be there? I prised it up. Fuck, yes. A mouldy pile of wank mags I'd bought in Camden Town with blazing cheeks and smuggled home with thumping heart. Blokes with permed hair, flowery shirts and erections sticking out of bell-bottom pants. Like the portraits downstairs, these faces were old friends. They'd have bus passes and prostate problems now, unless the plague had got them. I thanked them for the pleasure they'd given me and stamped the board back down. Rest in peace. I shook my head. All those years of fearful caution, then I'd blown it in a moment.

The cat and I climbed onwards till we reached the narrow wooden spiral that snaked up into the cupola; the highest point in a house that perched on the highest point in London. I lost myself in the view again, like I always had; the towers of Canary Wharf, the tip of Big Ben, the mast at Crystal Palace and, right below, the gardens, the woods and the wide green splash of the Heath. Up here I'd been King of the Castle. Impregnable. Safe.

The unlikeliest of faces now entered my mind and obscured the view. I hardly ever thought of my father. It should have been him standing here, not me. He'd only have been in his early seventies, my mother even younger. But Hector Blaine's life had gone off the rails long before he'd reversed his car into the drink. Under the iron rule of my grandfather, Archie, Blaine Shipping had been the biggest maritime empire in Scotland, but it had only taken Hector about five years to run it into the ground. After her brief, mysterious marriage to Archie, Granny had hurried back south to Mount Royal and the parental embrace. But she'd never abandoned the name of Blaine and, I'm guessing, couldn't bear the shame of her only son being a wastrel. So she'd poured Ashridge money into the shipyard but it was too late. What was left worth having was vultured by a rival and the Blaine flag was lowered over the Clyde after a century and a half. She'd never spoken to Hector again.

After that, my poor daddy didn't appear to have much talent for anything except self-indulgence. They'd lived at the gambling tables of Nice and Monte Carlo; I'd lived in a big villa in Kelvinside, looked after by a flush of nannies. I'd seen them so rarely that when they died the only difference was one of degree. Granny had considered me too young to go to the funeral and after our eventual trip to Mallaig harbour we'd rarely mentioned them again. We'd had each other after all. Granny was the last of the Ashridges, there were no cousins hovering to inherit; after her, the line would be extinct, a fact which seemed to nag her like a tooth. And I was the last of the Blaines, but of course that would be remedied in time; Granny had been quite confident of that.

'When I'm gone, it will be business as usual,' she'd said in the car that day as we'd driven away from Mallaig. 'You will carry on at Mount Royal, you will continue the line and I will look down on you proudly from my white fluffy cloud. Is that a deal, my darling?'

But at the thought of her loss, I'd erupted with violent sobs and clung frantically to her till we'd reached Fort William and had fish and chips for lunch. And now, fuck me if it hadn't happened; after all the years, after all the water that had roared under the bridge. Here I stood, up in the cupola, the master of Mount Royal. At least for a while.

'In Xanadu did Kubla Khan a stately pleasure-dome... and all that jazz,' said a voice. 'But this one needs serious re-pointing I reckon.'

'Vic d'Orsay, what the hell are you doing here?'

A snowy head ascended from the well of the spiral. He moved with some effort, the slight limp still there. We'd not met since Golders Green a couple of months ago.

'Her Ladyship's lawyer is an old buddy,' he panted, his belly rising and falling like a bellows. 'At lunch today, he let slip you'd

just taken possession. The security guy let me in. I came to con-
gratulate you. Hope you don't mind the intrusion.'

Maybe I should have done, but I suddenly felt glad to have him
there.

'Jeez, it's really something isn't it? Even in this state,' said
Vic, absorbing the panorama. I pointed out the landmarks and
Vic delivered the necessary oohs and aahs. There were some old
orange boxes lying around the cupola. Flicking the dust off one
with a blue silk handkerchief, he sat with his chins resting on the
top of his stick and fixed me in his gaze.

'Were you surprised she put you back in her will at the eleventh hour?'

'I didn't expect her to leave me a pot to piss in.'

'She didn't,' said Vic. 'I did.'

'Sorry?'

'As we'd both predicted, she'd left the lot to the loonies and
the lurchers,' said Vic. 'She didn't change her will, I changed it
for her.'

I sat down on another orange box, my mouth doing a passable
imitation of a goldfish. The cat leapt up onto a third and swivelled
its head between us as if it were at Wimbledon.

'I don't have many talents beyond my music,' Vic went on,
'but one of them was a boyhood genius for calligraphy. I can copy
somebody's handwriting two minutes after I've seen it. In this
particular instance, I employed it to spectacular effect.'

'How the fuck did you do it?' I whispered as if I didn't want the
cat to hear.

'One day before her second stroke, my friend the solicitor
brought her some important papers. She could still hold a pen
at that point and I helped her sign some stuff. Then, after her big
attack, I tracked you down, got to know you a bit, felt angry at the
wrong being done to you. The whole thing came to me when I was
trying to clip my toenails. Complete in every detail. I now knew
where she kept the will and one afternoon while she was totally
spaced, I dug it out, added the codicil, signed it in her handwriting and witnessed it in my own. Then I went into the sluice and
got one of the nurses to provide the second signature. It was done
and dusted in ten minutes. I was so chuffed with myself, I had a
meringue at tea.'

'Didn't the nurse suspect anything?'

'It was that surly Welsh one. A babe of strictly limited intel-
lectual gifts. Certainly too dumb to know you witness a signature
in the presence of the signatory and not while emptying out their
shit.'

'But why on earth did you do it? What's in it for you?'

There was a long pause.

'Well you see, the quacks say there's no reason why I can't have
another ten years at least. And I'd like them to be good years, not
just the fag-end of life, if you'll excuse the expression. But as I
mouldered in that lounge with poor old Dickie and the other
stiffs, it dawned on me that even passable health, the affection of
a million middle-aged ladies and an enviable portfolio of invest-
ments was unlikely to bring me what I really wanted.'

'Which is?'

He coloured a bit, looked away and stroked the cat.

'Oh toots, just the things most people are searching for. Say no
more.'

'And what's that got to do with me?'

Vic stood up and began to circle the tiny space.

'I came to this house once, donkeys years back. I remember
the magic of just being in those rooms. Before the rot set in,
of course. Not just the literal rot, but the bad things that Sibyl
allowed to happen here in later years. You remember too, don't
you? Well young Blaine, I have a plan for us to make it that way
again.'

'Us?' I said, with a prick of irritation. That wasn't a concept I
was used to wrestling with. 'What if I don't agree to this plan of
yours?'

'Well I could just go to the cops and confess,' said Vic. 'I could
say I felt your exclusion from Sibyl's will to be a grave injustice,
that I was depressed after my stroke and, under the influence of
my medical cocktail, I did a very silly thing and I'd now like to
cleanse my conscience. The quacks will testify on my behalf. Like
you, the cops will be unable to imagine any personal motive since
we hardly know each other and, as I'm a national treasure Grade
II, I'd bet I'll just get my ass kicked or at worst a suspended sentence and useful publicity for the sales of my back catalogue. Mr
Rory Blaine however will be disinherited, the loonies will get it as
planned then have to sell it and some gentleman from Jeddah will
move in with his fifteen wives.'

'So you're blackmailing me into going along with whatever you've dreamed-up?'

'Only in the nicest possible way.'

I was getting dizzy watching him circumnavigate the cupola. Granny's solicitor had said that the amended will, written just three days before her death, might normally have excited some suspicion. But since I, the new beneficiary, had not visited the home since the previous week and as one of the witnesses was no less than Vic d'Orsay, the celebrated singer, any thoughts of foul play had been instantly dismissed.

'Victor, for fuck's sake stand still,' I barked. 'What's this plan?'

'If my calculations are correct, you can only pay off the taxman, restore the house and pay its running costs if two criteria are met. The first is that you get a sizeable injection of extra dough. I can provide it. The second is that the house will have to work for its living. My scheme would not only enable it to do so but might even be a nice little earner.'

'You're assuming I want to keep this wreck.'

'I *was* assuming it, yes. Until ten minutes ago when I found you here and saw the look on your face. Now, I know you do,' said Vic. 'Anyway what was *your* plan? Flog it off, then fritter away what's left, chasing young Spanish ass in Marbella? You belong here, Rory.'

The old sod was dead right on both counts. I'd imagined selling both the house and the business then heading for the sunny villa with the jacuzzi and the hot-and-cold running boys. But to have Mount Royal again only to lose it for a second time was something I didn't think even Ms Prada could help with. I knew that for certain now I was back inside its walls.

I leaned back against the latticed glass and gazed out over the tops of the oaks. It had been a shock of course. Not Vic's crime, I'm ashamed to say, but the fact that Granny hadn't, after all, wanted to fix things at the last. In those final weeks, I'd made four or five trips to the white bed with the high railings. I'd worried that my presence might freak her out again, but she'd just lain there and stared. It hadn't been easy. I'd asked Vic to come the first once or twice, he seemed to understand the fractured sounds she made. But there were none for me. Still, I'd nattered on about anything; the years in Australia, the agency, the awards, wanting her to know I'd made something of myself even if she might not consider it much. I reminded her of dancing at the Savoy, freezing outside Edinburgh Castle, the day we'd won five hundred pounds at Ascot. But nothing. Oh well, Vic had said the words didn't really matter. The leaf-thin hand had lain still on the sheet. The final time I'd seen her, I'd let my own rest beside it, the fingertips almost touching. I'd told myself not to be pathetic. This might be my last chance. And it had been. And I'd not taken it. Then the inheritance had suggested that things had indeed been sorted and I'd been half-drunk on the joy of it. But now I'd discovered that was a sham. I stood here under false pretences.

'That big wrist-watch over there has stopped,' said Vic, peering down at the Clock Tower. 'What d'you say the two of us get it going again?'

It was hot as hell up here now. Vic d'Orsay waited, pushing the delinquent wave of hair back off his sweaty brow.

'Okay then,' I said finally. 'Let's hear how we save Mount Royal.'

He only spoke one short sentence but I laughed and laughed until I thought I was going to piss my nice new Paul Smith chinos. But the cat seemed to like what it heard and rubbed itself admiringly against Vic's dodgy leg.

*

The Saloon was lit entirely by candles. Thin as fingers in the wall-sconces, thick as arms in the giant torchères, they flickered against the Mogul tapestries, bringing a sort of half-life to leaping tigers and emperors on jewelled elephants. Milk-white roses frothed out of lacquered jars, their scent defeated by the smoke of cigars and the myriad perfumes of pampered flesh. While servants circled with coffee and liqueurs, the piano tinkled out Granny's favourite Cole Porter. '*You're The Top*' sang the pianist and few of those assembled would have doubted that they were.

Granny looked beautiful tonight in a long Givenchy sheath, her hair piled high on her head, clutching her jewelled Malacca cane. Around the long room opinions were being canvassed, plots hatched, flirtations begun; all of which might reverberate far beyond these walls. This was what Granny lived for. The unions may have been running the country but at Sibyl Blaine's parties all was well with the world as she had always known it.

I'd sat beside him at dinner. He never mentioned his name. He was a nice man, full of risqué jokes and anecdotes about famous

people. He was old enough to be my dad but he didn't talk down
to me. I was wearing my dress kilt and rattled on about my interest in clan tartans; he didn't seem bored like Granny usually did. I
told him that I hoped to be a writer one day. He promised to send
me a list of authors he thought I should get to know. If you want
to write, you must read, he said.

A few times I noticed Granny watching us. I felt the usual wee
jolt of fear, but that was familiar now, both here and at school. I'd
learned to be careful, to watch what I said, how I said it, even how
I moved my body. I always sat with my legs well apart, palms flat
on my thighs, elbows pointing outwards. I walked with a swag-
ger, I'd deepened my voice before its time and, to Granny's strong
disapproval, coarsened my Kelvinside accent to a degree not quite
welcome at Mount Royal. I'd also discovered a knack for making
people laugh, the age-old defence of the vulnerable. I'd scoured
joke books, learning them by heart, keeping them ready like a
quiverful of arrows. By sheer willpower, I'd even forced myself
to be good at rugby and, shamefully, to mock those who weren't.
And I'd found a role model; a Scottish folk-singer who appeared
every week on TV; strapping, bearded, thumping his guitar like a
man possessed. He'd been the reason I'd taken up the instrument
and fallen in love with the music. I dreamed about him regularly,
the evidence sticking to me when I woke. He was everything I
wanted to be, everything I was determined to show that I was.
His name was even Rory.

But the price of deception was eternal vigilance; a 24/7 aware-
ness of the thousand tiny ways in which I might betray myself.
One day I'd missed a try and been called a useless poof. I'd hardly
slept till I'd managed to persuade myself it'd been a meaningless
taunt. Tonight, at the dinner-table, why was Granny watching
us? What detail had I missed? What expression had slipped past
my guard? The fear was always there. It was locked in constant
combat with what I yearned for and sometimes it lost, but it was
always there. Me and my shadow.

The nice man poured champagne into my water-glass when
Granny wasn't looking. When I let my thigh rest against his, he
didn't pull it away. I offered to show him the gardens after coffee.

The night was humid. There had been a thundery shower and
the ground still exhaled a just perceptible mist. We circled the
Great Fountain, floodlit for the occasion. We dodged the spray

and laughed. Would he like to see our wee folly? He said that he would. I led him through an abandoned walled garden called the Wilderness, till we reached the little ruined temple. Inside the cramped, roofless chamber was a grubby statue of Apollo, his body scurvied with lichen. Despite the heat, it was dank and dark in here. The nice man found a stub of candle. He lit it and stuck it on Apollo's head.

At first, we didn't see Granny in the doorway, her long dress stained and slashed by the sodden brambles. It was only when her old spaniel ran in yelping that we turned our heads. The nice man hissed a soft expletive. He pulled up his trousers and, with an apologetic smile, tried to squeeze past her into the garden. But her hand shot out and clawed onto his collar.

'He's fifteen,' she said, spitting the words like grape pips. 'Fifteen. The scandal would finish your career.'

The nice man smiled at her again, but this time in a different, bolder way.

'And yours,' he said.

He wriggled from her grasp, smoothing his lapels. She stood aside and let him pass. I was still kneeling on the floor, calcified like a Pompeiian, my bare knees scuffed and dirty, my mouth wet. Granny looked down at me but said nothing. She was breathing heavily, leaning on the jewelled Malacca cane. Then suddenly the cane flew upwards. For a moment, it quivered in the air above my head, but then it froze and fell from her hand. She blew out the candle on Apollo's head and turned towards the doorway. The spaniel scampered ahead out into the night.

'Granny please,' I said.

But without looking back, she hobbled away and left me to the darkness.

FOUR

'Tonight, let me sleep in the lee of your thigh
Breakfast on the milk that seeps from the eye
The milk that makes me whole, the milk that feeds my soul
And nourishes my dream of you and I'

Filthy isn't it? Not to mention the shite grammar. It's today's 'Partner Poem' from Faisal. I get a few every week now, slipped under my cereal bowl or into my jacket pocket. He's got this book, *The Man-Love Manual: Same-Sex Solutions To Today's Partnership Challenges.* Among its touchy-feely suggestions is that we should write each other regular romantic verses, 'in order to express those deepest emotions so often left unsaid in our workaday world.' I tried it about twice, gave up and bought him a box of After Eights instead. He said it wasn't the same. Anyway, he's still churning them out at the speed of Barbara Cartland. He takes it all so seriously, it's like he's studying for another degree to add to the three he's got already.

Tonight before dinner, I was lying on the bed contemplating Faisal's 'south front'. It certainly deserves to be listed. As he trimmed his beard at the bathroom mirror, his buttocks jutted out from his lower back like two furry specimens of some Pakistani peach. I'd once tried propping the Shorter Oxford Dictionary on them to see if it could be done and fuck me it could. When I'd wandered online almost a year ago and seen the pic of him in tight running gear, his nipples like two tiny volcanoes, I'd almost cum in my pants. At 5'4", a bit too tall perhaps; but nobody's perfect. I was in there like a ferret.

DinkyDudes.com. Of all Internet sites, it's got me into the most trouble. I've never understood my sporadic fetish for teeny-weeny men. Ms Prada says it's an admirable manifestation of a caring response to perceived vulnerability, which was a relief as I'd been worried it was a wee streak of paedophilia. My platinum membership of Dinkydudes gives me access to an unlimited number of profiles and information about, *inter alia*, their sexual boundaries and the identity of their favourite actress, who is nearly always Dame Judi Dench. The Dinkydudes are graded by height, starting from 5'8" and working down in two-inch slots till you get to 5'0". Below that is a specialist 'room' where essentially we're talking midgets. But my fetish isn't that extreme or indeed exclusive; I've always been an equal opportunities predator.

When I'd messaged Faisal I'd got the standard cool response, but it had warmed up over a week or two although it was a month before he agreed to meet for coffee. This was a longer-term investment than I usually went in for and an instant dividend seemed unlikely as Dr Faisal Khan had made it plain he didn't sleep with anyone unless there was at least a tentative commitment to, as he phrased it, exploring possibilities. He'd accepted my invitations to dinner, the movies, even to the Varsity Match at Twickenham. He'd been perfectly amiable, but somehow quite detached. He wasn't that great at small talk either, work seemed to be his consuming passion. On every occasion, I'd reflexively tried to breach the bastion but he'd just slapped his little palm against mine and headed back to some tiny flat he rented near his hospital.

'Ah,' said a friend. 'The Anne Boleyn Manoeuvre. Hope he's worth the wait.'

One evening, I'd be given tickets for a concert by a gay choir and dragged him along. Not his sort of thing, he'd said. Not mine either; a hundred divas belting out an uneasy mixture of campy showtunes and right-on anthems about strength in the face of discrimination. But in the darkness, Faisal had reached out for my arm and I'd seen that he was crying, his shoulders shaking like an aspen in a gale. Hands from the row behind had patted him consolingly and, as we'd filed out, he'd been hugged by a black drag queen with dripping mascara. I'd been amazed; till then I'd assumed he was as hard as most of his generation seemed to me, hard as the Arab in The Catacombs. From that moment on he no longer scared me slightly like most of them did. And I think that was why I hung in there. That and the 'south front' of course.

That night I'd hoped my luck was in, but yet again he'd just vanished into the bowels of the Northern Line. What Stephen Sondheim couldn't achieve, Baron Haussman did. I'd taken him to Paris; he'd never been before and was dazzled. It was the corny candlelit dinner on the *bateau mouche* that'd clinched it. As we'd floated past the floodlit skirts of Notre-Dame, he'd confessed that, at twenty-nine, he'd never had a serious relationship and thought he wanted to try one with me. He'd felt our souls might travel in tandem. The waiter had overheard, said the wine was on the house and sent the violinist over to our table. I'd told the violinist to piss off.

I'd splashed out on a top floor suite in my favourite hotel in the Marais. For the first ten minutes, the sex had been ok but not sensational, which I put down to our having overdone the Louvre. But then Faisal had passed me the tie he'd been wearing and held out his fists. The night had been warm, the tall windows flung wide open. I'd attached him to the railing of the Juliet balcony and given it to him from behind in time to the midnight chimes of Saint-Germain-l'Auxerrois. It was utterly fucking amazing. These same bells had tolled for the doomed Huguenots on St Bartholomew's Eve. Were they tolling now to mark the end of Rory Blaine's confirmed bachelorhood? Was I about to let my hands be tied too?

I'd lain watching him as he slept that night, his hairy arm clamped tightly round my chest. Over the past few celibate weeks, I'd decided that he was, without a doubt, the most beautiful man I'd ever known. Not just physically, but in every way. He worked himself to death looking after the sick, helped run a soup-kitchen on the Embankment and visited his parents in Slough every Sunday. He was too good for me really, too good for this world in fact. He was Mother Teresa with an arse to die for. He was, as the saying goes, something else. It could never last.

But it's more than nine months since Paris and it's still going fairly well. He has a way of peering into my eyes like he really wants to know what's behind them. The reserve has gone too. In fact, he insists on opening up more and more bits of himself like windows on an Advent Calendar: his relationship with his father and mother, with his Uncle Raj and Auntie Shazia, being gay, being gay and Asian, being gay, Asian and a doctor. I feel pretty sure he's never opened these windows before. Why does that make me a tad uncomfortable? Is it in case he expects me to open mine too? I'm a bit out of practice with that, except with Ms Prada in the eau-de-nil room with the droopy azalea.

I've never totally understood this mass compulsion for partnership. I'd craved it that one time in Australia when I'd been little more than a kid, but it hadn't worked out. Okay, that's an understatement, like saying *Hamlet* gets a bit gloomy towards the end. As I've said, I gave it a few more goes but the only man I'd ever really wanted nattering first thing in the morning had been

Terry Wogan. That'd been why the strange toothbrushes had never stayed for long. When I'd needed company, I'd gone out and got it. I'd always been essentially alone. I'd never been scared of it. But was I scared of it now then? After the Arab kid in The Catacombs turned up the light? I'd realized that'd happen sooner or later, but nothing had quite prepared me for the pain of the fall. Mind you, I'd got straight back on the horse and gone off at full gallop, till I'd had to limp in and get Rod, my genito-urinary mechanic, to treat a nasty bout of 'recreational collateral damage.' I'd tried to convince myself the Arab was some sort of freak, but I'd known that from then on I'd probably fall a lot more often. Of course I'd run to Ms Prada afterwards and we'd set off on an in-depth exploration of self-esteem, hacking through the jungle of false perceptions, searching for new mental pathways that I just *might* want to consider taking.

Anyway. Whatever the murky middle-aged psychology, here I was in a relationship again, or at least test-driving one, though it seemed clear Faisal had already signed the purchase agreement.

'Hey, let's dress up a bit,' I said tonight as he came back into the bedroom, his coal-black hair still damp from the shower. 'Wear the Gaultier leathers.'

'Must I?' he replied, in the calm, almost sleepy voice that still carried traces of Slough. I felt a niggle of impatience. I'd frog-marched him into the coolest clothes shops in town but he rarely appeared in anything other than sweat pants and a T-shirt.

'Oh come on Faisal, it's his birthday. Make his pacemaker blow a gasket.'

'Has he got one? He's never mentioned it.'

'I've no idea. It was just a figure of speech,' I said. 'Though I guess we might get quite a few of those.'

'Possibly,' said Faisal. 'I'm going to need that sort of info before they're accepted. I'm sure you don't want them pegging out before their deposit's in the bank. Right, I'd better get started on this banquet.'

Still wrapped in his towel, he went upstairs to the kitchen.

The flat was in the low L-shaped block, once dairies and store-rooms, barnacled onto the east wing of Mount Royal. Out of it, we'd created several studio apartments for the live-in staff we'd need and, for myself, a two-storey maisonette nevertheless called 'the flat'. I'd wanted it to be cool, contemporary, a total contrast to the main house. Downstairs are two bedrooms and bathrooms and, at the top of a glass staircase, a big open-plan living area with a kitchen in one corner. The wow factor is a huge sloping picture window punched into the roof and looking south over the city. It's a kind of minimalist-Montmartre look. I've sent some stills to the interiors mags and there's a good chance of a feature.

Vic had seemed a bit baffled by the flat. He'd assumed I'd want to lay claim to my grandmother's old rooms. Was he serious? Anyhow, I'd always been clear that, when the house opened for business, I'd not want to be living right above the shop. Faisal had also been firm about our having private space if he agreed to move in. It had to be *our* home; he would pay rent and share the bills just like any other couple. At first, I'd pooh-poohed all that, but he'd got a solicitor to draw up two agreements, one formalizing his tenancy of the flat, the other his part-time employment as medical and nutritional adviser to Mount Royal Limited. I'd felt a bit uneasy when I'd signed the papers. They carried a *gravitas* the toothbrushes lacked. It seemed we were now bonded.

Upstairs Faisal, still in his towel, was chopping vegetables with the ferocity his ancestors had used to slice up mine in the Khyber Pass. One of the things I hated most about the younger generation of men was their nonchalant ability to cook. At school, Miss Elspeth Wishart had once found me with a book of recipes from the library. She'd given me a funny look, snatched it from my hand and ordered me towards the rugby pitch. Boys don't bother about such things, she'd said.

Tonight, Faisal had pulled all the stops out. On the long glass table beside the picture window everything shimmered; glasses, silver, china, candlelight.

'You trying to impress him?'

'Probably,' said Faisal. 'He hardly seemed overjoyed to meet me.'

'Tough. What's your being here got to do with him? He's my business partner, not my mother.'

It was true though. When I'd told Vic about my new relationship and that Faisal would be moving into the flat, he'd not exactly given us a Papal blessing. We'd been in the Red Damask Drawing-Room, the only one of the state rooms as yet habitable, poring over the plans for the new kitchens. The constant smile had remained in place but it sort of froze over, like the thinnest layer of ice on a pond, hardly noticeable till you looked really close. He'd knocked back half a glass of Sancerre in one gulp.

'Well I hope it works out,' he'd said. 'Now, these kitchens...'

When Faisal moved in a month ago, Vic had presented him with an autographed copy of his most recent compilation CD, *D'Orsay: The Ultimate Collection*, on which he was photographed leaning cheek to cheek against a sculpture in his namesake Parisian museum. Faisal had thanked him politely and then examined it with the same expression he no doubt used when diagnosing terminal cancer. It wasn't the response Vic was used to. Since then they'd had little contact, so I was pleased that Faisal was making an effort this evening. We were living at close quarters after all, our cheeks by Vic's jowls.

When I'd met Faisal, Vic and I had been about eighteen months into the restoration. I'd flogged my stake in Blaine Rampling. Thatcher's children hadn't been able to believe their luck; they'd raised the loot in twenty-four hours and been like bitches on heat till they'd got me out the door. A week after my farewell party, Blaine Rampling had become *Eclecsis*. Hey ho. *Sic transit gloria mundi*. But I'd not given a damn. I'd also sold Devonshire Street and was camped out in one of Mount Royal's dilapidated bedrooms till the flat was ready. Vic was here too by then, having cleaned up on his Chelsea place and taken possession of my grandmother's rooms. I'd not brought Faisal to the house at first. After Paris, we'd always gone back to his place; an anodyne studio near the Whittington Hospital. Eventually of course he'd asked to see where I lived, but I'd been right not to flaunt it in his face. The appeal of Mount Royal just wasn't on the radar of a fiercely left-wing doctor; all Faisal saw was a decrepit remnant of a discredited way of life. He toured round it with the feigned interest of the Queen in a widget factory.

'What on earth will you do with it?' he'd asked 'A hotel or something?'

I'd told him that Mount Royal was about to become Britain's first residential home for gay men. Zap! Bang! Pow! Faisal had gone straight from courteous disengagement to messianic fervour with no stops in between. I'd been drenched in admiration. He'd fast-bowled me paeans of praise and encouragement, lobbed pertinent questions, thrown in his own observations on the current state of care for the elderly and what he called the untapped possibilities for transformative advance. I'd felt myself being gently lifted onto a pedestal and I'd liked it.

'You've wasted your life in advertising,' Faisal had said. 'Now you're going to be giving, not just taking like you're used to.'

'Thanks a lot,' I'd said, remembering the hotel bill in Paris.

It didn't seem totally fair to be so praised for an action I'd been half-blackmailed into and which, in the wee small hours, still scared the shite out of me. Up in the cupola that day, when Vic had told me his plan, I'd thought he was crazy. But it had seeded in me and grown. I would save Mount Royal from the Chancellor and sad lonely people from a fate worse than death. If it worked at Mount Royal, it could be extended. It could make me a fortune, it could make me famous, revered even, like Jamie Oliver. My birthday might, at long last, be squeezed into that wee paragraph in *The Times*. In short, it could be a new beginning. Rory's Blaine's life would be moving upward. There would be no plateau and certainly no over-the-hill. That night, I'd had a nice dream about being knighted by King Charles III. Prince William had whispered in my ear that he batted for both teams and had slipped me his private number.

Of course, I'd not told Faisal about Vic and the will. He'd never have accepted our new life together being built on the foundation of a crime, natural justice or not. I'd simply told him that Vic was a friend of my grandmother's who'd come into business with me. Nor did I tell him it was actually Vic's idea; I was enjoying the view from my pedestal too much. But, for the last few months, it had been Faisal's enthusiasm as much as Vic's which had kept me on course as week by week, grant by grant, regulation by regulation, the project was being nudged into harbour.

Tonight, Faisal obeyed instructions and wore the black leather Gaultier pants, matching waistcoat and John Smedley knitted T-shirt which had once caused a cataclysmic collision between two waiters in the Wolseley. Vic arrived, slightly late as usual, with the star's instinct of keeping the punters waiting. He'd dressed up too; a shiny silk suit in dove grey; his matching shoes bearing a wee silver buckle in the shape of a treble-clef. We gave him a card and a case of a very rare Burgundy. He gave us another CD, *Vic Bites The Big Apple*.

'My attempt to crack the American market,' he explained. 'But Frank, Tony Bennett, little Andy Williams, they had it all sewn up. Don't regret it though; my chance to break out of the artistic straightjacket of British M.O.R. Dusty did exactly the same. This is my equivalent of her Memphis album; you'll find it rougher, bluesier than my British stuff. Bit of a cult album now in fact. Slap it on if you want, I won't mind.'

We sipped our drinks in silence as Vic's voice sashayed around the room. God knows why he thought it less syrupy than his usual output, every track could have clogged an artery. As Vic mimed along to his own voice, the cat jumped onto his lap. The cat was devoted to Vic; not only had he discovered it was actually a girl, he'd even given her a name. She was now Alma, after Vic's old friend, the late-lamented Ms Cogan.

'Shall we eat?' shouted Faisal after about four tracks, killing the music with the remote. I wondered if anyone had ever done that in Vic's presence before. He blinked rather rapidly but said nothing.

Faisal produced an exemplary meal but very little conversation. When he was tense, he had an odd habit of forgetting to talk. But Vic didn't seem to notice and we nattered aimlessly about the renovations. Tomorrow an expert in William & Mary porcelain was coming from Oxford.

'Faisal went to Oxford,' I said, trying to reel him in.

'Glorious town, isn't it doc?' said Vic, 'Did you go for the day?'

'No, I went for six years. I studied medicine there,' replied Faisal.

'Jeez,' said Vic, 'now there's a thing.'

As Faisal struggled to chat about his three degrees and his Blue for running, Vic's eyes drifted back and forth from him like a boat tugging at its anchor. I began to sense that Faisal, despite being young, gorgeous and intelligent, just didn't interest Vic very much. Whenever I'd dragged him to meet my other gay friends, they'd all salivated. Now here was this fat old man, smiling as usual, but utterly ungobsmacked.

I'd realized quite early that Faisal had little sense of humour. He never told jokes and often didn't understand them. And nobody could have said my gags weren't accessible. We weren't talking Noel Coward, witticisms polished like limousines; we were talking nuns and cucumber-patches. When I'd taken him to some stand-up in Islington, he'd been lost as a toddler in Tesco's. When I'd laughed out loud at his first 'Partner Poem', he'd not only been hurt but also unable to grasp why. Once, when I'd poured a lot of wine down him, he'd confessed that his work appraisals were often blotted by the feedback that his patients found him distant. He'd been really upset about it, because he cared about them all very much. I'd told myself that it hardly mattered against his other dazzling attributes, but tonight I felt that Vic detected some void in him too.

'So where were you born in France, Vic?' asked Faisal doggedly as he served the crème brûlée.

'France?' asked Vic. 'No doc, d'Orsay is only a stage name. Seventy-seven years ago today I first appeared on the world stage as Victor Emmanuel Aronson in Warsaw.'

'Ok cool,' said Faisal 'So what made you leave Poland?'

'Is the kid serious?' asked Vic, turning to me.

'Oh. Right. Sorry,' said Faisal, 'Do you have any family?'

I realized I'd never bothered to ask Vic these questions and that perhaps he'd thought that odd. But although he looked Jewish, he rarely referred to it; never telling Jewish jokes or peppering his speech with 'oy veys'. It was like he'd painted it over.

'Not any more. As far as I know anyway,' said Vic. 'There's still the wife of course. I always forget about her.'

'Fuck me, you've got a wife?' I said.

'We've been divorced for years now' said Vic, shovelling in the pudding. 'She drinks on a terrace in Ibiza these days.'

'Why the hell did you get married?' I asked.

'Oh c'mon toots,' said Vic. 'Ask Rock Hudson, though you can't now, bless him. It was what they call a 'lavender marriage'; an arranged union like I guess they still have in the doc here's community. Her name was Greta, she was a showgirl, as Mr Manilow put it. She got the fancy clothes, the big house, her face in the papers. I got the smoke-screen.'

'But what about sex?'

'She had her chorus-boys, I had mine,' said Vic. 'Sometimes we even exchanged them. Though there was one awful Christmas when we both got stoned and she tried to make me do it. Jeez. I could just about cope with the bits up north, but not down south. I had to finish her off with a Minton candlestick, a present from Johnnie Gielgud. It was the only thing to hand. I never told Johnnie though.'

Faisal left the table to make coffee. When he returned with the tray he had several spiral-bound folders tucked under his arm.

'I've got another present for Vic,' he said shyly. 'For both of you really.'

But as he filled the wee coffee cups, his eyes began to get their evangelical look, the one which appeared when he was talking about his work, the state of the planet or the life and times of Sir Roger Bannister.

'Vic, as Rory's already aware, I see a unique opportunity here,' he said. 'Mount Royal could be remembered not just as Britain's first gay retirement home but also as the template for living well as one gets older. A whole philosophy inside four walls.'

'Jeez,' said Vic, ignoring the coffee and topping up his glass. He was fairly well gone by now. Faisal handed each of us a folder. On the front cover was neatly typed *The Lazarus Programme: Unlocking Your Later-Life Potential.*

'As you know, my professional interest lies in the area of holistic medicine with particular emphasis on nutrition and preventative therapies.' Faisal continued, talking ever faster, his usually measured sentences sprinting off the starting-block. 'In this context, I believe that not only should we be offering our residents food and shelter but also, as far as is currently possible, the means to stop the clock and even to turn it back. That's why I call it *The Lazarus Programme*, a chance to rise again.'

'There are plenty of old guys who'd vote for that,' smiled Vic.

Faisal didn't get the joke.

'Vic, can I talk to you as a doctor rather than a friend?' said Faisal. 'You're seventy-seven today and, with respect, you look it. I suspect your biological age might be even higher. But with a combination of diet, nutrition, exercise, perhaps even some cosmetic surgery if you wanted to go that far, you could wipe ten years off the way you both look and feel. Maybe even fifteen.'

'Wow,' I said. 'Amazing. What do you say to that, Victor?'

'Let me be even blunter,' Faisal went on. 'When you sat down at this table, you let one go didn't you?'

'Sorry. Didn't notice.'

'You didn't? There are two problems then. First, if you weren't aware of the fart, you've slightly lost control of your sphincter muscles. That can be corrected with simple exercises. In six months, you could have the sphincter of a twenty year old.'

'Only if we've been introduced,' replied Vic.

Faisal didn't get that joke either. He refilled our coffee cups and sat down again, the eyes still flashing.

'The second problem is what your fart revealed to me' said Faisal. 'It's a bit like a connoisseur savouring the bouquet of a fine wine. In one whiff, I can guess roughly what's wrong with your diet. And in one glance I can see how that's affecting your health and appearance.'

'So what's the bottom line, so to speak?' asked Vic. The smile was still there but it was wobbling like a trapeze artist on a tightrope. I now wished Faisal would shut up.

'It's that you're the perfect example of an elderly man for whom *The Lazarus Programme* could be, literally, a life-saver.'

'But what if I'm quite happy as I am doc?'

'Surely you'd be a lot happier if your body were happier too?' countered Faisal with the smug tone of the expert witness. 'You're in this thing together after all.'

'Suppose my soul isn't too bothered about my body?' asked Vic. 'Suppose it's quite content to witness a gradual deterioration because that's in the natural order of things?'

'Even if it means you may die five or ten years before you need to?'

'Doc, in my seventy-seven years I've seen many people die long before their time. Knocked down by a bus or by some other goddam event that comes tearing round the bend. In even more terrible ways too, though I don't know you well enough to talk about that. But against all the odds, Vic d'Orsay is still here and I'm so grateful for that. But it's got to be on my own terms. So I don't want to rain on your parade, but please excuse me the gym, the lentils and the lipo-suction. Just let me sit in the Italian Garden on a summer's evening with a brandy glass resting on my gut and let me look at the bees buzzing in the honeysuckle. That okay with you?'

Faisal shrugged amiably, but looked a bit deflated.

'Well I think it's brilliant Faisal,' I said. 'Victor, *The Lazarus Programme* is a sensational add-on concept for our product. Nobody wants to get older, especially gay men for Christ's sake. It's a winner.'

'Do you remember Dickie?' Vic asked me. 'The old guy back in that nursing home? Babbling on about being fucked by The Master?'

'Sure. Poor old bugger.'

'Exactly. I wonder how many thousands of poor old buggers are in his situation? The Dickies of this world don't want biceps or Botox or sphincter muscles that could pick up a ping-pong ball. They just want a place to feel safe and to be themselves. Where somebody will be pleased to see them when they come down for breakfast, make sure they're okay when they've got the flu and be within a taxi-ride of the latest revival of *Lady Windermere's Fan*. This house is supposed to become a home, not a fucking boot-camp.'

There was long silence at the table, broken only by the purring of Alma the cat as she snoozed with her head against Vic's shoe with the treble clef buckle. Faisal was nearly always as placid as a duck on a midsummer pond but, when irritated or hacked off, he had a wee habit of pulling at his beard and he was tugging quite violently now.

'So you oppose what I'm putting forward?' he asked eventually.

'No doc, not at all,' said Vic, patting his arm. 'Just as long as it's not compulsory. Poor Dickie's old pal, the great Mr Coward, once summed it up nicely. "There's no point trying to bar the door against old age. Invite it in and give it lunch."'

Vic dabbed his lips with his napkin and wobbled to his feet. His chair clattered to the floor behind him, but he didn't seem to notice. I rose too, but Faisal didn't.

'Oops, I might have let another one go,' said Vic. 'I'll leave it with you doc. See what you make of it.'

He hoisted his waistband above his belly and trundled across the room. His copy of *The Lazarus Programme* lay abandoned on the table.

'Well if I don't pursue this, there's really no role for me here,' replied Faisal, trying to say it lightly, but not succeeding.

'Nonsense,' laughed Vic over his shoulder. 'You're Mr Blaine's paramour, to use an old-fashioned word. And a cute little one too. Jeez doc, what other role could any man want?'

He negotiated his way carefully down the staircase, as if he feared the glass might splinter under his weight. I followed with Faisal trailing behind. At the front door, Vic picked up a carrier-bag.

'Hey toots, I almost forgot, here's a present for you too,' he said, passing me a fat leather-bound album. It was filled with photographs and pages of neatly laid-out type.

'The result of a year's hard work,' said Vic. 'A year of exhaustive networking, carefully-phrased letters, delicate phone calls and discreet word of mouth.'

'Who are all these guys?' I asked, flicking through the images.

'They're Rory's Boys' said Vic.

FIVE

'One egg or two?' said Marcus Leigh, his gaze drifting past my right ear and out through the silk-draped window into Carlton Gardens. 'One egg or two. Not going to make it into any compilation of famous last words is it? Not going to be up there with "Kiss me Hardy" or "Bugger Bognor."'

There was a long pause. Vic squeezed his friend's pin-striped shoulder, then brushed off the dandruff which had gathered there.

'I was in the bathroom. He was making my breakfast as he always did. Then an awful cry. A thud on the floor. Cerebral haemorrhage. Bang. Dead.'

Marcus Leigh waved across the dining-room of the Reform Club at a sad-looking waitress.

'Not much of a goodbye was it?' he sighed. 'After thirty years, you'd have thought we'd have earned a gentler separation. A little warning, time for one final weekend in Florence, even just a death bed-scene for God's sake, a chance to say thank you. Not merely the sudden explosion of a blood vessel. Then full stop. Water under the bridge. Pull yourself together. Get on with your life. That's what they all said. I recommend the lamb cutlets.'

'I'll have the guinea-fowl,' I said. I'd only met him twenty minutes ago but I'd already clocked Marcus Leigh's way of making suggestions sound like instructions; well-meant, but instructions nonetheless.

'Apologies for getting morbid,' he said, when she'd plodded away. 'Bad form.'

'Not at all Marcus,' said Vic. 'I was so sorry when you wrote to me about it. I'm sure all your clients were.'

Marcus flashed him a short tight smile.

'Dear Vic, I have lived my life in different compartments. You are the only client of my firm who was ever *au fait*.'

'And that was just because I once got you pissed at the Dorchester and you slipped your phone number to a pretty sommelier.'

Vic gave him a blokey punch to suggest that Marcus could be a bit of a lad. Marcus dimpled and blushed but anyone less blokey would be hard to imagine. When the guinea-fowl arrived, it bore him a definite resemblance. Dried-out and all trussed-up, just like

Marcus in his buttoned waistcoat and tightly-knotted tie. It was impossible to picture him on the tube, shopping for loo rolls or in any environment that was completely marble-free.

The room was crowded, muggy and over-lit, which was a mistake as most of the diners had reached the age of needing soft focus. I couldn't spot a soul under forty, nearly all clones of Marcus with grey hair, florid faces, dark suits and a lightly-worn sense of superiority. There were a few females; a mix of sharp-shouldered boardroom types and wives up from the shires with no make-up and awful clothes. Marcus had followed my glance.

'Ghastly, aren't they?' he said quietly. 'I know I shouldn't feel that. I battle misogyny the way other people struggle with booze but, the blessed Margaret apart, I do feel the feminist pendulum has swung too far.'

He glanced round, then discreetly pulled a couple of dog-eared Polaroids from his wallet. A pretty Latin boy with a pencil moustache posed by the fountain in the Piazza Navona.

'Phwoar!' I said. Marcus's ruddy cheeks flushed again, but I could see he was pleased. 'So where did you two meet?'

'In Oddbins in North Audley Street on a pouring wet Sunday,' he replied. 'He disapproved of the wine I had selected and suggested one that came from his own region. Everybody else was gloomy and smelled of raincoats, but Ricardo was wearing a bright yellow sweater and a smile like August. He asked me to go for coffee and we sat in a scruffy place behind Oxford Street laughing our heads off. We were as different as people could be, but for some reason we fitted together like two pieces of a jigsaw. That night, a dull chartered accountant aged thirty-five lost his virginity and found everything he'd ever wanted. It felt like I'd taken myself out of storage and blown off the dust.'

Vic's eyes were already moist. It didn't seem to take much. I was never sure if it was genuine or some showbizzy Dickie Attenborough thing.

'He was an Italian actor from a council flat in Naples. Fifteen years younger than me,' said Marcus, easing the photos back into the safety of his wallet. 'So of course people said he was after my money. But even if he had been, I'm not sure I'd have cared. Ricardo was handing me his life on a platter and since nobody else had ever offered so much as a morsel of themselves, I thought I'd better tuck in. Wouldn't you?'

Marcus dictated that we should all have sticky-toffee pudding and this time I acquiesced, hoping that it might cheer him up. Afterwards, he marched us up a tunnel-vaulted staircase to the gallery that overlooked the atrium. It was even hotter up here than down below. I peeked into a vast library, jam-packed with huge polished volumes and piles of magazines and newspapers. All the information the members might possibly need to help them go on running the country. Marcus poured out the coffee with a nervy precision as if he expected some hidden menace lurking in the pot. We settled ourselves beneath the portrait of a particularly tight-arsed Whig.

'I suppose the reason I'm meeting you today is because Ricardo and I made one big mistake in our time together,' said Marcus. 'Neither of us really felt the need for anyone else. We saw ourselves as a respectable married couple and lived accordingly. We never went to parks, public conveniences or those fire-trap drinking clubs in Soho garrets. We ring-fenced ourselves from outside threats. And now he's gone, I'm still in there on my own.'

'I'm sure your chimney-piece is sagging with invitations Marcus,' said Vic.

'Not quite,' he replied. 'Most of my family has been culled too, except for a nephew who surfaces occasionally in the erroneous hope he might be in the will. My former colleagues rarely ring. My social life is All Saints, Margaret Street on a Sunday and the occasional livery dinner where you almost choke on the boredom.'

Poor old sod. I wondered if I should mention the pleasures of the websites and the chat-rooms where you could lead a perfectly acceptable, indeed riotous, social life without ever leaving your own fireside. I was just about to suggest DynamiteDads.com when Marcus sat forward in his chair and clasped me firmly in his gaze.

'Tell me Mr Blaine, is your beautiful house haunted? Mine is, you see. The chairs, the tables, the bath, the bed, even the way the plates are stacked in the cupboards. I should have moved of course, but the ghost was at least some sort of presence. But he'd not have wanted it to be like this. For the past three years, I've been feeling that old carapace creeping back over me, the one Ricardo had cracked open and thrown away. And that scares me. So if you'll forgive an old man getting rather fanciful, I wondered maybe if Vic's letter really came from Ricardo. As if he's showing me the way forward. I just need to be brave enough to take it.'

Marcus sank back against the wrinkled red leather of his chair. He looked away from us and straightened the knot of his tie. I sensed that this sort of confessional wasn't in his nature and that he'd found it an effort. He stood up very suddenly.

'Will you both excuse me for a moment? I've just seen the Lord Chancellor over there. We were at Marlborough together. He'll be offended if I don't say hello. Perhaps you'd care for a brandy?'

He snapped his fingers at a waiter then headed towards a tall wispy man in spectacles on the far side of the gallery. Vic and I watched as the brown-nosing began, Marcus's shoulders heaving at some legal witticism.

'I know he's a bit heavy-going,' said Vic. 'Got a good heart though.'

'He's also got the readies I suppose?'

'Leigh and Montague are among the sharpest accountants in town. It's partly down to Marcus that I'm loaded enough to bank-roll our little project. When he retired, he laughed all the way to Threadneedle Street. He's also got a very classy pad just behind the Connaught. I don't think we need to worry.'

'Sad about the boyfriend,' I said. 'He's gutted isn't he?'

'I guess you'd feel the same if Faisal dropped dead?'

'Sure, but I think I'd survive. Not sure Marcus has, are you?'

'Not in any meaningful way perhaps,' said Vic. 'I suppose that's the risk of a long-term thing. Not being two totally separate people any more.'

'Can't quite imagine that, can you Victor?'

'Oh yes I can imagine it toots. Never experienced it though; certainly not to the degree that Marcus has.'

'Yeah, I feel sorry for him.'

'Sorry for him?' asked Vic, waving for another brandy. 'Shouldn't we envy him? Better to have loved and lost...'

'Well he's really paying the price now isn't he?' I said. 'Is it worth it?'

'I reckon Marcus would say that it was. What would you say? You're the one who's just entered a serious relationship, after all.'

'I don't know,' I replied honestly. 'Thirty years together, then half an hour at the crem with Celine Dion and that fucking song from *Titanic*. Followed by sausages on sticks, being hugged by people you've never met before, then home alone to your haunted house, as Marcus calls it. I'm not sure I could take being disembowelled like that.'

'Maybe you need to become sure pretty damn quick.'

'So you reckon it's worth it then?' I asked.

'Oh yes, I'd risk it,' said Vic 'for the chance of the joy.'

I could see his eyelids beginning to droop as they often did at this time of the day, although Vic always looked like a man who'd had a good lunch even when he hadn't. Well I'd risked it years ago back in Australia, when I'd been too young to realize that any risk was involved. Disaster. Now here I was having a final go with Faisal, for the chance of the joy. But I was still a bit hazy as to what that meant exactly. I just assumed it was something worth having, some Nirvana shimmering on the horizon, where life could be lived on a higher plane. Or was that just a load of bollocks?

'Well let's hope Marcus can lighten up a bit,' I said eventually. 'Are all the guys in that album of yours this stuffy Victor?'

'Jeez toots, get real,' he replied 'Men well-heeled enough to afford our fees are likely to be sixty-five plus, hang out in places like this and take the *Telegraph*. They're unlikely to moisturize, exfoliate or pay much attention to their nasal hair. They might even dribble slightly from one or more of their orifices. So if you're banking on a house full of Tom Selleck lookalikes, you're in for a disappointment. Marcus, bless him, is our template. Deal with it.'

Marcus returned and led us back downstairs to the floor of the atrium.

'Thank you so much for coming to vet me,' he said, shaking our hands briskly.

'We'll be honoured to have you, old buddy,' said Vic, slapping his back and turning towards the cloakroom. But Marcus seemed reluctant to let us go before he was totally sure the judges had heard his plea.

'The thing is, gentlemen, I think I'm in imminent danger of becoming a sad case,' he said. 'I spend my days watching dreadful TV programmes about grandmothers who run off with teenage boys or spunky women who don't mind that their husbands wear their frocks. So I do hope you might take me in. Otherwise I shall be left sitting here rereading George Eliot, and Dorothea Brooke's just not as much fun as she used to be.'

Their faces were like two podgy beetroots now; the sticky toffee pudding, the brandies, the heat. As Vic clasped his hand again, Marcus suddenly swooned. I grabbed for him a second too late and the three of us ended up on the mosaic floor in a vaguely indecent tangle. People came running. We got Marcus up onto a chair, took off his tie, opened his collar and fanned him with a copy of *The Spectator*. His eyes fluttered back into focus.

'Take it easy Marcus. Breathe slowly and deeply,' I said, giving him a sip of water.

Marcus's hand flew to his throat.

'Where's my tie?'

'You needed air. We took it off.'

'In here? Good grief! Did the Lord Chancellor see?'

I glanced back up to the gallery where knots of coffee-drinkers were peering down on the unaccustomed commotion. The Lord Chancellor looked very concerned. Marcus's eyes followed my gaze.

'Oh my God, how could you?' He moaned and fainted again.

*

Okay, this is as good a place as any. This is where I make the big confession. Ms Prada would be thrilled. Here we go. I don't want to be a homosexual. Never did, never will. I've learned to accept it and I feel no guilt whatsoever because it wasn't my fault. But if they ever invent the 'straight' pill, I'll swallow it whole with a glass of champagne and shout 'yippee!' Sorry. I realize this is sad, pathetic and terminally uncool.

Yes I know there's never been a 'better' time to be gay. I know I'm not likely to be locked up or spat at in the street, unless I go on a mini-break to Belfast. In our shiny new Millennium, I'm not just tolerated, I'm chic. How many dinner parties in Putney have I been expected to liven-up as the token gay? At Blaine Rampling, it was one of the few things Thatcher's children approved of, convinced it helped bring in business. So hip, so happening, so now.

But I still regard it as a duff card in the pack. This sort of thing wasn't supposed to be on my CV. For Rory Blaine, scion of a shipping empire, it was supposed to be plain sailing from cradle to grave by way of Glenlyon School, Oxbridge, the Guards, the wedding, the patter of tiny feet and a fistful of non-executive directorships to see me out. Roughly what old Marcus Leigh had planned too I suppose. I just never imagined myself on the 'outside' of anything, I'm not the 'oppressed minority' type. Hey world, what I've got to offer you is worth having. Don't you dare condemn me just because of what makes my willy go hard. Even worse, don't positively discriminate in my favour. You can shove them both.

But the card was dealt, so I got on with playing it as best I could. I've never lied about it. I dragged myself on the requisite marches with the sandal-wearing types, which was not my scene at all. I once threw condoms at Mary Whitehouse. I got arrested for that. Maybe what worried me even more than being gay was the possibility of flunking it. If you have to be a poof, you might as well do it properly. And I'm pleased to report that Rory Blaine is now, without any doubt, an A-List gay. I give money to the right causes, I go to the right openings, I say all the right things. Except here of course, except now.

The other day I saw a man, half my age, walking ahead of me in the street, hand in hand with a wee boy. The kid said something; the man laughed and ruffled his hair. Suddenly I wanted to weep, then remembered that I couldn't. Okay I know, pass the sick-bag. But I've always wanted kids; it must be amazing, illuminating your soul like a million-watt lightbulb. The only time I'll be called 'dad' is by twinks with an older man fetish. How sad is that? Sure, the parent-child thing can go hideously wrong, but it would've been nice to have had the chance to fuck it up, that's all. Take old Marcus Leigh. By now, he ought to have children of my age, grandchildren in their twenties, great-grandkids even, all lined up in relays, ready to carry him on their shoulders for the rest of his days. Instead his only companion is the ghost from the Piazza Navona.

However dysfunctional my straight friends might be, at all those dinner parties I'd nearly always absorbed some sense of calm anchorage. I'd tried telling myself how rigid the itinerary of the heterosexual life. All the milestones so mercilessly laid out; no chance to wander off the path, take the road less travelled. By thirty, thou shall have monogamy and a mortgage. By thirty-five, thou shall smell of nappies. By forty thou shall look like shite and only have sex once a year. How turgid compared to the uncharted thrills of the gay journey with only your instincts to guide you. But I'd never entirely bought all that. Ms Prada doesn't either. She thinks that to mature properly people need those milestones, the generational yardsticks that children bring. And because most gays don't have them we never quite grow up ourselves. We just keep on dancing and arguing about whether Lesley Garrett is a great diva or just a vulgar populist.

Anyway, I think it's a bit too late to go chasing a lesbian with a turkey-baster. So just like Granny was the last of the Ashridges, I will be the last of the Blaines. The plug will be pulled on my prestigious gene pool and it will gurgle to extinction. It will not be business as usual as Granny had imagined. There will be no new portraits for the Gilded Hall. Oh well, hey ho. I've never given a fuck about the cause of sexual orientation. But whatever bit of bad wiring is responsible, it has lost me everything I cared about and brought me nothing I could value, unless of course Faisal manages to lift the curse. I don't want to be a homosexual. There, I've said it again. But I will never say it aloud, not even to Ms Prada. It is my shame.

*

Tonight I took myself out on the town. Faisal had dashed down to Slough. At Khan's Tools & Hardware, a two-litre can of Dulux Brilliant White Gloss had fallen from a shelf right onto his father's skull. I'd hoped it might be curtains for the bigoted old shite, but Faisal had left within three minutes of his mother's call; he worshipped his father.

Vic was in bed with a migraine and anyway for the last fortnight I'd spent nearly every waking moment in his company. He'd been right about Marcus Leigh being the template. Day after day, I'd been living in a melanin-free world inspecting a line-up of eminently respectable, grey-haired gentlemen. After lunch at the Reform, I'd sat through tea at the Athenaeum and dinner at the Garrick. I'd visited so many gracious apartments in Mayfair and Belgravia that when we'd travelled out to Fulham, it'd felt like slumming. The most fun had been when a retired Cambridge don had answered the door dressed like Alistair Sim as the headmistress of St Trinians. He'd wanted to be open with us right from the start he'd said; we'd have to take him or leave him. We'd not quite decided yet.

But tonight I really needed to get out of Mount Royal, to get away briefly from this thing that I'd allowed to take over my life. And La Ronde was this year's 'kewl' bar. I'd been too busy to get to the opening but I didn't want to start losing touch. I'd no intention of trying to pull. With one bizarre exception, of which more later, I'd been faithful to Faisal since the night I'd tied him to that balcony in Paris. Monogamy was fine, really it was. I just wanted to check the place out. I'd scarcely been into Soho in months and certainly not to anywhere gay. Faisal never wanted to go on the scene. I'd once frogmarched him to a club but his utter boredom had shrouded both of us in a pall of peevishness. He'd had one Diet Coke and refused point blank to dance, not even to Abba. We'd been home by midnight.

'Why on earth do you and I need places like that now?' he'd demanded as he'd brewed the herbal tea he always took to bed.

At the door of La Ronde the bouncer greeted me like a long-lost brother. I knew him from other clubs he'd worked at. He was a Muscle Mary; emphasis on the latter word.

'And where have *we* been all this time?' he asked, kissing me on both cheeks. 'It's just like Dolly Levi returning to the Harmonia Gardens Restaurant.'

The interior was the shape of a huge drum. On the ground level was a dance floor and bar; above it, three tiers of pillared galleries connected to each other by teeny spiral staircases. The galleries were furnished with fake Baroque sofas and big gilt-framed mirrors hung at crazy angles on the curving walls. The mirror glass was made of some material that distorted reflections; faces, bodies, colours and lights were twisted into weird, almost frightening shapes. It was all achingly hip, but of course just the same as any other bar I'd been in during the last twenty-five years. The sets, the costumes, the hairdos changed, but the script never varied. Yet these were the stages where metropolitan gay men were programmed to perform. Whatever other parts you played in your life, however brilliantly you played them, it was against this backdrop that you'd be reviewed by your peers as a *bona fide* homosexual.

Sorry to stretch the metaphor, but Rory Blaine's appearances on such stages had always been a triumphant success. From my debut in the late Seventies, my appeal had been simple; I'd appeared to have stumbled into the wrong play. Back then, they couldn't quite believe I was gay. Even in the first heady years of liberation, it had still been a sub-culture whose icons were Quentin Crisp, Julian and Sandy and drag acts in grubby pubs. But I'd personified what most of them imagined they'd failed to be. Despite the golden locks, I'd been what old Quentin had once called The Great Dark Man, the unattainable possessor of unforced masculinity. But I was in fact attainable; disgracefully so. And in that fashion, giving away little pieces of myself like fragments of the true cross, I'd passed some of the best years of my life. It'd been a far cry from how Miss Elspeth Wishart had hoped her boys from Glenlyon School would behave.

'You're chipping away at your very soul,' she'd say when any of us wandered from the simple clear Calvinist road she'd been determined we should follow. And boy, had I chipped.

I got a beer and cruised the galleries. I saw three or four faces I recognized but nobody said hello. I'd long since forgotten their names but, oddly, I could still remember wee glimpses I'd had into their real lives, their lives away from places like this. I remembered suburban flats, hideous wallpaper, tropical fish, dishes in the sink. I remembered bathroom cabinets which I'd checked out, as I always did, to see if they had gum problems or fungal infections. Once or twice I'd discovered such a suspicious regiment of pill-bottles that I'd faked a sudden headache and got the hell out of there. Otherwise, for a couple of hours, we'd hopped off the world together, then we'd travelled onwards. *A bientôt. Hasta luego*. See you later.

I stood on the topmost gallery and looked down on the dancers. The body-heat rose and hit you in the face. It was like looking into a cauldron seething with gorgeous grubs, slithering around each other, high as kites on fuck-knows-what. Apart from booze, I don't do drugs. Never understood why anyone would want to lose control. Give me a man who sticks to three pints of Guinness and stops while he can still get it up.

The ghetto stereotypes were all there: the skin-deep machismo of the leather men who probably worked in the fabric department of John Lewis, the pot-bellied bears with their beards and tats, the shaven-headed, anorexic waifs, the screamers in eye-liner. Every one of them instantly flagged their sexuality to the world and his wife without embarrassment, defiant in their right to be respected. And wasn't that exactly what my lot had battled for? Why should I be jealous of that? Fuck it. I still deserved a place here. I'd earned it.

I got another Becks, went downstairs and shoe-horned myself onto the dance-floor. *Honky-Tonk Women* rose from the grave. I made eye contact with a circle of scally lads and gave them my

Jagger. They grinned at first but melted away one by one till I was dancing alone. I saw them regroup on the far side of the floor. Christ, why on earth had I come here? I'd been eyed by a couple of obvious renters, but otherwise hardly a glance. I spotted a couple more faces I knew, still on the prowl, just that wee bit older. They had a curious quality for me now, ghostly almost, though not like Marcus Leigh's precious dead Italian boy. These were worthless ghosts. Once we might have offered each other something, but none of us had bothered to search for it. It hadn't been the name of the game. Anyway, at that point, I'd not been willing to play any other.

But hey, I'd come out unscathed right? I did have a relationship now and with a decent man, who trailed youth and beauty behind him like a fur. I had my trophy, the evidence of my continuing appeal. Why, as Faisal had asked, didn't I just walk out of places like this forever? Why go on clinging to the carousel? Would it really be that awful to let go? Mightn't it just conceivably be a glorious release? At exactly what point did the Great Dark Man turn into the Sad Old Fucker? I'd feared it had happened that day in the sauna when the Arab kid turned up the light. But maybe that had been a false alarm. Maybe it was just tonight, a minute ago, as I strutted my ageing stuff like a demented chicken? Or perhaps I could hang on till next year or even the year after that? I'd always prided myself that I would know.

I bought the one beer too many and sat at the bar. Near me was a boy I'd already noticed a few times. Most people had. A broad, strong olive-skinned face with full lips and a flattened nose beneath a mop of tousled hair. No more than eighteen. Straight out of Caravaggio. But he sat alone, the handsome face blank, the body tensed, feet perched on the highest rung on the bar stool, knees drawn up against the chest, foetal almost. He'd thrown up an invisible wall that everybody could see, so they'd left him in there. Mostly he just contemplated the depths of his drink but occasionally his eyes would dart around for a moment before retreating again. On one such expedition they caught mine and stayed there. At first I felt the reflexive surge of vanity. The Great Dark Man lived. But as we looked at each other, I realized it wasn't attraction I could read in his eyes but curiosity. Then suddenly he untangled himself from the stool and vanished into the crowd.

I headed for the exit via the loos. The urinals were crowded. I hated peeing in gay bogs. I could never manage it unless I stared at the porcelain and conjured up some deeply unerotic image. Like Glenda Jackson stark naked in that old Ken Russell movie about Tchaikovsky. I was just focussing on Glenda when a gruff voice murmured in my ear.

'Shame to waste that mate.'

A big leather guy beside me had pushed an empty half-pint beer mug under my cock. Oh what the hell. The management had hung one of their distorting mirrors in here too and I watched my warped reflection pissing into the beer mug, chipping away at my very soul.

'Cheers mate,' he said.

'Cheers,' I said.

Outside, a sharp spring wind made me realize I'd overdone the booze. As I walked back to the Merc, I saw the Caravaggio boy standing under a lamp post smoking a fag with tears running down his cheeks. He turned his head away.

'Are you all right?' I asked.

'Yes thank you. I do not have problem,' he replied. The accent was Mediterranean, maybe even Italian after all.

'Can I do anything to help?'

He shook the tousled head. I headed towards the Merc. Then his voice called after me.

'Answer me a question, yes?'

'Of course.'

'I do not wish to be rude, but I think you have been gay for many years now?' he said. 'I am just beginning. Tell me please. Is this all there is?'

I retraced my steps and stood under the lamp post.

'I'm still trying to decide about that,' I said. 'I think it probably depends on who you are. And if you want there to be, then there can be.'

A Starbucks cardboard mug was rolling in the gutter. I scribbled my mobile number on it.

'If you ever want to chat any time, call me.'

The handsome face wrinkled up, like he'd smelt something bad.

'Gesu,' he said, wheeling away from me and tearing off along the street.

'But I didn't mean...' I shouted after him. 'Really...'

*

I swung the car into the East Court with more luck than judgment and only just missed Faisal's scruffy old Peugeot. Bugger. I'd not expected him back tonight. But then I felt pleased that he was. Lights blazed out of every window. I suddenly thought of old Marcus Leigh sitting in his flat behind the Connaught crying over the past and the Caravaggio cutie on the windy pavement crying over the future. Blearily I vowed that I would try to embrace my present and the possibilities that it offered, both for obliterating what had gone before and for creating the shape of things to come. I pictured Ms Prada clapping her chubby wee hands with glee.

Faisal was in the kitchen in his bathrobe, brewing his herbal tea. His father had been released from hospital, the accident much less serious than first thought. He gave me a cursory glance and made the correct diagnosis.

'Black coffee perhaps?' Faisal never ceased to be solicitous; it was a reflex action and mildly irritating.

'Just took myself out for a drink. Was getting a bit claustrophobic.'

'I see.'

'Just a few beers.'

'After which you drove the car. The behaviour of a thick teenager, not of a supposedly intelligent middle-aged man.'

Faisal thrust the coffee in my face. His rebukes were always delivered as serene statements of the blindingly obvious with which the guilty party must be moronic not to agree.

'Yep. Sorry.'

'Anyway, I was just leaving you a note. There's a visitor waiting in the house.'

'At this time of night? Who the fuck is it?'

'No idea,' said Faisal. 'Vic phoned across. He said they'd be in the Red Damask Drawing-Room. Better go at once, if you're capable; they've been there at least two hours.'

Faisal and his herbal tea headed towards the glass staircase.

'And by the way, you stink. Of booze, sweat and, unless I'm mistaken, urine. I shudder to think why. I'll be in the spare room.'

Oh dear. There were a couple of yellowish stains on my chinos where I must have missed the beer mug. Something told me I'd not be getting a 'Partner Poem' in the morning. I imagined him tucked up in the spare room flicking through *The Man-Love Manual*, in search of 'scene addiction' and 'inability to commit'.

I let myself into the house, weaving my way through the scaffolding and the paint pots, the furniture in its dustsheets looming like icebergs. I stopped at the door of the Red Damask Drawing-Room. I could hear Vic's mid-Atlantic drawl and a soft female voice I couldn't quite make out. I opened the door. Vic and the visitor turned around.

'Dearie me, Rory Blaine,' said the visitor. 'Just look at the state of you.'

On a richly gilded Napoleonic sofa, on which the Empress Josephine would happily have parked her arse, sat a slight elderly woman who looked like an extra from *Dr Finlay's Casebook*. Her back was ramrod straight and her eyes pierced into me like the two knitting-needles clicking away in her bony fingers. Allow me to properly introduce Miss Elspeth Wishart; spinster, Elder of the Church of Scotland, retired matron of Glenlyon School, Perthshire and keeper of my conscience.

And sitting close to her was a large and exhausted suitcase.

SIX

He zoomed under the Clock Tower astride a lilac scooter. He was in full red leathers, about six feet six and constructed along the lines of a public library. He was much too big for the scooter and it scrunched to an erratic halt no more than a metre from Alma the cat, Miss Elspeth Wishart and me, sending a cloud of gravel-dust over the East Court. Alma fled, I leapt back, but Elspeth Wishart never flinched.

Under the helmet was a man in his mid-twenties with a fat sweaty face the colour of melting butterscotch.

'Hello *doux-doux*,' he boomed to Elspeth in a deep West Indian voice. 'And how are we on this lovely spring mornin'?'

'We're covered in dust now laddie,' she replied. 'You should have dismounted at the main gate and pushed it.'

'Pushed it *doux-doux*?' the big man grinned and patted his mountainous crutch. 'Don't be wishin' no hernia on me now.'

The initial *Ol' Man River* impression was somewhat undermined by a distinctly camp demeanour. It was an odd combination.

'What's that name you're calling me?' asked Elspeth.

'It's a term of endearment back home in Trinidad,' he said 'I used it cos the moment I saw you I knew we was goin' to get on like a friggin' house on fire.'

I now noticed that the giant was carrying a human rucksack. A young girl unfolded herself from the back of the scooter. She was a beautiful creature, with a slim athletic figure topped by disproportionately big tits. Her thick spiky hair was black as Faisal's against a pale white skin; her lips a tarty red to match her long fingernails. She wore high heels, a padded silk jacket and expensive-looking black pants. Men must have been stacked over her like planes waiting to land at Heathrow.

'Who are you both please?' I asked tersely. I had a bitch of a hangover.

'The record shows that I was baptised Francis Albert Beckles, but my intimates call me Big Frankie and I hope you'll soon be among their number. I met this pretty lady at the gates and gave her a lift. We are both here to be interviewed by a Mr Vic d'Orsay.'

'I'm Dolores Potts,' said the girl, flicking the dust off her trousers. 'I've come for the position of landscape gardener.'

'A gardener called Potts?' I said. Never did a woman look less likely to wield a spade.

'I've heard all the jokes,' she replied in a husky voice with a strong hint of *The Archers*. 'Are you Rory Blaine?'

When I confirmed it, her dark eyes swept over me with a bit more intensity than seemed appropriate.

'And why are *you* here, Mr Beckles?'

'I'm your new chef, boss,' bellowed Big Frankie. 'I'm dreamin' last night I'd be the successful candidate and my dream scenarios are never wrong.'

I pointed to the door in a corner of the East Court where we'd set up an office.

'You'll find Mr d'Orsay in there. Good luck to you both.'

Big Frankie used his sleeve to polish the dust from his helmet and winked at me in a way that was slightly suggestive. He and the girl turned towards the office. He was surprisingly light on his feet.

'In my day, chefs were usually delicate wee men with moustaches,' said Miss Elspeth Wishart staring after him. 'Can you imagine those hands making a trifle?'

'I don't imagine chefs of his age do trifles,' I said.

'Aye, you'll be right no doubt. Over-familiar too, did you not think?'

I smothered a smile. Why do we assume people are likely to alter with the passage of time? 'Oh he's not changed,' we say with surprise after a long separation. We're amazed when they appear unmarked by the terrorist attacks of life. If we ourselves are among the walking wounded, we might reflect smugly that experience has taught them nothing, that they've not grown as we have. We rarely allow that they might feel they'd learnt all the big truths way back when and simply stopped there.

Miss Elspeth Wishart was a supreme example of the species. Though we corresponded quite often, I'd not actually seen her since my last trip north nearly ten years ago. In that time, I'd have expected at least some superficial alterations. But Elspeth Wishart's appearance and character seemed to have set like Superglue around 1955. She must be pushing seventy now, which meant she couldn't have been much more than thirty-something when I'd first seen her. She'd been grey-haired even then; these days it looked like stuffing ripped out of an armchair and worried at by a terrier. The Calvinist jaw remained set firm against all forms of wickedness and the reed-thin figure still moved with the bustle of someone who believed that if you wanted something done well, it was best to do it yourself. And though you'd maybe not have called her masculine, she sure wasn't very girly either, as if gender had passed her by, having taken a long look and deciding it wasn't going to have much of a role in her life.

Whenever I thought of Miss Elspeth Wishart, it was in monochrome. She would always be flint grey walls against matching skies, rugby pitches and tepid showers, iron bedsteads and linoleum floors. Only her eyes had much colour; they were a bright limpid green and her smile, on the rare occasions when she bothered to use it, could light her up like Blackpool Tower.

Elspeth it was who'd long ago infected me with that streak of Low Church morality which came out like a rash at the least appropriate moments. Elspeth who'd switched off the dorm lights every night with a brisk injunction against 'playing down below'. Elspeth whose door was never closed and who, when I'd needed it, had let me hide from the world behind those tweedy skirts. Ms Prada had decreed that Miss Wishart was of course a mother-substitute figure and asked if I ever thought about her breasts. I'd reacted with such disgust that Ms Prada had allowed herself a knowing smirk. I'd nearly taken my neuroses elsewhere.

This morning, Vic reported that Elspeth had been up since half-past six. None of the other bedrooms was habitable, so Vic had given up his and slept on the sofa in his sitting-room. He'd given her dozy directions to the unfinished kitchens and told her to help herself. When he'd eventually staggered down, she'd already cooked herself the full British Rail breakfast, mopped the floor and re-arranged the contents of the cupboards into a more logical arrangement which she claimed would reduce meal preparation time by up to twenty-five per cent.

In fact it'd been Virgin Trains that had brought Elspeth to my door. The line to Glasgow had been closed by a derailment. Knowing nobody else in London and genetically reluctant to pay for a hotel, she'd travelled up to Hampstead on the tube, then pulled her big suitcase on its little wheels half a mile uphill through dark streets in a city she didn't know.

'What are you doing in London, Miss Wishart? You've not been out of Scotland for years,' I'd asked last night in the Red Damask Drawing-Room, trying to enunciate as clearly as possible.

'I've been down to Brighton to visit Morag Proudie, my junior matron at Glenlyon. You'll maybe not remember her now?'

Morag Proudie. Wow. The long-buried power of that name had flushed my cheeks even more. I'd once convinced myself I was in love with Morag Proudie.

'Her husband's got the biggest jacuzzi business on the south coast. Much good may it do her now, poor lassie,' Elspeth had said. 'Breast cancer. Five and a half-stone. I just wanted one last wee blether before... you know.'

I said how sorry I was and she reminded me, as she always had, that the Lord moved in mysterious ways.

This morning I was showing her round the house. She gave no sign of being overwhelmed; the High Anglican flamboyance of the Chapel evoking a pout of distaste and the comment that John Knox would turn in his grave. It wasn't the best day for a tour. Less than three months from our projected opening, the workmen were everywhere; electricians, plumbers, stonemasons, roofers, floorers, painters, decorators, Uncle Tom Cobley and all. Over the last two years Mount Royal, starved of attention for so long, had displayed a ravenous appetite for cash. Into its hungry mouth, I'd thrown the proceeds from Blaine Rampling, the sale of Devonshire Street and Granny's liquid assets, though the last would hardly have paid for weeding the gardens. I'd also sold off some minor pictures and mediocre furniture. But it had been Vic's seemingly limitless ability to write cheques full of zeros that had really made things possible. I'd begun to wonder if it was all, well, kosher. He'd hung out with Mr Sinatra after all.

But I'd been too hard on Granny; her house had been in better shape than it looked. The exterior stone was dire but the roof was fine and most of the state-rooms just needed delicate redecoration. The major headache was the creation of the new apartments on the upper floors, including twenty en-suite bathrooms. I'd soon discovered that we couldn't so much as fart without permission from English Heritage. In return for a few spindly grants, they descended on us like genital warts, just a couple at first then you had dozens of the bastards; experts in stonework, woodwork, metalwork, in marbelling, panelling, gilding, in furniture, fabrics, tapestry and antique carpets. Male or female, straight or gay, they were *prima donnas* all.

By a stroke of luck however, the *Obergruppenführer* was a

young aesthete called Robin Bradbury-Ross. By day, he'd be on all fours checking the wainscotting in the stately homes of England. By night, he'd be in much the same position, attached to a lead with a collar round his neck in the fetish clubs of Vauxhall. It was in the latter context I'd met him, during one of my sporadic expeditions to discover my sexual boundaries. Robin had praised my skill at dripping hot wax on his nipples and given me his card. It hadn't really been my thing and I'd never called. But now my ten quid admission to The Sling turned out to be worth every penny.

Robin's powers over what we could do at Mount Royal were vast but discretionary. In a trivial dispute, I'd let him have his way. If it were more important, we'd stare at each other across the architect's plans and begin to haggle. There was a sliding scale. For an extra water tank, he got to toss me off. For a big new boiler, he'd been allowed a blowjob. But for the controversial installation of a lift, I'd had to bend him over a Sheraton table and provide the full Grade 1 seeing-to while calling him a cheap middle-class whore. Obviously I didn't tell Faisal about this arrangement but nor did I regard it as unfaithfulness, merely as a business matter; though Robin undeniably had me, so to speak, by the short and curlies.

This morning as he gave Elspeth a Walter Raleigh bow, I realized how appropriate it was that she should, so unexpectedly, be beside me as Mount Royal came slowly back to life. It was only to Elspeth that I'd painted proud pictures of these extravagant rooms when I'd taken refuge in her spartan quarters at Glenlyon. Only to her that I might have betrayed how much I missed it. No doubt I'd bored her to death, but she'd let me rattle on while she'd knitted endless pullovers for the children of cousins she scarcely knew. When I'd stopped returning to London for the Christmas and Easter vacs, she'd never asked me why. She'd have been instructed that Rory Blaine was now sentenced to join the other sad souls, with parents far away, who were year-round prisoners. In the summers, I was sent on outward-bound courses or educational cruises to assorted ruins. Elspeth herself had always returned to the Isle of Bute, to the cottage her father had retired to when he'd left the manse. But wherever I was, I'd get a weekly postcard of some loch or ruined castle and a no-nonsense message.

'Rory Blaine, are you behaving? Make sure you do. The weather here is wet. Miss Wishart.'

I'd loved those postcards. For years, I'd even kept them.

Today, we ended our tour up in the cupola. Elspeth gazed down on the vans and trucks in the carriage circle, the figures scurrying up ladders and across scaffolding. Bruce Willis, whom I'd hired in a moment of weakness as a permanent security man, was on his fat stomach checking under vehicles, presumably for incendiary devices. Vic was guiding Dolores Potts and Big Frankie Beckles around the grounds. Spring sunshine bounced off the latticed windows of the cupola; the skeletons of the oak trees would soon be shrouded in a becoming green, softening the constant cackle of our ASBO neighbours, the rooks.

'You'll be a happy man now, I'm thinking?'

'And what about you, Miss Wishart? How's life in your lovely cottage by the sea?'

'Och, it's a simple existence. I walk into the village twice a week though I hardly know a soul there now. All second homes, couples from Glasgow in those huge cars crammed with screaming bairns. They'd never even nod to you, let alone pass the time of day. But there's still the kirk and teaching at the Sunday school. A woman minister now, would you credit it? A wee lassie, pleasant enough, black nail varnish. Not sure I'd want her holding my hand at the last.'

'Miss Wishart,' I said, taking my courage in both hands. 'Excuse my asking, but are you okay?'

'Oh aye,' she said. 'Wee bit of arthritis in the fingers and a cataract in one eye means *The People's Friend* is no longer the joy it was. Otherwise, fit as a fiddle.'

'No I mean, um, money-wise. Because if not, I could, you know...'

'Away with you, Rory Blaine,' she said. 'The thought is kindly meant, but misplaced. Besides, Elspeth Wishart has never taken a penny-piece without having worked for it.'

I doubted that my thought was misplaced at all. Her flat brown shoes were creaky and scuffed and Vic had whispered that the last time he'd seen a coat like hers it'd been on Ena Sharples. I imagined her pension from Glenlyon would stretch gentility till it screamed.

The rail line to Scotland was clear again. Elspeth's taxi was due soon, but there was just time to show her the gardens. Alan Titchmarsh would still have wept, but the worst of the jungle had been cleared, the paths weeded and the grass re-sewn. The Great Fountain had been sealed and re-tiled, the Orangery fumigated of junk and long-dead plants. Elspeth and I sat down on a bench and contemplated the south front.

'Mr d'Orsay tells me you're opening an old folks' home,' said Elspeth. 'Not a business I'd have imagined you in Rory Blaine, you being so trendy.'

'The house has to become a business so that I can keep it, Miss Wishart. And I'm not planning on making the beds myself.'

'Well if I win the Lottery one day, maybe I'll book a room,' said Elspeth.

I took a very dusty, thirty-year-old bullet from my pocket, raised it to my lips and bit firmly.

'I'm afraid you'd not be eligible, Miss Wishart.' I said. 'All the residents of Mount Royal will be male.'

'No women at all?' asked Elspeth, her eyes panning my face in search of clues. 'Is it some sort of Masonic thing?'

'No, nothing like that.'

As the realization dawned, her eyebrows rose so high that her forehead looked like a concertina with liver spots.

'Good Gordon Highlanders,' she said. 'Will the police not close you down?'

'It's not a brothel, Miss Wishart. It's perfectly legal.'

'I'm from the Isle of Bute, you'll have to make allowances. Are there many such places these days?'

'We believe it'll be the first in the UK. We're rather proud of that.'

Elspeth Wishart pulled her cardigan round her. She rose from the bench and sniffed at the daffodils sprouting out of an urn.

'So Morag Proudie was right then,' she said. 'She told me it hadn't worked.'

'What the hell do you mean, Miss Wishart?' I felt my face flush and my heart begin to thump. After all these years. How crazy was that.

'It was me who sent her to you,' she said, her cheeks reddening also. 'To see if it wasn't too late to...'

'To save me from myself?'

'Aye, something like that,' said Elspeth.

'Jesus Christ.'

'An unorthodox action I admit,' she said. 'But I wasn't sure about you, you see, as you got older I mean. Sometimes you'd be quiet and withdrawn, other times you were like a coiled spring. I knew something was going on with you, though I wasn't sure what. You weren't like the other wee jessies; the ones who were no good at rugby and couldn't wait to put on their kilts for kirk on the Sabbath. You seemed like, well, a real boy. And at that age, these things are sometimes a phase, are they not?'

'So you got Morag Proudie to find out? What about sex outside marriage then? Your strict religious code Miss Wishart?'

'We both saw it as God's work, the lesser of two evils. Morag was extremely devout, did you not ken that? She was always happy to do it.'

'You mean she did it a lot?' I asked.

'Jings no,' said Elspeth sharply. 'Maybe just once or twice a year. And she was on the pill thing, so there was no risk of an unwanted bairn.'

'Bloody hell,' I said. 'And what exactly did Morag report back in my case?'

'That you were on a one-way trip to the cities of the plain.'

Elspeth was now examining a bed of tulips. She appeared to be having trouble looking at me directly which wasn't like her one bit. I felt the bile rise up.

'I didn't have much choice in my destination, Miss Wishart. That's the ticket I was handed. That's the way these things work.'

The trauma of the scene came charging back at me. Morag Proudie had been rough as guts and thick as two short planks, but warm and pulsing with life. There had been a big shed at the back of the boarding-house, where luggage was stored. Morag had taken me to a dark corner where someone's huge leather trunk could be used as a sort of couch. I'd instinctively sensed she'd been there before. She'd kissed me, let me fondle her big tits then parted her chubby thighs and led my hand towards her minge. I'd rummaged round aimlessly for a bit, as if it had been my sock drawer. Then Morag, with a casual expertise that wouldn't have disgraced a courtesan in Second Empire Paris, had managed to coax a semi-erection which she'd promptly taken in her mouth. My visible lack of excitement was increased by Morag releasing a burp which smelt strongly of the haggis we'd just had for tea. I'd attempted penetration but my cock had shrivelled in terror.

'Dinnae worry yersel,' she'd said cheerfully, re-doing her lip-stick. 'We'll ha'e anither wee go next term if ye's want. Think of it like yer drivin' test. One failure disnae mean ye'll nae pass at the next go.'

But I'd been devastated. I'd asked her not to tell anyone else, given her money to buy something nice, then raced off up the glen and hidden myself in the heather. I'd never had any trouble get-ting a stiffy when MacPherson in Form 3 sucked me off. By a mer-ciful paradox, such encounters were quite allowable in the culture of Glenlyon; not considered indicative of sexual orientation, just the scarcity of the real thing. Like Elspeth, I'd been confident of the phase theory; it had permitted and excused me the nervous pleas-ures of the past couple of years; not just the safe ones at school but the dangerous ones when I'd still been living under Granny's roof. The wanderings in Hyde Park, the loo off Oxford Circus, the nice man in the folly. This would all pass, then I'd be able to live the life I was expected to. When I got a chance at the real thing, I'd be fine. When I'd been sent away from Mount Royal, I'd been deter-mined to find it and, right on cue, Morag Proudie had miracu-lously materialized, sunbeams around her, like St Bernadette. But no apparition was Morag; she had been the sweating, pulsing real thing and I'd failed miserably. Maybe she'd been right though, maybe it was just first-night nerves. And I'd clung to that pos-sibility through years of repeated attempts, till I'd admitted to myself that the ability to achieve penetration while thinking of Donny Osmond's legs around my back probably wasn't the way most men did it. Alas, poor Morag. Hers were the first tits I'd ever touched. Now they were gone no doubt and soon she would be too. I hoped she'd had a good life among the Jacuzzis.

Elspeth turned back from the tulips. She looked me squarely in the eye again which was a relief. Seeing Miss Wishart on shaky moral ground had been oddly unsettling, apocalyptic even, like the fall of the Roman Empire or something.

'Mr d'Orsay said you share your flat here with a foreign doctor fellow. Is he your ...?'

She reached for the appropriate noun from those displaying themselves in her mind like chocolates in a box. I offered her 'partner' and she was able to swallow that. She'd not met Faisal; he'd gone off to work early in a bad mood. She asked if we were happy.

'I'm hoping it'll work out,' I said.

'Well at least he's someone with a qualification,' she replied.

A cacophony met us round at the front of the house. Big Frankie Beckles was roaring round the carriage circle with Vic riding pillion, his arms clamped round Frankie's huge waist but failing to meet in the middle. Workmen cheered from the Portakabins. Dolores Potts sat smoking on the steps. When the lilac scooter stopped in front of us, Vic slithered off, breathless with pleasure.

'Hey toots, we've found ourselves one terrific chef,' he gasped, sweeping back the avalanche of snowy hair. 'An excellent CV; he knows Marlow and Bray like the back of his hand. And a charming horticulturalist in Ms Dolores Potts here. Wouldn't she be the loveliest rose in our garden?'

Big Frankie dimpled till he was on the cusp of a simper. Dolores tried to hide a mocking smile behind a puff of smoke. I felt the prick of my increasingly familiar irritation with Vic's presumption; he'd fixed these interviews without my knowledge and had now made the decisions. I knew he meant no harm, it was just his reflex to put himself centre-stage. But was the position of master of Mount Royal to be a job-share? In the financial sense I guess it already was, but I'd not put up with it in any other. I was the Ashridge, I was the Blaine.

'Mr d'Orsay and I will discuss both your appointments later and we'll let you know shortly,' I said.

'I'll be sittin' on top of the phone,' gushed Big Frankie in his *basso profundo*. 'Poor old phone I'm hearin' you think.'

I picked up a small book that had fallen to the gravel when the scooter had braked. *The Poems of W. H. Auden*.

'Thanks boss, I'd have died to be losin' that,' said Big Frankie. 'Just look at his face. Isn't it amazin'?'

'Like a dodgy prune from Asda,' I said.

Big Frankie looked hurt. 'Well I'm thinkin' it's the most beautiful face I've ever seen,' he said, squirreling it away inside his red leathers and revving up again. Dolores Potts climbed onto the pillion. Then he smiled sweetly at Vic.

'One of them anyway.'

As the scooter banked round towards the front gates, the girl stared back at me. I was sure I'd never met her before, but I somehow felt that I had.

ALAN CLARK

'It's your decision of course,' Elspeth murmured. 'But I'd not be happy about a man of that size over a hot stove. Can you not see the sweat dripping in the batter?'

The taxi was due at any time. Elspeth's tired old suitcase was waiting just inside the Gilded Hall. But it had become quite nippy again in that indecisive spring way, so Vic took her by the arm and led her inside to a pair of George II armchairs parked at the foot of the staircase. I was left to stand.

'Now listen honey, I've been lying in wait for you,' he said. 'I so enjoyed our chat last night, hearing about your fascinating life and career in Scotland. And it set me thinking. Miss Wishart, I'd like to offer you a job.'

He leaned forward and patted her bony knee, which was instantly pulled out of his grasp.

'Och you're havering, Mr d'Orsay. Have you taken a dram this early? And what job might that be?'

'Call it what you like, but essentially the job of matron at Mount Royal. The boys a bit older than you're used to, the surroundings more opulent, but basically the same work. I've been scouring London for somebody to run the domestic side of things. To supervise the cleaning staff, make sure the interior of the house is perfection and the whims of our residents catered for. Somebody with experience and authority. Honey, you could do it standing on your head. It came to me this morning while I was on the john.'

'But Victor, Miss Wishart is retired now, enjoying a life of leisure,' I said in as light-hearted a tone as I could muster. Elspeth's eyes were locked on Vic, so she couldn't see that mine were imploring him to shut the fuck up.

'Well she could come out again. Mr Sinatra did it several times.'

'I'm sure Miss Wishart would never consider leaving her lovely island, would you Miss Wishart?' I said.

'Aye, I'm a bit set in my ways now Mr d'Orsay,' she replied.

'Nonsense. The work wouldn't be physically demanding, you'd be living rent-free in this great house and the salary would be substantial. Honey, you're perfect.'

I decided I'd kill him later. Vic had no idea of the role Elspeth Wishart had played in my life. The woman about whose breasts, if she'd had any to speak of, Ms Prada had asked if I ever thought.

78

Elspeth and I would always be bonded, but she belonged to another time and place. The boy she'd waved off from Glenlyon was lost in the mists. When I'd visited Granny on her deathbed, I'd been eager for her to see who Rory Blaine had become, though that had been for all the wrong reasons. But from Elspeth Wishart, I somehow felt the necessity of hiding him. I sensed instinctively that she might not take to him. He would fall short, be a disappointment and I didn't want to see that. I certainly didn't fancy her critical gaze every day, damp and drear as a Lowland November. I already had Ms Prada's helium tones advising me on my inadequacies, I didn't need it in stereo. Luckily however, Elspeth Wishart was shaking her head.

'Mr d'Orsay, I'm not insensible to the compliment you're paying me,' she said. 'But I'm a woman who teaches bairns in Sunday school. I rip the headphones off their wee ears, make them hear the words of the Old Testament and sing the hymns of William Blake. I know the world has sailed on, but Elspeth Wishart has not. I am left clinging to the flotsam of my faith. So with absolutely no offence to you or anyone else of your persuasion, I'm the least likely candidate for a job looking after rich old jessies in Hampstead. Dearie me, no.'

Relief flooded through me like a nip of brandy on a winter's day in the stand at Twickenham. When the taxi arrived, I put the old suitcase inside. I'd wanted to go with her to Euston, but she'd pooh-poohed that.

'Cheery-bye, Rory Blaine,' she said. 'Nice to see you again.'

I kissed her on both cheeks, something I'd never done before. She looked surprised but kept hold of my hand for a second or two longer than she needed.

'You're more than welcome to visit us any time,' I said.

'Yes and if you ever change your mind...' called Vic from behind me.

Thankfully though, her taxi was now creeping round the carriage circle towards the front gates. Bruce Willis was standing by his caravan, preparing the salute he gave to everyone who passed through.

'Shame,' grumbled Vic. 'That woman has balls of steel.'

'Yeah and if she'd lived here she'd have cut ours off inside a month,' I said. 'What on earth possessed you, Victor?'

But instead of turning out of the gates, the taxi continued on round the the circle and back towards the front door. The passenger window buzzed down.

'A substantial salary, Mr d'Orsay?'

'£35K a year. Free accommodation, meals and private health care,' called Vic. 'And there's a Presbyterian church just down the road. The minister is a cousin of Ewan McGregor.'

'I see. Thank you.'

She peered from one of us to the other, then at the house like she was weighing it up. But then the window buzzed up and the taxi moved off again. Elspeth glanced back through the rear window. I waved cheerfully as it slipped through the gates, which began to swing shut behind it. The booze from last night was probably still washing around my liver, but I thought a glass of champagne might be in order.

But as we headed back inside, I heard the mechanical whirring of the gates again. Bruce Willis replayed his salute. The taxi was rolling back round the carriage circle. It seemed to come towards me in slow motion. The window buzzed down.

'Right then, you're on,' said Elspeth.

One of my hands took on a life of its own, floating up to cover my mouth.

'Welcome aboard honey.' Vic, the smile at full blast, helped her from the taxi as if she were the Queen Mother. Elspeth fixed him in her gaze.

'Aye, well I run a tight ship, Mr d'Orsay. Make no mistake about that,' she said. 'And you can stop calling me honey. I'm an Elder of the Church of Scotland, not some Las Vegas floozie.'

She eyed me sharply.

'You're looking peely-wally Rory Blaine. The excesses of last night no doubt. Bring my case inside. I've got something that might settle you.'

Vic offered his arm and the two of them climbed the steps to the front doors. The deed was done. There was no way now that I could, or would, protest. She seemed to be living just the remnants of a life. If she wanted to be here, I'd have to take her in. She'd always done the same for me.

Miss Elspeth Wishart turned round on the threshold of Mount Royal.

'The suitcase, Rory Blaine.'

SEVEN

I stood, a daft grin glued to my face, as a procession of wee Oriental people filed past for my inspection. They all shook my hand, some even bowed. I felt like Deborah Kerr in the *March of The Siamese Children*. Faisal made formal introductions, providing superfluous career details.

'And this is Key-Yong from Shanghai. He is a gastroenterologist, specializing in alcohol-related hepatitis.'

'Hi Key-Yong,' I said. 'I'm working on catching that, so it's great to meet you.'

Today was Faisal's thirtieth birthday and these were, apparently, his friends. Everyone seemed to come either from the Whittington Hospital or the soup kitchen where he still spent two evenings a week. At least three quarters were East Asian, South Asian or Afro-Caribbean. Few looked old enough to be out without their mummies.

On a cool May evening, we stood in a slightly awkward knot outside the old County Hall; Faisal's mates, Faisal and me. And, by special invitation, Vic d'Orsay the King Of Croon, Miss Elspeth Wishart, Big Frankie Beckles and Ms Dolores Potts. The last three were now employees of Mount Royal Limited and had each moved into the studio flats around the East Court. There were also two old Ozzie mates of mine, here on holiday, whom I'd asked to make up the numbers as we'd been slightly short.

'Mr Blaine's party?' said a voice. A short dapper middle-aged man thrust himself into our midst. 'My name is Stephen and I am your host for tonight's magic trip on the world-famous London Eye. Will you please follow me?

We morphed ourselves into a line and shuffled towards the huge white stilts that held up the wheel. Faisal suddenly squeezed my arm and kissed my cheek. I felt myself flush as usual. Despite my years on the demos, I'd never lost my discomfort about public displays of male-on-male affection, still half-expecting to be spat at, stoned or bundled into a police van. I knew such a thought would never have crossed Faisal's mind and envied him for it.

'Thanks a million for fixing this,' he said.

'Anything for you,' I replied.

I almost meant it too, can you believe that? Apart from the blip of a month ago when I'd come home pissed from that bar, we were doing okay. I felt we'd both been making an extra effort to connect. We'd ferreted around in each other and come across a few more things in common. Running was the big one of course. Now we went out on the Heath every other morning or whenever his shifts permitted. Naturally he could out-run me, my compensation being the pleasure of watching that arse a few metres ahead and knowing it belonged to me. But it was quite Mills & Boon too; all soft-focus, wind-blown hair and the early sun sparkling on the ponds. All that shite. Nice though, really nice.

And the sex had been getting better and better. Faisal wasn't the least embarrassed about his wee fetish. He never even referred to it, but just dragged out an old doctor's bag with the harnesses, ropes and other paraphernalia and expected me to get on with trussing him up in the way he liked. I'd had a discreet word with Ms Prada who'd suggested it was about the relief of abandoning responsibility, often found among the caring professions. And right, he was a doctor after all; if he wasn't bothered, why should I be? Though I could've done without the weekend in Gibraltar when he'd decided to stay in the hotel room while I went to see the apes. He'd asked to be left tied up. But I'd forgotten to put out the 'Do Not Disturb' sign, the chambermaid had screamed, security had come running. When they'd pulled the gag off, he'd had trouble convincing them it was just a bit of fun. Such things didn't happen at the Rock Hotel, the manager had said; the late Sir John Mills had been a regular guest. They'd moved us to a table in a far corner of the dining-room.

'The exclusive Champagne Capsule for Mr Blaine's party is now approaching the ground,' called the dapper little man. 'Please board with due regard for your safety.'

As soon we began to drift up from the Embankment, Dapper Stephen opened the bottles.

'Well I've seen cleaner glasses,' muttered Miss Elspeth Wishart, grabbing a napkin and beginning to polish. 'That looks like a wee bogie stuck to the rim of this one. I hope we get a discount for dysentery.'

Faisal told her that there were no known cases of dysentery by bogie but she didn't look convinced.

It was twilight now and lights were winking on all over the city. The Siamese Children oohed and aahed in their own lingo and snapped away on their digi-cams. Vic was doing a great

job, pointing out the landmarks, sketching the history, betray-
ing only the teeniest hint of condescension towards them for not
being lucky enough to be born British. Big Frankie, in gold lurex
baggies and a T-shirt reading *Smitten Kitten*, hung on his every
word. He'd quickly bonded with the teeny Oriental girls and was
photographed lifting one under each arm. Quite soon it began to
get a bit rowdy. I saw Dapper Stephen wrinkle his nose.

My Australian buddies, in their late fifties, surfing days long
gone, were chatting up Faisal's male friends, on the ancient principle of gay till proved straight.

'You have such beautiful fingers,' one of them murmured to
his target. 'It'd be a joy to have my prostate checked by you.'

The Oriental boys smiled politely; the white guys tolerated
it for a minute then walked away, usually in the direction of
Dolores Potts, who was looking ethereally beautiful, as if she'd
just stepped off a passing low cloud and were hitching a lift.

'Tell those Aussie creeps to back off,' whispered Faisal.

'Are all your mates straight then?' I asked.

'I have no idea,' he replied.

'How well do you actually know these people?'

'I see them at the hospital and the soup kitchen.'

Apart from a less than historic meeting with his mother, tonight
was the first time I'd been introduced to anyone in Faisal's life. I
was beginning to suspect there weren't many to meet, not significant ones at least. One of the latter was bearing down on me now.
Her name was Ruby. They'd met at medical school. He spoke of
her often, though saw her rarely since she worked for Oxfam in
various depressing corners of the world. A bit older than Faisal,
she seemed to be some sort of big-sister figure. She was certainly
big; reminiscent of Ms Prada but on a Primark budget.

'I've been watching you,' said Ruby, nibbling on a canapé.
'And I've decided you have to be an iceberg; most of you hidden
below the surface.'

I caught the unmistakeable whiff of disapproval, oozing out of
her like the sweat that stained her beefy armpits.

'Because judging by the visible portion, I can't work out why
you and Faisal are together.'

'You're very direct,' I said.

'No time to be otherwise,' she replied, dropping crumbs down
her cascade of chins. 'Tomorrow night I'll be in a tent in the

Sudan. I care very much for Faisal and I don't want him to get hurt.'

'He's thirty today,' I said. 'I reckon he can make his own decisions.'

'Maybe, but emotionally he's still about eighteen,' said Ruby, grabbing another canapé off Dapper Stephen's passing tray. 'You appear to be his first serious relationship and I'm baffled by the choice.'

'Cute and reasonably well-off doesn't count then?' I said as lightly and as quietly as possible. The capsule was too cramped for this sort of conversation.

'Money isn't part of Faisal's landscape; I'd have thought you'd know that by now. As for cute, well you're no spring chicken are you? That's why there must be more to you than meets the eye.'

It was nearly dark outside now and the big wheel had reached the top of its revolution. Planes sinking towards the airport seemed dangerously close and the cars on the Embankment were like electric ants scurrying along the black snake of the river. Vic and Big Frankie were doing a double act as the life and soul of the party. The Siamese Children were knocking back the champagne, which was probably in short supply at the nurses' home. The straight boys were less interested in the view of the city than of Dolores Potts' knockers, which could have breast-fed Southwark. Even Elspeth was having a glass, forgetting for a moment that John Knox was always watching her. Everyone seemed to be having a good time except me, pinned against the safety-rail by a gorgon on a mission.

'I hope you realize how nuts he is about you?' Ruby was saying. 'I get endless letters about the wonderful Rory Blaine. It's just that I can't see him with a rich, middle-aged, advertising man in a stately pile in Hampstead, getting the flab off a bunch of old queens. It's ludicrous miscasting.'

'Where exactly do you see him then?'

'In the Sudan like me or in some similar environment. Failing that, in a nice little flat with some gentle guy of his own age. A teacher, a social worker, another doctor maybe. Faisal's work is the heart of him. Do you understand that?'

'I think so.' I smiled. 'I call him Mother Teresa with a cock.'

Ruby gave me a look that could have curdled milk. She didn't seem to do jokes any more than Faisal did.

'You're not a very serious man, are you?' she said. 'Faisal is you see. But I guess he's looked beneath your surface and found something worth loving.'

She screwed her eyes up as if trying to discern what it might be.

'And look at how he's dressed tonight. That's not the Faisal I know. Your doing?'

I'd coaxed him into a new Ozwald Boateng three-piece dark-blue suit with a collarless pale-blue linen shirt. He looked stunning. I wondered if mentioning Ozwald might win me a sliver of Ruby's approval; an African boy who'd got on.

'Anyway, Faisal Khan is one of the good guys. And if you hurt him, I will personally come and cut your balls off. Is that clear?'

Ruby waddled off towards her next canapé.

'Lovely party by the way,' she called over her shoulder.

What a fucking nerve. So I wasn't good enough for him? What about me then? Supposing I was the one who got hurt? Why the assumption that being middle-aged and having a few bob makes me a bastard?

But Ruby hadn't been the only one giving me the once-over. I'd clocked several of Faisal's friends exchanging smiles and whispers. I'd tried chatting to some of them down on the ground. The Siamese Children had given monosyllabic answers, the British were polite but stiffly formal; they'd all appeared vaguely uneasy at being there in the first place, though now they seemed happy to get through my booze as fast as Dapper Stephen could pour it.

I was feeling more and more like a parent hosting a children's party, at it but not of it. The further the big wheel revolved, the further the groups polarized. Faisal's friends slowly drew away from me, Vic, Elspeth and the Australians. Because we weren't of their generation, did they view any engagement as pointless? Did it never occur to them that our stories might be worth hearing or that we might even be good for a laugh? I wondered at what precise point how you looked, how you dressed, the music that moved you, the way you saw the world suddenly made you irrelevant to a huge swathe of your fellow men and your value as a member of the human race crash like shares on Black Monday? Why was it that just because the last song I'd really liked had been *Careless Whisper*, all my other opinions were equally crap?

But how come Faisal wasn't infected by this ageism? If, as

Ruby decreed, I was so totally unsuitable, what *did* he see in me? I'd considered the father-figure option when we'd first met. But he already had one who could do no wrong, so I'd doubted he wanted a spare. Or maybe it was part of his wee fetish; maybe for some reason I was the perfect 'top', his sexual fantasy in the same way he was mine? I could hardly complain if that were the explanation. Or was I perhaps just a suitable case for treatment, a quasi- patient to be cured of my imperfections by the saintly doctor? Possible I suppose, if so, I could give Ms Prada her P45. But if none of these were the answer, that only left the option of love didn't it? There was affection between us, that was clear, but the other thing, the big thing? Was it conceivable? I looked over at him, Ruby's chubby arm draped possessively around his shoulders. After decades of panning through most of the shites in gay London, had I actually stumbled on my own wee nugget of gold? Could I take the risk of believing that? If I could, I'd show them all; fat Ruby and those smirking kids. I'd never hurt him. I'd cherish him. I'd not get it wrong. He turned round just then and smiled at me. For a split second I thought I might blub, but of course I didn't do that.

'Toots, is it my imagination or has this gadget stopped?' called Vic above the chatter. He'd been telling the Australians how he'd taught Frank Ifield to yodel.

The capsule was on its descending arc, but still a long way up. Peering down at the ground, something was clearly going on. The crowds who'd been ebbing round the wheel had vanished. Now it was populated by police cars and fire engines, headlights strobing the darkness. There was no traffic clogging Westminster Bridge, no trains creeping out of Charing Cross. Dapper Stephen announced that we weren't to panic. A metallic voice squawked from a speaker.

'Dear Guests, we hope you are enjoying your trip on the London Eye. Unfortunately, we have been notified of a possible security issue and the London Eye has been stopped while this is investigated. There is no cause for alarm. We are confident the situation will be resolved quickly. In the meantime, just relax and enjoy these spectacular views. There will be no additional charge for your extended time aboard the London Eye.'

But it wasn't resolved quickly. An hour later we hadn't moved. A couple of the wee Oriental girls were getting a bit tearful.

'Whatever happened to backbone?' Elspeth muttered. 'That's what we British can teach the world.'

Then the real trouble started.

'Jeez, I've got to take a piss,' said Vic to me, his face flushed. 'I can't hold it much longer.'

The Australians overheard and said they did too.

'Shite Victor, why didn't you all go before you got on?' I asked.

'We did. But that was an hour and a half ago,' said Vic.

'Can't you hold it longer than *that?*'

Vic raised his eyebrows to heaven.

'Well you can't piss on the floor. For fuck's sake hang on.'

I informed Dapper Stephen of the problem. He replied smugly that there wasn't one. Every capsule carried an emergency pack, containing water, blankets, glucose tablets and a portable commode. But when he looked for it, it wasn't there and he remembered that the operative responsible had taken the day off because his pit-bull had died. Fifteen minutes later, Vic demanded one of the empty champagne bottles, turned his back on everyone and pissed into it with a theatrical sigh. He'd forgotten he was in full view of the adjacent capsule, from which now came inaudible applause and punching in the air.

'Go for it Papi,' said Big Frankie, an odd glazed expression on his face.

The Australians demanded two more bottles and did the same. Then some of the Oriental girls succumbed. It was harder for a woman to hit the target but Dapper Stephen had an inexhaustible supply of paper napkins. A system developed where a ring was formed round the pisser, shielding him or her from view. When a bottle was filled, it was passed to Dapper Stephen who, now wearing plastic gloves, deposited it in the crate like it was a Molotov cocktail. By now, we'd been up there the best part of two hours now and it was getting a wee bit unpleasant. Dapper Stephen announced there was only one champagne bottle left.

'You all right Miss Wishart?' I asked.

'I'd rather die,' she said.

I felt the same. None of the younger guys had needed the bottles; there was no way I would either. Then hallelujah, the wheel began to move. When the capsule reached the ground, the paramedics were over us like ants from a skirting-board. Dapper

Stephen, looking a lot less dapper, struggled off with his crate. Nobody volunteered to help.

'Thanks for an unforgettable evening Stephen,' I said. 'I know a club in Vauxhall where you could take that crate. You'd be quids in.'

'That's the last trip I make on this fucking wheel,' he snapped 'I'm going back to EasyJet. Nice meeting you.'

The security alert had been a false alarm; a suspicious holdall under a bench near the entrance to the wheel. It'd turned out to contain a woman's knitting.

'I suddenly felt daft having brought it,' Elspeth whispered, 'so I left it there till we came back. I didn't think anyone would steal half a balaclava.'

'Jesus Christ, Miss Wishart.'

'Don't blaspheme Rory Blaine,' she said. 'Had I better confess do you think?'

'You've stopped the London Eye, Miss Wishart,' I said. 'Do you really want your face staring at everyone in Bute as they eat their porridge in the morning?'

'Nothing to be gained from that,' said Elspeth firmly.

We were way too late for the restaurant I'd booked and the party was spoiled anyway. Faisal seemed to be in deep conference with Ruby and the others. He beckoned me over.

'Listen, the guys would prefer to skip the meal. They want to hit some club in Covent Garden now.'

'Fine, but I don't think Vic, Elspeth or the Aussies will fancy that.'

'Course not.'

'Um, well they're your guests too...'

'Yes sure, but...'

'All right, let me organize a couple of cabs for them, then we can get going,' I said.

'Oh you're coming then? Cool,' he said. He seemed surprised and the tiniest bit uncomfortable.

Faisal's friends were grouped behind him, some of them look-ing a bit sullen now. Vic, Elspeth and the others were behind me. Faisal and I stood in the middle, like those officers who'd come out of the trenches at Christmas on the Somme. I caught a look that passed between two of the Siamese Children.

'Okay, you go off with your friends,' I said.

'No no, you're very welcome to come. Really,' he said.

'Thanks a lot but I don't think so Faisal. I'll stick with your other guests. Enjoy the rest of your evening.'

His eyes darted back and forth from one group to another. I could see he didn't know what to do and I got mean pleasure from that. I turned away and steered Elspeth and the rest towards the Festival Hall to find a taxi.

'Hey Frankie, Dolores, you wanna come with us?' shouted one of the Oriental girls.

'No thanks sweet-bread,' Big Frankie called back. 'I'm with my buddies here.'

'Don't let us keep you from all your admirers,' I said to Dolores Potts.

'God no,' she replied from behind the usual cloud of smoke. 'The white boys are pompous prats and the Orientals, well have you ever come across one with a decent cock?'

'Not since you come to mention it,' I said.

I glanced back and saw Faisal still standing there, watching us go. Then Ruby slipped her arm through his and pulled him away.

Vic gave me one of those smiles Princess Diana no doubt used when she visited hospices. If he'd clasped my hand and told me to be brave, I'd have punched his lights out. He insisted we should all go and eat at the Oxo Tower. I didn't think he'd get a table at this short notice, but he called them and he did. I was beginning to realize that Vic's celebrity wasn't a totally extinct volcano; it was still capable of giving a rumble and blowing open the occasional door. Because the pretty boys had dumped us, the Australians did so too and it was just Elspeth, Dolores, Big Frankie, Vic and me. We walked under Waterloo Bridge and past the National Theatre. Just before the Oxo Tower was a clump of cheap eateries and take-aways.

'How about saving a couple of hundred quid?' said Vic. 'Fish and chips all round?'

I was ordered to phone the Oxo Tower and say he'd just had an acute anxiety attack. He returned with five cardboard boxes from Fishy Business and we sat in a line on a bench looking out over the river. A strong breeze had whipped up now and the dark oily water was surprisingly rough, as if protesting against its neat urban confinement.

'Shall we all join hands together?' said Big Frankie before we could open our cardboard boxes. He bowed his head and began what was possibly the first grace ever spoken over cod and chips on a Southwark Council bench. It wasn't a short one either. Frankie not only thanked God for what we were about to receive, he also thanked the fishermen who'd risked their lives on the deep and the farmers who'd planted the spuds. Passing Londoners looked away with their 'Oops, there's a loony' reflex. This really wasn't the night I'd had planned.

'Och that was lovely, Frankie,' said Elspeth, looking at him anew. 'I'd not have marked you down as a religious man.'

'There are many roads to Jesus, *doux-doux*,' he said, still holding her hand. 'But bikers get there faster.'

Elspeth favoured him with one of her occasional smiles. Big Frankie asked Dolores Potts if prayer had a place in her life. Not as a rule she said, only when her period was a few days late. She was eating chips with one hand and smoking with the other.

I suddenly realized that I felt absolutely knackered. Not to mention pretty fucking upset. Why was I sitting on a chilly bench eating fish and chips? Why wasn't I in some club with my so-called partner on his birthday? Because he'd pissed off and left me, that's why. And not more than two seconds after I'd actually started to believe he might be the one, a blessing from my own humanist god. Nice timing, Paki boy.

I began to feel a Milton coming over me like a big black cartoon cloud, so I sat back quietly and let Vic rabbit on. All you had to do to make Vic happy was give him an audience, wind him up and watch him go. He wasn't bothered how small it was as long as he got a good review. Tonight it was Rat Pack anecdotes. Big Frankie was clearly dazzled that Vic had known them all personally and had once resisted the advances of Lauren Bacall.

Elspeth sat silently nibbling her chips. Was she possibly in mild shock, having been single-handedly responsible for a major terrorist alert? But no, she was hanging on Vic's every word as he painted pictures of worlds that had never touched her. That day when she'd agreed to take the job, she'd gone on a later train back to Scotland. I'd wondered if we'd ever see her again; half-hoped, shamefully, that we wouldn't, that the sight of the hills of Bute might calm her apparent brain-storm. But maybe it was one of those Lowland days when the clouds are no higher than the bus-stops and for which the anti-depressant has yet to be invented.

Anyway, inside a fortnight she'd packed her bags, rented out her cottage, left her Sunday school kids to Satan and was back in NW3. Perhaps this was her Nureyev moment, leaping the border like he'd leapt the barrier at Le Bourget.

Vic was now teasing her gently, demanding to know which of his songs she'd danced to. When she answered none, he overstepped the mark.

'Okay, which have you made love to then?'

'Dearie me Mr d'Orsay, I'm a maiden lady.'

'I only meant a kiss and a cuddle Miss Wishart, nothing more.'

'Not even that I'm afraid,' said Elspeth, flustered, dabbing at her lips with a paper napkin, as if trying to wipe away his imputations. 'Sorry to disappoint you.'

Vic looked genuinely sad.

'Jeez, you do disappoint me, Miss Wishart. The last slow dance, strong arms around you, me on the turntable singing *Moonlight In Amalfi*.'

'A wee bitty late now,' said Elspeth.

'Nonsense honey,' he replied, seizing her spindly wrist 'You just come here with me.'

He dragged her to where the terrace jutted right out over the river. The disco boats, over-laden with fairy lights, lurched across the swell and the dome of St Paul's, floodlit like some bloody great tureen, still managed to dwarf the pretentious pinnacles that soared around it.

'Look at that,' Vic shouted, throwing his arms wide to embrace the panorama. 'London. The centre of the world. Dirty, dangerous, expensive, exhausting. But throbbing with people being who they want to be and to hell with what anybody else thinks. A place to make a fresh start Miss Wishart, even at our age. While you've still got time, there's everything to play for.'

'I'm not sure *who* I want to be Mr d'Orsay,' Elspeth said. 'It hadn't occurred to me I could be anybody else now. Anyway I've been reasonably content being Elspeth Wishart, school matron.'

'Content? But you've never been held tightly and danced to Vic d'Orsay singing *Moonlight In Amalfi*? Well, you're going to now.'

Vic grabbed Elspeth round the waist. She was too surprised to resist. He began to sing some horrendous Fifties crap about fishing-boats bobbing, seabirds swooping and a girl with eyes like amethysts. It was obvious that Elspeth had hardly danced in her life, but Vic's skill carried them both. Her eyes stayed mostly on the ground like some teenage wallflower, only occasionally meeting his with an embarrassed grimace, as anybody would when being sung at full in the face. As he steered her around the terrace, I stopped noticing that they were old; that he was fat and she was dowdy. Okay, we weren't talking Gene Kelly and Cyd Charisse but, by some alchemy, they began to look almost beautiful. We could all see it; Big Frankie stopped eating his chips, Dolores Potts let the cigarette burn away between her fingers. At the end of the song, Vic kissed Elspeth's hand, bowed to a few applauding tourists and give two fingers to a hoodie on a skateboard who'd yelled abuse. Big Frankie leapt up and whooped, his huge arse vibrating like a tumble-drier on maximum spin.

'That's friggin' star quality, ain't it boss?'

'I guess it is,' I said.

Dolores now demanded to be danced with too and the performance was encored. I didn't imagine any of the strolling tourists knew who Vic was, but they knew he was Somebody. He certainly wasn't like elderly men were supposed to be. It had obviously never occurred to him to disengage with the world, to step back and leave life to the younger generation. He never stood on his dignity either so somehow, however he behaved, he kept it. When I'd first met him, he'd seemed quite a simple character; impossible to imagine Vic d'Orsay in the eau-de-nil room as Ms Prada peeled off the geniality in search of the layers underneath. But over the last three years, I'd come to sense that those layers were present, even if I had no idea what they were. Ours was an odd association, based on a chance meeting, cemented by a well-intentioned crime. And now I saw him every day in life. We rubbed along like Elspeth's blasted knitting needles, putting together this odd enterprise of ours. I'd tried to maintain a certain distance though; I'd not been used to rubbing along with anybody much. My private life was mine and his, whatever it might be, was his. There were no net curtains twitching around the East Court. Nevertheless I could no longer quite picture Mount Royal without him. Like Granny, he had surrendered to the house, painted himself into its canvas, as much a fixture now as the statue of Old Father Thyme or the fluted pilasters that framed the great front doors. As Vic twirled Dolores round the terrace, I was glad of that.

I looked past them at the forest of lights across the river and wondered where exactly Faisal was. Perhaps he was dancing too, with Ruby or one of the Siamese Children. He'd refused to dance for me when we'd gone to that club, but it was his birthday after all, so maybe he'd do it for them. I was aware of an odd feeling in the pit of my stomach. Not the bloody gastric reflux thing, but something else. I missed him that was all.

We climbed up the steps onto Waterloo Bridge, Big Frankie offering Elspeth the assistance of his monumental arm. To my surprise she accepted and I worried in case tonight had been too much for her. No doubt the usual excitement of her day was the paddle steamers passing the Isle of Bute.

I ran ahead to flag down an approaching cab, but saw it was occupied. As it went past, the woman passenger peered out, long straight hair and cadaverous cheekbones, a dead spit for the great Joni Mitchell, Canada's only decent export till Keanu Reeves. One of Joni's best songs surfaced in my mind; about relationships being like snakes and ladders. Just when you think you've finally got up there, some shite happens and you slither all the way back down again. So you drag yourself up one more time then hey, guess what? She'd never been a looker old Joni, but she knew her stuff all right.

EIGHT

'TERROR GRANNY HALTS THE EYE' – *Guardian*
'KNITWIT NEEDLES LONDON' – *Daily Mail*
'GREAT BALLS OF WOOL!' – *Sun*

I spread the papers over the breakfast table. Elspeth's coverage
was quite extensive. If she'd left her knitting outside Tesco on
Heath Street she'd have got a small para on Page 12, but she'd
gone for an iconic target on her first time out. You had to hand
it to her.

I wasn't sure whether to show her or not. She'd refused to have
a telly in her wee flat. A cesspit of stupidity she'd called it, an
insult to the genius of John Logie Baird. But she was addicted to
what she called the Home Service, so I imagined she'd have heard
at least some of the fuss. Her first night out in London had been
quite something; causing a major bomb scare, waltzing with the
King Of Croon. I'd pop over later and see if she was okay.

Though it was past ten, I was breakfasting alone. Faisal, usually up with the rooks, hadn't yet emerged from the spare room.
I'd heard him come in at god-knows-when, soon followed by the
retching, honking and flushing. So how was I going to deal with
last night then? I considered the options over my salty porridge.
Option One was to delete it from my memory and go forward as if
nothing had happened. Option Two was the wounded fawn rou-
tine. Option Three was the all-guns-blazing, tits-out row. Which
road would the well-balanced, anger-managed person have taken,
the one Ms Prada would have applauded? Probably Option One,
realizing that the other party is as flawed as oneself and forgiv-
ing them. Except hang on, Faisal was Mother Teresa wasn't he?
He wasn't supposed to have flaws; his job was to point out mine.
Option Two, the sad victim number, exposed your vulnerability,
letting them know they had the power to hurt you. A dodgy strategy but with the possible advantage of speeding the healing process and walking into the sunset hand in hand. Or there was Option
Three, which could make things infinitely worse, the immature,
pointless and stupid option. I just loved Option Three.

'About a thousand quid, give or take a tenner.'

'Sorry?' said Faisal, who'd just crept up the glass staircase and
headed for the Douwe Egberts.

'The invoice from the London Eye. What your birthday shindig cost me last night.'

'Wow,' he said, his eyes half-shuttered against the morning sun. 'Big hug. Very grateful.'

'Really? Then why did you fuck off?'

He grimaced; but there was resignation in it. Like when the dentist finally hits the nerve; you know it's coming but it still hurts.

'Don't put it like that, Rory. The evening had been a bit spoiled for everyone, so when Ruby suggested going on somewhere, I felt I had to go.'

'I realized your dilemma, Faisal,' I said, 'but the nasty truth is that your buddies didn't want me, or any of the other oldies, along. It was hanging in the air like one of Vic's farts. And you smelt it didn't you? Look me in the eyes and tell me I'm wrong. You had a choice to make. Right there, right that second. And you chose to go with them.'

He came over to the table with the cafetière and his bowl of organic muesli.

'Yes I know,' he said quietly. 'I've been lying awake half the night.'

'Bollocks. You've been snoring half the night,' I said. 'Look Faisal, if you're going to dump me sooner or later, because of the age thing or any of my other inadequacies, then do it sooner and let's get it over with.'

'Oh Rory, stop over-reacting. I don't care about the age thing.'

'Well you let it separate us last night, a night when we should have been together. Was that fat cow Ruby behind it then?'

'Hey, that's not fair.'

'Fair? She wasn't very fair to me. Before she'd even met me, she'd decided I wasn't right for you. Is that the vibe the others were giving you too? Last night, I felt like a poodle on parade at Crufts. I obviously didn't get very good marks either.'

Faisal sprinted from the table and deposited his organic muesli into the sink. I flung open a window. I knew I should probably stop there but I also knew I couldn't.

'I've committed myself to you Faisal,' I yelled at his heaving back. 'Do you have any idea how long it is since I did that?'

He pulled his head from the sink and dabbed his beard with kitchen roll.

'Committed? Really? So what about that night last month when you came home smelling of piss? And... and... if you're so committed to me, how come your profile is still on fucking Dinkydudes?'

Oh dear. Faisal never ever swore.

'I forgot to take it off. And why were you on there anyway?'

'Checking to see if *you* were, and yes, there you still are! "Scotstud. Age Forty." Ha! "Looking to play with like-minded guys. No holes barred. I don't bite unless you want me to." I know it by heart. And don't tell me you forgot to remove it. That site shows when the user last logged on. You were there three days ago.'

He was glaring up at me, tugging at his beard, oblivious to the bits of sick still nesting there.

'You walked away from me last night Faisal,' I blustered back. 'You walked away.'

I swept the cafetière off the table; I'd always been one for the grand gesture. Unfortunately, the contents sprayed all over a Berber rug that Faisal had owned for years and was very fond of. But I didn't care. No, that's not honest. At that moment, I was happy to be causing him pain.

I flew out into the East Court, slamming the door with such force that some dozy doves having a lie-in came wheeling out of the Clock Tower and precision-bombed the Merc. I tripped over a reel of cable an electrician had left there days ago. I snatched it up, tracked him down in the Gilded Hall and flung it at him. He walked off the job on the spot. Fine. Fuck him. I roamed the house, looking for people to growl at. Robin Bradbury-Ross was up a ladder in the Chapel cleaning one of the fat marble putti on the reredos. A pile of mucky tissues was scattered on the floor, as if he'd been changing its nappy.

'We need to talk about the lift my sweet,' he called down. 'English Heritage has more issues.'

'I thought we'd resolved all those,' I shouted up. 'Over that desk in the Library? Don't you remember?'

'I remember all right,' he smiled, 'but Simon Jenkins has written a letter.'

'Fuck Simon Jenkins.'

'Who's a grumpy girl today then?' he yelled at my back.

I strode outside to the Great Fountain and threw pebbles at

my new Koi carp till it struck me that they might be traumatized; they'd cost an arm and a leg. I sat down on a bench and did one of Ms Prada's relaxation exercises. I had to imagine all my troubles trapped inside a cheery yellow balloon which I could then release and watch disappear into space. It didn't work very well today, but the peace of the gardens helped. The re-seeded lawns were sprouting fast and the giant urns dotted across them were now inhabited by pyramids of box, fringed with purple pansies and white tulips. Along the perimeter walls, the lines of small topiary yews, sitting it out like matrons at a ball, had had their crinolines clipped and spruced up. Dolores Potts had made order out of chaos in an amazingly short time. Perhaps she could teach me the principles so I could apply them to my life.

'Would you fancy a wee walk out on the Heath?' asked a voice just behind me. That had always been one of Elspeth's tricks; materializing suddenly beside you like Mrs Danvers in *Rebecca*.

But Elspeth's wee walk turned into a marathon. After a lifetime of climbing hillsides up to her arse in heather, she took the pathetic undulations of Hampstead in her steely stride. It had warmed up into a lovely May morning and the place was knee-deep in psychotic roller-bladers and Filipino nannies with screaming brats. For a while we trekked along without talking. I didn't feel much like chatting and she seemed to sense that, just like she'd always done.

I carelessly led her to the brim of Parliament Hill to take in the view. A mistake really, because it was impossible to miss the bloody London Eye. I asked how she was feeling this morning. She sighed. She'd heard the radio she said, but she'd already apologized to the 'top brass' before getting into bed and it seemed superfluous to repeat it to anyone of lesser rank like the Commissioner of the Metropolitan Police. She wondered if there was any way of getting her knitting back. I said I thought it best to let sleeping balaclavas lie.

We turned and wandered up the east side of the Heath to the wedding-cake walls of Kenwood. The only empty bench was engraved with the words 'In fond memory of Augustus and Mollie Parker-Smith. They loved this view.' It felt impertinent to sit down and block it, but I was tired, I'd not slept well. Elspeth announced an urge for 'a wee pokey hat', so I bought two small but outrageously expensive ice-creams. We licked in silence, contemplating the lake with its daft fake bridge. Past us paraded the matrons of Hampstead and Highgate, the ladies who strolled then lunched; huge hair, high heels, make-up you'd need to sand-blast off. I saw Elspeth eyeing them and wondered if, deep inside the soul of the spinster, there was a yearning for a facial, a mud-wrap and a couple of hours in Harvey Nicks with an Amex Platinum.

If I glanced over my shoulder I could see into Robert Adam's sensational Library. At Mount Royal, only the Gilded Hall and the Saloon were in its league. But everything here seemed lifeless, a great dead house lying on a slab of grass. At least, I was saving Mount Royal from the cafés, the litter-bins and the ghosts of Augustus and Mollie Parker-Smith.

'You've not had a good day so far, I'm thinking,' Elspeth said eventually. Her flat was at right angles to ours and her windows were often open. She'd probably heard most of the row.

'Well Rory Blaine, it's not my place to comment so I will let the Lord do it for me. Forgive us our trespasses as we forgive those who trespass against us. And you're not without trespasses I'd imagine.'

'No, Miss Wishart.'

She could see I didn't want to discuss it. She was an odd mixture old Elspeth; briskly insensitive one minute, the antennae of a Lakeland poet the next.

'Tell me more about the last thirty years then,' she said, changing the subject with a great crashing of gears. 'I know the outline of course, but there's not much room on a Christmas card is there?'

So I found myself on an unexpected canter across my five years in Australia, making a name as a hot kid-copywriter, winning every award going, then getting an offer I couldn't refuse from a big agency back in London, at that time the world capital of creative advertising. I told her about starting up Blaine Rampling and gradually becoming a big cheese in the business. Elspeth listened with slightly baffled attention.

'And did all that make you happy?' she asked. Calvinists always cut to the chase.

'When I was younger it was fun, glamorous even. Sometimes you even think it matters, then it dawns that it's not much of a job for a grown-man.'

'Well at least you made your own way,' she said. 'Most lads who left Glenlyon had it all mapped-out for them. Not you though. I used to worry whether you'd sink or swim.'

'Oh I soon became a swimmer, Miss Wishart.'

'A lonely thing though, swimming on your own, is it not?'

'No need to weep for me Miss Wishart,' I smiled. 'I had a nice lawyer who administered my trust fund. And you'd always been kind to me too. I've not forgotten that.'

'Och that was just my job.'

'Well you did a good job for me,' I said. We were both awkward now, neither of us much use at this sort of stuff, our eyes fixed firmly on the pampered pooches with private medical insurance skittering around fetching balls. Elspeth broke the silence.

'And what happened to you becoming a real writer? That was your dream was it not?'

'I got waylaid,' I said, a tad sharply, the old self-loathing kicking in. Nobody had ever asked me that before. Nobody else knew of course.

'A question in return?' I said 'I've always wanted to ask it. What happened to you becoming a real mother?'

I froze. Fuck. The censorship mechanism between thought and word had crashed totally. Miss Wishart had never tolerated the smallest impertinence and this was off the scale. I tensed myself to take the blow, but none came.

'I wasn't able to have children,' she said. 'I had an illness as a lass which put paid to that. In those days, that was a cause of shame. It put men off you.'

'I'm really sorry. Was there never anyone who didn't mind that?'

'My list of suitors was hardly extensive,' she replied. 'Lana Turner I was not. Anyway, my misfortune was common knowledge on the island. My father had seen to that. With my mother gone, he wanted to keep me at home.'

'Bastard,' I said.

'Language, Rory Blaine,' she clucked 'No, he wasn't really. My looking after him, supporting him in his ministry, he just never thought that might be less than totally fulfilling.'

She told me about an American sailor from the Polaris base on the Holy Loch. He'd come to her father's kirk one Sunday on a big motorbike, then every Sunday after that. Charlie was his name. He'd been tubby, funny, kind. Once he'd brought a spare crash helmet and they'd zoomed all over the island. Aged twenty, Elspeth had fallen in love. It had probably shown in her face, she said. The Reverend Wishart had taken Charlie to one side. But Charlie had told him he didn't care that Elspeth couldn't have children because he'd no intention of proposing to her or any-one. Then he'd taken her for a long ramble, explained that he respected her very much and would always be her friend but that he wasn't the marrying kind. Soon after, he'd been sent back to Georgia. He'd written regularly for a while, then it had stopped. Eventually a letter had arrived from Charlie's sister. Charlie was dead. They'd found him in a park in a seedy quarter of Atlanta, far from where he lived. Beaten to a pulp. Nobody among his family or friends could figure out what he'd been doing there.

Soon afterwards, Elspeth had seen the small ad in *The Lady* and Glenlyon had become her true home for the next forty years. Her father had never quite forgiven her.

'In short, I've not been a person very much has happened to. As I told Mr d'Orsay last night by the river, I'm just Miss Wishart, school matron, retired. Not a lot else to say.'

We returned their eternal view to Augustus and Mollie Parker-Smith. Outside the gates of Kenwood, the sun was surpassing itself for mid-May and only the shyest of breezes dared ripple the blossom in the house-trained gardens of the stockbroker villas. After we'd passed The Spaniards pub Elspeth, without warning, veered off into the West Heath. Come on, she said. She loved the woods, just like a fairy tale. She never spoke a truer word. On a fat old Falstaff of an oak somebody had spray-painted the word 'cock' underlined by a helpful arrow.

The woods were quite dense here, the treetops wrapped round each other in a tangled skein of branches, grasping for the light. Down below, the sun, diffused by the foliage, was no more than a hazy yellow wash. But if Elspeth had been seeking a sylvan idyll, she'd been mistaken. There were just as many bodies here as at Kenwood and all of them better toned. A West Highland terrier raced up to our ankles, stumpy tail throbbing.

'Och, it's a wee Westie,' beamed Elspeth. 'What's that in his mouth?'

The dog obediently dropped his grubby trophy for our inspec-tion; a pair of top of the range Calvin Klein underpants.

'Dearie me,' said Elspeth. 'Why would anybody leave those here?'

'Shall we turn back?' I asked hopefully.

'Jings no, come on.'

The pathways of the West Heath interlaced like a bucolic Spaghetti Junction where men circled endlessly without any interest in finding an exit. Some, with the confidence to present themselves for more considered perusal, might create a tableau in the style of Manet or Seurat, lolling under a tree, pin-spotted by a shaft of sunlight, with a Pret A Manger baguette and decaf latte, perhaps even a slim volume of romantic verse. Though it wasn't quite sun-bathing weather yet, most had their shirts off and I wondered how long it'd take Elspeth to register the infinitely higher concentration of nipple-rings than at Kenwood. As we ploughed deeper into the wood, it became necessary to tread with more caution. Among the long-dead leaves were used condoms, torn sachets of lube and tissues crumpled up like dirty snowballs. I saw Elspeth blushing, so I did too.

And it was then that I saw him.

Hanging by his arms from the low branch of a beech was a tall, thin, crop-headed man in aviator shades, naked but for a microscopic pair of cut-off denim shorts. I told myself it couldn't possibly be but, shades or not, I knew instantly that it was. The same body, the same tilt of the head, maybe even the same cut-offs. Jesus Christ. Across nearly thirty years and several oceans, it was my Lancelot, my Cruel Deceiver, my Man That Got Away. It was Matty Rice. Of all the cruising-grounds in all the towns in all the world, he walks into mine. The gastric reflux awoke from its slumbers. What did I do now? Grab Elspeth's elbow and force her to change course or seize the opportunity to face up to the past, metabolize the pain and move forward as Ms Prada would wish me to do? I saw her serene fleshy face with one eyebrow lifted, challenging me to rise to the occasion.

I asked Elspeth to wait and walked over to the tree.

'Hi Matty. How's life?'

He dropped to the ground and smiled carelessly from behind the shades.

'Hey mate. Where do I know you from? Here the other night?'

'Sydney, 1982,' I replied.

'Cripes,' said Matty. 'Long time no see then. Lost your name I'm afraid.'

Even this close up, Matty looked pretty much as he'd done thirty years ago. Lean as a whippet, cheekbones you could hang your laundry on. But then he took off the shades to get a better look at me. That blew it. All those Joan Rivers jokes sprang to terrifying life. Matty had been under the knife. The grin was now a vaguely chilling version of the original. The lips I'd kissed so fiercely were plumper than before. He made Joan look like a Great Dane. He had to be pushing sixty by now.

'It's Rory Blaine,' I said.

'Ah yeah, that's right,' said Matty.

'What are you doing in London?'

'Just here for some fun and to check out a few rellies. Make sure I'm still in the will, you know? What you up to these days?'

'Oh this and that.'

'Sounds good mate.'

I couldn't think what to say next. What do you say to a ghost? The morning on the beach when I'd first laid eyes on Matty Rice had been in another lifetime. He'd come trotting out of a sea-mist on a black horse, bare-chested, tanned as his saddle, a bandana round his shaven skull, in ripped white jeans. Honestly, no joke. I'd just turned nineteen, how was I supposed to resist? You don't often get that in Perthshire.

I'd not long been in Sydney, the ultimate destination in my year-long whizz round the globe after I'd left Glenlyon. The money my parents hadn't pissed or gambled away by the time they'd sunk to the bottom of Mallaig harbour had gone into a trust. It hadn't been huge but big enough to let me wander off in search of fuck-knows-what. I'd not really known where I was going; only that the world was my oyster and that, in one context or another, I must make myself into some sort of pearl. I'd had no interest in university; I'd had enough of institutions. Anyway, I'd been average academically. Few subjects had made much impression, only the joy to be found in words had branded itself onto me. I guess it had started with Rory Blaine schoolboy comedian, polishing my arrows, and gone on from there. I became a junkie; books, plays, poetry, anything. But any vague notions of being a writer were just that; something to be thought about later. In the meantime, I'd ached for a new place to be. And I'd been dazzled by Australia. Not just by the light, the colour, the size, but by the roughness of it, the whole 'Ocker' thing. They were direct, unfiltered people, not unlike the Scots with class consciousness removed, and that had helped me feel at home. I'd taken to it like the proverbial duck. Then Matty's black horse had come out of the mist.

On the surface, you'd have taken him for a one brain-cell beach-boy, but he'd turned out to be a teacher of backward kids, living in a small flat with a tortoise called Joan Sutherland. He used to cook me dinner and talk about his dream of opening his own school. The walls had been lined with photos of his family in Brisbane; though his father had beaten him up when he'd discovered his only son was a poofter. I could still see their faces. I could still see clothes Matty had worn back then. I could still see the bedroom where I'd been screwed for the first time. I remembered all this because I'd loved him.

During our time together, the places and people I'd come from had been airbrushed from my consciousness. Matty was my present and my future. He'd introduced me to the guy who gave me my first job as a copywriter. The pay had been about ten dollars but I'd turned out to be good at it, very good. It had been my start in the business, the start of my life proper as I saw it. The pearl had begun to form.

I'd have done anything for Matty Rice. Danced naked on top of the Opera House. Sheared a sheep. Moved into the wee flat with him and Joan Sutherland. But he'd never suggested that. When Matty wasn't in the classroom or on the beach, he was in the bars. After about three months, the excuses had started, the calls not returned, then the fibs, then the rows. From Matty the anger, from me the tears. Back then it had seemed like a tragedy, now I knew it was just the usual farce.

'Cripes, is it the custom here to bring your mum to these places?' he asked, seeing Elspeth hovering behind me. 'That's kinda nice.'

She shook his hand cautiously with the expression she'd had when skirting the Durex Extra Strength. Matty explained he had a dodgy back and that his physio wanted him to hang vertically as much as possible to stretch the spine.

'So I thought, why not do it where there's fresh air and the chance to meet some like-minded people. It's amazing who comes up to chat.'

I said our goodbyes as quickly as possible, Matty clearly unbothered about whether we bumped into each other tomorrow or never in this lifetime. I prayed it would be the latter. He trotted back to his branch and hung from it again, a sagging Tarzan.

'By the way, did you ever open your school?' I called.

'I'm in real estate mate, have been for twenty years.'

'The school for backward kids?'

Matty dropped back to the ground and peered at me again.

'Christ, how did you know about that?'

It was like a punch in the face. I took Elspeth tightly by the arm and hurried her away. There was a shout.

'Hey shit, I've remembered you now!' he yelled, grinning the rictus grin. 'All the best mate.'

I knew Elspeth could see something was wrong, but she didn't ask. We walked on a short way then sadly, like Eurydice, she made the mistake of looking back.

'Good Gordon Highlanders,' she said.

Matty, hanging from his branch, head flung back, was enjoying a vigorous blowjob from a young guy in running gear. He'd not even bothered to wait till we were out of sight. But the young guy suddenly glanced in my direction. It was the Caravaggio boy, the kid crying under the lamp post that night I'd left the Soho bar. He stilled his bobbing head and held my gaze. I heard Matty demanding what his problem was, then Elspeth's voice behind me.

'Let's get away from here.'

The beams of sunlight had melted away; the woods seemed drab and dank now. I saw Elspeth shiver. Neither of us spoke till we reached Whitestone Pond.

'I suppose it's the unfortunates who go there?' she asked. 'The ones who've not found anybody?'

I shrugged as if I didn't know. I didn't want to disabuse her of that notion, to tell her that lots of nice respectable people found places like this unbelievably exciting, a brief liberation from lives inhibited by conscience, religion, partners or wives. Nor was I going to tell her that some regarded it as an untouchable part of their human rights, a grubby Mecca to which every self-respecting gay had to make at least one pilgrimage. I wasn't sure she'd be able to grasp the sophistication of that argument just after she'd had, presumably, her first glimpse of fellatio and been up to her knees in used johnnies.

'Well I'm glad you've got a special friend,' she said, 'A good person I'm thinking. Worth holding onto.'

'Don't worry,' I said. 'Things are going pretty well on the whole.'

As we turned into Spaniards Road, Elspeth looked back towards the West Heath.

'There's work to be done here,' she said, almost to herself. 'Work to be done.'

She was walking slowly now, not at her usual cracking pace, her gaze on the pavement. She said nothing more till we reached the East Court.

'When Charlie's sister wrote from America to tell me he was dead, the letter said they'd no idea why he'd been attacked. But I did. I knew. That was why I never wanted you, or any of the others, to follow in those footsteps. I thought maybe you could be stopped and re-directed along the right road.'

'The Morag Proudie Plan?'

'Aye,' she sighed. 'Didn't work though, did it?'

'I wanted it to work even more than you did, Miss Wishart,' I said 'But it never could. Life's not always a matter of choice, you know.'

'I've learned that now,' she said. '*The People's Friend* is getting quite progressive these days. But there's still a choice in the way you lead that life, is there not Rory Blaine? I'd not want to think of you being like that man back there in the woods, being like an animal.'

She fumbled in her bag for her keys.

'They could only identify him by dental records,' she said without looking at me. 'Och, it was such a nice face.'

*

Back in our flat, there was no sign of Faisal. I made myself a coffee and sat down by the big picture window. Alma the cat was curled up on the Berber rug. Faisal had tried to clean the stains and only made it worse. Where was he then? I wondered if I should go and see if his stuff was still in the wardrobes, but that seemed melodramatic. It was quiet in the flat. Not a sound from outside either. It was the workmen's half-day. Elspeth would be preparing her frugal lunch, Vic taking his midday nap. Big Frankie had zoomed off to Brighton with the Gay Scooter Group. I could just see Dolores Potts digging in a distant flower-bed. I stuck my iPod in my ears; I'd been struggling to update my musical tastes so Faisal would stop mocking me. I was working on Kanye West and Lady Gaga at the moment. God, it was shite.

I wondered if Matty Rice was still hanging from his tree, just half a mile away. I let myself fantasize that tonight, in some hotel room, he might think of me, letting memories drift back, maybe even a regret or two? Yeah sure. He'd be in a club, cocaine up his nostrils, dancing his tired old tits off, clinging to that damned carousel. And why should I care anyway? It was all history. I'd long since vaccinated myself against the Matty Rices of this world by absorbing some elements of them into myself. Just like a flu jab. From then on, I'd been immune. I might decide to use them but they'd not been able to hurt me any more. Let them walk away if they wanted, let anyone walk away.

The Rory Blaine who'd flown first-class out of Sydney back to London wasn't the one who'd sailed in five years earlier. By my early twenties, there were few traces of either the shy orphan from Kelvinside or the abandoned grandson from Mount Royal.; I'd shed them both like a snake-skin, drained their bruised blood and replaced it with something of a stronger proof. By then, the performance first sketched out at Glenlyon, the walk, the talk, the jokes, the costumes, had solidified into the role of a lifetime. The accent had been retained of course, more refined again now but still a crowd-pleaser on all continents. Amazing how, in the perceptions of many, the queer Scotsman remained an oxymoron. The Braemar Gathering had a lot to answer for.

Naturally, the great fucking irony was that by the time I'd perfected the performance, it was no longer necessary. Times had changed. The pretence had become pointless, shameful even, and there had been no denying the sheer relief of that. Gradually, I'd delivered my soliloquies of confession to the punters and found it made no difference. They still enjoyed the character and I'd seen no reason why I couldn't play him forever. So the fear had begun to lift, slowly at first then more and more quickly till it had almost gone.

But the anger had never left me. That outrage at the dealing of the cards. The worst times were when, as happened now while I stared out of the window, the anger spun round and turned on me. Why, in the deepest part of me, could I still not manage to accept the damn thing? Like the world assumed I did and as everybody else seemed able to? Like Matty Rice always had, even all those years ago. Like Faisal had succeeded in doing, despite the greater taboos in his culture. Like Vic appeared to, despite the lavender marriage and the wiles of Lauren Bacall. Why couldn't I even bring myself to discuss it with Ms Prada and make the bitch earn her money? She knew all about what happened with Granny, she'd got that out of me quickly, triumphantly almost, like a surgeon with a tumour. But I hadn't let her get to the root of me yet. To the rogue and shameful cell. Once, I'd hoped that time itself might be a sufficient healer but the bad stuff was still in there. I knew it. Yet I allowed it to remain. What sort of tosser was that?

A wave of irritation rose and choked me. I considered throwing my coffee against the wall, but I'd already ruined the Berber rug today and the place would be a wreck at this rate. So I ripped off the iPod and threw Kanye West and Lady Gaga instead. It buggered the iPod but it did the business. I fetched the guitar from under the bed and treated Alma to my cover of *A Man's A Man For A' That*.

Faisal appeared at the top of the glass staircase, holding a big plastic container.

'Hi,' I said.

'Hi,' he said. 'You all right? Where have you been?'

'Went for a walk with Elspeth,' I said. 'What's that you've got?'

'Heavy-duty carpet cleaner. Been to Homebase.'

We looked down at the Berber rug, like policemen examining a corpse.

'Really sorry about that,' I said. 'Let me give you a hand.'

Faisal mixed the stuff into a basin of water and found two sponges. We got down on our hands and knees and began to scrub gently. We worked in silence for a few minutes, then he stopped and looked up at me.

'Look, I just made a mistake. A bad one I know, but still just a mistake,' he said quietly. 'I've so little experience of these things.'

'It's okay,' I said. 'Come on, let's see if we can sort this.'

And the two of us bent our heads again and kept on scrubbing.

NINE

It was all because she'd looked a bit like June Whitfield. Darling Junie as the daft old sod called her. Neatly tailored, comfy white hair, just the sort you'd imagine writing for *Saga* Magazine. That was why he'd let his guard down. She'd been doing one of those 'alive and kicking' pieces. Vic agreed to these sometimes, usually in some posh restaurant on the assumption that they'd pick up the bill. But he'd had a chesty cough and asked her to come to Mount Royal instead. From the comfort of the Red Damask Drawing-Room, with Vic dosed up on Benylin, they'd set off on the usual Cook's Tour of his life and career. They'd ascended his peaks and sunk into his troughs. They'd hacked through the jungle of statistics on his Top Ten hits, album sales and Royal Command performances. They'd bumped into the usual crew; Frank, Dino, Sammy, Larry and Viv, Noel, Johnnie Gielgud, and of course the blessed Alma, the singer not the cat. They'd even waved, from afar, at the ex-Mrs d'Orsay in sunny Ibiza.

Naturally, the woman had asked about the house and Vic had described his current business project, renovating it into apartments for retired people. Then, just as Elspeth had done with me, she'd gushed that she'd absolutely adore to live here one day.

Vic had tapped the side of his blocked nose, winked and croaked, 'Bachelors only honey.'

Later, he'd blamed the combination of the Benylin and the two stonking glasses of Rioja he'd had at lunch. But in those three words, he'd outed both Mount Royal and himself. Bugger Saga, the woman must have thought as she started dialling numbers in Wapping.

Three hundred years ago, my fat-cat ancestor had named his house after the legend that Henry VIII had bolted up here to slaughter some deer after his first glimpse of Anne of Cleves. That was now to be changed at the click of a mouse by some wee spiv at an Apple Mac in Docklands. The next morning, for eight million *Sun* readers crunching their Shreddies and lighting their first roll-up, Mount Royal was re-christened *Withering Heights!*

Under that banner, the sub-head read 'Queen of Croon? Vic d'Orsay opens old folks home for gays.' The rest was no more than a scissors-and-paste job about Vic's career, Granny's loony doings and a couple of lines about me. But by lunchtime, nearly every other paper, TV and radio station had picked it up. The office phone rang non-stop. Eventually I pulled it out of the wall, but that just transferred the problem to the front gates. Bruce Willis waddled into the office, sweating heavily as usual. There were about twenty of them outside plus a few more with cameras up in the oak trees. The rooks were furious. Bruce said he'd threatened them with garrotting, disembowelment and other tricks picked up in *Die Hard With A Vengeance*. But he'd feel a lot happier with back-up from his mates Lance and Jason, ex-territorials who didn't take no bull from nobody. Then he flushed a little and said that though he himself was a thousand percent red-blooded male, his philosophy was live-and-let-live; his neighbours in Dalston were two lovely lads with the neatest garden in the street.

With all the fuss, I'd forgotten to tell Elspeth what had happened. She'd gone down the hill to get her magazines and had to fight her way back in.

'One wee tyke asked me if I was a lesbian,' she said on reaching the sanctuary of the office. 'But *The Lady* can deliver a hefty whack.'

She was more concerned about having had her picture taken, in case it might be seen back in Bute. Vic promised her it was really pictures of elderly gents they were after, preferably in full drag cutting roses. Elspeth wanted to know what we were going to do. I asked if she had any suggestions. She looked hard at me, in the way she'd always done if I'd posed a question to which any decent Church of Scotland boy should have known the answer.

'If you believe in this place, then tell the truth and shame the devil', she said. 'I'll away and make us a wee pot of tea. A lesbian indeed. Do I *look* like a lesbian?'

There was the sudden roar of an engine. Big Frankie rode the lilac scooter across the East Court and out onto the carriage circle. Cameras starting flashing in the oaks, making them look like Christmas trees. He stopped just inside the gates and leaned back in the saddle. He pouted and preened, teased and tantalized, both hands dangling in his crotch. He opened the neck of the red leathers and slowly pulled the zip lower and lower till his great black belly spilled out like a hernia. The oaks went berserk. Then he blew them a kiss and rode back into the East Court.

'I'm not sure that was helpful, Frankie,' I shouted from my hiding-place in the office doorway.

'Ainsley Harriott's like a busted flush,' he grinned. 'There's a vacancy for an ethnic celebrity-chef. Why not Big Frankie Beckles? We're famous boss. We got fifteen minutes. Enjoy!'

He wasn't wrong. We made all the tea-time news bulletins, usually as the last item, the 'would you believe it?' slot, often occupied by skate-boarding dachshunds or disabled kids who'd done a bungee-jump.

I didn't sleep well. Faisal, thank God, had gone to a conference in north Wales. I hoped they were all too wrapped up in their microbes and viruses to see newspapers or watch TV. My brain was buzzing like a hedge-trimmer. I kept getting up to peek out the window in case a reporter had his nose pressed against it. It was reassuring to see the light in Bruce Willis's caravan, though he'd be safe back in Dalston now. At night we'd acquired a young bloke, tall and skinny with piercings, tattoos and a deathly pale skin. He only grunted the odd monosyllable and I'd decided he sat in the caravan drinking the blood of virgins or pulling the wings off bats. Tonight though, I was glad the Vampire was out there.

Next morning, we were even in the broadsheets; I'd finally got myself in *The Times* after all. But poor Frankie; there were no pix of him anywhere and Elspeth had been spared exposure on the Isle of Bute.

Marcus Leigh called on my mobile.

'Well, this is a jolly bad show isn't it?' he said briskly. 'I bumped into the Lord Chancellor in St. James's Square. He asked if I'd put my name down for "Withering Heights."'

'Did you tell him you had?' I asked.

'I most certainly did not.'

'You still with us then, Marcus?'

There was a long pause.

'I very much want to be with you, as I made clear at the Reform,' he said slowly 'But I simply couldn't cope with being an attraction in a media circus. That's not what I was looking for at all.'

He offered his advice. As with his suggestions on what to order for lunch, this came across as compulsory. Like Elspeth, he said there was no point in denying the truth. If we did, they'd be

crawling over us like midges forever. We must issue a bald statement verifying the essence of the article, then refuse to comment
further.

'I'll have to see how things develop,' he concluded, 'before
committing myself further. Frightfully sorry, but I'm sure you
understand.'

By the middle of the next day, seven potential residents had
called to cancel their interviews. None made any bones about
why.

'I'm perfectly happy to be open in private,' said one member
of the House of Lords, 'but not to the world, his wife and his feral
children. I have non-executive directorships to protect. Several of
the companies do business in the Middle East. It's just not on.'

'Listen toots, you have to understand how things used to be for
these guys,' Vic said when I'd put the phone down. 'They were
criminals till they were thirty or forty. Some of them have never
got the chill of that out of their bones, however cosy things might
be now. The shame may have gone, but the embarrassment's still
there like a ball and chain. They learn to drag it around, but they
never entirely lose it.'

We'd always realized that our plans for Mount Royal would
be newsworthy. There were dozens of such places in the States
and a few in Europe but for your deep-fried British bigot we
could be a freak show. We'd never expected to keep it secret in
the longer term, sooner or later, we'd be outed, but we wanted it
later. Not that we weren't proud of what we were doing; I'd had
a nice dream about Prince William coming to cut the ribbon, Big
Frankie bobbing as he presented the bouquet, Elspeth with her
hair actually done, that sort of thing. But Vic and I had agreed
that, until everybody had been planted-in and well watered, we'd
keep the species of our elderly flowers to ourselves. Anyway, the
sort who could pay our fees would expect discretion like they'd
expect their hotel bed turned down and a chocolate on their
pillow.

But now this. So far, I'd stayed remarkably calm. I'd not lost
it with Vic like I'd lost it with Faisal. Not gone for Option Three.
Not called him a silly old bastard who'd just fucked up everything. All the more admirable since he'd not actually delivered a
proper apology. The less convenient side of Vic's sunny disposition was an ability to delete bad stuff from his consciousness; the

glass couldn't just be half-full, it had to be up to the brim with a cherry and a wee paper parasol. Admittedly though, he had seemed a bit subdued today and there hadn't been a Rat Pack anecdote for forty-eight hours. But by the evening, we'd notched up fifteen cancellations and just as I put down the phone on the latest *refusenik*, Vic strolled back into the office with a bottle of whisky and two glasses.

'What's up toots?'

The gastric reflux heard its cue and made its entrance. Yep, here we go.

'I'll fucking tell you what's up. How could you have been so idiotic? You've been giving press interviews for fifty years and you slip up now. All this work. All this time. All this money; most of it your own. And at the eleventh hour, you've blown it because you'd overdosed on Benylin. Jesus, Victor. *Withering Heights!* Well done.'

'It would have come out somewhere along the line. We always knew that, didn't we?'

'Yes, but not now!' I yelled. 'Not one punter has signed on the dotted line. Not one. This whole thing could yet go down the toilet and you'll have flushed it, you stupid old man.'

Vic's smile snuffed out completely. I'd often been rude about his age, but never seriously, never cruelly. But I mean, well, was I wrong? He said it was the Benylin, but wasn't it maybe just the brain cells dying? I was used to working with sharp, clever operators in their prime. For the first time it hit me that I'd soon be surrounded by people who might be starting to lose the plot. Would senility leak silently into the air like carbon monoxide, till I started taking a nap in the afternoons and going to bed at half-past ten? Christ, what had I done?

Vic picked up the whisky bottle from the desk.

'Think I'll find a quiet corner of the garden and finish this off. Might put a slug of Benylin in it too.'

'Try an overdose,' I snapped.

*

Dolores Potts stood framed in the office doorway, the evening sun shimmering in a halo round her dark head. *Madonna With A Trowel.* She'd developed a habit of popping in, usually at the end of the day. She'd always have some excuse, but I sensed that was all they were. I'd give her a glass of wine and we'd chat about her plans for the gardens. She was clever, sparky, a laugh. I'd come to quite look forward to it.

'Bad moment?' she asked. 'Got some invoices from the nurseries.'

As well as *The Archers* vowels, she spoke in the new received pronunciation in which the letters *t* and *g* were dead and gone and *r* was in intensive care. It was a shame. For some reason I couldn't explain, I yearned for Dolores Potts to be without a flaw. She was so beautiful that even the smallest imperfection seemed like an outrage.

I snatched the invoices, rammed them in a drawer and grabbed a bottle from the fridge.

'One of those reporters asked me if I was a lesbian,' she said. 'Do I *look* like a lesbian?'

'Don't take it personally, they're asking everyone,' I replied. 'Are you a lesbian?'

'Oh no,' she smiled, draping herself across a chair and staring at me with her big eyes. 'I tried it once but it made my teeth chatter. Besides I like cock too much.'

'Fuck, you're coarse,' I said, my Calvinist gene stirring in its sleep. 'Are all your generation like that now?'

'I expect so,' she said. 'Don't really bother with them as a rule. I've always gone for older men. Mind if I light up?'

She didn't wait for permission. My impulse was to stop her, but Dolores Potts carried an odd kind of authority. As if she were the boss and I the employee, as if this were her house, not mine. Whenever we talked, she always deflected questions about her background. She claimed to be just a country girl from the middle of nowhere. Except that she wasn't, I'd have laid good money on that.

'So you don't like women any more than I do then?' she said.

'That's an odd question on a day when I'm all over the papers as a card-carrying poof,' I replied.

'Well I tried it. Just wondered if you ever had?'

'A few times actually,' I heard myself say, aware that I said it as a boast.

'I bet you broke some hearts.'

'I doubt it,' I smiled.

'Oh I'm sure you broke at least one or two,' she teased. She flicked her ash into an empty coffee-cup, never letting the big eyes leave mine. For a moment, I imagined I saw something hard and cold in them, but then it vanished.

There had been more than a few women in fact. A dozen maybe. After Morag Proudie, it'd taken me several years to try again; not till I was in Oz and Matty Rice had broken what I'd thought of as my heart. It had been planned as a major plank of my reinvention. At first it hadn't been a total disaster, physically at least. I'd closed my eyes and thought of dinky Dustin Hoffman or that other Rory, the hunky folk-singer of my teenage fantasies. I'd closed my eyes and tried to kid myself. It had sort of worked for a while then, like a medicine you take too often, it gradually lost its power and you learn to accept you're incurable. Since then, as my charms and my bank account had reached their zenith, I'd often been chased by women whose ears hadn't been whispered in. I'd always been flattered even though I'd decided never to unhook another *Ann Summers* crotchless suspender-thong. But I wondered if it were happening again, here and now. *Madonna With A Trowel* was gazing at me through her veil of cigarette smoke. Despite what she knew of me, did Dolores Potts want my body?

She asked how serious the press exposure was. I said I didn't know yet, but it might be. She said I should try to relax. I went to the fridge to get us a second bottle.

'Don't do that,' said the husky voice behind me. 'I know a better way.'

She reached for my hand. Shite. But then she led me from the office and out into the Italian Garden. We stopped at the long flowerbed below the Orangery; she'd been planting here, spades and forks rested on the grass, their day's work done.

'Do what I do,' said Dolores Potts.

She pushed up her sleeves and lay flat on her stomach at the edge of the lawn. Closing her eyes, she plunged both arms elbow-deep into the newly-turned ground. For a few moments, she held them there then pulled back out and began to knead the rich dark soil like flour, letting it run through her fingers and back to where it belonged. Then she submerged her dirty brown limbs once again.

'Do it,' she said, her eyes still shut. So I did. Together we lay face-down on the evening grass, half-buried in the earth of Mount Royal.

'Feel better?' she asked after a while.

'Yes,' I said.

'Hold on then,' said Dolores Potts. 'Just hold on to what you're feeling now. The rest doesn't matter a damn.'

*

Later, I ate alone in the flat. Faisal was still somewhere among the men of Harlech, presumably in blissful ignorance. I'd thought about calling and crying on his shoulder. That was what partnerships were for, wasn't it? In good times and in bad, in sickness and in health? I'd not had many shoulders available as a rule, so I might as well enjoy the perk. He was going to find out sooner or later and might be cross I'd not rung. But for some reason I didn't.

I made cheese on toast and gave Alma had her usual fishy muck. I imagined mild reproach in her slitty eyes and wondered if she expected fresh fish, being a cat from Harrods. Oh dear, I really ought to learn to cook. After that day at school when Elspeth had snatched away the recipe book and ordered me into my rugby kit, I'd steered clear of it, like a rock on which my machismo might founder. But it was never too late. Maybe Big Frankie would teach me a few simple dishes.

Big Frankie. I wanted a word with him. I'd not been taken with that wee bout of exhibitionism yesterday. His references were immaculate and he wasn't a bad lad, but I sensed a cuckoo in our nest and his wings needed clipping now. I looked out into the East Court. The lilac scooter was there, shiny and vulgar in the setting sun. He answered his door breathless and flustered.

'Good timing boss. I could use your help.'

I followed the huge arse up the narrow stairs to the studio on the first floor. The room was woozy with dozens of candles, punctured only by a harsh shaft of electricity from the half-open bathroom door. There was a pungent smell of sick. In the loo, propped on a stool with his head resting on the basin, was Vic. He seemed to be only semi-conscious and ponged like Sauchiehall Street on a Saturday night.

'He's ringin' my friggin' bell fifteen minutes now. Pissed as a fart, pants all muddy, he must've fallen in the garden. I got him upstairs but he wouldn't stop moppin' up the liquor, cryin' too. That's whisky for you'

Big Frankie insisted that Vic should be put to bed there; that he had to be watched in case he threw up again in his sleep.

Somehow we got most of his clothes off and carried him onto the bed. Frankie wiped his face gently with a cold flannel and smoothed his hair.

'Thanks boss, I'll look after him now. Don't you fret none.'

I headed for the door but Frankie pressed me to stay for coffee. I'd not been here since he'd moved in a few weeks back to supervise the installation of the new kitchens. The room was meticulously tidy, corseted even, such a contrast to its great wobbly occupant. In one corner, close to the bed with the snoring drunk, was a small table laid out as a shrine to The Virgin Mary; candles, incense, flowers, the statue with the halo, the works. At the window was a big fat telescope on a stand. While he made the coffee, I peeked through it, but you couldn't see any sky from this angle, only the East Front of the house. Cheaply-framed photos took up every available space; Prince Philip, David Attenborough, Nelson Mandela, Michael Parkinson, Bill Oddie and the poet whose book had fallen from his bike that day. His heroes presumably. There were family pictures too. A teenage Frankie, an uninflated version of the way he looked now, but still towering over several other children, his arm round the shoulder of a younger boy, a tiny girl clinging to his hand. A lean, clenched middle-aged man stood beside Frankie. There didn't seem to be a mother. Then I sort of sensed that Frankie was the mother.

'She died givin' birth to my little sister,' he said. 'I was twelve. It was hard, specially for my father.'

'Are they all still in Trinidad?'

'Only my father. He's married again now. Rest of us scattered on the winds. We emailin' now and again, but the family not really there no more.'

'It'll always be there,' I said, 'even if you sometimes can't see it.'

'You think so boss?' asked Frankie. 'I'd like to feel that.'

He went and dabbed Vic's brow with the flannel.

'I never see him sleepin' before. Isn't he lovely?'

'He's old, fat, pissed and smells of sick.'

Big Frankie spun round, anger flaring in his eyes like two gas rings.

'How can you say that? Mr d'Orsay is the most beautiful person I know.'

The Tupperware bowl that Frankie had rested on Vic's belly in case he puked again was rising and falling like Captain Pugwash's ship on a stormy sea.

'Look boss, his whole story there in that face,' said Frankie. 'It fills my eyes, it really does.'

'Well that's a nice feeling to express Frankie,' I said. I guess there was a penny sticking in the slot on top of my skull and refusing to drop. Maybe because there were so many things whirling in my head today, there just wasn't room for anything more.

'And the first time I get him into my bed, he no damn good to me,' said Frankie. 'Ain't life a bitch?

I stared up at him, then at Prince Philip, Michael Parkinson and the rest. All the pennies dropped with the noise of a jackpot in a one-armed bandit.

'Shite kid, you're a...'

'A gerontophile,' said Big Frankie with a wide grin. 'Cool word, don't you reckon? Like somethin' you can study at university. Ger-on-to-phile.'

He blew out the syllables proudly, like bubbles from a wand.

'Why don't you like guys of your own age?'

'Oh they're like newborn puppy-dogs, smooth and wet, all lookin' the same,' said Big Frankie. 'It's only when men get older that you can tell them apart, only then is the real beauty appearin'. You never been to *The Last Resort*?'

'The old guys' bar? No I fucking haven't.'

'When I first arrived in London, it was like being let loose in a sweet-shop. I had a special T-shirt printed. It said *Steradent Provided.*'

He embraced his massive knees and rocked back in his chair.

'Never fails to break the ice. Humour is the best aphrodisiac.'

He pulled his chair closer to mine. I caught a faint whiff of Vic's puke off his shirt. The big face clouded over.

'You know, back in Trinidad we respect the old folks. They still livin' with their families, only in a home if they really sick. They sit at the head of the table. They wear nice clothes in happy colours. They stroll out in the evenin' to meet their friends at the cafes. They still have joy. But here, they all seem so sad. Everybody makin' jokes about them or just pretendin' they ain't there. They're just fadin' away into black and white, like turnin' down the colour on your TV set, like they ashamed to still be here.'

Big Frankie shook his head sadly then smiled over at the bed.

'But Mr d'Orsay's not like that. He's still in Technicolor, that one. I love him like a hog loves mud.'

I walked over to the window. I had no idea what to say or how to deal with this. I'd given a gerontophile a job in a home for old blokes. My hand rested on the telescope.

'You can only see the house from here surely?'

Big Frankie gave a pantomine wink.

'Yep, just settin' it up for all these lovely old men movin' in.'

'Do you think there's maybe something the matter with you Frankie?' I said. 'I know someone you could talk to...'

'How come you're sayin' that Mr Blaine?' he replied coolly. 'There's beauty in every season ain't there? Beauty in the leaf that goin' to open, but also in the leaf that goin' to fall? More perhaps, because soon it'll be gone forever. Maybe that's why I'm drawn to it and want to cherish it while it's still here. So if that makes me sick, then that's how God made me. I real surprised that you, of all people, should be talkin' like that. A man who create this beautiful haven where the old leaves can float gently to the ground when the time comes.'

'So you're quite happy as you are then?' I asked.

'Sure, why not?' he said.

'What does The Virgin Mary say?'

'Our Lady well understand that I'm filled with love and that's all she needs to know,' he said. 'Okay, I'm livin' my life to a different set of chimes from most, but they're still the ones I hear in my soul, the ones that tell me right from wrong. And every time I put a great big smile on some baggy old face, I hear those chimes go ding-dong and I know that Jesus and his mum blessin' me for it.'

'And you don't want to know why you're like this? Or change it if you could?'

Big Frankie looked at me like I needed to be sectioned.

'Change the way I find love? What the hell for boss?'

There was coughing and mumbling from the bed. Frankie hurried over. I followed. Vic was chattering in his sleep.

'Stupid... old... stupid... stupid old man...'

Frankie went and soaked the cold flannel again.

'I'll do that,' I said and wiped the forehead and pasty cheeks. I couldn't have done it if his eyes had been open. I'd have been too ashamed.

Big Frankie was unrolling a futon on the floor. I headed for the door.

'Does Vic know how you feel about him?' I asked.

'Oh no boss, and promise me you'll keep it secret,' he said. 'Mr d'Orsay thinks I'm just a star-struck queen. But I'd never even heard of him to be honest; though don't you go tellin' him that neither. You noticin' I don't even use his first name yet? I mustn't push things. But the planets are workin' on my behalf, I'm sure of that.'

'Why?'

'Today, I burned that T-shirt I wore in *The Last Resort*. I don't be wantin' it again. I've found my daddy and I'll be faithful to him. And now here he is in my bed. Not in the way I imagined it, but tonight we'll sleep under the same roof with me watchin' over him. It's a sign I'm not wrong to love this man.'

Big Frankie began blowing out the candles, except those on the shrine. The light flickered over Vic's sleeping figure.

'Goodnight boss,' he said. 'If you don't mind my sayin' so, you're going to be a really beautiful old man. I can see that even now.'

'Even now? Thanks a bunch, Frankie.'

'And don't go worryin' over all this publicity. It'll be cool. I've already had a word with The Virgin and first thing tomorrow I callin' the Poor Clares. I worked in the convent kitchen when I first came over from Trini. I'll get them to pray for us.'

'You expect nuns to pray for a houseful of gay men?'

'They'll pray for anyone, boss,' said Big Frankie 'They're not proud. That's why they're friggin' nuns.'

Out in the East Court, the only lights came from the flats; the house itself was in darkness, a great black shape crouched against the purple-pink glow of the city sky. So now it was to be *Withering Heights*. Oh well, better that than the reputation it gained in my grandmother's time. Maybe there was something in its genes that predisposed it to notoriety. Ok then, so be it. Elspeth had said to tell the truth and shame the devil. I went into the office and emailed The Press Association. I said that we were proud to confirm recent reports that Mount Royal was shortly to open as a retirement home for gay men. The directors of the management company were Rory Blaine, descendant of the builder of the house, and Vic d'Orsay, the celebrated singer. I emphasized that we would have no further comment to make at any time.

I locked the office and turned towards the flat. It was nearly midnight. The moon had appeared out of nowhere and lit Mount Royal in a silvery-blue wash. Way up there in the cupola, on that first day back in Mount Royal, Vic had said that I belonged here. He'd been even more right than I'd realized then. Now it was inconceivable to be anywhere else. That was my excuse for today. I'd apologize to Vic in the morning. Of all people he would understand.

'It's going to be all right,' I said. 'The Poor Clares are praying for us. Whoever the fuck they are.'

I took a quick shower. The soil from Dolores' flowerbed was still clogged beneath my fingernails but I left it there. I banged out a swift one and fell asleep like a baby. In the middle of the night, I sensed something furry resting against my chest. I thought it was Faisal, quietly returned, and felt a dozy surge of pleasure. Then there was a gentle purr followed by a fishy fart. I cupped my hand round Alma's wee body and felt the beating of her heart. I synchronized my breathing with hers and we both slept through till Chris Evans clicked on, urging us to leap out of bed and embrace the day, whatever it might bring. So we did.

TEN

What do you give to the woman who doesn't have everything? Who has absolutely nothing in fact and likes it that way? Today I found myself in the unusual position of wondering how to thank thirty-five nuns. Heathen as I am, I had to admit that within a few hours of Big Frankie ringing the Poor Clares, something in the universe shifted gear and nice things began to happen. At Frankie's suggestion, I sent them a small donation for their chapel roof. He wasn't sure if they had a problem with their roof but they could put it away for a rainy day.

There was nothing else in the morning papers, no more reporters in the oak trees. Bruce Willis cancelled his reinforcements and Elspeth resumed her outings without fear of being asked if she were a muff-diver. Above all, there were no more cancellations from prospective residents. Instead the post brought over two hundred enquiries from men who were keen, in some cases frantic, to take their places. Most of the letters were formal and businesslike, but a few were emotional and embarrassing to read. Later, Bruce Willis brought another batch that had been hand-delivered at the gates, some of them marked 'urgent'. By the end of the day, we could have filled Mount Royal ten times over.

My email contained requests for interviews from The *Guardian* and The *Sunday Times*. *Newsnight* wanted us to appear with some African bishop who'd just told the Synod that homosexuals should be fed to the hippos. The Minister For Equality and Diversity messaged to praise our 'thrilling social experiment', reassuring us of the government's 'ongoing commitment to same-sex issues'. And somebody wants me to do a commercial for a shampoo-conditioner. They just totally love my look.

I'd not seen Vic all day, I'd not had time. Big Frankie said he'd been pretty rough this morning and stumbled off back to his own bed. It wasn't till early evening that I climbed the staircase and knocked on the double satinwood doors to my grandmother's old rooms. A voice called 'come'. The old shiver ran through me.

I'd half expected to find him still in bed with the Tupperware bowl, but he was draped across a sofa, merry as a carnival float, in a long silk dressing-gown with the phone in one hand and a wine-glass in the other.

'Hair of the dog, toots,' he whispered. There was no hint of a chill in the air.

While he took his call, I wandered to the windows. Granny's former suite had the best views in Mount Royal, directly south over the city. It had been slept in by William Gladstone and Oscar Wilde, though not of course together. The drawing-room, decorated by Wyattville in a spectrum of greens and golds, was dominated by a massive chimneypiece in white marble, the lintel held up by two caryatids strongly resembling a pair of lesbian truckers. It was a room to rattle round in, but Vic wasn't a rattler; he expanded like a jelly to fill whatever space he was in.

He'd certainly erased all traces of Granny, banishing all her furniture to the attics, even the huge State Bed once used by Queen Charlotte. He'd not sleep in Sibyl's bed he'd said, in one of his rare oblique references to his crime. His own stuff fitted perfectly. To look, or indeed listen, to Vic d'Orsay, you'd imagine his taste would be neo-Weybridge, but he had Chippendale tables, George II armchairs and some nice modern art including, centre-stage over the chimney-piece, a Lucian Freud of himself in which he looked startlingly like that old chorus-girl who'd been Speaker of the House of Commons. Books were packed into newly-built cases like commuters on a tube-train. There were dedicated shelves for classic literature and contemporary novels, fat tomes on art and architecture, volumes of history, philosophy and other spiritual stuff. He seemed pretty big on Buddha; perhaps some affinity based on shape. CDs and old vinyl albums were lined up in battalions; I flicked along all the usual suspects but hey, look here. I pulled out a faded sleeve of a burly man in Highland dress playing a guitar up to his knees in heather. And wow, it had been autographed. *'To Vic. Thanks for a night to remember baby.'* Jesus. Rory McCulloch had been a kilt-lifter? The man I'd wanted to be had been as much of a fake as I was? Irony could go no further. I had to sit down. I wasn't sure whether to be heartbroken or overjoyed. I think I was a bit of both.

Vic was still on the phone to some woman called Wendy, telling her that just because he was gay didn't mean they couldn't go on having their annual lunch at the Savoy. He assured her that the Savoy had an open-door policy towards gays these days. Yes, he hoped that all his fans in Shropshire would stay loyal despite the terrible shock they'd suffered. No, he'd never had sex with Graham Norton or Will Young, though he confessed to having goosed Russ Conway when they'd been on *The Billy Cotton Band Show*. He said he still loved her to bits, blew a few kisses down the phone and cut her off.

'Wendy runs my fan-club and website,' he explained. 'From a council house in Ludlow, I think it is. She had no idea I was "like that", she just thought I was theatrical. She was a bit weepy. Silly cow.'

I'd been so focused on Vic's having outed the house, I'd forgotten he'd outed himself at the same time. But he was undaunted by the wobble in Wendy's devotion because, between sobs, she'd provided him with some interesting facts. In the last forty-eight hours, the website (www.kingofcroon.com) had received over a thousand hits and nearly three hundred emails. Apart from some abusive ones from the usual nutters, they'd been overwhelmingly supportive of Vic's 'singing the song of sodomy' as one of the nutters had put it.

'I've even had offers of sexual congress apparently,' said Vic. 'Some of them suggesting things unheard of in Ludlow. I think poor Wendy's reeling but very possibly aroused.'

His agent had been on the line constantly. On Amazon and in the big music stores, sales of Vic's precious CDs had gone from a flaccid ten or twelve a month to a throbbing fifty-plus a day. There had been lots of interview requests including *Saga* magazine asking to re-do their original piece from a 'more contemporary slant'. *Gay Times* wanted to pastiche its usual front-cover of chiselled chest and washboard abs with Vic's big belly and hairy man-boobs. There were enquiries about cabaret spots in several gay venues. Vic's agent, who specialized in representing artistes in the last act of their careers and who rarely got into his office before eleven, said he'd not been this excited since the rumours that Matt Monro wasn't really dead.

When he paused to draw breath, I told him about the avalanche of interest from prospective punters.

'Jeez, that's terrific, toots,' he said.

'I think I need to say sorry, Victor.'

'Well I do too,' he said, clasping my hand. 'Anyway, it seems to have been a cloud with a distinctly silver lining, so let's move on, shall we?'

Vic's phone rang. It was his agent yet again. As he listened, the smile went up to maximum voltage.

'Elton's people have been on,' he said, a little catch in his throat. 'He's doing another album of duets and he wants me.'

'Wow,' I said. 'What's the song to be?'

'Elton's put some music to a Shakespeare sonnet.'

'Which one's that then?'

Vic gave me an oblique, almost shy smile. He crossed to the window and began to address the statues down in the garden. He spoke the words wistfully, almost in a whisper.

'Shall I compare thee to a summer's day?

Thou art more lovely and more temperate . . .'.

Twelve lines later, he turned back towards me, his eyes spilling over. I wondered if Big Frankie, despite what he'd said last night, had declared himself today after all? And did his elderly squeeze reciprocate? Had the Poor Clares, beseeching the heavens to look kindly on Mount Royal, gone a prayer too far? At the very moment of his unmasking, had The King of Croon also fallen in love?

'Elton says his tune's a classical-rap fusion,' said Vic. 'Any idea what that means?'

'Oh yeah,' I lied. 'Cool.'

*

Last night Vic d'Orsay went on television and gave the performance of his life without singing a single note. The BBC switchboard was deluged and this morning he got the best reviews of his career.

Big Frankie had invited Elspeth and me to his flat for a 'Sevillano fork-supper' so we could all watch together. Dolores Potts had been asked too but, as usual, she was going what she called 'up West'. Nibbling our tapas, we sat through items about hygiene standards in massage parlours and a Tory MP who'd invented a 'humane' birch. Vic, as he'd have expected, was to be top of the bill.

Of course it helped that the Bishop was a caricature of a third-world evangelical; slamming the table, eyes rolling like a Black & White Minstrel, a few resolutions short of a conference. He condemned the concept of a home for elderly homosexuals as an obscene contradiction, demanding that they remain as outcasts in any God-fearing society. He also laid into Britain's secular decadence in general citing, as examples, scratchcards, *Strictly Come Dancing* and the novels of Jilly Cooper. The interviewer, a hard-faced Geordie woman known to the tabloids as Stroppy Tits, let her perfectly-plucked eyebrows slowly rise into Norman arches.

Vic, in a powder blue suit and a pink tie with matching hanky, lolled back as if he were about to doze off and let the torrent of bigotry wash over him. Then he sat up very straight and began to reply. Stroppy Tits, notorious for her aggressive interjections, didn't cut in once.

He told the nation he'd been born Victor Aronson and that he'd been a child in the Warsaw Ghetto, followed by two years in Treblinka. He'd watched his father and brother die there; he had no idea what had become of his mother and sister, but he guessed they'd perished too. Christ, I didn't know any of this. He'd only ever said his family had died in the war.

'But even as we faced this horror, we still had each other to turn to,' said Vic. 'If you're Jewish, Muslim, black or any other group that gets a rough deal in our world, you've still probably got your family to lick your wounds and allow you your dignity. The glaring exception to this principle is the gay minority. It's a lot better now of course but, for my generation at least, the last people you'd confide in were your own folk, in case they might stop loving you. So most of us began to live in constant fear of being found out. Your home, the one place you should be able to feel safe, could never be quite the same again. And for many people, these fears were totally justified. When their secret came out, they did lose their families, either by being literally ejected or just by the silent withdrawal of the love they'd once imagined they could always take for granted. And it still happens today, even in these shiny pink post-Millenium times.'

In Big Frankie's little flat, I had a mouthful of *bocorones* that I couldn't swallow.

The Bishop said that decent families had the absolute right to reject children who were an abomination in the eyes of the Lord. Keeping one under your roof would be like having a Trojan horse filled with the soldiers of Satan. Stroppy Tits' eyebrows arched from Norman into Perpendicular Gothic.

'Lots of gay people spend years trying to rebuild some sort of family unit,' Vic went on. 'Some manage it, by finding partners or by creating a circle of loving friends. But some never do. For many old guys like me, the gay life hasn't been that easy. The simple idea behind our project is to give at least a few of them a space to be themselves. And we're hoping it's an idea that might catch on.'

'It's over forty years since the law changed in Britain,' said Stroppy Tits. 'Elton's out, George Michael's out. What's kept you?'

Vic sighed and smiled.

'Honey, my sexuality has never been a problem to me. It was no secret to my friends, colleagues or indeed to my darling ex-wife, but I baulked at telling the wider world. I felt I'd earned a break from discrimination. And it was another time then. Lord Montagu, Johnnie Gielgud, the great Alan Turing. Even after the law changed, sodomy didn't sell records, at least not to the lovely ladies who appreciate my sort of music. But I'm ashamed of that now and I'm sitting here trying to make up for it.'

'Why can't you love gay people?' demanded Stroppy Tits of the Bishop, who claimed that he did love gay people, but believed that they should be chemically castrated to help them find their way to God.

Vic replied that he wasn't a huge fan of God's. He wasn't impressed by God's CV he said, God having not turned up for work a few too many times; Vic himself having been present on the most notorious occasion when God had overslept. The Bishop called him a blasphemer as well as a pervert. Vic shook his head and sighed again.

'For most of my life I've gone around singing songs about love,' he said. 'And I really do believe in moons in June, red roses for a blue lady and dancing under the starlight. Aren't those the moments that we tuck under our arms as we head towards our graves? It's what separates us from the beasts of the field, among whom the Bishop reckons I should be numbered. But I see no love in this man here or in people like him. He is the abomination, not me. And I will stand up to be counted against him and his sort until my dying day.'

Big Frankie punched the air.

'Yeah Papi, you tell that fucker! Beggin' your pardon Miss Wishart.'

The Bishop slammed the table a bit more, chucked in Leviticus and declared that buggery would destroy the planet faster than global warming.

'One last question Vic d'Orsay,' said Stroppy Tits. 'Before your parents perished, did they find out you were gay?'

Vic opened his mouth but nothing came out. He took a slow sip of water, then another. Stroppy Tits waited then repeated the question.

'There was a boy in my hut,' he said. 'A few years older than me. About seventeen maybe. A pink triangle on his jacket. Alone. No family. A nice kid, always smiling in a place where there was little reason for that. My brother told me not to talk to him, but we became friends nevertheless. One day, my brother found us in a corner of the hut together. Our fingertips were touching. That was all. But my brother saw. He must have told my father. My father died about a month later, my brother very soon after. Neither of them had spoken to me during that time.'

In front of the TV, Big Frankie began to shake. Elspeth lowered her eyes and fixed them on her plate. I just felt a weariness sweep over me like the flu. A weariness at the whole damn thing.

'Now honey,' Vic was saying on the box. 'My thoughts are turning to a free night-cap in your green room. Will you join me?'

'I'd be delighted, Mr d'Orsay,' said Stroppy Tits. They both pulled off their mikes and abandoned the table, leaving the Bishop on his own as the credits charged over him like stampeding cattle.

Big Frankie was crying and laughing at the same time. Elspeth sat silently finishing her food. Every now and then, she'd been giving me odd sidelong glances. But there would be no more conversation now. I got up and said goodnight.

In my own flat, I poured myself a large whisky. I'd decided to wait up for Vic. There was no way I'd be able to sleep without seeing him, saying something, though I'd no idea what that might be. Those layers I'd sensed in him went deeper and darker than anything I could have imagined. But he'd survived. How come I couldn't quite say the same?

There was a ring at my door. Elspeth asked if she could come in. I led her upstairs. She peered at me with those wee green eyes.

'That's what happened here, is it not?' she asked.

'Sorry?'

'That's what happened here, to you. What Mr d'Orsay was talk-ing about on the television. Your grandmother found out about you, disowned you, barred you from this house? That's why you never left Glenlyon in the holidays. It all makes sense now. Is that not true?'

I stared back at her. The flippant denial was on my tongue but it stuck there like a toffee and wouldn't come out. Apart from Ms Prada, I'd never admitted it to anyone. Not sure why. For Christ's sake, it shouldn't have been that difficult now, when a tsunami of water had gone under the bridge. Vic had just bared his soul to tens of thousands. And it would be good to tell somebody who wasn't paid to listen, who wouldn't glance at their watch to see if my hour was up yet. But the truth I needed to tell her wouldn't come either. Instead I felt my throat close, my mouth contort and my eyes begin to glaze over. Fuck, it was going to happen.

'Och, Rory Blaine,' said Elspeth. An arm encased in a baggy green cardigan reached out towards me.

*

I waited for Vic on the front steps of Mount Royal with Alma and the bottle of whisky. The night was mild and still; the rooks were asleep. The soft hum of the small-hours traffic out on Spaniards Road seemed to come from another world. I suddenly realized I'd not been beyond the gates for nearly a week. When we'd been under siege, I'd been too anxious to desert the house, as if it might somehow be gone when I returned. This was my watch after all.

I was back in myself now. Elspeth had said we needn't speak of it again if I didn't want to. I'd told her I'd like to leave the option open if that was okay and she'd said that it was.

It was nearly one o'clock before Vic's taxi swept through the gates. Big Frankie bounced out across the grass like one of those balloon things that chased Patrick McGoohan in *The Prisoner*. He hauled Vic from the cab, insisting he needed a nice cup of cocoa before bed, but Vic declined with a pale smile. He was tired as a toddler home from the beach, but too excited to sleep.

'Perhaps a very small whisky though,' he said, eyeing my glass. Frankie looked crestfallen, till Vic kissed his big hand and thanked him for waiting up. We went inside to the Red Damask Drawing-Room. But instead of sitting down, Vic opened the jib door that led to the Chapel Gallery.

'You're going to drink in there?' I asked.

'Toots, for a man of noble lineage you're amazingly middle-class sometimes,' he said.

The Chapel Gallery was dominated by two Baroque thrones from which previous Ashridges had looked down on their servants and the rest of the world. Vic threw on the lights, slumped into one of the thrones and put his feet up on the velvet balustrade. He reached for the bottle and took a slug.

'I often sit here,' he said. 'It's such a glorious place, way too good for the likes of God. It pisses me off the way religion was always able to hijack art. Paying half-starved geniuses to cloak its superstitious bullshit in such incredible beauty.'

We drank silently for a while. Robin Bradbury-Ross's electronics boys had done an impressive job, brushing Laguerre's ceiling with light and shade as subtly as he'd done with his paint. Cibber's alabaster reredos sparkled like sugar, the fat putti looking like they could easily fly off their pediment and join us for a nightcap.

'So how did I do?' Vic asked eventually.

'I don't think you need me to tell you that'

Alma was splayed out across Vic's belly as if it were a hearth-rug. He had a talent for inducing adoration that was vaguely annoying.

'I'm really sorry about what happened to you in the war. You'd never mentioned any of that.'

'Well some stuff is so goddam grim that talking about it seems redundant.'

'But you talked about it tonight. To the nation even.'

'I'd not planned to,' he replied. 'Maybe it was that African asshole or maybe just one of those moments when such things needed to be aired, shaken like a dusty old blanket.'

I had a question though I wasn't sure I had the right to ask it.

'How do you cope with what your father and brother did?'

'Do you remember that first day we met? You asked how I could care for your grandmother with her awful views and I said there comes a time when you just have to forgive everything? It's fucking hard of course, but it's best in the long run or you can eat yourself away. I guess my father and brother saw my sexuality as one more staging-post in their humiliation. They were both dead within weeks. I used to wonder if that was my fault. Anyhow, whatever sin they committed against me, they expiated it pretty damn quick.'

He stretched out an arm and I topped up his glass.

'Try to forgive, Rory. Like I did. It really helps. It's one of the few things the Bible-bashers have got right.'

'Lost you,' I said. 'Forgive who?'

'Your grandmother.'

'What do you know about that?'

'Educated guess,' said Vic, tickling Alma's tummy as he sipped the scotch. 'You've never said and I've never asked, but am I wrong?'

'Nope,' I said. It was clearly my night for telling the world.

'Maybe you could start by remembering the extenuating circumstances in your case.'

'Lost you again.'

'Your grandfather.' Vic scanned my face and saw nothing there. 'Jeez, is it possible?'

He gently detached Alma, heaved himself up from the throne and circled the Gallery, the glass in his fist.

'Sir Archibald Blaine swung both ways, with a very pronounced swing in our direction. I can't believe you never knew that, it wasn't exactly a state secret.'

Christ. I could only shake my head.

'He married your grandmother for the Ashridge loot. It was The Depression. Shipbuilding on the Clyde was having a shit time. Everybody knew about Archie Blaine but they somehow forgot to tell Sibyl and her parents. He clearly managed to get it up at least once or you wouldn't be here now but then it was back to the wee laddies in Kelvingrove Park. Unfortunately Sibyl had married for love. She was a proud girl from a proud family and she'd been tricked, used, humiliated. She grabbed your infant dad from his nursery and fled back here to mummy and daddy. Apparently she never saw Archie Blaine again, though people like the Ashridges didn't divorce in those days. So Sibyl sat in Mount Royal, inherited it, turned herself into a social lioness, took the occasional discreet lover and eventually went slightly batty. Anyway, hell hath no fury; that's why she hated gays. Wouldn't knowingly have them in the house. One of them had scorned her big time and nobody did that to Sibyl. I got all this decades later from Wallis Simpson. Sorry to name-drop.'

I reached for the bottle. A piece of a jigsaw, big as a meteor, had come out of nowhere, smacked me in the face and fallen into its rightful place.

'You okay?' asked Vic.

'Yep.'

And I was. As I glugged the whisky, I felt a sudden easing; as if some tiny muscle which had been in spasm for years had relaxed itself. Her cruelty had been irrefutable, but she'd had some sliver of excuse. It hadn't been just my crime, but somebody else's too.

Vic looked suddenly knackered. He'd had a big night after all. We both had. We went back into the Gilded Hall.

'We've nearly done it, haven't we toots?' he said, looking round the echoing space, the gilding shining as it hadn't done in three hundred years. 'The goddam house is coming alive again. We're going to be okay, aren't we?'

'Sure we are, Victor,' I said.

'Toots, whatever anybody else hits you with, you've always got yourself to fight back with. Remember that. It works.'

I watched him till he'd reached the top of the staircase. He'd drunk more than was good for him and the leg affected by the stroke still occasionally gave way.

So I've got myself to fight back with he says. Fine, except I've not yet got a clear picture of who that is. All those years ago in Oz, after Matty Rice had gone, I'd set out to bury myself, just like I'd tried to bury Granny. That had been the big mistake of course. That was why I went to the eau-de-nil room with the droopy azalea. Was I getting anywhere? Fuck knows. But two remarkable things had happened tonight. I had wept in the lap of Elspeth Wishart and discovered that my story was more complex than I had known it to be. I was still filled with the sense of easing that had come over me in the Chapel, the sense that I'd just put down a burden and that the ache would soon begin to fade. I crossed over to the portrait of the young princess with the sapphires in her hair and whispered up to her.

'Granny, I'm sorry. Sorry for what happened to you in your life. And I'm sorry that my being what I am hurt you even more. But it wasn't my fault. Could you not have understood that?'

Then I threw all the switches and left her in the blackness.

*

I've never been able to recall the nice man's face, not even vaguely.

I suppose I'd just blotted it out; a common post-trauma response according to Ms Prada. But I'd been fifteen back then, hormones raging. I'd have sucked off anyone, age and looks immaterial as they say on the more desperate websites these days. When I'd offered to show him the folly in the Wilderness, my heart had been bursting under my velvet jacket. I'd never taken such a risk. Never.

That night had been my last under the roof of Mount Royal. There had been no further scene, no drama at all. In the morning she'd merely sent a servant to my room with a note saying I'd been booked on the noon train back to Glenlyon. I would be spending the rest of the vacation there. I'd scrawled a long, dishonest reply pleading I'd had some champagne, had never done such a thing before and never would again. There was no response. Like me, Granny had always had a temper, but her rages usually passed like summer storms. I'd waited in the Gilded Hall with my suitcases for the minicab to come. The great space had looked oddly different that morning, not quite as I recognized it. I'd glanced round at all the familiar things; the chandeliers, the tall mirrors; the faces in the portraits I'd known for so long. But at that moment they'd seemed like a jury after it had passed its verdict; shifty, uncomfortable, wishing I would go away. And I had, in a Ford Capri with seats of cracked beige leather, driven by a sweaty man with a moustache. I'd gazed back at the house till it had vanished inside the oaks. It had taken me in, protected me and I had let it down. An air freshener thing swung from the rear-view mirror, pumping out the sickly smell of lilies, appropriate for a sort of death.

I'd written another letter when I reached the dormitory at Glenlyon with the iron bedsteads and linoleum floor. Miss Wishart had been surprised to see me, asking if my grandmother had been taken ill. I wasn't summoned south that Christmas as usual. I'd sent a card and a present, but nothing arrived in return. It had been almost a year before I'd understood that I might never see her again. The loss of belonging had begun.

ELEVEN

The stars above Mount Royal, re-arranged by the Poor Clares, continued to shine down benignly upon us. All Vic's press notices were excellent. In the *Guardian*, Polly Toynbee said she'd wanted to marry him since she was twelve and saw no reason to change her mind now. Countless bouquets arrived at the gates; Dolores turned his rooms into Kew Gardens and Big Frankie produced an Afro-Caribbean breakfast that occupied three trays.

At lunchtime, a statement was issued from Lambeth Palace and a copy hand-delivered to Mount Royal. The newly-appointed Primate Of All England, the youngest-ever incumbent, said that he 'understood where his African brother was coming from' and empathized with 'the struggle to reconcile traditional values in a "whatever" world.' He wanted to stress however that his brother's views on chemical castration might be at odds with the Church of England's policies on inclusiveness. He added that, though he and his wife were die-hard Spandau Ballet fans, he was sure they had a Vic d'Orsay CD somewhere in their collection. Vic was delighted and within the hour Big Frankie and the lilac scooter were roaring across Lambeth Bridge with Vic's entire recorded *œuvre* tied up with a pretty red ribbon.

I rang Ms Prada to tell her that I'd cried in Elspeth's lap. Well I didn't mention the lap actually in case she went careering off down the wrong track. She'd seen the media coverage and had been expecting a call.

'Things are really moving,' she said. 'Come in tomorrow.'

Then, at last, Faisal phoned from Wales. He'd been shut up in his conference centre discussing lipoproteins and running up mountains. But now he knew what had happened. He spoke very softly, even for Faisal. He wanted to know why I'd not been in touch. Was I okay? I told him things were fine and not to worry.

'It was my parents who told me,' he said. 'They'd seen the papers.'

'Ah. What's the reaction?'

'Oh, they're thrilled to bits. Just a bit disappointed that my name wasn't mentioned.'

'Seriously? Hey, that's progress.'

I heard a long ironic exhalation, which was unusual because Faisal didn't really do irony any more than he did jokes.

'They're hysterical, Rory. I've been summoned back to Slough. I'm just setting off now.'

'Shite, what did your father say?'

'A lot of stuff. None of it very nice and most of it at a high volume. He's given me an ultimatum.'

There was a pause.

'If I don't leave Mount Royal, and you, he won't ever speak to me again.'

*

There's a glaring omission in *The Man-Love Manual*. Where's the chapter on 'Meeting His Mother'? Not a bloody word. Surely it's more important than all the stuff on tantric massage, sharing a bathroom and the symptoms of syphilis rolled into one? I mean it's a difficult area, right? Not only are you responsible for shattering the poor woman's dream of grandchildren, but the chances of shopping together for a bra are minimal. The omission was regrettable because Mrs Khan had been my first 'mother' and I'd screwed it up good and proper.

The setting itself had not been conducive to success, a cramped corner table in a coffee-shop near Baker Street tube. I'd suggested the bar of the Groucho, which I always proposed when I couldn't be bothered to think. Faisal had shaken his head in disbelief and also nixed tea at The Landmark. His mother would be more comfortable in a place she knew. The coffee-shop was where they met every Wednesday, on his afternoon off from the hospital. His father didn't know, believing she was with a housebound friend. So there we were, surrounded by intense people jabbing at laptops and school-kids giggling into mobiles.

Faisal had told her about his new friend and she'd said she'd like to meet me. She'd been a sad-looking wee woman, dressed in a drab full-length Muslim thing with the headscarf to match. Not unlike a version of Elspeth in fact. But I'd been as nervous as she was and I'd over-compensated. I'd tried to kiss her hand, which was a major boo-boo. When the coffees arrived, I'd wittered on about my brief spell working on a Peruvian plantation and the subtleties of growing the arabica bean. Basically I'd given her the full charm offensive and it'd had the opposite effect. Her face had gradually frosted over like a car windscreen on a winter afternoon. Then, when she'd spilt her coffee, I'd made a loud fuss because the waitress had been slow in bringing a cloth and that had only made things worse.

I'd watched Faisal trying to dredge up subjects we might have in common, but the conversation had eventually floundered, gasped for breath and then expired. I'd ended up ogling a guy on the next table, while Mrs Khan gave Faisal the gruesome details of his Auntie Shazia's radical mastectomy. She'd refused a second cup of coffee. She'd had to be getting back because Khan's Tools & Hardware was having a sale of paints and Faisal's father was coping on his own. We'd walked her across to the tube, her arm slipped through Faisal's. She'd kissed him and shaken my hand from as far away as possible in case I'd tried any further intimacy. That was when she'd bowled the googly.

'Are you a good man, Mr Blaine?'

'Um, well, a work in progress at least.'

'Will you be a good man to my boy?' the little woman had asked as the commuters heaved around us. 'I need to know that he has someone in his life who will look out for him. He tells me that it's you. So I thank you for that. And you have a nice head of hair. That will stand you in good stead.'

Then she'd evaporated into the Circle Line.

'Mum lives in a very small world,' Faisal had said as we'd walked back to the car. 'Just Dad, the family, the store. Today was a big step for her.'

'And I messed it up.'

'Next time try Force 2 instead of Force 8. She'll cope a lot better.'

Faisal had come out to his parents about a year before we'd met. His precious father had said nothing, just got up and left the room. Then a letter had arrived at the hospital asking Faisal not to come home for the time being. The photo of their son the Oxford graduate had been taken down from its position above the shop counter. A few days later, Mr Khan had taken a swig from a bottle of white spirit instead of the mineral water standing right beside it on the counter. The white spirit had been on special offer. An unfortunate accident, the police said. For a few hours, it'd been touch and go. When Mr Khan had surfaced from the painkillers, his son was by his bedside. After that, it had never again been suggested that Faisal shouldn't darken their door. Since then, he'd made a pilgrimage to Slough for Sunday lunch.

While his mother washed up, he and his father would discuss the cricket. Faisal hated cricket, but every week he mugged up on it so he could debate the latest triumphs or disasters at Lord's or Edgbaston.

'That's all we can talk about now,' he'd told me. 'Or what's happening in the store or at the hospital. The rest of my life is firmly out of frame. There will never be any questions.'

Tonight, he'd texted me to pick him up off the Slough train at Paddington. He'd never done that before; Faisal rarely asked anybody for anything. I found him on the concourse, sitting on his suitcase. His hair and beard looked uncombed, the black Moschino jeans I'd bought him were crusted with Welsh mud. Instead of the usual bear-hug there was a tepid pat on the arm.

I suggested dinner at a gastro-pub nearby, but he wanted to go to Mamma Rosa's. I hated Mamma Rosa's. He'd taken me there a few times in our early days. In a parade of scruffy laundrettes and mini-markets in Tufnell Park, it was a basic Italian joint; chequered table-cloths, faded prints of the Amalfi coast and a menu that Mussolini would have recognized. The only frills were on the cheesy shirts of the paunchy, middle-aged waiters. Its charm was totally lost on me, but Faisal had been coming here since he first went to the Whittington.

Tonight though, he could scarcely raise a smile when Mamma Rosa herself, an obese old biddy with a spiv's moustache, pumped his hand and welcomed '*Il Dottore*'. He asked me to order for him and sat looking around at the other tables; mostly students or hen nights getting ratted on Lambrusco. It was bloody noisy. He watched me toying with an avocado that was as dry as the tits on an Egyptian mummy.

'If a restaurant's not been reviewed by Michael Winner, your swallow reflex just shuts down doesn't it?' he said.

'Hey, that was in the foothills of being a joke, Faisal,' I replied. 'You must be really stressed.'

Questions about Wales got monosyllables in return. After he'd abandoned his saltimbocca half-eaten, I asked after his mother. He'd not seen his mother; not to speak to anyway. His father had ordered her to stay in her bedroom. Faisal had only glimpsed her peeking out from behind a curtain as he'd left the house.

'But why wouldn't he let you see her?'

'It was Mum who saw the stuff in the paper about Mount

Royal. I imagine she must have choked on her Rice Krispies and he wormed the whole thing out of her. I think he suspected I lived with someone, but he'd no idea where or with whom. Then she confessed she'd even met you as well. When I got there today, he went berserk, screaming abuse. He was shouting at Mum too, through the bedroom door. Said she'd betrayed him and the family.'

Mamma Rosa waddled up to our table with the pudding trolley and spent two full minutes describing the joys on offer. When we turned her down, her wee moustache pouted in disappointment.

'So now it's me or them?'

'Basically,' Faisal sighed. 'The person my Dad assumed me to be was his achievement in life, his reward from Allah for decades of hard work and self-sacrifice. My son, the doctor. When I came out, it was like I'd stripped him of his medal. They could at least keep it from the rest of the family though. But any chance of my name getting in the news like this, well, shame, dishonour, the usual mantra.'

'This ultimatum then . . .' I said. 'I assume you'll tell them where to shove it.'

Faisal suddenly found the pattern on the floor tiles of consuming interest. On the next table was a trio of tarty women, huddling over bowls of steaming risotto like the Three Witches in *Macbeth*. Well past fifty, they all had long dyed blonde hair and dresses showing things that should no longer have been revealed. They'd just started a hellish rendition of *Three Coins In The Fountain*, but all I could hear was the silence coming from the rickety wooden chair beside me.

'It's not that simple,' he said at last.

'Of course it fucking is.'

Faisal gripped my forearm in his hairy wee fist and leaned forward till his face was inches from mine.

'Rory, I love my Mum. I love my Dad too, in a messy sort of way. And he loves me; even though he's behaving like a monster right now. You just don't know what a family is. That's why you've led a rudderless life.'

With Faisal, despite his saintliness, there were never any spoonfuls of sugar. And sometimes you need those. I'd have chosen somebody else to tell me I had three weeks to live.

'You don't know anything about my family,' I snapped.

'That's because you've never chosen to share much of it with me.'

I couldn't deny that. I'd only ever given him the settings and chief characters of my life; I'd always stonewalled on the twists and turns of the plot. So, as the Three Witches sequed into *Arrivederci Roma*, I told him everything there was to tell. The grip on my arm slowly relaxed then turned into a gentle stroking motion with the tips of his fingers. The Three Witches nudged each other and we became an object of interest.

'Then you, of all people, can understand what losing them would mean to me?' he said.

'Listen Faisal, if you're thrown over the cliff, you can either fall or fly. I flew. And the more you fly, the stronger you get.'

'Ha! Is that really how you see yourself?' said Faisal, giving me his first real smile of the evening. 'Remember my friend Ruby? She just couldn't understand why I was interested in you. The answer is that, underneath all the jokes and the cool guy bullshit, I thought there was a person worth knowing. I thought I might try giving him some affection and see if I could get through to him. But if you're sitting here implying that you can get along quite well without love in your life, then I'm wasting my time, surely?'

I couldn't think of an answer. Faisal looked at me for a long moment.

'You're not much of an advertisement for being an orphan, Rory, so please don't try forcing it onto me.'

The Three Witches had stopped singing and were sipping their drinks, pretending not to listen in.

'So do you love me, Rory?' he asked.

One of the women leaned across to me, her lipstick smeared, her breath smelling of cheap wine.

'Go on darlin'. Tell him you love him. There's not enough of it in this world.'

'Would you mind your own fucking business?' I said, as amiably as I could. 'Just piss off and treat us all to another song. I'm not answering the question until you do.'

I sat back, folded my arms and waited. There was a brief discussion of repertoire, so it was a minute or two before they got going on *The Wind Beneath My Wings*.

'Well, Rory?'

'I don't honestly know. But I know that I want to.'

'Okay,' said Faisal.

'Do you love *me*?'

'As I just said, I want to give you love,' he replied.

'That's not the same thing, Faisal.'

'I know it's not.'

'Where do we go from here, then?'

There was a sudden commotion at the top of the stairs leading down to the kitchen. A waiter rushed over and begged *'Il Dottore'* to come quickly; Mamma Rosa had collapsed. The waiters went round apologizing that no more food could be served. People moaned and groaned; a few left, the others grabbed at their compensatory bottles of wine. Flashing lights appeared outside; paramedics dived below. Then a stretcher, at an angle of about 60 degrees, was negotiated up the narrow stairs bearing Mamma Rosa. It looked like removal men dealing with an awkward sofa. Faisal came over, his brow damp with sweat.

'Heart attack. A big one. I'm going in the ambulance.'

'You have to?'

'Not really, but I want to,' he said. 'She's a nice old girl. Baked me a birthday cake once.'

'Shame. We were having a pretty important discussion,' I said, walking out with him to the ambulance. 'But I understand.'

'Oh yeah?' he said.

Any answer to that was impossible. The sirens had started to scream and Faisal leaped into the ambulance like John Wayne into the saddle. In ten seconds it had vanished towards Archway, as if it had never been there at all.

Back inside the waiters, some of them tearful, busied themselves giving out more wine to people who didn't care. I went back to our table and waited for the bill. The Three Witches took pity.

'Gone off, has he, darlin'?' asked the one with the smeared lipstick. 'Come and have a glass with us. We're in need of a handsome man at this table, even if he ain't going to give us what we old girls need.'

The others cackled and made way for me to pull my chair in. Oh, what the hell.

'He's a doctor then, your boyfriend?' said one. 'Those dark lads usually are though, aren't they? In their blood, like being able to dance, innit?'

'I think you're confusing Asians with people from the Caribbean,' I said.

The Three Witches called for yet another bottle. During its consumption they mused on the origins of love; rejoicing in its ecstasies, bemoaning its pitfalls and illustrating their theses with lurid episodes from their past lives, much of which seemed to have been spent horizontally.

To my surprise, I heard myself telling them about the Khans and their ultimatum to their son. The Three Witches were disgusted. Live and let live, they said. One had a mother who'd been a dresser for Danny La Rue. Another had a brother in the Merchant Navy, who now lived with his friend on Hayling Island. The third lived next door to Asians who'd never even heard of Vera Lynn. Fuck the Khans, she said. We clinked glasses to that. The consensus though was that I should try to make a go of things with Faisal because, as they bluntly put it, he was a looker, had a well-paid job and at my time of life I'd be lucky to do much better. Besides, I'd be amazed how soon the day would come when I'd be glad of somebody to look after me. When I got up to leave, they took my pic on their mobiles.

Like a fool, I drove the Merc back to Mount Royal but I wasn't leaving it in Tufnell Park. As I parked in the East Court, the bell in the Clock Tower struck midnight and I saw a shadowy figure coming through the archway beneath. It was Elspeth. She was clutching a carrier-bag which seemed to be quite heavy. She'd just been out for a wee breath of air, she said.

'For goodness' sake Miss Wishart, you'll get mugged or worse,' I said. 'This isn't the Isle of Bute. Where on earth have you been at this time of night?'

'I'm over twenty-one Rory Blaine, so I'll thank you to mind your own concerns,' she said, fumbling for her keys. 'Cheery-bye to you now.'

The door was firmly closed in my face. As she'd pulled her keys from her pocket, I'd noticed something fall onto the gravel. It was a packet of Mates Endurance.

A note was lying at the bottom of the glass staircase. Faisal had gone to sleep in the spare room, as he didn't want to disturb me. He was wiped out and wanted to lie-in. Mamma Rosa hadn't made it. He'd see me when he surfaced. There was a big X.

*

Window-cleaners perched on precarious ledges whistling cheerful ditties. Florists scampered up the front steps submerged in armfuls of gladioli. Wine-merchants and caterers lugged their wares to the cellars and the kitchens. A few milkmaids and chimney-sweeps and we could've done the Act Two opening of *Oliver!* Tomorrow was Preview Day at Mount Royal and our prospective residents were coming en masse. After nearly three years, we still had lots of dotted lines but not a single signature.

Through the open basement windows, I could hear Big Frankie thundering at the delivery people; he wasn't always camp and docile, he could be camp and fierce too. Elspeth was striding about, hectoring a squad of cleaners and polishers. Dolores Potts and her gardeners were raking gravel and deporting even the tiniest weed that had dared to immigrate to her flowerbeds. Vic and I toured around like 'nice' and 'nasty' policemen; I created troubled waters, Vic poured the oil. He said he told them I was at an awkward time of life. Hot flushes, that kind of thing.

It was a knackering day but some sort of Dunkirk spirit carried us through to the end. In the evening, when all the vans had gone, Dolores Potts strolled into the office. But she'd not come for her usual chat, she had a treat for Vic and me in the Italian Garden.

'Stand there,' she ordered. 'The engineers finished this afternoon.'

Dolores disappeared down the horseshoe staircase into the gardens. Behind the steps were some electrical junction boxes; machinery could be heard to whirr and whine. From the direction of the Great Fountain there was gurgling and burping and then, with a violent hiss, a plume of water shot thirty feet into the air, a sight I'd not seen for more than half a lifetime. From the height of the terrace, we could see right down across the Italian Garden to the Orangery and, beyond that, out over the tops of the trees to the city skyline. Dolores had emphasized it would be several years before the gardens looked as good as they once had. But they seemed pretty fine to me. I found myself wishing that Granny could have seen them.

'Enjoy!' shouted Dolores and disappeared. I wanted to yell that that verb was transitive, but doubted she'd have a clue what I meant. Vic and I went down and rubbernecked the fountain. The Koi carp had vanished under the lily-pads, sheltering from the sudden downpour. A light breeze skittered the spray beyond the rim of the basin, showering our faces and hair. The evening sun was slowly dropping away behind the plume, lighting it up like some gigantic watery sparkler. We sat on a safely dry bench.

'Personal question?' I asked after a while. 'You know what you were saying on TV, about your love songs, all that stuff. I've been wondering. Did you never find anybody?'

'Not really. Ironic, isn't it?' he replied. 'Though I loved my ex-wife actually, in a funny sort of way. We were good chums and without that things never work out. But in the end she wanted the full monty. Otherwise, most of my relationships have been, well, casual. Early on, that was to do with the times. Later, when it was all a bit easier, some nice people hung around for a while. A few star-fuckers of course, but others seemed to like me for me. But I found I always wanted to move on. Part of it was the old cliché of being in love with the audience. It's quite true, all that, you know; hard for any one person to compete with. But maybe part of it was being scared I'd lose them, like I'd lost my folks. I suspect you can relate to that.'

He glanced at me for an answer but I didn't give him one.

'And besides, I was waiting for the trumpets,' he said. 'My old buddy Stevie Sondheim once wrote a song about how, when lurve comes along, there won't be trumpets, choirs of angels, thunder-claps. It'll just be kind of ordinary, creep up on you like a cold. But Stevie and I differ on that one.'

'You heard the trumpets?'

'Oh yes, just the once. The whole goddam regimental band,' he smiled.

'And the other party?'

'Sadly not,' he replied. 'I guess you've heard them loud and clear though. With Faisal?'

'Oh yeah, sure,' I said. I wondered whether to tell him about the Khan's ultimatum, the freeze-frame life I was living in the flat. But I didn't. There had been so many confessions lately, to Elspeth, to Faisal and to Ms Prada as always. I didn't want to become an emotional incontinent.

'That's nice. I'm sure it's not always easy though,' he said. Had he sensed something? His antennae were as sharp as Elspeth's.

'So there's never been anybody else?' I asked 'Where there's life there's hope.'

'No toots, never anybody else,' he said with a shrug. 'Never will be now.'

I looked at his face for evidence of lying, but found none. I guessed I'd been mistaken and that Big Frankie hadn't yet declared himself after all. I felt a wee surge of pleasure at what lay in store for Vic; like a parent before Christmas with the Playstation wrapped and hidden under the bed.

The plume of water suddenly faltered and collapsed. Dolores shouted her apologies, explaining that she had to run it in gently, like a Volvo. As the ripples in the basin were soothed away, the Koi carp began to re-emerge from beneath the lily-pads. The biggest one appeared first, like a scout, followed by his smaller, more timid cohabitants. Silence fell on the garden again.

'You remember that day in the Reform Club?' I asked, 'With Marcus Leigh and those photos of his dead Italian boy? You said everything was worth it for the chance of the joy.'

'And I believe it,' said Vic. 'How about you?'

'Yes, of course,' I said.

'An early night I think toots,' said Vic. 'Showtime tomorrow.'

'Showtime,' I said.

I headed back to the flat. I'd no idea whether Faisal would be there or not. There were staff shortages at the hospital he'd said; he had to do extra shifts. During the brief periods he'd been around, I'd felt he was keeping his distance, only talking about trivia, not something that came naturally to him at all. In bed though, he'd clung to me fiercely, his bearded face on my shoulder, his hairy bicep across my chest. There had been no actual sex, no reaching for the doctor's bag with the ropes and straps. I'd been quite glad of the break from all that, it wasn't great for my back and had now become just a wee bit boring. Maybe it was because it felt like his ghastly father was in bed with us, though there had been no further mention of the old bastard or the ultimatum. I certainly wasn't going to ask what decision he'd come to, it was up to him to tell me. Besides, I was pretty sure he'd not reached one. He was constantly restless, no longer seeming interested in what was happening with the house. He remembered to ask an occasional polite question but the days when the project thrilled and inspired him appeared to be gone. He'd not mentioned *The Lazarus Programme* in weeks.

As always, he was amiable enough with everyone; but he'd

formed no friendships here, never really connected with any of them. I'd watched Vic, Elspeth, Big Frankie and others reach out to him then slowly retreat back into the necessary civilities and no more. He'd promised to be on parade tomorrow but I'd had to more or less go on my hands and knees.

While the rest of Mount Royal pulsated around us, our life in the flat was holding its breath. Maybe my pedestal had crumbled from under me when I'd not been looking.

TWELVE

'Whadda fuck ya doin' here, ya low-life motherfucker?' the podgy American yelled across the room.

Vic's welcoming smile withered away.

'Cos this is my territory, ya piece of shit!' he shouted back.

'Well I'm takin' it over now, ya sonofabitch.'

'Latino scum!' roared Vic, 'Get back to Puerto Rico with the other cheap whores.'

On a table in the Gilded Hall was a display of weaponry from the Battle of Worcester. Vic grabbed a dagger and the American did the same. They began to circle each other like wrestlers, their blades flashing in the sunlight that spilled through the open front doors. Faisal tried to move between them.

'Guys please, what on earth?'

'Back off Paki,' the American snarled like an alley-cat, 'it ain't your fight.'

A small thin man accompanying the American found his voice too.

'Sir, I believe there's some awful mistake,' he called to Vic. 'Beaumont is from New Orleans but has no Hispanic blood whatsoever.'

'Stay out of this faggot,' said Vic, brandishing his knife, 'or these eight hard inches go right up your Yankee ass.'

The podgy American crumpled into laughter.

'He'd think Santa had come early. These days, the only thing he gets up there is his colonic irrigation tube,' he said, dropping the dagger and throwing his arms around Vic. 'Oh babe, it's so wonderful to see you.'

'My dear Beau,' said Vic, hugging him tightly. 'Is it really forty years?'

'Las Vegas seventy-one. *West Side Story*. I was just a Shark and you were the first Jewish Tony. You still recognized me after all this time?'

'Of course, though maybe now not so much a Shark as a whale?'

'Well pardon me,' replied Beau, 'but when did you turn into the fucking *Hindenburg*?'

'Beaumont, won't you introduce me to your friend?' said the small thin man, with a smile so tight you could have plucked it like a violin.

'Vic, may I present my partner, Professor Curtis Powell?'

Vic looked him up and down like he was on a butcher's hook. Curtis's skin was stretched taut across his cheekbones as if he'd not wanted to pay for the amount required to cover them. His slate-grey hair was pulled back into a pigtail which might have been classless in New York but in London marked you down as a mini-cab driver on the verge of retirement. Beau, despite the performance he'd just given, was a big dozy thing with an expression like an anaesthetized cow. A few remaining strands of dyed black hair were draped across his skull in a Jackie Charlton. Both were expensively dressed but with that over-pastelled golf-cart look which most American men eventually adopt.

'You're a lucky man, Professor Powell,' said Vic. 'I remember when the name Beau Styles made cocks twitch on every chorus-line on Broadway.'

Curtis's parchment-pale face reddened into a shade vaguely approaching being alive. Beau and Vic couldn't stop hugging each other. The other introductions were made and Beau apologized for calling Faisal a Paki. He wasn't a racist he said; he'd once had a small part on *The Bill Cosby Show*. He'd been the postman.

'My god, that's Grinling Gibbons over there,' said Curtis, his eyes ricocheting round the Gilded Hall.

'You wanna go say "hi"?' asked Beau.

'Grinling Gibbons was England's greatest wood-carver,' snapped Curtis. 'You've been taught that already Beaumont. I do apologize, Mr Blaine; I went looking for Gatsby and ended up with Myrtle, the slut from the wrong side of the tracks.'

'Get a life, Grampa,' said Beau.

Curtis Powell gazed up at Verrio's ceiling, almost wetting himself with excitement. According to Vic's briefing notes, he was a retired history professor who'd written a series of coffee-table books on the great houses of Europe for the posh American market. He'd once dubbed Mount Royal 'the lost palace'.

'You must be very proud today, Mr Blaine,' he said. 'Your restoration appears highly sympathetic, though I won't hesitate to criticise if I find fault.'

'I'd expect nothing less, Professor Powell. After lunch, everyone will be given a tour by the expert from English Heritage in charge of the work.'

Robin Bradbury-Ross had agreed to do this wee favour. The

price had been three of my jockstraps, in different colours, recently worn and unwashed.

So here they were at last, coming through the door in ones and twos; the men Vic insisted on calling Rory's Boys.

So far, I'd not exactly have claimed Preview Day was in full swing; there was too much nervousness in the air for that. But maybe that wasn't so surprising; about forty people, mostly strangers, at a party that might never end. If they decided to live here, these were the faces they'd see day in, day out, perhaps for years to come. In the Saloon, where drinks were being served, they were pacing round each other in a shy gavotte, making brief, gracious contact before wheeling away again into a different space. In this they were accompanied by the musicians of *Strings Attached*, a quartet of hunky gay boys on violins and cellos whose website promised that 'When we fiddle, you'll burn'.

But Curtis Powell was correct. I did feel proud. Today you could stand in the Gilded Hall and look right through the Saloon out onto the terrace where the tip of the water plume from the Great Fountain was thrusting itself into a clear blue sky. In spite of Robin's hysterical protests, I'd ordered the blinds raised on every single window and summer light was pouring into the house in a way it hadn't done for years. The bad smells lingering on its reputation could be blown away at last.

Today's guests were a mixture of those on Vic's original list who'd not fled after the publicity and the most promising of those who'd contacted us because of it. There had been no time to interview any of the latter group in person, only to check their credit-worthiness and, thanks to an old shag of mine at New Scotland Yard, their absence from the police computer. But today was critical. Maybe that was why, after his obsessive vetting of the original candidates, Vic was surprisingly relaxed about these unknown quantities. If they could hold a basic conversation about the works of Christopher Wren or the music of Perry Como, we'd not go far wrong, he said.

When each punter arrived, he was announced by a waiter. This turned out to be none other than Dapper Stephen from the London Eye, who'd failed to get back into EasyJet and was now working freelance. As they approached one by one it felt like some bizarre beauty pageant. I should be holding a mike and declaring their vital statistics to the waiters and the string quartet. They would shyly tell me that their ambition was to travel or work with kiddies in Botswana. But I watched the parade with growing unease. These were the people I might be glimpsing daily as they passed the windows of the flat. They'd be sitting in my Red Damask Drawing-Room, reading in my Library, strolling in my Italian Garden. They'd be living under my roof. I began to wonder, really for the first time, just who they all might be.

Marcus Leigh had arrived first, on the dot of twelve. We'd suggested smart-casual on the invitation, but Marcus was wearing a tie. He'd been highly useful with some last minute financial issues, refusing any fee, perhaps trying to make up for having wobbled in the wind of the tabloids.

'The Lord Chancellor's already here, Marcus,' I said. 'He's saving you a cocktail sausage.'

Marcus's ruddy smile froze.

'He's just come out. Hadn't you heard?

'Most amusing, Mr Blaine.'

After a while, the attributes of the grey-haired lovelies began to blur, but they all had the faint but unmistakeable sheen of material wealth. Not one would have known the price of a pint of milk, the route of the 29 bus or how his washing-machine worked. It did my heart good to see that.

A slight Chinese man in pebble glasses, announced simply as Mr Lim, shook my hand, peering up at me intently. I remembered he was some posh orthodontist.

'That's Roland Snape, isn't it?' he asked. 'Your upper bridge-work?'

'Wow, how did you know that?'

'I'd recognize Snape's work anywhere,' said Mr Lim. 'He drinks, you know. That's the problem. You really can't go around looking like that.'

He reached up taking my chin in one hand and pushing up my top lip with the other.

'The mouth is like a magic garden from which spring the fruits of civilized thought, the words of poetry and passion, the sound of sweet music. What a shame if the garden gates are grubby, uneven or coming off their hinges. We'll talk later.'

To illustrate his point, Mr Lim gave me a broad smile. Not like Vic's at all, it was slightly mechanical and bypassed the eyes altogether but in terms of wattage it was right up there with Marti Pellow's.

There was a sudden ripple of commotion at the front doors. Standing beside Dapper Stephen, who was failing hopelessly to suppress laughter, were two tiny identical old men. From a distance they seemed interchangeable; round as thimbles, Persil-white goatees, light brown suits and hardly more than five feet off the floor. But as I hurried over, I could see that the expressions were chalk and cheese. One of them was shy and benign, the other wasn't. It was the latter who rounded on me.

'We are Jasper and Jacob Trevelyan,' he said, in an unexpectedly deep West Country voice. 'A fact which this pansy here seems unable to announce. We're not impressed so far, are we Jacob?'

'Jeez, no need for any announcement of who you are,' cried Vic with his hand outstretched. 'Jasper & Jacob's Fowey Fudge has been clogging my arteries for years. At least that's what the quacks reckoned when I had my little stroke.'

'The policy of Trevelyan's Toffees has always been to promote the occasional confectionery treat as part of a balanced diet,' the little shy one recited. 'We are committed to supporting a healthy lifestyle, which should include twenty minutes of aerobic exercise three times a week.'

Jasper and Jacob Trevelyan, widely known as The Toffee Twins, appeared in dire but iconic TV commercials in which they sat in wing-chairs by roaring fires giving sweeties to the cherubic kiddies perched on their laps. In a country hysterical about paedophilia, the Toffee Twins went on year in, year out presenting a child molester's fantasy and nobody said a word.

'I'd been afraid,' Vic was saying, *sotto voce*, 'that, as treasured national figures, you might have been put off by our recent publicity.'

'I've been discreet for the last fifty years,' snorted Jasper. 'But we've just sold out to Nestlé and pissed ourselves laughing all the way to the bank. Now I don't give a toss who knows I like a lad's arse from time to time. That right, Jacob?'

Jacob blushed and smiled again, shaking his wee silvery head.

'They're *both* gay?' Faisal murmured.

'Presumably,' I replied.

'I wonder if they're on Dinkydudes,' he said.

We reckoned everyone had arrived and turned to follow Vic and the Toffee Twins into the Saloon. Then an extraordinary voice, light, fluting but with surprising power stopped us in our tracks.

'I am Lord Vale.'

Framed in the front doors was what looked like an exotic bird that had lost its way over the Tropic of Cancer and taken a wrong turn northwards. Tall and spindly, it wore a white Moroccan djellabah, the neck and sleeves ornately embroidered with gold thread. There were rings on its fingers and jewelled sandals on its feet. Its skin was light brown and corrugated by the sun; above a large hook nose sat a candy-floss of dyed gold hair, whipped up to conceal its sparseness.

'I am Lord Vale,' the voice repeated, lobbing the perfectly-formed syllables the length of the Gilded Hall, like one of those old actors who could hit the upper circle without breaking sweat. We'd almost forgotten the man Vic had described as our biggest catch, the one who'd give Mount Royal a cachet that the nouveau-riche bank accounts of Curtis and Beau, Mr Lim, the Toffee Twins and even Vic himself could never deliver.

Lord William Vale, second son of the Marquis of Matcham, known to the international jet-set as Lord Billy and, for forty years, also bearer of the title Queen of Marrakesh, where he'd ruled the expatriate community of artists, writers and Eurotrash with an iron-fist holding a cocktail-shaker. He'd returned to England just recently and was living in flat in Bryanston Square. He glided towards us, the djellabah billowing behind him in the breeze from the open doors.

Vic reminded him that they'd last met at the Windsors' in the Bois de Boulogne, when Vic and Nancy Mitford had duetted on *Buddy Can You Spare A Dime?* while sipping Puligny-Montrachet.

'I remember it well, my dear,' said Lord Billy. 'Wallis said, "Oh look, two Nancies." She had more wit than she was given credit for.'

We led Lord Billy into the Saloon. It was strange to see it full of people again, smelling of their breath, their flesh and the slightly dated fragrances of Jermyn Street. It had come alive in other ways too. William and Mary armchairs now had to rub snooty shoulders with modern sofas in crisp white covers and table lamps with soft silk shades. Papers and magazines lay on the lacquered tables, prominent among them, at his insistence, Vic and his hairy man-boobs on the front cover of *Gay Times*. Elspeth directed the waiters like they were an especially irritating bunch of juniors at Glenlyon, while keeping a beady eye on the cleanliness of Dapper Stephen's glassware. Alma the cat worked the room, weaving her way among the forest of ankles, lubricating the conversation. We'd not be allowing pets so she might be a selling-point. I must remember to mention she came from Harrods. They'd like that.

After a while, we ushered everyone back out to the Gilded Hall. I climbed a short way up one branch of the staircase. Vic and Faisal stood just behind me like a couple of heavies. I'd wanted Vic to do the speech, but he'd refused, saying it was my right. I was atypically nervous. I'd made countless presentations in my career, but this was different. I thought I'd start with a gag so I asked if anybody needed to pee before I began, boasting that we'd installed enough loos for everyone to go simultaneously should the need ever arise. The bathroom suppliers had given me what they called a Prostate Discount. Beau Styles laughed but nobody else did.

'For fuck's sake, toots, get on with it,' hissed Vic at my shoulder.

So I threw my head back, flung my arms wide and flooded my eyes with wonder. I'd seen Charlton Heston do it as Moses parting the Red Sea and felt it worked well. I'd been practising in the mirror.

'Gentleman, look around you. You now have a unique opportunity to live in one of the great houses of England; to live alongside the genius of Wren, of Gainsborough and Reynolds, of William Kent, of Jeffrey Wyattville. Yet only recently, all this was under threat and might easily have been lost. Mount Royal has been a sleeping beauty. The fact that it now has the chance to wake again is due to all of you. I want to thank you formally now; many others will want to thank you in the centuries to come.'

I wondered if I sounded up my arse, but they seemed to be rapt.

'As you will all know, Mount Royal has been in the news lately. Our pioneering project has been mocked, condemned even, by some, but applauded by many many more. And when communities like ours are taken for granted, people will perhaps look back and recall that famous phrase in our island story, "never was so much owed by so many to so few".'

I'd intended that line as another gag, but I noticed Marcus Leigh tighten the knot of his tie and several slightly curved spines perceptibly straighten. Heads grey, dyed, bewigged and bald turned to their neighbours with smiles of tentative camaraderie. I signalled to the waiters to start giving out champagne.

'Over the top?' I muttered to Vic.

'By several battalions,' he replied, 'but I think they're right behind you.'

'Gentlemen, a toast,' I said, raising my glass. 'To Mount Royal.'

The words were boomeranged back to me amid the pinging of crystal. It wasn't just a polite murmur either; it was loud, gutsy, aggressive even. Beau whooped and punched the air till Curtis grabbed his arm and forced it down.

Just then I caught my grandmother's eye. She was, as portraits do, staring straight at me. I lost myself in those eyes for a few seconds, till I noticed that everyone had fallen quiet and was waiting for me to speak again. I knew I had to announce lunch, but the sentence wouldn't come. Luckily it was provided by Elspeth who'd done her Mrs Danvers thing and materialized beside me. She'd made no concessions to the occasion and was wearing something that would've looked grim on a wardress in *Prisoner Cell Block H*.

'Will you all come away and get your lunch?' called Elspeth 'It'll be spoiling in a minute and there are others less fortunate who'd be grateful for it. However, since I've got you assembled, I'll just say a few quick words about the standards of behaviour we'd be expecting to see at Mount Royal. My name is Miss Wishart and I am matron of this establishment. So if you'd kindly give me your attention...'

Without warning, Elspeth launched into a lecture covering, *inter alia*, punctuality at meals, the frequency of the changing of sheets, the ban on smoking anywhere in the house and acceptable dress codes for different times of the day. I knew I should stop her, but listening dutifully while Miss Wishart delivered instructions was an ingrained habit and interruption was unthinkable. I was about to wish that I had.

'Lastly, a wee word about gentlemen callers,' she said, her face flushing slightly. 'Respectable visitors, your family or friends, are of course welcome here, though they will be restricted to certain hours and certain parts of the house. It's a big place to keep clean and I'll not be wanting too many people under my feet. However, we're not going to be having any scruffy scallywags of uncertain parentage whom you met five minutes ago coming into Mount Royal and stuffing the silver spoons down their breeks. So let's get that clear right from the start. I run a tight ship here, lads.'

Oh dear. Marcus Leigh's nostrils flared until I thought he might whinny. Little Jacob Trevelyan bit his fingernails and didn't know where to look. Lord Billy's high-pitched laughter tinkled up towards the cupola.

'You just relax babe,' called Beau. 'The only gentlemen callers most of us are gonna get will be the paramedics or the morticians.'

As I led the procession towards lunch, Curtis Powell tugged at my sleeve.

'Congratulations on having a transgender person on the staff,' he said. 'I relate to your progressive outlook. She sure could do with some tips on hair and make-up though. I'm sure Beaumont would be pleased to help.'

On the long walnut table in the State Dining-Room, the crystal and silver sparkled in the midday sun streaming in from the gardens. Big Frankie, in full chef's gear, was waiting with a tits-out buffet. When the old guys filtered in, his mouth gashed into a grin that could have floodlit the Heath.

A few people were already ladling out their lobster bisque when a cadaverous man named Archdeacon Brownlow silenced the chatter by announcing that he would say a grace. Big Frankie sank to his knees. The Archdeacon, with a concave face like an Easter Island statue and halitosis bad enough to fell trees, looked down at him in alarm.

'Are you an evangelical?'

'No, Sir, a Roman.'

'Thank goodness for that.'

The Archdeacon warbled away in that colourless tone copyrighted by clergymen everywhere, his head tilted towards heaven. It was like Birnam Wood up his nose and it was definitely on the move to Dunsinane; much longer and he'd have the beginnings of a moustache. My own gaze drifted upwards too. On the ceiling there was another party going on; a painted feast of gods, nymphs and satyrs draped over clouds, plucking lyres, admiring each other's perfect pecs and rosebud nipples. As a boy, imprisoned at Granny's formal dinners, I'd imagined myself up there with them, jumping across the clear blue void from cumulus to cumulus with a basket of shiny red apples. They'd been peering down on the long walnut table for three centuries and I wondered what they were thinking today. Were they laughing even more heartily than usual?

'I was the first to realize the Snowdons were in trouble,' I heard Lord Billy telling Curtis and Mr Lim. 'I said to her mother, "Sorry Ma'am, but you've only yourself to blame. Dear Peter would have been perfect for her." It was ten years before I saw the inside of Clarence House again.'

Curtis was shitting himself because Lord Billy had known the Queen Mother. Mr Lim lamented the terrible decline of Her Majesty's teeth in later life. He had written to her personally outlining his ideas for improvement, but had only received a brief reply from a secretary.

As I walked past Elspeth and The Toffee Twins, she was telling them how infection rates for syphilis, herpes and chlamydia were going through the roof.

'So if you're going to play, play canny,' she said to the little shy one.

Big Frankie cantered about, making sure that plates were filled and glasses full.

'You've got the loveliest eyes, mister,' he informed Marcus Leigh. 'But I expect people tell you that all the time.' Marcus blushed and muttered something into his meringue glacé.

I watched Vic schmoozing from group to group, giving each person just enough time to make them feel important, then moving on while they still wanted more. He seemed to assume everyone he met was either a fan or about to become one. A nice philosophy really. I might raise it with Ms Prada and see if she felt it was psychologically sound.

I finally managed to corner Elspeth.

'You were a bit heavy back there, Miss Wishart,' I said. 'The sexual health stuff? Where did all that come from?'

'You're now looking at a proud member of an organization called Rubber Duckies,' she said. 'We go to those places frequented by misguided men and give out the wee condom things. I got in touch with them via that magazine with the awful picture of Mr d'Orsay on the cover.'

'Is that where you'd been the other night? Out on the Heath?'

'It was indeed.'

'Are there many mature ladies in Rubber Duckies?'

'No just me,' she said 'But they've got something called an open-door policy so they took me in. They're mostly peely-wally lads with tattoos and earrings. Dreadful to look at, but not bad boys on the whole.'

'Please tell me you don't go alone?'

'Dearie me, no, I'm buddied with a chap called Shane. He works in Fortnum & Mason. Very nicely spoken.'

'Well, ok, Miss Wishart,' I mumbled, at a loss for anything more coherent. 'Just be careful.'

'There's work to be done out there, Rory Blaine,' she said 'I told you that before. Anyway, I've not got the Sunday school now and it's really not that different. Just spreading a message.'

When lunch was over, Robin Bradbury-Ross asked everyone to follow him on his guided tour of the state rooms.

'I'm wearing one of your jocks,' he whispered as he led the punters out. 'And it feels *so* good.'

'You're a very sick boy, Robin,' I replied.

'You love it,' he said, leaving me worried that I actually did.

Elspeth and Big Frankie were down in the kitchens, organizing coffee for later. Faisal had vanished somewhere as soon as he politely could. I went back into the Saloon, planning a catnap on a sofa, but there sat Lord Billy Vale in solitary splendour, his sandals slipped off and his long legs tucked up under him.

'Not taking the tour then, Lord Billy?'

'I've seen it before, my dear,' he said, 'I used to come here as a child with my Mama. She was a friend of your grandmother's. It's not exactly Matcham of course, though it's still quite something.'

He described the family seat in Wiltshire, even grander than Mount Royal. Lord Billy's nephew was now the Earl. They invited him to christenings, that sort of thing, but he didn't often visit. He embarrassed them before the good burghers of Salisbury. The pink sheep of the family.

'The trouble is, these great houses, they're not like a three-bedroomed semi in Dartford, are they?' he said, gazing round at the Mogul tapestries. 'They begin to define who one is. Nowhere else can quite compete. I suppose it's all the insistent beauty. You are lucky Mr Blaine to be still living in yours.'

I explained that I'd been estranged from my grandmother for most of my life and hadn't expected to ever return to Mount Royal, let alone inherit it. He peered at me as if I were some rare specimen in a jar.

'How incredible for you,' he said. 'I have never slept a night at Matcham since I left England over fifty years ago. A guardsman in St James's Park, such a frightful cliché. I just can't bring myself to do it, even though one longs to. There's no real affection for me there, so it's just a house now rather than a home. Oh dear, I sound like one of Vic d'Orsay's sugary songs, do I not?'

From the folds of the djellabah, he produced a teeny mother-of-pearl box. He carefully counted out a row of four or five tablets and washed them down with water. Then he uncurled his endless legs and asked for the nearest loo. My little joke earlier had been cruelly perceptive, he said. Turning in the doorway, he pointed a long, arthritic finger in my direction. The sun caught on a big fat ruby ring.

'I was watching you at luncheon, my dear,' he said. 'You were perfectly charming to everyone, but you were talking at us like a double-glazing salesman. One realizes this is a commercial venture but unless you trouble to engage with these strangers wandering round your marbled halls, then this house will remain as empty for you as Matcham now is for me. A stage-set, nothing more. Think on't, I beg you. But if I don't go now, I shall piss on your Aubusson.'

When Robin's tour had finished, I herded everyone upstairs to see the apartments, now ready for occupation. Most were still empty shells but we'd furnished and propped one as if it were already in use. The four-poster had been turned back and a fluffy bathrobe spread across it. The scent of expensive soaps filled the ensuite bathroom and freshly-made coffee wafted from the galley kitchen. Chopin played on the sound system, books were piled on the bedside tables and, in absurd defiance of the season, we'd lit the fire. There was a gratifying buzz of approval, though Jasper Trevelyan snorted that at these prices he'd have expected a rent-boy in the bed, already lubed-up.

Then I led them out to the Coach House where they were

shown the gym, the small pool and the site of our imminent jacuzzi. Poor Morag Proudie had finally died a few weeks back and bequeathed Elspeth a top of the range installation. Faisal gave a brief, tense presentation of *The Lazarus Programme*. He talked about diet, nutrition and the incredible benefits of exercise particularly, as he put it, for those on the last lap of life.

'Can you give me my arse back?' one man called out. 'It used to be quite famous in certain parts of Portsmouth, but now there's a staircase leading down to my thighs.'

Faisal said he felt sure that the staircase could, at the very least, be turned into a ramp. People laughed and Faisal looked perplexed, not understanding why.

Dolores Potts guided everyone round the gardens. She was impressive; sketching the history of the British garden and Mount Royal's place in it, explaining the stages of the replanting, painting a picture of how it would all look one day. She knew her stuff all right but then, if her CV was kosher, she'd won every prize going at horticultural college. She'd told me it was the formal garden that turned her on; she loved the tidiness and symmetry because she'd come from a messy family, an English father who was a farmer and a Spanish mother who'd thrown things. The fact that Gertrude Jekyll's lot had been terribly establishment explained the wild abandon of her borders; That was the way it worked, Dolores thought, parental rebellion in horticultural form. When she'd finished her tour, she'd curtsied deeply to her audience like she was Maria Callas. I watched her enchant them with my eternal feeling of having known her somewhere before.

Preview Day was to end with coffee in the Orangery. A regiment of miniature orange trees in white wooden tubs guarded the tall glass doors, folded back to let in the warmth of the afternoon. The long shallow interior was now decorated with oleanders, camellias and ceiling-high palms. In the centre was a restored Edwardian aviary, newly tenanted by linnets and canaries. I was surprised to see that the Bechstein baby grand, usually in the Red Damask Drawing-Room, had been transported here too. Dapper Stephen and his team swirled around with coffee-pots while the punters cooed at the birds and Big Frankie fluttered around the punters. He'd changed out of his chef's gear into a pair of silver satin baggies and a T-shirt reading *There's No Tool Like An Old Tool*. I'd get him for that later.

Eventually, Vic tapped his cup with his spoon, thanked everyone for coming and expressed the hope that we'd be seeing at least some of them again. We'd agreed this bit in advance, but then he moved to the piano.

'Gentlemen, it's not over till the fat man sings. It's more than forty years since I first performed this lovely song from *West Side Story*. Today, I'd like to sing it again for all of you but with a special dedication to my old friend Mr Beau Styles.'

'Oh babe,' cried Beau.

'And on keyboards, direct from the parish church on the lovely Isle of Bute, please welcome our very own Miss Elspeth Wishart.'

There was a smattering of applause. Elspeth slid onto the stool, looking as if she wished the earth would swallow her, an emotion I was relating to quite strongly. Vic moulded himself into the curve of the piano.

'My pal Stevie Sondheim wrote these beautiful lyrics, which encapsulate everything I feel about what's happened here today.'

Vic segued into that song about there being a place, somewhere, for us all. I felt my shoulders start to heave. Dolores Potts, having a ciggie in the doorway, choked on her smoke and had to slip outside. Shite, what was he like? He had his faults all right, but nobody could say he wasn't a laugh.

I looked around me, ready to share grins with all and sundry. But nobody else was grinning. Vic wasn't singing the song for laughs, as an advertising jingle for the attractions of Mount Royal, he was doing it straight, meaning every soppy word, as he'd insisted that he always did. And Elspeth's playing, hesitant at first as she tried to pin down his rhythm, soon became fluid and assured. Sundays at Glenlyon, when she'd thumped out hymns on an asthmatic organ had shown no sign of any such gift. But every eye was bolted onto Vic, even those of the smooth young waiters, at an age when I'd have thought them inoculated against sentimentality. For once in his career Vic was underplaying. Keeping it simple. No frills. And it worked a treat.

'*Somewhere*'. The last long note hovered in the air then evaporated into the highest fronds of the palm trees. Vic lowered his head slowly and contemplated the innards of the piano.

There was silence in the Orangery. Even the birds had stopped chirping, as if in awe of a classier act. Then somebody started the clapping, but it was almost reluctant, the sort you make when it doesn't seem quite appropriate but is expected of you. Something had moved in the room; I wasn't quite sure what it was, but there was a presence now which hadn't been there before. Lord Billy was standing at my elbow.

'Point made, I think,' he said.

I could hear gulps and sniffles from several quarters. Beau's chubby cheeks were flooded by a confluence of sweat and tears. Marcus Leigh's gaze was fixed on his tiny Sèvres coffee cup. And, for the second time that afternoon, Big Frankie had fallen to his knees in worshipful wonder. But it was Faisal, his features struggling to corset themselves together, who suddenly turned on his heel and vanished out into the gardens.

THIRTEEN

It was one of those rare but awful summer nights when London tosses and turns and gets up grumpy in the morning. The jolly for prospective residents had been the last comfortable day. For seventy-two hours, the heat had been building up, weaving itself into the pollution and thickening into one vast Twelve-Tog duvet you couldn't kick off. There wasn't a whisper of wind. All day, the rooks had made only the odd token caw but tonight the foxes were screaming with more than their usual hysteria. It can't have been much fun in a fur coat.

The windows around the East Court were thrown wide open. Lying naked on top of the bed, I could hear Big Frankie snoring in his. From our new improved security HQ in the basement of the house came the distant pulse of the Vampire's grungy music; I'd put a stop to that tomorrow. Even the scent of the jasmine round my window seemed oppressive and unwelcome.

Faisal, sod him, was dead to the world. Nothing ever kept him awake; the legacy of grasping at straws of sleep during a thirty-six hour shift. The blinds had been raised to tempt in some air, bathing the room in a monochrome glow from the lamps outside. Despite his wild black beard, it made Faisal look about fifteen. I reached out and stroked his hair. In this light, the back of my hand was bleached a smooth virginal white; no longer the coarse alien thing it was slowly morphing into. It was only when I noticed Faisal's skin against mine that I ever felt like a dirty old man. We were still living in our state of suspended animation. After he'd walked out of the Orangery, I'd wondered if a decision might have been triggered. But he'd said nothing more.

I must have drifted off eventually, because when I half-opened my eyes I was blinded by the early morning sun. There was a body on top of me and I could hardly breathe.

'Get off, Faisal,' I gasped, 'you're killing me.'

I looked at the arm draped across my chest. It was clothed in a cheapish pin-striped fabric and it wasn't Faisal's. I twisted my head round to look into the face of a total stranger, an elderly brown-skinned man, his eyes shut, blood trickling down from a gash on his temple.

Somehow, I hauled myself out from under him and fled to the nearest corner where I stood panting, wild-eyed and starkers. In the opposite corner was Faisal, naked too and shaking from his shiny black head to his dinky wee toes. In the open doorway was Vic, fully-dressed but slumped on the floor, as if he'd slithered down the lintel like a drunk. The three of us gaped at the rumpled bed where the man in the cheap suit was sprawled unconscious. He was small, slight man with a *Psycho*-sized knife clutched in his hand.

'Meet my Dad,' Faisal said.

Vic said he'd glanced out from the house and seen a stranger peering through the windows in the East Court. He'd hurried outside in time to see the man going into our flat, followed and found him standing at the foot of our bed, the knife raised in his fist. Having once had a affair with an ex-commando and learnt some basic self-defence, Vic had flung himself at the intruder and pulled the legs from under him. The man had bumped his head on the bed post as he'd fallen. The ex-commando had been called Trevor; it had been quite an exciting relationship, Vic said.

'And I'm okay by the way. Thanks for asking,' he added.

A low moan from the bed thawed Faisal from his spot. In a whirlwind of professionalism, he stripped the bed, checked his father's pulse and heartbeat and cleaned his wound.

'How the hell did he get past the Vampire?' I asked.

'There's a big van inside the gates,' said Vic, pulling himself to his feet. 'The guys with that Jacuzzi Elspeth's inherited. I imagine he slipped in with them.'

At last Faisal remembered the two of us. He insisted on checking Vic over. He seemed shrivelled with embarrassment, unable to look us in the eye. There was a small knife-wound in my shoulder, sustained when the body had fallen on me. I began to realize how much worse it could have been and felt a bit sick. I wondered what the symptoms of delayed shock might be, but it seemed wimpish to ask. Faisal bandaged my cut, then took his father's pulse for the umpteenth time. I made us all some coffee. We drank it in silence watching Mr Khan drift back towards the shores of consciousness.

'Why's he wearing a goddamned suit?' Vic asked.

'Don't know,' replied Faisal. 'It's usually just for special occasions.'

'I guess he thought a double murder qualified,' said Vic. 'Shame to spoil the suit though.'

Panic flooded Faisal's normally placid face. He stared at Vic as if he'd only just registered what had happened. Then at last Mr Khan's eyes flickered open. He took one look at his son, turned his face into the pillow and began to weep.

'Right then,' I said, 'we'd better call the police now.'

Faisal leapt as if I'd nudged him with a cattle prod.

'No!' he bellowed, like a small but very mad bull. 'There's no need for that.'

'He tried to kill us both, Faisal,' I said, as gently as I could. 'If it hadn't been for Vic, it could have been Quentin Tarantino in here.'

'It would finish my mother,' he said. 'What would be gained from it?'

'Well it might dissuade some other homophobic Muslim nutter from an honour killing,' I said. 'Isn't that what we're talking about here?'

Faisal, still kneeling by the bed, tugged violently at his beard. Just then his mobile rang and he began talking in Urdu. It was obviously his mother, hysterical. He covered the mouthpiece.

'Dad left her a note,' he said.

At first, he seemed to be trying to calm her then gradually he buried his face in one hand and reached towards his father with the other. It was a hesitant movement like he expected to be brushed away. But the older man's fingers wrapped themselves round Faisal's and clung on for dear life.

'Okay Mum, try to relax now,' Faisal said in English, presumably for our benefit. 'I'm going to bring him back home.'

'I don't think that's entirely your decision, Faisal,' I said quietly, when he'd closed the mobile. He didn't reply but took his father's pulse yet again.

'Dad didn't come to harm us,' he said eventually. 'He came to harm himself. His note to Mum was a suicide note. He planned to kill himself in front of us. So yes, it was to be what you call an "honour killing", but not the sort you imagined.'

I didn't know what to answer. Vic clearly didn't either, asking if Mr Khan might like a brandy. Faisal shook Vic's hand and formally thanked him for stepping in. Then he went out to bring his car up to the front door. There had now been a definite change of gear in the group dynamic. Vic seemed to feel that Mr Khan should be treated as some sort of guest; uninvited and not exactly welcome, but a guest nonetheless.

'Mr Khan? Hey, I'm Vic d'Orsay. You may have heard of me? Look buddy, sorry about the dramatics, but I got the wrong end of the stick. No offence I hope.'

Faisal's father turned his head away, but Vic wasn't to be prevented from making amends.

'I don't expect you've had any breakfast? Or did you get it on the train? Is there anything we could tempt you with? Something light? An omelette maybe? We have an excellent chef here.'

'For fuck's sake Victor, drop it,' I muttered. Mr Khan turned and looked straight at me for the first time. My instinct was to avoid his gaze, but I was damned if I would. He was in my bed, in my house and he had brought terror over my door. So I stared right back at him and challenged whatever it was in his eyes. Hate? Disgust? Fear? I hadn't a clue, but he wasn't going to see any of those in mine.

Faisal came back and struggled to get his father onto his feet. I went to help but Mr Khan gestured me away, then Faisal did too. The old man was somehow shoehorned into Faisal's old Peugeot.

'Hope to see you again sometime,' said Vic, leaning into the car.

Faisal went inside once more, returning with a holdall.

'Listen, I'll see you when I see you.'

'Sure.'

'Look, I'm sorry about all this.'

'It's okay,' I lied, 'you're not to blame.'

'Yes I am,' he said. 'The other day I posted Mum and Dad a reply to their ultimatum. I guess they got it all right.'

It took me a moment to grasp what he was saying.

'Hey,' I said, touching his arm.

'Why is it that who we are seems to cause so much pain to some other people. I'll never understand that. Never,' he said, in a voice clogged with despair. 'Dad was prepared to end his life, to die for heaven's sake. Why? Can you tell me that?'

'Just take him home Faisal,' I said.

His father's bandaged head lay back against the neck-rest, the eyes staring blankly ahead. Through the window, Vic was telling Mr Khan that buying a cheap suit was a false economy and that he'd send him the name of his tailor. Faisal buzzed it up; a neat little metaphor for their relationship. They could see one another quite clearly but neither was much interested in what the other had to say.

As if he'd read my mind earlier, Faisal rattled off the symptoms of delayed shock. Then the Peugeot spluttered off under the Clock Tower and was gone.

'Come on, let's go and get Big Frankie to make us some breakfast,' said Vic.

'Nobody else needs to know about this, Victor,' I said.

'Whatever you say, toots.'

Vic went first as we headed down the narrow kitchen staircase.

'It's not your fault, you know,' he said, turning and blocking my path as if he could block the thought as well. 'It really isn't.'

'So why do I feel like it is?'

'Because that's the way they programme people like us,' he said. 'However sorted we think we've become, deep down they can still make us feel we have something to apologize for. Well we fucking haven't. So come on, I need a bacon roll. Frankie hates making anything so common and I enjoy ordering him to do it.'

*

By eleven o'clock, the humidity already hit you in the face like a damp, sweaty sock. The sky was a vile yellow-white and the city beneath it ached for thunder. After my bacon roll, I wandered over to the Coach House to watch the installation of the Morag Proudie Memorial Jacuzzi. Elspeth was giving out mugs of tea to Morag's husband and his team who'd come up from Brighton bearing a bells-and-whistles number called The Cleopatra. A pale sliver of a man in his late fifties, it was hard to imagine him married to the earthy junior matron. His wife had never stopped talking about Glenlyon and the lads she'd taken care of there. I caught Elspeth's eye and she had the grace to blush. Morag's husband said it would mean a lot to him if I'd allow a small plaque to be attached to the wall. In fact, he'd brought it with him.

This jacuzzi is dedicated to Morag "Bubbles" Proudie. 1951–2011.'

The wound in my shoulder was starting to nip like a terrier. I wondered what was happening in Slough. It must be pretty horrendous. Surely I should be there with him at a time like this? Isn't that what it's supposed to be about? But of course I'd not have been welcome, not even to Faisal. In this relationship, there were places I just couldn't go.

Back in the house, I was accosted by Vic, sweating in the heat like an old pug-dog. We needed to sit down urgently and draw up the short-list of residents. We couldn't keep people on tenterhooks any longer. Our doors were due to open in a couple of weeks. Come on, it would take our minds off things. I was frog-marched to the office.

Every single person who'd come to Preview Day wanted to move in. After all our anxieties, this was a wonderful problem, but a problem nonetheless. Vic kept wittering on about the importance of 'the mix' but for me the major criteria were still that they had the readies and hadn't done time in Pentonville for flashing at wee boys. Otherwise, I wasn't hugely bothered. I certainly wouldn't be choosing them on their looks.

With small variations depending on the size and position of the apartments, the financial mechanics were simple. There would be a deposit, roughly equivalent to the purchase price of a sea-front flat at Eastbourne. This would, with a hefty annual deduction, be returnable on departure or death, whichever came first. On top of this, a monthly rent would be charged to include room-cleaning, laundry, and electricity. Three gourmet meals a day would also be included, with refunds given for absences. Bar bills would be extra, as would participation in *The Lazarus Programme*. And it was made clear to everyone that we weren't a nursing home; at the onset of any serious long-term illness the unlucky resident would be expected to move on. So coming to live at Mount Royal wouldn't be cheap, but it wasn't a rip-off either. Vic and I had thrashed out the business plan with my old finance director from Blaine Rampling, who'd done it in return for an all-expenses-paid week in Phuket, where he went for the Thai lady-boys.

We pored over names, faces and bank references and by lunch-time we'd whittled it down to twenty-five. In the afternoon, we phoned or emailed the acceptances or rejections. The latter were hard to do. We lied and said it was on a first-come, first-served basis. Most people were stoical but some were clearly upset, a few even offered higher fees than we'd been asking. It was tough, but Vic insisted we stuck to our original choices.

I'd sent Faisal several texts, but by teatime there was still no word from Slough. It was hellishly humid. I took a quick shower and, as I was drying-off, I was aware of feeling massively horny. Heat always did that to me. Damn. I slapped my own wrist and went out to the Great Fountain to check that my Koi carp hadn't fried; I loved those fish like they were my own flesh and blood. Through the open doors of the Orangery, soft piano music trickled out onto the lawns.

'I've not thanked you properly for playing the other day, Miss Wishart,' I said, when she'd stopped. 'I'd no idea you had such talent.'

'Dearie me, it's only a very small talent,' she said, rising quickly from the stool like I'd caught her at something shameful. 'At least that's what my father always told me.'

'That's bloody nonsense,' I said. If there really was an afterlife, I hoped to meet the Reverend Wishart and bang his head against some celestial wall.

'Aye well, I had dreams of the Royal Scottish Academy, but most of us get our wings clipped a bit in this life, do we not Rory Blaine?' she said. 'One way or another.'

'Well you don't play like somebody with clipped wings,' I said.

'Och, Big Frankie's been giving me something for the arthritis in my fingers' she said 'Some sort of herbal cigarette. I've never smoked in my life, but it works wonders. A nice perfume too.'

Morag Proudie's husband and his men had brought sleeping bags and would be dossing down in the Coach House so they could complete the job tomorrow. Big Frankie was laying on an informal supper in the kitchen, but I begged Vic to host instead, using my aching shoulder as an excuse.

'You noticed any symptoms of delayed shock?' I asked him.

'I just watched a repeat of *Midsomer Murders* and found it quite exciting. Could that be it?'

'I seem to have to have a semi-permanent stiffy for some reason.'

'A spontaneous erection? Wow, I remember those,' he said. 'Any news from Slough?'

'Nothing.'

'Jeez, I think he might have called, if only to ask after your shoulder.'

I shrugged it and it hurt.

I went back to the flat, sent Faisal another text, fed Alma and scavenged in the fridge for myself. By then, I felt so randy I could've snogged that scrawny Archdeacon with the bad breath. Faisal and I hadn't had proper sex for about three weeks. I logged onto the web; never was a facility more accurately named.

I'd not been on Dinkydudes since the night Faisal had thrown a wobbly about my profile still being there. I'd deleted 'Scotstud' at once and was now 'Highland Fling', no face pic, just a fetching series of images of me in a kilt, in various stages of exposure. Instantly, I felt that old Christmas Morning thrill. About forty messages had piled up, not a bad haul. I trawled through them and zeroed in on a Japanese guy. His profile name was 'Tenko'. Shaven-headed, eyes like teeny scissor-cuts on pale yellow silk and a hot smooth little body. If he had a single hair on him, it must have been up his nose. He was 'currently online' and 'lookin' to meet for no-strings play'. He described himself as a 'power-bottom' with a fetish for tight foreskins. We started to message.

His name was Ng. It wasn't clear if that was his first or last name, but at least it was easy to remember. Ng wanted to know if I had any military gear. When I said not, he suggested I wore a black T-shirt above my kilt, so he could pretend I was a member of some Highland Regiment. Ng's thing was to be dominated by British soldiery as penance for Japanese brutality in World War II. Hence the profile name. He ran a florist's in Kentish Town Road and lived above the shop. Would I like to come over? Did I have a pen to take down his address?

I opened the drawers of the little desk Faisal and I both used. No luck in my drawer, so I looked in his. I was scrambling around under some official-looking papers, then I saw what the papers were. I messaged Ng to hold on as I'd left the bath running.

'Kewl,' he messaged back.

Lying on the bottle-green leather top of the desk were some forms sent to Dr Faisal Khan by Camden Council. They were forms to register an intention to enter into a Civil Partnership. I flopped down at the desk and stared at the papers. Well well. He was certainly throwing his eggs into my basket. He'd always made it clear he wanted commitment, in that earnest, slightly scary way he had. But now he was going as far as it was possible to go. Telling his parents, his dad at least, to fuck right off. What more could I ask of anyone?

So how come I didn't feel flooded with joy, pole-axed with emotion? Why didn't I message Ng that the bath had overflowed, the ceiling collapsed and we'd have to postpone? Why did I look at those pieces of sterile paper and feel my stomach tie itself into a reef knot? Why Ms Prada, why? Tell me for God'sake, there's a bonus in it for you.

I remembered the Three Witches in Mamma Rosa's. A real looker they'd said. Got a good job. Somebody to take care of you.

'Do you love me?' we'd asked each other that evening, agreeing that we'd like to. Was that all it was then? Liking the idea of it? So *did* I love him? *Do* I love him? I was going to have to decide pretty quick.

It hadn't just been our post-ultimatum celibacy that bothered me. Even before that, the sex had begun to wither a bit. The fatal worm of duty had wriggled under the bedroom door and into our bed. Of course, the 'south front' remained stupendous. Once, in an empty first-class compartment, the thought of it had made me jerk off into a Virgin Trains serviette. But I guess my perspective on it had changed; I was just used to it now.

But hey, when the sex fades there's the companionship, right? So how many marks would we get for that? *Cinq points*? Maybe only *quattre*? Despite the homoerotic runs round the Heath, we'd not excavated much more in common. There were pinpricks of irritation and resentment too. Faisal always dismissed my career as a waste of a life while I was expected to venerate his, as indeed I had. Mind you, I'd never been exactly mesmerized by Faisal's folksy anecdotes of growing up in a hardware store in Slough; they fell a bit short of the fascinating social document he imagined they were.

I'd sometimes thought back to Vic's birthday dinner in the flat, when I'd sensed he found Faisal dull. Back then, it had put my nose out of joint but I'd gradually begun to understand the judgment. I teased him about having no sense of humour but it really wasn't funny at all. And the age difference? Did it matter? I'd not forgotten the London Eye; the antipathy of Ruby, the smirks of the Siamese Children. Were our mutual denials that it wasn't an issue just pretentious crap? Were we trying to battle on, heads bowed against an irresistible fact of nature? Odd thing here though. With Vic and me, the age-divide works differently. When there's a new band I've never heard of, Faisal patronizes me, shuts me out; when I tease Vic about his cheesy old songs, he doesn't do that. He pulls me into his times, shares them, makes them accessible, interesting. Faisal often seems like a foreign country with the frontiers sealed. And now, this morning, his deranged old Dad had tried to commit hara kiri all over the duvet. I was happy to let cultural diversity enrich my life, but that was a bridge too far.

And I did care for Faisal. There was no doubt of that. I wanted him to be happy, I wanted him to be happy with me. And let's be honest, that's a major step forward for Rory Blaine. Count your lucky stars. That's what Ms Prada, Elspeth Wishart and the Three Witches had all said with varying degrees of subtlety. But was it a good enough reason to fill in the forms? And if there wasn't a Faisal, what then? Who then? Anyone? The papers from Camden Council stared back at me.

The Dinkydudes message bar was flashing. Ng had left me three breathless entreaties. He was oiled and lubed. He was ready and waiting to atone. Was I coming or not? Well was I? While my significant other was dealing with a major crisis, was I going to go and shag a meaningless stranger as I'd done so many times before?

To hell with the texts. I called Faisal's mobile this time, but the voicemail cut in and asked me to leave a message in that sleepy, disinterested tone he sometimes used. My hackles rose. Why hadn't he been in touch? He must have known how worried I'd be. Whatever was going on, he could have found thirty seconds to text. How fucking thoughtless. And anyway, I was only flesh and blood. I'd always had a high sex drive. Why should I be blamed for that?

I messaged Ng to say I was on my way. I put on my kilt and the dark T-shirt. I prayed that everyone would still be in the kitchens and that I'd make it to the Merc before somebody glanced out and wondered why a member of The Black Watch was creeping across the East Court.

*

The storm, when it finally broke, mistimed its entrance. Had it possessed any sense of drama, it would've been crackling over the florist's as I'd punished Ng for the sins of his fathers. It certainly had a tropical intensity that might have recalled those POW camps in the jungle. But when I got to Kentish Town Road, the evening was still calm and sickeningly heavy, the smells from the take-aways coating the paralysed air.

I knew at once I'd made a mistake. Ng opened his shop door in a loin cloth, but the body I'd fancied online was covered in weals and scratches and not the sort you get from wrapping a dozen Golden Showers. He said my long hair would have to be tied back as it wasn't military enough but the kilt was well-received and, when I took off the T-shirt, he just loved the wound on my shoulder. He handed me a long willow cane and bent over his Ikea sofa. He asked what my rank was. I said corporal but he didn't laugh. I had to be at least a major. I gave him a few light whacks. He started apologizing over and over and I tried calling Hirohito a slitty-eyed bastard, but my heart wasn't in it. I'd got used to Faisal's wee fetish but this was something else. I'd come here for simplicity after all, for that glorious, no-strings fusion I'd once found so sustaining. But this was complicated and not my scene at all. Ng didn't seem to be enjoying it much either; his miniscule cock as soft as a jelly-baby. He begged to be hit much harder, to shed blood for the crimes of his people, but I threw down the cane and apologized for wasting his time. As I went out through the shop, I bought a couple of bonsai trees. It seemed the least I could do.

I hurried along Kentish Town Road to the car. A young black couple with two little kids were coming towards me. The boy pointed and laughed, asking loudly why the old man was wearing a dress. The father was embarrassed. I stopped and explained why it wasn't really a dress. It was his birthday, the boy said; they were all going to Burger King and did I want to come? I said I had to be getting home, but would he and his sister like the bonsai trees as a present? They were thrilled; they'd never seen bonsais before. The parents thanked me awkwardly, eager to move on. They had me down as a weirdo and maybe that's exactly what I was tonight. It was certainly what I felt like. I'd started the day with one nutter trying to top himself and ended it thrashing another one above a florist's. Not exactly what you'd have called a normal life and, whatever that was, I suddenly yearned for it again as I'd done so many times before. I waved the kids off into Burger King, conquering the urge to accept their invitation after all. But that would never have done.

On the drive back up to Mount Royal, the heavens finally split. It wasn't the sort of storm that played fair, issuing a civilized warning from afar, giving you time to run and hide. This was a mean bastard, furious, apocalyptic. It exploded with a nuclear flash followed by bang that rattled even the Merc, a car from a Wagnerian country after all. Wind began to tear through the trees and then the rain came, heavier than I'd ever seen it in London. The wipers were next to useless and I crawled all the way up the hill. When I turned into Spaniards Road, a woman was running along the pavement. It was Dolores Potts, drenched to the skin. I shouted her into the car. She shook her hair like a drowned rat, spraying my upholstery. Her make-up had run and from the neck up she looked about sixteen. From the neck down though, with her wet shirt plastered to her tits, she looked like the calendars they hang in an MOT garage. She asked me why I was wearing a dress.

The oak trees outside the walls were lurching to and fro like a panicking crowd; the rooks must have been clinging on for dear life. When we reached the East Court, we dashed towards our respective front doors. But I'd dropped my keys somewhere by the car and couldn't find them in the dark. As I fumbled in the gravel, I realized how good the driving rain felt on my face. I stood up and let it soak me, hose me down, wash me clean. My hair hung down my neck, limp as spinach and the water turned the kilt into a lead weight. I stood there for minutes, watching the storm batter the old house on the Heath, as if it were King Lear in stone, slate and glass. The bell in the Clock Tower, tumbling in the gale, had lost its senses and tolled without rhyme or reason.

Suddenly Dolores, wearing only a towel, sprinted out and dragged me into her flat. She asked if I'd gone mad. I was pushed into her loo with orders to strip, shower and put on her bathrobe. I took the longest shower I'd ever had. When I came out, she was sitting on the sofa, still only in the towel. She'd opened a bottle of wine. She handed me a glass.

'So where were you on this hot sticky night?' she asked. 'And dressed up in that gear? A gathering of the clans?'

'Mind your own business.'

'Out on the prowl, I reckon,' she said.

'Just like you no doubt.'

'We're a couple of cats then, aren't we?' she said, lighting a fag.

'Why the fuck do you do that?' I said, parking myself beside her on the sofa. I'd never let myself ask before in case I seemed uncool.

'Because it's dangerous,' she smiled. 'Gardening tends to be a bit low-risk. The worst you can do is tread on a rake and knock your front teeth out.'

'You like a bit of danger then?'

'I sure do,' she said. 'It must be my Spanish blood. Running the bulls and all that bollocks.'

'What else do you like that's dangerous?' I asked, aware of sounding like Leslie Phillips with his pencil moustache and the dark blue blazer with shiny buttons.

'I'm not telling you that,' she grinned, tightening the towel around her.

We smiled at each other over the rims of our wine glasses and I knew I was going to kiss Dolores Potts. Well she'd been making it clear for weeks that it would be a welcome advance. Okay, she was an employee and it was shitting on my own doorstep, but what the hell. Okay, she was a woman and I was supposed to be gay, but so what? I'd worry about that tomorrow. Or maybe I wouldn't worry. Suddenly, to kiss her seemed the most natural thing in the world. I leaned across the space between us and tilted my head.

Dolores Potts leapt up, spilling her wine and almost losing her towel.

'What the fuck are you doing?'

'Christ I'm sorry,' I spluttered. 'I didn't mean… I thought you liked me…'

'I do like you. But not like that. Jesus.'

Dolores had fled to a chair in the opposite corner. She grabbed her fags and lit another. The match quivered in her hand. I'd never seen her flustered before.

'Look, I just misread the signals. Really stupid. I know I'm old enough to be your father.'

'No, it's not that' she said.

'What is it then?'

Dolores took a long slow drag from her cigarette. She stared down at the carpet, then up at me, then back at the carpet. The bell in the Clock Tower tolled once more.

'You *are* my father,' she said.

She gave me that odd, searching look she'd used ever since the day she'd first slithered off Big Frankie's bike. With the make-up gone, the map of her features was easier to read. Now I realized where I knew that face. The nagging ache of vague recognition was stilled. Why on earth hadn't it clicked before? It was the same face that gazed down from the portrait in the Gilded Hall.

'Hello Daddy,' she said.

As suddenly as the storm had come, it was gone. Through the half-opened window, I could smell the steaming earth, the sodden walls and the scent of battered jasmine. The wind had bustled off on its way to the sea, the oak trees composed themselves again and the bell in the Clock Tower stopped its drunk and disorderly clanging.

Fourteen

I have a child. If it weren't so vulgar, I'd type those words in huge capitals of red and gold, encrust them with diamonds and sweep them with floodlights. I have a child. I am the father of a young woman called Dolores Potts. She smokes, she has a regional accent, I suspect she is as sexually promiscuous as I ever was and I love her beyond my wildest imaginings.

Sleep of course had been a non-starter. I'd lain for hours, listening to the bell in the Clock Tower strike, its equilibrium regained as surely as mine had just been lost. I'd not woken till gone eleven, with Alma standing on my chest, squeaking gently, which meant that her saucer was empty. But I'd remained a while longer staring at the blank canvas of the ceiling. The room looked exactly as it had yesterday; the framed copies of my best ad campaigns, my regiment of suits hanging alphabetically from Armani to Zegna, Faisal's running-shoes abandoned on the floor. But everything had now seemed vaguely foreign, props from another time. Nothing would ever be the same again. I'd felt more excited than I'd ever done in my life. Even before I got out of the bed, I'd felt my heart pounding. Should I call Roger, the mechanic responsible for my mitral valve murmur? As a dangerous stress factor, the sudden appearance of an unknown child must rank right up there with bereavement, moving house and tantric sex. Or should I call Ms Prada? But Ms Prada was there to talk about my problems so why on earth would I need her now?

Last night in Dolores' tiny flat, the storm gone, the revelation made, a silence had sat waiting to be filled. But I'd not known what to do or say. Who the fuck would? I'd just sat there, running my hands through my damp hair and spluttering half-formed questions. I'd got up and paced around, sat down again then paced some more. Dolores had looked a bit worried and offered me one of her ciggies. Should I try to embrace her or would she leap away again? She'd certainly made no attempt to do anything so sentimental. But not for a second had I doubted what she'd claimed. I only had to look at her.

After her nervous declaration, Dolores had quickly returned to her usual self and taken charge. She'd ordered me to sit still, poured more wine, then summarized the major facts of the matter in a brisk *News At Ten* sort of way.

Dolores Potts was the illegitimate daughter of Cristina Gomez, a baker's daughter from Seville. In her youth, Cristina had spent a year in Sydney where she'd had a brief fling with a Scottish boy. Later she'd discovered she was pregnant. She'd not told the Scottish boy because she knew he didn't love her. Soon after the birth, she'd met an English tourist who'd asked her to marry him and offered to take on the child. He'd taken them both back to Oxfordshire where he ran a farm. Cristina Potts had died a year ago, after finally telling her daughter the name of her real father. Her mother had had no idea where I was or even if I were still alive but Dolores had googled me. It was that simple.

As she spoke, I'd rifled my memory to find Cristina Gomez. I'd managed to get a snapshot of a small dark girl but the face wouldn't come into focus. She'd worked as a temp in the ad agency where I'd started out. I'd scarcely known her. After Matty had gone, she'd just been one of the bodies with whom I'd tried, yet again, to prove myself. A member of that honourable line begun by Morag Proudie in the luggage-shed at Glenlyon. Nothing more. She'd not crossed my mind in centuries.

'Why didn't you just write to me or call?' I'd asked. 'Why all the stuff with the job?'

'After Mum died, I wasn't sure if I wanted to track you down or not,' she'd replied. 'My Dad, Mr Potts that is, was all for it when he found out you were loaded. In times like these, farming really is a heap of shit. I'd still not decided when, surprise surprise, I heard about this job on the grapevine. Wicked one for the CV. I couldn't resist.'

'Why the fuck didn't you tell me before?'

'Because I still hadn't made up my mind whether I'd tell you at all,' she'd said. 'But I'd not reckoned on your making a pass. What *was* all that about? You've got your footprints in the Poofters' Hall of Fame now surely?'

'So you just came to take a look at me? Is that it?'

'Yeah,' said Dolores with a shrug. 'I suppose that's about it.'

The conversation had sort of stalled there. She'd gathered my soaked clothes from the bathroom and stuffed them in a bin-liner. I'd bolted down the last of the wine. At her front door, I'd wondered again if I should embrace her and sensed she'd been wondering the same. She'd stopped being cool and looked like an awkward kid. Then she'd extended her hand.

'Bit of a shock right? You okay?'

'Yes, yes, I'm fine. Thanks.'

I'd shaken her hand and opened the door.

'Nice to meet you,' I'd said.

'Yeah, you too.'

*

This morning, I stood drinking coffee at the picture window. Dolores was in the Italian Garden, grooming a box pyramid. I noticed again how gracefully she moved, despite those breasts. *Madonna With A Trowel.* I watched her for a full ten minutes, then dressed quickly and went outside. The grass was still damp from the deluge, but the sky was a fresh-blown blue. We were both awkward again, hiding it behind nonchalance. I said hi. She asked what was up. I wondered if she were free tonight and she said she might be. Would she like to have dinner?

This evening I took my daughter to The Ritz. We had a window table looking onto Green Park, still crowded with people lolling in the sun. It was a ludicrous confection of a room, its femininity at odds with the all-male tables of Japanese businessmen, but I wanted to flag that this was a celebration. To my amazement, the waiter greeted Dolores by name. She didn't fancy anything on the menu she pleaded, grabbing his hand as if her life depended on it. Could he possibly rustle up an omelette and chips? I ordered the same. My kid might have grown up in the sticks but she had style.

'They seem to know you here,' I said, a tad deflated.

'Yeah, a friend brings me quite often,' she replied 'A property developer. I design his gardens for him.'

'Really?' I said.

'Hey, I'm not a hooker on the side,' she said, with a needle-sharp look. 'I just like men a lot.'

'Something we've got in common then.'

'In your case not exclusively, it seems,' she said, 'or I'd not be here.'

'That was all a long time ago,' I replied.

'And now it's back to haunt you,' she smiled. 'How you coping?'

'I'm just fine,' I said.

I ordered champagne, but the wine waiter remarked that Mademoiselle usually preferred Pouilly-Fuissé. We raised our glasses.

'What's the toast then?' I asked.

'My mother, maybe?' she said.

I paused. In the ragbag of feelings I was dealing with today was a cold blade of resentment at Dolores' mother for hiding my child away from me. Even before the internet, I'd have been easy to track down. I'd become well-known in advertising, the agency in Sydney could have told her how to reach me. How dare she not tell me I had a daughter? It had been my right surely? Last night Dolores said her mother had known I'd not loved her. What sort of fucking excuse is that? I'd have given my kid everything. But at least Cristina Gomez had done the right thing in the end. I raised my glass.

'To your mother then,' I said. 'And to you and me too.'

She didn't answer but we clinked the crystal. Then, over the next hour, I made Dolores Potts talk; though in my mind I'd already deleted that cloddish surname and replaced it with my own. I bowled every question I could think of. The farm she'd lived on, the school she'd gone to, the Catholic church her mother had marched her to every Sunday in a town miles away. I found out about the names of her dogs and cats, the GCSEs she'd taken, the attack of meningitis that had nearly killed her at the age of twelve, how she'd only got into gardening because of a teenage passion for Diarmuid Gavin. He'd presented her first-prize medal at horticultural college. She'd done it all for him she'd told him and attempted seduction at the reception afterwards, the only time she'd ever been rebuffed. She'd been taking revenge on married men ever since.

I listened, missing all that stuff which, till last night, I'd not known I should have had. All those years when I'd felt my life had been at full throttle, the awards, the travelling, the parties, the shagging; in truth, nothing of consequence had been happening at all. And all those years, just fifty miles up the M40, Dolores Blaine had been happening.

It was only when I asked more about her mother and, as I now thought of him, her stepfather that she clammed up a bit. No, she didn't see that much of Mr Potts now, though she phoned regularly to check he was okay. Yes, he was a decent sort of the whole. No, she had no Spanish relatives still alive; her mother had been an only child. And if I had any more questions, would I submit them in writing and she'd get round to them when she'd finished planting out the kitchen garden.

I asked to be allowed one more. She seemed to go 'up West' almost every night of the week. Was there a serious man in her life?

'Serious? Shit no,' she laughed. 'I've seen the damage that can do.'

She gave me another of her long unsettling looks.

'What about you?' she asked.

'Of course,' I replied 'Extraordinary question.'

'Sorry,' she said. 'But you and the pretty doctor. Wasn't quite sure what the score was.'

'Well we're living under the same fucking roof.'

'Bit of an odd couple though, aren't you? Hard to see the connection.'

'Why's that?'

'Well he's sort of there, but not there,' she said, 'if you see what I mean. He's quite hard work isn't he? Only ever speaks to me when he's bumming ciggies.'

'But Faisal doesn't smoke.'

'I think you'll find he does,' she said.

Pudding came. A quartet of overweight Latino musicians began to play sleepy cha-chas and rumbas. Over-dressed elderly couples crept around the floor. I asked Dolores if there was anything she wanted to know about me. Not really, she said. Not right now anyway. The internet had already filled her in on me, the Blaines and of course Granny.

'The resemblance is amazing,' I said 'That was why I always thought we'd met before. But it just didn't click.'

'A bit of a horror, wasn't she?'

'Not always,' I said. 'Only later.'

At the next table, two bishops in full purple were having a fierce debate on the morality of giving money to beggars. Dolores was irritated. Addressing them as 'guys', she ordered them to pipe down, saying her Dad here was just back from Afghanistan where he'd got shell-shock and was hyper-sensitive to noise. The bishops were contrite, muttered, 'Jolly good show,' and sent us over two brandies. I'd been searching for some trace of me in her and there it was. Cheeky wee bitch.

'Is that what you're going to call me from now on then?' I asked, staring into my coffee. All day long I'd imagined her using the word.

'Let's stick to Rory for now,' she replied, knocking back the brandy in a couple of gulps. This girl would be dead by thirty. 'And I'd rather we kept this to ourselves for a while, yeah? Get to know each other a bit more? Nobody else's business after all.'

'Cool,' I said, trying not to show my disappointment. In the shower tonight, I'd mentally composed a notice for *The Times*. To Rory Blaine, a daughter. I was gagging to tell Vic, Elspeth, Bruce Willis, anyone who passed me on the street. As I followed Dolores from the restaurant, the waiter gave me a man-of-the-world smile.

'You're a lucky man, Sir,' he murmured.

'She's my daughter, arsehole,' I said.

'Yes indeed, Sir' he replied.

He was right of course. I went to the loo and returned to find Dolores waiting in the Palm Court, perched on a tiny gilt chair. She'd taken off her shiny black stilettos and was gently massaging her feet. Every eye was on her. Where was Mario Testino when you needed him? In that moment I knew that I would give myself totally to her. I felt no reservations or fear of getting hurt. There was no agonizing, no endless weighing up of the pros and cons as there had been, and still were, with Faisal. I presumed it was just a reflex, the natural instinct of a parent towards a child. But what did I know? I realized that there might many new emotions heading my way now; good or bad I didn't care. That old feeling of having been short-changed in life had suddenly gone. Whatever was coming, bring it on.

We got a cab home; I'd left the Merc as I'd not wanted to risk my daughter with a drunken driver. I asked Dolores to come inside the house for a minute. I led her across the Gilded Hall till she stood beneath the portrait at the foot of the staircase. Apart from the eyes and hair, where her Hispanic genes had triumphed, she was Granny to the life.

'You're a Blaine now; an Ashridge too, of course. The lines go on with you,' I said quietly.

'No,' she replied 'I'm just Dolores Potts. And I was Dolores Potts first.'

'Well maybe one day,' I said. 'Give it time.'

We smiled at each other, the awkwardness there again. Then I made my second pass at Dolores Potts. Naturally it was more hesitant than the first but this time she didn't leap back. I kissed her forehead then put my arms around her. But though I held her lightly, I felt her body stiffen. Maybe it was just the unfamiliar fit of our new relationship, but I sensed something else too, something that hadn't yet been said but would need to be.

As I rested my cheek against the spiky black hair, trying to breathe her in, my glance drifted up the staircase. Vic was standing on the top landing. I wondered how long he'd been there and, despite the fifty feet between us, what he might have heard. Behind Dolores' head, I smiled up at him. But he didn't smile back or call down to us. He just turned away and disappeared inside his room.

*

By ten o'clock, removal vans were drawn up round the carriage circle like wagons in a Western. Bruce Willis was trying to make about thirty grumpy Neanderthals grasp that they couldn't all park right outside the front doors. Some seemed to go into mild shock; others were calling their bases to check on their terms of employment. Big Frankie tried to cool things down by going out with jugs of barley water and expressions of endearment.

'I never have guessed you did this work,' he boomed to one wizened Cockney. 'You got the hands of a concert pianist. Do you play at all?'

'Only a bit... Chopsticks an' that.'

'Well you be takin' care of those precious hands today, you hear?'

Professor Curtis Powell and Beau Styles had been the first to arrive. At the front door, Curtis knelt down and kissed the step.

'Did you find that vulgar, Mr Blaine?' he asked. 'Well that's just the way I feel today. I was part of the Stonewall riots in '69 on the day that Judy died and now I'm part of this. Wherever there's a barricade, you'll find Curtis Powell right there, ready to break it down.'

Beau called to a removal man with a black bag stuffed precariously under his arm.

'Careful with that babe, it's Professor Powell's colonic irrigation kit.'

'If it wasn't for me, Beaumont,' said Curtis with a desiccated smile, 'you'd not be moving into this magnificent mansion but a home for clapped-out chorus-boys in Yonkers.'

'Yeah, grampa, and without me you'd be sitting alone in that gloomy apartment in The Dakota with your tits covered in cob-webs like the old broad in *Great Vibrations*.'

'*Expectations*.'

'Whatever.'

The residents weren't the only new faces at Mount Royal today. The team we needed to make the place work was now up and running. Under Elspeth's charge was a squad of general helpers. Working in shifts, their duties would combine cleaning the apartments and public rooms with waiting at table. I'd sent Elspeth off to House Proud!, a gay domestic agency. She'd been looking for evidence of maturity and stability she said later, so had given preference to clean fingernails, religious convictions or live-in relationships of over six months' duration. It hadn't been easy, but she'd eventually hired ten such paragons. To a man, or rather boy, they were Scottish. She called them her Chamber-Laddies.

Down in his state-of-the-art kitchens, Big Frankie now had five shaven-headed urchins under his command. He took no shite from anyone, firing and replacing three of them inside twenty-four hours. I'd once interrupted a lecture on the preparation of broccoli. He'd glared at me and pointed to that day's T-shirt. 'Fuck Off. Man Cooking', it read. So I had.

One by one the removal vans regurgitated their contents.

'That is a Rossetti, young man,' trilled Lord Billy Vale to a tat-tooed juvenile lugging in a frame. 'Not a Rolf Harris.'

Wee Mr Lim, the Chinese dentist, showed me his Smile Album, page after page of extreme close-ups of celebrity bridgework. He couldn't tell me their names he said; the tabloids would kill to get hold of it. Pride of place was given to the lip-sticked mouth of an elderly woman. Mr Lim was sure I'd recognize that smile any-where, perhaps when opening a computer-chip factory, drinking tea with a council house tenant or, at its most fixed, watching a display of bare-breasted Patagonian dancers. He still had the mould he'd taken; he kept it in a velvet-covered casket. Perhaps I'd like to hold it sometime? I said that'd be great.

From the top of the stairs, I watched a fat oaf bash upwards with two ancient suitcases that could've been up the Euphrates with Wilfrid Thesiger.

'That panelling's seventeenth-century,' I yelled. 'Not fucking MFI.'

A mistake. The fat oaf seemed to be of a nervous disposition and dropped both cases. The geriatric locks gave way and at least a hundred DVDs were scattered like confetti the length and breadth of the stairs. With that unerring sense of inconvenient timing for which she'd been renowned among the boys of Glenlyon, Elspeth had just appeared on the lower steps and now had gay pornography licking round her ankles.

'Mercy upon us,' she cried, raising her eyes to heaven like Joan of Arc at the stake.

The fat oaf bent over and picked one up.

'*PIG-malion*,' he declaimed from the box. '"An upper-class muscle-daddy searches for sleaze among the street-boys of Covent Garden. The ultimate in inter-generational action." Takes all sorts, dunnit?'

I hurried down the stairs as Archdeacon Brownlow walked into the Gilded Hall. His face turning the same red as Elspeth's, he rushed to help me stuff the filth back into his broken cases. Elspeth looked down at him as if he were a cowpat.

'No wonder they never made you a Dean,' she said and marched out of the front doors. I imagined her in her bathroom, scrubbing her ankles with a loofah.

It was two weeks now since that morning Vic had dubbed The Day Of The Long Knives. The day after, Faisal had finally got round to calling me back. Things hadn't been that great in Slough. Mr Khan had wandered off at Heston Services and been nearly knocked down by an Eddie Stobart lorry. Once home, he'd had a complete collapse at the sight of his distraught wife. He was now in a psychiatric ward under suicide watch. Faisal was staying at home to look after his Mum and shield her from their horrified relations. He'd not been sure when he'd be able to get back. Was there anything I could do to help, I'd asked? No, he didn't think so. He'd not even asked about my shoulder. I'd left supportive voicemails every day since then, but he'd not returned them.

I'd hardly cared. Isn't that awful? For the last fortnight, all I could see and think of was Dolores. After the Ritz, our actual encounters had been casual and hurried as, day by day, the atmosphere in the house had become more febrile with the imminent arrival of the first punters. I'd tried to find excuses to slip out into the gardens, but Vic, Elspeth, Big Frankie and a hundred others had been leeched onto me from dawn till dusk with endless questions or demands for arbitration. I'd powered through it all, fuelled by a new sense of purpose. This project really had to work now; there was an heir to Mount Royal. At night I dreamed of Dolores, ten years older or so, strolling in the gardens with a litter of well-scrubbed kiddies scampering around her legs. She smiled indulgently and spoke to them in a voice which, miraculously cured of its bucolic vowels, sounded exactly like that of her great-grandmother. I was there too, sitting by the Great Fountain, remarkably unaltered, receiving the posies of buttercups my grandchildren had picked and patting their shiny wee heads.

But perhaps these frantic days had been a good thing, giving us both time to tread water, to soak up the presence of the other without the need to move anything forward. Though I still yearned to tell the world, I knew Dolores had been right in forbidding it. As I flew around the house, from the cellars to the cupola, the glow of our secret had warmed me like sunshine.

'You sickening for something toots?' Vic had asked one day.

'Don't think so. Why?'

'You've not garrotted a plumber all week.'

And then she'd fallen off the ladder. Vic had been rabbiting on about the latest drama, but I'd been watching Dolores training the *Hydrangea Petiolaris* along the side of the Orangery. She'd only fallen about three feet, but was lying on the ground not moving. I'd screamed at Vic to call an ambulance and sprinted the length of the Italian Garden. Her eyes were open but she'd been moaning and clutching her head. She'd tried to get up but I'd made her stay still. I was already convinced she was about to need Extreme Unction and where would I find a priest in time? Vic had managed to get down on his knees and was holding her hand and cooing about his 'poor rose'. I'd wanted to push him out the way.

'Jeez, calm down,' he'd said, as I circled Dolores like a tiger with a wounded cub. 'She'll be fine.'

The paramedics had concurred, though Dolores must be put to be bed and watched for any dizziness or nausea. They'd strapped the swelling ankle and put her on a stretcher. I'd ordered her taken into my spare bedroom. Elspeth had helped her into bed and given her the painkillers the paramedics had dictated. Dolores insisted she felt okay but it was clear she was shaken. I'd left her to rest, leaving the bedroom door open, creeping down every ten minutes to check. She'd seemed to be sleeping soundly, but maybe she was slipping into a coma? Then she'd given a violent snore. Did people in comas snore? I'd called Faisal's mobile for a second opinion but got the voicemail as usual.

A while later there had been a soft knock at the front door. It was Vic. I'd shooed him out into the East Court, my finger to my lips.

'Right then, toots,' he'd said. 'I think it's time you told me.'

'Told you what?'

'Who is Dolores Potts?'

I'd known at once I was going to tell him. And I'd felt really happy that he'd be the first to know. A smile had spread across my face like honey on a crumpet. For a moment, I'd savoured the three words forming on my tongue. I'd known they'd never taste this good again. So it was odd that a different three words spilled out into the warm evening air.

'She's the future' I'd said.

∗

'A bull in a china shop,' Robin Bradbury-Ross had declared one day. 'I don't wish to be unkind but that is literally what you are in this house. How much do you weigh exactly?'

'Twenty-five stone,' Big Frankie had replied in a tone that was, well, bullish.

'My God, is it your glands?' asked Robin, whose hips weren't much wider than one of Frankie's thighs.

'My glands are just fine, mister,' Frankie had snapped. 'It's a lifestyle choice.'

Robin had then taken him by the horns and tugged him round the state rooms, decreeing the chairs he must never sit in, the tables he must must never lean against, the china he must never so much as breathe on.

The armchair in which Big Frankie now reclined had been approved for his occupation. It was a burly Victorian thing, but Frankie's arse still landed on it like a double scoop of ice-cream on too small a cone. He'd begged me for a quick word. It was hardly the best of moments. Another flock of removal vans had arrived this morning, herded by an even worse bunch of tossers than before. The final group of residents were now in possession of their apartments; Mount Royal was full to the rafters. Most of them were upstairs taking a nap, having a bath or feeling nervous. Tonight there would be a posh dinner in the State Dining-Room.

Faisal had agreed to come up from Slough specially, though he'd be going back in the morning. Big Frankie should have been in his kitchens right now, but he'd looked so troubled that I'd whisked him into the Red Damask Drawing-Room.

He was in a state about Vic. One day Papi was his sunny self, the next diggin' the blues, as Frankie put it. Did I think Vic might be bi-polaroid?

I'd noticed it too though. Vic was usually the sort who swatted the glooms away like a wasp. That evening a week ago when I'd told him about Dolores he'd been gobsmacked of course but typically sweet, shaking my hand and promising to keep the secret. Since then, I'd not seen that much of him. He was normally such an emphatic presence but recently he'd almost been an absence, despite the fact we had plenty of teething troubles to wrestle with. A few times when I'd needed to track him down, they said he'd left the house telling nobody where he'd gone. When I'd eventually cornered him, he'd seemed a bit disengaged, as if these were somebody else's problems. Once I'd seen him sitting outside the Orangery with a bottle of whisky, watching Dolores and her gardeners. He'd still been there hours later, slumped on the bench.

But this evening I told Frankie not to worry, that we'd all been under stress. And Vic was getting on a bit; we had to remember that. I promised to keep a close eye on him and asked Frankie to do the same. The young chef's eyes glazed over.

'A close eye?' he asked, the deep voice cracking. 'He's all I see boss, all I see. But he hardly seems to notice me. Twenty-five stone of lovin' man. It's not that I'm easy to miss, is it? I'm proppin' sorrow here, boss.'

'Sorry Frankie,' I said and meant it. 'Perhaps, with everything else, he's just not realized how you feel. Perhaps you need to make it more obvious.'

'I know boss. But I'm kinda scared of doing that in case... you know. In case he doesn't like me.'

'Come on Frankie, butch up,' I said. 'Faint heart never won fair geriatric.'

'But I'm no shrinkin' violet am I? It's just that Papi's different to all the others. There's nobody like him, is there boss?'

'You really feel he's the one for you then?'

'Oh yes. I want to give myself to him for the rest of his years. And there can't be that many can there? That's the shit part of being a gerontophile. It's like livin' in a short-term rental. You know you'll have to move on again soon.'

Big Frankie heaved himself up from the chair.

'Oh well, even if he doesn't want me as a lover, I'm always goin' to be his friend.'

'That's nice, Frankie,' I said. 'And chins up, you've always got Jesus.'

'The perfect life-partner in every way,' he sighed, 'except he never grows old. Forever thirty-three. Such an uninterestin' age.'

I was just about to warn him against feeding Elspeth too much marijuana, when there was an almighty crash on the ceiling.

We were directly underneath Vic's rooms. Within thirty seconds I was outside his door with Big Frankie puffing up behind me. The door was locked; I hammered hard. Just as I was wondering if I should kick it in, it was flung wide open and I stared into a handsome young face with tousled hair and panic in his eyes. The boy outside the club. The boy blowing Matty on the Heath. The Caravaggio boy. Over his shoulder I glimpsed Vic crumpled up on the floor at the feet of the lesbian caryatids. Oh Jesus.

At first Caravaggio tried to struggle past me then spun round in search of another way out. I chased, we tussled, he kneed me in the balls. I yelled at Frankie to stop him but, like an oil tanker, Frankie found it difficult to change direction and the boy dodged from his reach.

'Get him boss, he's friggin gone and killed Papi.' The big face was sweaty with terror as he rushed to where Vic still lay motionless. My own fear twisted itself into a rage.

I grabbed at something from a table-top, a statuette, some Variety Club award of Vic's. I lunged and struck him hard on the skull. It slowed him down but it didn't fell him. His escape route now clear, he lurched out onto the landing. Pole-axed with the pain in my crotch, I hobbled after him. But the boy was now just standing at the head of the stairs, no longer trying to flee. For a moment he swayed like a sapling in a storm, then he began to fall. His arms flailed at the empty air, clutching at a picture-frame, tilting it to a crazy angle. Then a long high scream ricocheted round the Gilded Hall as Caravaggio rolled down the length of the staircase and came to rest below my grandmother's portrait.

As I saw him lying there, I knew the scream must have stopped but I could still hear it in my ears. The pale carpet was now streaked with blood. Christ, I'd hit him much too hard. From somewhere below, a figure ran towards the broken body. It was Faisal. He felt the pulse in the neck, put his ear to the chest, then looked up at us and shook his head; just like they do in the movies.

Big Frankie panted to my side with the news that Vic had opened his eyes. Then he looked down.

'Shit boss,' he said. 'We got trouble in the camp.'

There was a groan from behind us. Vic was propped up groggily against his doorway, tie askew, jacket ripped and a reddish weal blossoming under his right eye.

'Did you catch the little bastard?' he asked. 'I found him trying to pocket my Fabergé egg.'

'We caught him,' I said.

At the sight of Vic, Big Frankie sank to his knees as usual, trembling like a jelly just turned out of its mould.

'Blessed be the name of the Lord,' he said.

At the foot of the staircase, the tousled head was now surrounded by a crimson halo, wide as a Japanese sun.

FIFTEEN

The body lay in state in the Library. Facing north with dark green walls, it was conveniently sepulchral; a mossy pond of a room where you could hide beneath some leather-bound tome like a tadpole under a rock. From the tops of the bookcases, a congregation of distinguished busts bowed their marble heads: Homer and Pliny, Spenser and Shakespeare, Dickens and Trollope. Dostoyevsky looked especially sad, but then he always did.

Out in the Gilded Hall, peering down from the landing, I'd been paralysed till I'd known that Vic's obituaries could snooze on undisturbed. The sight of him, battered but breathing, had pumped into me like a drug. I'd raced down and begun to lift the boy in my arms. Faisal had tried to pull me off, insisting that the body wasn't moved till the police arrived. I'd snatched his mobile and flung it across the chequered floor.

'There will be no police,' I'd hissed, slinging the corpse over my good shoulder, feeling the bloody wetness seep into my shirt. By some miracle, nobody else had appeared in the Gilded Hall. I'd barked at Faisal to find something to cover the stained carpet. In the Library I'd spread newspapers over the floor and laid the boy down. Faisal was soon yelping at my heels. Who was this guy? What on earth was I doing? We must call the police at once. He was a doctor; he had to follow the correct procedures.

'No police,' I repeated, bending my knees to look him straight in the eye, a movement I'd perfected long ago. I knew he hated my doing it, though he'd never said so. 'There were no police with your father, there will be no police today.'

Big Frankie appeared, half-dragging Vic under his arm like a couple of drunks on a Saturday night. It was only now Vic realized the boy was dead. He groaned and sank into a high-winged chair. I ordered him to start talking.

He'd been for his annual lunch at the Savoy with Wendy from Ludlow, the woman who ran his fan club. On his way back, he'd stopped the cab at Whitestone Pond and gone into the woods for a breath of air to clear away the brandies. The boy had been friendly, intelligent, a third cousin of Sophia Loren no less. He'd asked him back for coffee. He'd known it was risky, but the kid had such nice manners, offering his arm on the slope up to the road. Vic's eyes never left the body as he spoke. Then he covered them with his hands, moaned and pulled himself deep into the shelter of the chair. Big Frankie stared down at him in desolation, shoulders slumped, looking several inches shorter than he usually did.

I closed the half-shutters so nobody could see into the room. Faisal examined Vic but, apart from the embryonic shiner, he'd escaped with a couple of bruised ribs. Then Faisal turned to the dead boy. The neck had been broken in the fall, he said, though the blow to the skull might have been the cause of death. Only a post-mortem could confirm which. Big Frankie joined Vic in moaning and groaning; it was like the fucking *Trojan Women*.

The door was thrown open. Elspeth was searching for Frankie; there was a hissy fit between two of the queens in the kitchen over a salmon mousse. Then she saw the body.

'Good Gordon Highlanders!' she said, dropping to her knees. 'It's the wee Italian. What on earth?'

She took Caravaggio's pale hand in hers and knelt there while she was given the salient facts. He was one of her regulars from the Heath; a frequent user of the Rubber Duckies product range. A nice boy she said; a religious boy; that's how they'd got to talking beyond the usual exchanges on such occasions. He'd come to London to work as a waiter, but the jobs had dried up.

'He was a second cousin of Sophia Loren,' she added.

'Third,' said Vic.

'Did I not specifically warn against gentlemen callers in my wee talk?' she exploded. 'And if it wasn't for men like you, these poor lads would never stoop to such things.'

'Hang on *doux-doux*,' said Big Frankie. 'It was your friend who attacked and robbed Mr d'Orsay.'

'Aye well, just look at him,' she replied. 'Skin and bone he is. Not adjectives that could be applied to either of you. Judge not that ye may not be judged.'

Elspeth and Frankie, usually such buddies, now even praying regularly together in the Chapel, began ping-ponging the scriptures at each other till I yelled at them to shut up. Elspeth looked at me in amazement. I'd never spoken to her like that in forty years. I went and locked the door.

'Listen to me,' I began. 'This boy's death was an accident, but if we call the police we'll have photographers in the trees just like before. But this time it'll be different. Vic's CD sales will drop faster than a bride's knickers and I could end up being buggered in Pentonville. Mount Royal won't be a symbol of progress any more, it'll be a symbol of sleaze. I don't think our new residents will like that very much, do you?'

Had anyone seen Vic with the boy? He didn't think so; the cruising area had been deserted and he'd sneaked him in through a small ivy-clad gate in the perimeter wall. The CCTV company had overlooked it and there was no camera there yet. Bruce Willis was supposed to be on the case. They'd not met a single soul on their way towards his rooms.

'Nobody knows he was here then?' I asked.

'What are you suggesting?' Faisal asked, beginning to tug at his beard. 'Planting him in the garden?'

'It's an option.'

'I hope that's one of your jokes, Rory,' said Faisal, flicking open his mobile. 'Every minute we delay is making this worse. And then my career will be as dead as he is.'

'But you can't go bringin' him back Doctor Khan,' said Big Frankie. 'And he's safe with Jesus now.'

'And what about the people who would spend the rest of their lives wondering what happened to him?' asked Faisal.

'I'm not sure there would be any,' said Elspeth. She spoke hesitantly, as if forming the words in spite of herself. 'He had no close family in Italy at all. I think he'd been living in some hostel place lately. He was pretty much alone, poor bairn.'

'They're lovely gardens too,' Vic piped up. 'He could do a lot worse.'

Faisal and I glared at each other across the body of the rent-boy. I wasn't sure what I was reading in his eyes. Like me, there was panic certainly; like Elspeth, there was unaccustomed self-doubt, though not of course a lot.

'Faisal if you make that call, everything here might be lost,' I said.

Now I saw despair creep into his gaze, weariness even. He threw his mobile across the room where it clipped Lord Byron's marble ear.

'We're doing this all wrong,' said Vic. 'The five of us locked in here. We have to go to the whole house, tell them everything. This should be their decision too.'

'Faisal, do you agree to this?' I asked.

'No. I certainly don't,' he said, 'but for you, Rory, I won't stop it. Which could be the worst decision I've ever made.'

I heard voices going past in the corridor. I'd almost forgotten the rest of the building existed. In half an hour everyone was gathering for drinks before the grand dinner.

Faisal unlocked the door.

'You don't have long,' he said, 'In a few hours, he'll be as stiff as yesterday's croissants. And it might be nice if you found something to cover him up.'

'I want all of you in the Saloon in thirty minutes,' I said. 'Frankie, go and tell your guys to hold back the meal.'

Elspeth went too, leaving Vic and me in the dusk of the Library.

'How the fuck could you have been so crazy, Victor?' I said quietly. 'Were you on the Benylin like last time?'

'I knew it was stupid but...' his voice trailed away.

'But?' I said, as gently as I could manage.

'I just wanted somebody, toots,' he said. 'Somebody to touch me. Even as part of a commercial transaction.'

'You could have had Big Frankie without even leaving the premises.'

'Never,' he said. 'Frankie cares for me, I'm aware of that. But I'm afraid I don't reciprocate. He's a sweetheart, but no trumpets there. So I really couldn't use him like that.'

'But you've put everything in jeopardy,' I said 'And we'd only just pulled it off.'

'It suddenly didn't seem so important any more,' he replied. 'Not enough.'

'I thought it was what you wanted more than anything,' I said.

Vic just sat staring down at Caravaggio's body.

'If you were feeling low, you should have told me,' I said. 'We're buddies aren't we, you old git?'

'Yes, toots,' he replied. 'Buddies.'

'So why didn't you then?'

'You've had other things on your mind lately,' he said 'I didn't think there would be room for me as well.'

Shite. But he'd seemed pleased for me when I'd told him about Dolores. I'd really wanted him to share my happiness and I knew he was fond of her too. I'd even confided some plans I was hatching to get to know her better. A trip to Australia where I'd met her mum, maybe round the world even. Only once the house was up and running of course. I could get a manager in to help Vic for a few months. I'd not leave him in the lurch.

'You know, it's a funny thing,' he murmured from the shadows of the winged chair. 'Every night, my bed seems to get bigger and bigger and I lie there getting smaller and smaller. Shrinking like Alice. Maybe one morning, I'll just be gone altogether.'

Big Frankie reappeared, carrying a long chef's apron. He was sorry but it was the only thing he could find. It was bright yellow with an illustration of an open sack of small potatoes. *Jersey Royals. Smooth and succulent from the sun-kissed soil. It's the way our farmers grow 'em!'*

He knelt down and laid it delicately across Caravaggio's face, the olive complexion now bleached to a papery-white. For a few moments Frankie stayed on the floor, head lowered, eyes closed. When he got up again, Vic reached for the big hand and kissed it. Briefly, Frankie let his fingers rest against Vic's cheek then he pulled them away.

*

'Well Beaumont, our first week living in a great English mansion and now there's a body in the Library,' I heard Professor Curtis Powell murmur as everyone filed into the State Dining-Room. 'I die of pleasure.'

The trial of Rory Blaine, for in a way that's what it was, took place around the long walnut table at which Queen Victoria herself had once stuffed her already podgy wee frame. It had been laid for our first formal Mount Royal dinner, but this meal was going to have to wait. Perhaps it might never happen at all.

They'd gathered in the Saloon at the appointed time; everyone in dinner jackets except for Lord Billy Vale, a bird of paradise among penguins, glittering in a thousand-watt djellabah. I'd just thrown on a clean shirt above my jeans; the one stained in Caravaggio's blood had been safely disposed of.

A few of the Chamber-Laddies had been circulating with the Sancerre. Elspeth had chosen well and I'd rather taken to the whole gang of them. They were young, fresh and unreserved, with a sunny openness about them which my generation had never been relaxed enough to achieve and the familiar burr floating round the house was oddly comforting, like being back in the dorm at Glenlyon. But tonight I'd ordered them from the room and called for everybody's attention. I'd announced briefly that a visitor to the house had met with a fatal accident, that the body now lay in the Library, but that the emergency services hadn't yet been summoned. There would now be an urgent meeting of the residents of Mount Royal. They could bring their drinks with them. Beau had asked if they could take the nibbles too; he was so hungry he could eat a whole baby.

I sat at the head of the table with Faisal at the opposite end; everyone else took the seats allocated to them by the crisp cards which stood on the white plates like little tents in the Antarctic. Big Frankie had put his kitchen into suspend mode and was sitting behind me on a small gilt chair which had certainly not been passed for his usage. Elspeth was in another. Vic, still shaky and silent, had draped himself over a chaise-longue by the window like Elizabeth Barrett Browning. The one missing person was Dolores. I'd wanted her to be here tonight, sitting on my right, her status unacknowledged but beside me nonetheless. But she'd rumbled me on that one and wasn't playing. She was going out to hear some girl-band called Manic Vagina. I was glad of that now.

I stood up and outlined what had occurred.

'The last embers of lust,' said Lord Billy, shaking his head. 'How often they can cause a conflagration.'

As I presented the options, Marcus Leigh buried his head in his hands. I asked for a communal decision on how to proceed.

'But there is no decision to make,' interrupted Marcus, his voice rising so high that the last syllables were more like squeaks. 'If we sanction your ludicrous idea of concealing this death, every one of us becomes a criminal.'

'Oh my goodness,' said wee Jacob Trevelyan, twisting his tiny wrinkled fingers.

'Criminals?' asked Beau. 'As in jail? As in *Shawshank Redemption?* Holy shit.'

'Calm yourselves,' said Jasper, bowling his twin a contemptuous glance. 'Let's stop flapping around like a flock of old nancies.'

'But my dear, we *are* a flock of old nancies,' said Lord Billy.

'Actually, Marcus is right,' I said. 'So if anyone wishes, they are free to leave the table now.'

'It's too late for that,' said Marcus. His left hand was trembling, the ice-cubes rattling in his gin and tonic. 'If your crazy scheme is implemented then even those who reject it will be accessories after the fact.'

'I'm just asking you to examine the option,' I said. 'No real moral crime would be committed, simply an act which would be against the law.'

'Oh well, babe, that's different,' said Beau, grabbing another fat fistful of peanuts. 'I started doing *those* aged twelve with the kid from the next trailer.'

'Anyway, the little bastard got what he deserved,' said Jasper Trevelyan. 'I vote we plant him out.'

There were vociferous objections to this remark and it lit the fuse of an ethical debate that would not have disgraced the General Synod or Radio 4. I was now joined in the dock by the deceased. Various witnesses were called on both sides. The Archdeacon summoned God of course. Faisal summoned Allah and Elspeth called John Knox. Somebody spoke of the playing fields of Eton and Beau recalled a similar storyline in an episode of *Perry Mason* in which he'd been an extra: *The Case of The Unhappy Hooker*. I noticed Marcus Leigh's hand still trembling and his face getting redder just like it had before he'd passed out on the floor of the Reform Club. Then amazingly, he undid the top button of his starched shirt and pulled off his bow-tie. Maybe he felt that if civilized values were about to collapse, it just didn't matter any more.

Like Vic, Lord Billy had said nothing. He'd counted out the tablets from his mother-of-pearl box and swigged them down with white wine. His hook nose was tilted up towards the ceiling, to the alternative gathering of nymphs and satyrs, no doubt thinking it looked a lot more fun.

'I'm frightfully sorry Mr Blaine, but I'm quite lost,' he said eventually, stretching the final vowel like it was on a rack and making it rhyme with 'toast'. 'What exactly have you done wrong?'

'Well nothing really,' I replied. 'Not deliberately anyway.'

'Then what on earth are you afraid of?'

'Dragging you all through it. Dragging Mount Royal through it.'

'Do you imagine that if there's trouble we'll not stand by you?' asked Lord Billy. 'That we'd pack our valises and run for the hills?'

'Yeah babe,' said Beau, 'what sort of guys do you take us for?'

I realized I didn't know the answer to that question. Up till now I'd not been very interested in finding out. I suppose I'd decided that though they were all gay they were all pretty straight as well; that they'd been used to lives that ran smoothly, used to putting themselves first. Just like I always had. I certainly couldn't imagine any of them in Ford Open Prison. Not many touring opera companies out there.

'Well yes, I thought you all might vote with your feet,' I replied. 'I'm sure none of you want to go through a scandal.'

'My dear, how many gentlemen of our age get even a sniff of scandal?' said Lord Billy. 'I've not been near one since I was in Mustique with Margaret and Roddy. I was so cross to be cut out of that picture. And this one has everything; sex, violent death, lovely interiors. I believe the modern expression is "bring it on."'

Curtis Powell reminded us yet again about having been at the Stonewall riots in '69. The Archdeacon mentioned he'd been a friend of Jeremy Thorpe and would always remain so, dead dog or no dead dog. Beau wondered if there might eventually be a TV movie. He thought that Daniel Craig could play me; though he'd need to grow his hair and Beau reckoned Daniel's was thinning so a wig might be necessary.

A shy hand rose from the ranks. The big lumbering man beside Lord Billy asked if he could speak. His name was Jim McLatchie, once an admired New Zealand cricketer, known as Gentleman Jim because of his courtesy on the pitch. Decades back, he'd got caught with another player in the showers at Lord's. All over the papers. Kicked off the squad. The other guy had hanged himself. But afterwards, Jim had stayed in the UK, gone into property and made a fortune. He'd given lots to charity, got a gong. Now he stood up, his knuckles gripping the edge of the table.

'Rory mate, not a great one for public speaking but hear me out. Long time back, when I got myself into big-league trouble, the folks I thought would support me buckled under the strain. Somewhere on the other side of the world, I've got an ex-wife and grown-up kids. Grandkids too I guess; I don't really know. I've sent a thousand letters and never had a reply. Not even now, in the brave new world blokes like us are supposed to inhabit. It's like a bloody great hole was punched in my belly, excuse my language Miss Wishart, and I've never really managed to fill it.'

Gentleman Jim took a gulp from a glass of water.

'Well I came to your beautiful house to see if that hole might somehow shrink and maybe even heal, while that's still just possible. There's no way I'm going to pack my bags and leave now. I want to stay and get to know you all, care for you maybe. Even when you're seventy-five, you need possibilities. Otherwise, you just feel that it's all over bar the shouting. Rory, what happened to this poor kid tonight is a tragedy, but let's not allow it to be ours too. What you did you did from the best motives right? Even if it's got you in the shit, you've got nothing to be ashamed of, unlike that daft old arsehole lolling over there, begging your pardon again Miss Wishart. So come on mate, let's call the cops. Most of us old nancies, as Lord Bill here calls us, have been through a lot worse in our day. None of us is going anywhere and Mount Royal isn't going down the gurgler.'

Gentleman Jim sat down awkwardly and stared at his empty soup-bowl. In the neighbouring bowl was a droplet of bright red blood from Lord Billy's finger. He'd been toying with his big ruby ring and had twisted it till the skin had broken.

'You're quite delightful aren't you my dear?' he said, patting Gentleman Jim on the arm. 'Where have you been all my life?'

Vic, looking cowed and still a bit dazed, rose from his chaise-longue and shuffled over to my chair.

'Hear that, toots? Nobody's walking away,' he murmured in my ear. 'Not this time.'

Faisal looked at me and raised an eyebrow. I nodded. He flicked open his mobile. Marcus Leigh patted his face with his hanky and slowly retied his tie.

'For Chrissakes,' said Beau. 'Are we ever going to *eat?*'

*

'It's all go here, innit guv?' said the paramedic. They were the same guys who'd come when Dolores fell off the ladder. 'What's it gonna be next week? Mass ritual suicide?'

It was past ten now. The police had finished for the night though they'd be back in the morning to take detailed statements, fingerprints, photographs. Before they'd arrived, Vic had finally agreed not to hide the fact he'd brought Caravaggio into the house. For a while he'd wriggled on the hook, but Elspeth had reeled him in. It would be disgraceful to pretend the boy was just a burglar, unknown to any of us. At least we could show him that small mark of respect. She'd not be party to it anyway; she'd tell the police exactly who he was and what he did for a living. So that was that. And I sensed Vic was glad of it really; confession being the first step on his road to forgiveness.

As Faisal feared, the police had raised their eyebrows at the moving of the corpse. I'd taken the blame, saying I'd not wanted our elderly residents upset by the sight of it. Faisal, used to dealing with the police, had been his crisp professional self, but he'd tugged at his beard like it was on fire. One of the policemen had recognized Vic; his mum was a huge fan and had a signed photo in her guest loo. Vic had offered him a CD but the man said it wouldn't be appropriate to accept it at this point.

Faisal had given Vic some painkillers and ordered him upstairs. Elspeth, grumpier than I'd ever seen her, had taken charge of getting him undressed and into bed. I doubted if the drugs would help much against the onslaught of full-blown Calvinist outrage.

A late supper was eventually served in the State Dining-Room. It was hardly the celebration planned; quite a few had already disappeared to their rooms. Faisal had returned to the flat; he'd be going back to Slough first thing. In contrast to the turbulence of the earlier sitting, small talk now becalmed the long walnut table. Lord Billy was reminiscing about his youthful stint as an extra in Hollywood; James Dean had once invited him to stub out a Marlboro in his navel. But Billy had fled Tinseltown due to an unrequited passion for Tab Hunter; he was still unable to watch any of Tab's movies; not, he said, that any were worth watching in the first place. Beau, not to be outdone, talked about being in the chorus of *Mame* with Angela Lansbury. He'd walked Angela's little dog between shows on matinee days. When the pooch had passed away, she'd named its successor after him. They still exchanged cards at Christmas.

But as the booze took effect, the tales got darker. Lord Billy pushed back the candy-floss hair from his temple to reveal a large pinkish scar from the day his father's doctors overdid the electric shocks. There was a collective intake of breath, a sympathetic silence, then Archdeacon Brownlow silently displayed a matching wound. Well pissed by now, he started apologizing for his halitosis; no doctor or dentist had ever been able to pin down the cause, probably just nerves they'd all said. Wee Mr Lim patted his hand and said he knew a very good man in Queen Anne Street; he'd be happy to take the Archdeacon there himself. Mr Lim didn't say much as a rule but tonight he talked about escaping from communist China in 1948 with, naturally, only a toothbrush. He was an odd, intangible creature. He'd probably been quite cute once, but now his little rosebud lips were beginning to crinkle with age. I wondered if they'd ever said anything more intimate than 'next Tuesday at three suit you?' Then Gentleman Jim spoke about his friend who'd hanged himself. It was sobering stuff, so more port was poured.

The conversation doubled back to Vic and his rent-boy. Liberated by the temporary absence of his twin, Jasper Trevelyan regaled us with tales of similar encounters; he'd never been with anyone without paying for it he said quite proudly. So much simpler that way; let you get on with what mattered in life, like making toffee better than anyone else. Marcus Leigh failed to cloak his sadness at such a point of view. Shyly, he introduced Ricardo and their life together. The wallet was opened, the dog-eared Polaroids passed around.

Somebody began to moan about getting older, about the invisibility that was descending over them all like a mist. Let loose by alcohol, anger now stalked round the long walnut table, only thinly veiled by humour. Stories were told of discrimination, insults, condescension.

'Well of course the world no longer looks one in the eye,' said Lord Billy. 'It's much too scary for them. If they do deign to notice one, one is expected to be two-dimensional; a cardboard cut-out of a nice old soul. As if one is expected to shed one's complexities along with one's hair and teeth. Well, bugger that, as ghastly old George V would have said.'

Beau confessed his terror of farting now; in case it turned out to be something slightly more substantial. There was laughter, but Lord Billy turned on him.

'If that is true my dear, then keep quiet about it,' he said 'Don't make yourself into a music-hall joke. There is nothing funny about one's physical decline. Nothing.'

'But surely that's a fair way of coping with it?' I asked.

'Rubbish,' said Lord Billy. 'Ageism is at its most terrible when one turns it against oneself. We have earned dignity through our achievements and the kindnesses we have shown to others. We may be old men but we are still men. Forget that and one might as well turn one's face to the wall.'

The shy gavotte of Preview Day had come to an end; they were looking at each other now.

'In the depths of winter, I found within myself an invincible summer,' said Gentleman Jim. 'I think that's Albert Camus.'

'Indeed it is my dear and in saying so you prove my point,' said Lord Billy 'Who'd have thought a great lumping cricketer would have read Camus? We are each of us surprising and fascinating till our last breath. You really are quite adorable.'

The bell out in the Clock Tower struck one; eyelids were drooping, the party broke up. I hoped they'd all be okay. They were old guys after all. This sort of evening hadn't been in the brochure.

I was tired too but knew I'd not sleep. I headed for the Coach House and the Morag Proudie Memorial Jacuzzi, as I quite often did these days. 'Going for a Morag' had now entered the phraseology of the household; it seemed fitting that she should bring me comfort in later life when she'd caused so much trauma in days gone by. But the lights were already on, the windows steamed over. Faisal lay immersed, head flung back. He smiled but said nothing as I undressed and slid into the froth. This was the first time we'd been alone since the morning he'd driven his father away; the first time since I'd discovered I had a daughter. I'd have to tell him soon. He had the right to know. But not tonight. I asked about Slough.

'Dad's still in a hospital bed with drugged-up eyeballs.'

'And your mother?'

'Drugged up too. Terrified. Above all, ashamed. She keeps apologizing to me. And to you, come to that. There's a bunch of straggly roses waiting for you in the kitchen.'

He was trying to get counselling for them both when the worst had passed. He'd not found anybody yet to run the hardware shop so he'd be taking more leave from the hospital. His parents needed the income.

'So much hurt, Rory,' he said. 'And the big irony is that it's all supposed to be about love isn't it? Dad loving me, Mum loving us both, me loving you.'

'You'd decided you did then?'

'I guess I had,' he said, making patterns in the froth. 'But then Dad and now all this tonight. I'm just so tired, you know?'

'I found the papers in the desk,' I said. 'The partnership thing.'

'It seemed like a good idea at the time,' he smiled.

'Not any more though?'

'Let's get all this stuff over with, shall we? Then we can take a few steps back. See where we are. Okay?'

'Cool,' I said.

We snuggled under the blanket of bubbling water. I watched him through half-closed eyes, still stirred by his beauty. I leaned across and brushed his lips. For a few minutes we held each other, lightly kissing, instinctively beginning to use the little tricks we'd learned over our time together. It was the first time we'd touched like this in ages. Then I lifted his lower body above the surface of the water. It was over in less than a minute and it was wonderful. So why did we both look so sad?

Faisal climbed out of the jacuzzi and began to dry himself. It wasn't the best of moments, but I needed to lance the boil.

'You disappointed me tonight,' I said, keeping my tone as careless as the circumstances made appropriate. 'I've maybe killed a guy and you seemed to care more about your career than you did about me.'

Any post-coital languor vanished in a second. He bent over, thrust his hairy arse in my direction and slapped it hard.

'When you bought what you like to call my "south front", you bought the rest of me too,' he said sharply, fixing me with those black eyes. 'I've never been quite sure you grasped that. I only know how to do what I think is right.'

He wrapped himself in a robe. He was off to the spare room he said; he needed to get up early, give his statement to the police and get back to his mother as soon as possible. He didn't want to disturb me. Then he turned in the doorway.

'It's who I am Rory,' he said. 'The work. It's always been there. Rock solid, in the midst of whatever stuff is blowing all around. Try to understand.'

I nodded and tried for an empathetic smile.

'Like I said, let's get all this stuff out the way,' he repeated, 'then see where we are.'

'Cool,' I replied, though I'd begun to wonder if our points of contact were getting fewer, like a shirt with too many buttons missing to be wearable much longer.

'You really shouldn't use that expression you know,' said Faisal, closing the door behind him. 'It's a bit pathetic.'

I switched off the Jacuzzi jets. In half a minute, the bubbles had popped and vanished and the noisy froth evaporated into a still, limpid pool. If only life could be that simple. I soaked in the calm water, trying to blot out all thoughts of what might happen when the cops came back tomorrow. And I wanted to see Dolores. Where the hell was she at this hour? She should have been home by now. I wondered who was shagging her tonight. I felt myself get grumpy and parental, then I remembered she was twenty-six and that I had no rights over her. None at all. I'd missed out on that like I'd missed out on the meningitis, the first boyfriend and the college graduation. She might have been my daughter, but she'd never be my child. Hey ho.

Since the night of the storm, Dolores had filled my mind, blotting out everything else. I'd been drunk on her or at least drunk on the idea of her. Till then, nothing had mattered to me more than the survival of Mount Royal. Not even, I realized now with a jolt, the survival of Faisal and me. My house, his career; there had always been four of us in the marriage. And now, though he didn't know it yet, there were five.

Tonight though, Mount Royal had asserted its dominance. As I'd watched Caravaggio tumble down the staircase, what I'd seen had been the end of it all. It would be snatched away from me again. There would be a second exile, from which there would be no return. As the boy had died at her feet, Granny had stared out at me from her frame, challenging me to do something, to prove myself worthy. And I guess I'd gone a wee bit bonkers, lost the plot. But the old men had been there. I'd not reckoned on them or on what they might be willing to give. The old men had made things all right. The old men had been titans.

But there had been something else tonight too. I didn't want to let it enter my mind but I knew it was already there, wormed in forever. Gentleman Jim had said that I'd done what I'd done with the best motives, that I'd nothing to be ashamed of. But that wasn't quite true. When I'd seen Vic lying on the floor, not sure if he were dead or alive, I'd not simply wanted to catch the boy, I'd wanted to hurt him. Really hurt him. And I had, though much more than I'd ever intended. Even if it had been the fall and not the blow that killed him, even if nobody else blamed me for his death, I'd always blame myself. I'd always wonder about the road that had led him to the callous pavements of Soho, to the grubby woods of the West Heath, to the top of my staircase. And of course I'd never know. Maybe that was to be my punishment.

'Is this all there is?' he'd asked me that night outside the club.

And I'd understood exactly what he'd meant. For most of my life, that'd been how I'd felt. But now I knew that, for me, it was no longer the case. Whatever happened when Faisal and I sat down again and looked hard at each other, when Dolores finally opened herself up, when Vic let me understand this sadness that had entered him, I'd never need to ask myself that question again.

Back in the East Court everything was dark. The house was asleep but it was a different sleep now. Hearts were beating inside its walls again; it was sheltering them like it had sheltered this child all those years ago. And that's what a house is for after all. Now it has a purpose.

'Hang on,' I said. 'We're not finished yet.'

Out on the blue-black abyss of the Heath, some insomniac stray was barking against the night. I took it as a sign and, whatever the morning might bring, I resolved to do the same.

Sixteen

We didn't need the Poor Clares to get us out the shite this time, though Big Frankie had put them back on prayer alert. Our saviour was a member of the Royal Family; a minor one admittedly, but he still took paparazzi-precedence over the likes of us. On the very day the pack had gathered at our gates once more, a statement had been issued from one of the less prestigious apartments in Kensington Palace, which sent them scrambling westwards. A pair of plucky Royal Highnesses had just announced that, for the past year, their younger son had been living as woman, working on the beauty counter in Boots, cohabiting with an electrician in North Acton and was now about to undergo the surgery of no-return. His/her ducal parents were totally supportive of his/her lifestyle decisions and had been to tea with the electrician's family. As a gay scandal we were instantly second-rate; just a couple of paras on Page Six. Beau and Lord Billy had been more than a bit disappointed.

The morning after the accident, the police had returned to take our statements. Then an initial post-mortem revealed that Caravaggio had indeed died from the fall and not from the weight of Vic's statuette. And since the poor lad hadn't eaten a decent meal for a while it was harder to pinpoint the hour of death. So the lost ninety minutes before we'd called the cops would remain lost forever, soaked up into the walls of Mount Royal and never mentioned again. We'd have to appear at the inquest of course, but legally it was all over bar the rubber-stamping. So I'd not be slopping out as old lags eyed up my arse nor standing in the dock while Ms Prada, as a witness for the prosecution, told the world about my anger management issues. As predicted everybody told me not to blame myself. The policeman, the one whose mum was a fan of Vic's, opined that if the boy hadn't had the lousy luck to get dizzy at the head of the stairs, he'd have been right as rain by bedtime and back on the Heath by the next afternoon. The policeman now thought it acceptable to ask Vic for an autographed CD and was presented with a copy of *Vic's Smoochin' Summer*, on the cover of which Vic larked about on a beach with a surfboard and a bevy of big-breasted lovelies.

The same morning, in an attempt to limit any damage, we'd issued a short press statement outlining the facts and describing the boy as a fan of Vic d'Orsay who'd been invited into the house and then attempted a robbery. We deeply regretted what had happened and were making a donation in his memory to a charity set up to repatriate EU workers who'd fallen on hard times. Naturally, the idea of an Italian kid being into Vic's music wasn't swallowed by your average tabloid hack but they'd only just begun to sniff blood when the first case of trans-sexuality in the British Royal Family had hit the fan. And that, by and large, seemed to be that. Crisis averted. Like the truck that misses you by inches as you step off the pavement then vanishes like it had never been there at all. So you cross the road safely to get on with your life. Only later, in the chill of the night, does it roar into your mind again and you shiver for a moment. If only I'd been able to grab him before he fell. I still heard the scream in my sleep.

But almost everyone in Mount Royal was marked by the death of Caravaggio. The shifting of gears I'd sensed that night, as the port had circled the long walnut table, hadn't been a tipsy aberration. I heard first names being used more often. Croquet balls were scudding across Dolores' perfectly-striped lawns. There was more chatter in the corridors and on the staircases. The old men were melting into the house. I wondered about making some gesture to thank them for their support. Maybe hire a coach and go to Brighton. They'd like that. With the exception of Beau, they weren't exactly your kiss-me-quick types but they'd enjoy The Pavilion, The Lanes and the pretty bums on the beach. They might even like a paddle. I'd talk to Vic and see what he thought.

Trouble was Vic wasn't saying much at the moment. His bruised ribs were less painful now and the shiner was creeping across its usual spectrum of reds, purples and browns. But day after day he'd been holed-up in his suite looking out at the gardens and taking in whisky on a constant drip. Alma the cat never left his side, Dolores had filled the place with flowers and Elspeth bustled around doing her matronly thing and watering down the booze when his back was turned. Briefly he'd perked up when Big Frankie, having sulked for nearly a week, breezed in with a tea-tray that would have thrilled Billy Bunter and nattered away if as nothing had happened. But it had been a short renaissance.

The old men knocked shyly on his door and tried to josh him out of it. Beau danced constant attendance; but even his filthiest showbiz stories, the ones he'd never tell in front of Curtis, hadn't done the trick; not even the one about Tallulah Bankhead and a Yorkshire terrier. Wee Jacob delivered a regular supply of Trevelyan's Toffees, especially Fowey Fudge, which was Vic's favourite and, Jacob proudly told him, that of Mrs Thatcher. Mr Lim took in The Smile Album, actually whispering the celebrated identities and letting him hold the bridgework mould of the very great personage kept in the velvet-covered casket. But Vic's own smile, he reported to the others downstairs, flickered like a candle in the wind. Everyone was worried. I called Faisal back in Slough; he faxed me a prescription for anti-depressants but Vic wouldn't take them. Whisky would do quite well he said. Then I rang Ms Prada; she felt she should make an urgent evaluation of Vic's mental state with a view to a long-term course of treatment, though not this week as she'd be in Lanzarote.

I'd been looking in on him most evenings. Tonight, he had his own photo albums out, scattered across the spindly Regency armchairs. Great. Something we could talk about. But soon as he saw me he snapped them all shut. It was odd. The only photos displayed in this room were from recent years, nothing from his youth or middle age at all.

'Come on Victor. Give us a look.'

'No no,' he said, 'that's all the past.'

'Well of course,' I said, 'that's what photo albums are for.'

But they were all returned to the safety of the bookshelves. It was stifling in here, a fug of booze and sweat. I threw up one of the sashes. From the terrace below, laughter and cigar smoke clambered up into the room. I helped myself to a whisky and sat on the floor below the window to get some air.

'Listen, Victor, you hear that? Everybody's cool. You're not a pariah. This is so unlike you and it won't bring the boy back.'

'The boy? What boy?' he asked. 'Oh yes. Poor kid. He's our new resident, isn't he? He will never leave you or me now.'

'I suppose not.' I replied.

'Jeez, with all the drama, I've not really thanked you properly have I, toots?' he said. 'For racing to my aid that night.'

'It's okay,' I replied. 'I'd have done the same for anybody.'

He looked at me for a long moment then filled his glass again and raised it in my direction.

'I guess so. But cheers anyway.'

He turned away and ran his fingers over the red leather spines of the photo albums.

'All the past,' he muttered again. 'Neat and tidy. On a shelf.'

There was a great scurrying down on the terrace and the sound of closing doors. A sudden sharp shower ricocheted against the window panes. I slammed down the sash. Vic still contemplated his bookshelves. This was a waste of time.

'Looks like I'm going to get drenched before I reach the flat,' I said, draining the whisky. 'Wash my sins away maybe.'

'Oh I doubt you've got many worth speaking of,' he replied, wheeling round to face me again. 'Not beyond a short fuse, too much fucking and a few naff adverts.'

'Cheers for that Victor.' I smiled and headed for the door.

'Well perhaps there's just the one,' he said. 'Somewhere along the line, you laid aside some bits of yourself, didn't you? Some of the best bits too. But that wasn't totally your fault, was it? Luckily, I think you know it, and that's half the battle, isn't it, toots?'

He shuffled over to me, took my chin in one hand and patted my cheek with the other.

'You're a fine man, Rory,' he said. 'Has nobody ever told you that?'

He walked away towards the bedroom, Alma scampering ahead. I'd been called plenty of things in my time, some of them complimentary even. But no, nobody had ever used that particular word. Not Elspeth, not even Faisal. Never 'fine'.

*

'Always the bridesmaid,' Elspeth had said, when I'd asked if she'd be a witness, 'But aye, all right then.'

I'd invited Dolores to be the second, but she'd politely refused, on the grounds that Faisal would surely prefer one of his own friends. So here I sat, ponced up in my best Hugo Boss, between Elspeth and one of the wee Siamese Children who'd been on the London Eye. Her name was Soo-Yi, she said. She was in obstetrics and smelt faintly of disinfectant.

The waiting area for those undertaking a civil partnership ceremony suffered from an identity crisis, given that Camden Council required it to multitask. Not only did it embrace gays and dykes with buttonholes and shining eyes, it also catered for newly-minted parents registering births and the recently bereaved doing the opposite. To cover all eventualities, the decorators had gone for buttermilk in a big way; walls, carpets, curtains, bowls of anaemic primroses. The same principle was followed by the teen-age apparatchik behind the desk who neither smiled nor frowned, but had opted for a basilisk stare and a speak-your-weight deliv-ery. I hated the place and wanted this over and done with as soon as possible. But as yet there was no Faisal.

He'd been already dressed in his suit and tie when he'd come up the glass staircase and said there'd been an urgent call from the Whittington. A patient under his care had gone into a coma. He'd given me a long, tight hug. I wasn't to worry; he'd be there in good time for our appointment at twelve. It was now five-to.

The morning after the accident, as soon as he'd given the police his statement, he'd rushed back to Khan's Tools & Hardware, to the serenity of the nuts and the bolts, the paints and the bath plugs. But at least from then on he'd called me most evenings. His precious father had come home again, but still sat staring at the walls. His mother had calmed down a bit but was constantly weepy. Faisal had been running the shop, just like he'd done as a teenager. I'd offered to pop down and see him, but he'd thought it best if I didn't. He'd hoped I'd understand.

Then one night he'd paused, cleared his throat and mentioned the papers in the desk. What did I think? Should we give it a go maybe? He'd taken his few steps back, had been thinking hard about 'us'. We'd been through a lot lately but perhaps it was some sort of test? Things between us had come a bit unstuck, his fault as well as mine, but he reckoned making it legal might be the glue we needed. I'd wished he'd gone for another word.

I'd told him about Dolores. It was easier on the phone. He'd been shocked of course but, to my surprise, seemed as pleased as Vic had initially been. He liked Dolores he'd said; not the sort of girl he knew as a rule. Good fun. Did my having a daughter alter anything between us? I'd heard myself saying that it didn't, though I'd known I was lying. Dolores had altered everything, even the strength of the morning sun.

He'd repeated his question. Should we give it a go? I'd felt like one of those people who report being strangely drawn to the edge of Beachy Head or the railings of the Eiffel Tower. Faisal gave his life to easing people's pain. Now the physician needed healing himself and he was self-prescribing this piece of paper. Could I deny him that? Should I jump?

I'd jumped. Though I'd made it clear I wasn't having any of that gay 'marriage' shite; morning dress, exchanging rings, calling each other husband, trying to beat the straights at their own game. Luckily, Faisal didn't either. So one day he'd come up from Slough and we'd gone to the town hall to register our intentions. He'd written me a special 'Partner Poem' to mark the occasion. It'd been just as awful as the rest but I'd pretended to be deeply touched. Now, a week later, we were back to do the deed. Or at least I was.

I'd thought it right to discuss the business implications with Vic; what would happen if I went under a bus etc. I'd asked him to come for a chat in the office. His mood still hadn't lifted much. Big Frankie had agreed to slip the anti-depressants into Vic's meals, but they'd not stood much chance against the amount of whisky he was swallowing too. Our meeting had been a bit bumpy. After all the money he'd put in, after all we'd been through, he wasn't going to sit back and let anyone else wreck all that. Not Faisal, not Dolores. I was acquiring next-of-kin at an alarming rate. He'd insisted our talking to the lawyers as soon as possible. He'd wanted what he called 'legal battlements' around the project and he'd wanted it done right away. Only when he'd been going out of the door, had he tossed limp congratulations back over his shoulder.

'It's one minute to twelve,' said Elspeth. 'You'll miss your slot if he's not here soon.'

A chirpy middle-aged woman popped out of the room where the ceremonies took place. I explained that my partner was a doctor and on his way from an emergency. She flashed a dazzling smile, tinged with the steely glint of officialdom. The absolute latest we could begin would be twelve-fifteen, after which the proceedings would have to be aborted. I called Faisal's mobile but got the voicemail. Why hadn't he phoned or texted? Just then swing doors flew open. It wasn't Faisal, but an Oriental guy I recognized from the London Eye. Soo-Yi leapt up and greeted him. He looked uncomfortable. I asked where Faisal was. He said he wasn't exactly sure, then handed me an envelope and skedaddled.

'Golly,' chortled the woman. 'Maybe you've been left at the altar, so to speak. That'd be a first here, I believe.'

I opened the envelope. Many a true word spoken in jest, as Elspeth often said. She looked at my face and said it again now.

As I fled the room, an old crone with orange hair and a scruffy terrier grabbed my hand and squeezed it.

'Don't take on now, luv,' she said, 'you're a nice-looking boy and there's plenty more fish in the sea.'

Outside, I shoved Soo-Yi in a taxi, hoping I'd never lay eyes on her again, then called The Groucho and cancelled the table for lunch. Elspeth had vanished to the loo. When she reappeared, I don't think she knew what to say. Neither did I. The words inside the envelope hadn't totally transmitted themselves from the paper to my mind; they were floating in some limbo; understood but not yet absorbed. I hailed another cab. Elspeth and I sat in silence till we reached at Mornington Crescent, then I asked if she wanted to see the letter.

It was insultingly short. Faisal declared he'd been awake all night and had decided it would be a big mistake. Like trying to put Elastoplast on a severed artery, he said. There had been too much bad stuff going on and he just couldn't think straight. He might be going away for a while. He would come and get his stuff from Mount Royal shortly, if that would be convenient. He'd wanted to tell me this morning, but couldn't. He'd had no idea what words to use. The emergency call from his hospital had been a lie. He was really really sorry. He still loved me in his way.

'Well dearie me, I'd not have marked him down as a cowardy custard,' said Elspeth stuffing her reading glasses back in her bag. 'He should have done it to your face. Funny how we think we have the measure of folk.'

'I've always imagined you had the measure of everyone Miss Wishart,' I said. 'Always so certain of things. Life in black and white.'

'Oh aye, that'll be right,' she replied.

She stared out the window as we crawled past the lurid shabbiness of Camden Market with the grungy music shops and revolving racks of cheap leather jackets. A million miles from the world she'd always known. Then she turned and looked me hard in the face.

'Rory Blaine, when I came that evening to Mount Royal, not having seen you for so long, I was disappointed by the man I found.'

'Oh thanks Miss Wishart,' I said. 'Hit me when I'm down.'

'Och, the old charm was still intact,' she said. 'And despite the passing of time, you looked much the same. The same voice, the same walk, all that. But somehow you, the you I carried in my mind, wasn't there. Like you'd gone off somewhere and hired an actor to impersonate you. And he'd not quite caught you. Just a caricature. Shallow. No substance to it.'

I looked sulkily out the window on my side. A drunk was swigging sherry with one hand and pissing on the road with the other. What she was saying upset me as much as anything in Faisal's letter. It had been the reason I'd not wanted her to come to Mount Royal.

'But over the last while, I've begun to see you peeping out at me again,' she continued. 'Just occasionally mind; a long way still to go. I'd imagined it was all down to the wee Paki. So I'm sorry that it's not worked out. I really am.'

'Maybe I'd begun to feel a bit less alone,' I said.

And it was true. For a time at least Faisal had given me that, even if I'd not been certain he was the right provider. That night on the *bateau mouche* in Paris, he'd said he felt our souls might travel in tandem. I'd found that a bit over the top at the time, but I suppose it was what we'd been trying for. And now the chance of it was gone. The chance of the joy, as Vic always put it.

'Well there's no reason you shouldn't find someone else one day,' she said.

'Actually, there's already someone else, Miss Wishart,' I said, feeling that she deserved some good news.

'I kenned that,' she said, slapping her knee, her mouth tightening into a smug wee line. 'I've watched you together.'

'You guessed then? I reckoned you might. She means everything to me.'

'She? You've lost me, Rory Blaine.'

I told her about Dolores.

'But Morag Proudie said...'

'Yes well it's possible to do it without being it, Miss Wishart,' I replied.

Once over her surprise Elspeth, like Faisal and Vic, seemed happy for me. Dolores was a spunky lass, she said; though far from the sort of girl Elspeth had been trained to be. Rarely back home till the small hours though. Elspeth had had a wee chat with her about safer-sex techniques but had been pleased to discover Dolores was highly condom-literate. Elspeth's criteria of respectability seemed to have broadened of late.

'Dearie me, a bairn of your own,' she said finally. 'You're blessed. Whatever the circumstances. I hope you know that.'

'I know it, Miss Wishart,' I replied.

We didn't speak again till Hampstead High Street. Then Elspeth expressed one of her regular longings for a 'wee pokey-hat'. I paid off the cab and got the ice-cream. As we passed the newspaper kiosk by the tube, a young Rasta called out from behind the counter.

'Hey babes, how's you today?'

'It's how *are* you, Floyd,' Elspeth replied. 'You'll never get on in life with bad grammar.'

'Okay, babes, whatever,' said the Rasta. 'Don't forget your *Scooter World* will be in tomorrow.'

The Rasta clocked me and grinned, displaying a wraparound set of Daz-white teeth that would've had Mr Lim moaning with pleasure.

'What a woman, ain't she?' he said. 'She your mum then?'

'Yeah, sure,' I replied.

We licked our way up the brae, as Elspeth called Heath Street, past the trendy design shops, the art galleries, the well-heeled pubescent girls sexualized into tarts from a flasher's fantasy. Was it just my fancy that she was looking younger? Was it another that the fuzz above her upper lip had mysteriously vanished?

'You take *Scooter World* these days?'

'Aye, it's a good read,' she said. 'Big Frankie's been teaching me to ride his machine.'

'You're kidding. What on earth for?'

'Somebody started to teach me long ago,' she said. 'My American friend Charlie? The one who was killed, remember? Well we never got round to it before they sent him home. Suddenly I saw a second chance and I decided to take it. It's a new principle I'm adhering to these days.'

'Are you glad you came to us Miss Wishart?' I asked. I'd never bothered to ask before. 'Not homesick for your islands and lochs?'

'I have come to the conclusion, not without an ache in my heart, that being Scottish isn't all it's cracked up to be,' she replied. 'I feel I may have overvalued the importance of heather, good shortbread and, as you phrased it in the taxi, seeing the world in black and white.'

'Wow Miss Wishart,' I said. 'They'll be gutted at *The People's Friend.*'

'I no longer read that publication,' she replied. 'Dolores suggested I try *Marie Claire* and it's certainly opened my eyes. Do you remember, that night by the river, when Mr d'Orsay said I'd not done enough dancing in my life? Well there's a class starting at the community centre next week. For the over-sixty-fives. Something called salsa. I've put my name down.'

She pulled out a hanky and dabbed ice-cream from the corners of my mouth.

'I'm sorry I disappointed you when we met again Miss Wishart,' I said.

'Och well, perhaps we should both see ourselves as works in progress, Rory Blaine,' she replied. 'And is that not exciting? *Marie Claire* says we can achieve anything we want if we want it enough, though usually they're talking about a clitoral orgasm.'

I blushed and was rewarded with one of Elspeth Wishart's indisputable laughs. It was quite a dirty laugh too. Well well.

'A bairn of your own Rory Blaine,' she said again. 'You are blessed.'

As we approached the gates of Mount Royal, a pair of cherubs was clinging to the pillars. Close-up, they turned into Jacob and Jasper Trevelyan, precariously balanced on stepladders, trying to dismantle a necklace of bunting.

'Oh dear,' sighed Elspeth. 'They'd organized a surprise lunch. I was meant to whisk you both back here instead of going to that restaurant. I called Big Frankie from the Town Hall and told him what had happened. I'd asked for all this to be cleared by now.'

Wee Jacob waved from his wobbly perch. He tried for a sympathetic smile. From the opposite pillar his twin yelled down.

'Fuck 'em and chuck 'em, Rory. That's always been my policy.'

'Oh Jasper, really,' said Jacob.

A new architectural feature had been added to the North Front. Red, heart-shaped helium balloons; thirty or more, tied all along the balustrade that fringed the leads. I could see Vic and Big Frankie up there, one cutting the strings, the other collecting them in a bunch. When they noticed me they ducked down behind the parapet. But there must have been a sudden gust because the captured balloons now broke away, slowly rose up past the cupola and floated free into the hazy blue sky.

'He's no oil painting but you could do a lot worse,' said Elspeth.

She gave me one of her sharp-jawed, meaningful looks. I remembered her confusion in the taxi when I'd said there was already someone to fill the gap left by Faisal. I'd been referring to Dolores, but she'd thought I'd meant somebody else.

'A lot worse,' she repeated, gazing up to the roof.

Christ, me and Big Frankie? Surely she was barking up the wrong palm-tree there? After Vic's betrayal of his devotion, Frankie had returned to his booming self with surprising speed. Recently, he and Gentleman Jim had started batting practice behind the Coach House and his latest T-shirt said *Sticky Wicket*. So my money had been on Jim not me.

'I'd have to buy a wider bed Miss Wishart.'

'Whatever his faults, he's a good soul and that's all that matters.'

Elspeth and I stood watching as the red hearts disappeared over the house and lost themselves out above the Heath. But one, perhaps deflated by the outcome of the day, drifted downwards and crash-landed near my feet. On it had been printed, in intertwining capitals, the letters 'F & R.'

*

Hugo Boss would not have been a happy bunny. I'd just slept for three hours, fully dressed in one of his most expensive little numbers. Elspeth had suggested a wee lie-down and she'd been right. I'd switched off the mobile and crashed straight out on top of the bed. When I'd switched it on again, there had been five calls from Faisal. I decided he could wait.

The internal phone rang. It was Elspeth. She wondered if I wanted her to come over; she could bring her knitting. I said I was fine. The phone rang again. Big Frankie wondered if he could bring me something to eat; I'd probably not feel like cooking for one. I said not to bother, I was fine. The doorbell rang. It was Marcus Leigh. The chaps all wondered if I'd like to join them for a spot of croquet? I said no thanks, I was fine. He touched my arm shyly, his eyes lowered. He said he understood how I must be feeling; the sudden loss. If I changed my mind later, they'd be in the Saloon after dinner and would be so glad to see me for a nightcap. There was a note on the doormat: '*Lucky escape. Dolores X.*'

I made some coffee and sat by the picture window. It was nearly six by now. If I craned my neck, I could just see them playing croquet; flannels, blazers, white trilbys, the occasional sweater draped across the shoulders and knotted at the front. There were cries of 'Damn fine stroke', 'Hard cheese, old chap', and 'For god's sake Beaumont, it's not golf.' There were now eight calls and three texts from Faisal, asking me to ring him. Okay then, so how much did I mind about this? Ms Prada will want to know exactly. Hurt, humiliated, angry, relieved, down-on-my-knees thankful. They're all in there baby; you sort it out, you've got the diplomas. The mobile went again. I didn't answer. Maybe I would some-time, but not now. I did one of Ms Prada's deep breathing exer-cises then went and got the guitar, but I only played a few chords; *Marie's Wedding* just wouldn't happen tonight. I must have sat there for an hour or more then I scavenged in the kitchen; I'd had nothing since breakfast except the ice-cream with Elspeth. In among Faisal's muesli bars and organic porridge, I found a jumbo bag of kettle chips and demolished the lot.

The croquet players had drifted away towards their rooms. Baths would be running, the evening news on TV, smarter clothes laid out for dinner. In the kitchens Big Frankie would be yelling at his slaves; the Chamber-Laddies laying the long walnut table. The house would be buzzing but from my chair all I could hear was the distant splash of the Great Fountain and the soft purr of Alma as she dozed against my ankles. The sun was still shining in a streaky-bacon sky, but the shadows were lengthening across the croquet lawn. Summer was quietly passing its peak and begin-ning the cruise downhill towards September. I was just thinking about taking a shower and going back to bed with a DVD when the bloody doorbell rang again. It was Vic. He said I looked like shit and a walk round the gardens would do me good. I said I was fine, but he was insistent. I warned him not to expect much conversation.

He was moving fairly well again, the black eye almost gone. Over the past few days, his melancholy had seemed to fade a bit too but tonight I sensed it again. Or perhaps, like Marcus, he was just trying to empathize with my sad loss. We slowly circled the Great Fountain and sat down outside the Orangery. We didn't speak, just watched the evening; we'd known each other long enough now for silence to be comfortable. I remembered that night when Vic had told Faisal to stuff *The Lazarus Programme*, to just let him sit in the Italian Garden and contemplate the bees buzzing in the honeysuckle. I understood what he'd meant now. I could have sat here for ages, forever even, but suddenly Vic got up.

'Toots, I know you've had a tough day, but there's something we have to do.'

I groaned a protest but he'd suddenly become tense, agitated even, so I trudged after him between the ornamental cherry trees, past the fat yews towards the edge of Mount Royal's grounds till we reached the wall of the long-abandoned garden called the Wilderness. I realized he was heading straight for the crumbling doorway that led inside. I told him I didn't want to go in there; it was dangerous, a jungle, and besides it was nearly dusk. Vic said he really wanted to show me something. I protested again but he became even more fractious. We'd been handling him with kid gloves for the last few weeks, so I obeyed.

Dolores had got quite shiny-eyed when she'd come across the Wilderness with the wee ruined folly, the long thin finger of man-made water, the ornamental bridge that crossed over it. An amazing project she'd said; one for the horticultural magazines, an award-winner maybe. She was itching to get hold of it. But I'd told her no, to leave it locked, to forget it. We'd argued. She'd wanted reasons. I'd refused to give them. She'd sulked for days. I'd not been in there for more than thirty years.

But now I was wading through the thigh-high grass. Buddleias had grown as big as bungalows and blowsy rhododendrons, squashed together like people in a lift, pushed skywards desperate for air and light. Vic was leading the way, walking faster than I'd imagined possible. The going got tougher by the yard; gangs of psychotic brambles clawed at Hugo Boss. It was ridiculous; I could really do without this tonight. And of course the tableau had started to flash in my mind; the one I'd spent a lifetime trying to erase. We skirted the finger of choked-up water, where a rowdy colony of underclass toads were having some sort of do among the reeds. I yelled out that I wasn't going any further but he shouted back that I must come. The usual drawl had corkscrewed into a rasp.

Then, on the far side of the decrepit bridge, I saw it. Half-buried in foliage, its classical lines blurred and softened, it seemed almost harmless now but still I shivered. As we got closer, a flurry of birds panicked from the ivy, fleeing up and away through the tangled branches. I hung back, heart pounding, wishing I could do the same. But Vic had battled ahead and vanished inside. I shouted after him to come out, that it was a death-trap. Then the gloom in the little chamber was dispelled by a pinprick of light.

'Rory, come inside,' he called.

'I don't want to, Victor. Let's go back now.'

'No, you must come. I know why you don't want to, but you must come.'

'What the hell do you mean by that?'

I crept towards the open doorway at an angle, as if something might leap out at me. Something did. The smell of the place, just as I remembered it; a pot-pourri of rotting vegetation and mouldering marble, even more intense now with three more decades of dereliction.

Inside the chamber, Vic had stuck a candle in a bottle. It flickered over the crusty face of Apollo on his plinth. Vic was standing beside the statue, his arm draped around its shoulders. He didn't look at me or say anything. He just stood there, frozen. The tableau.

I suppose my mouth was hanging open, which made it easier for the projectile vomiting of the kettle chips onto the flotsam of soggy leaves and the atrophied corpses of long-dead toads. Vic reached an arm out towards me, but I backed away and sagged against the crumbling door frame. I had an overwhelming urge to run but my knees wouldn't work. I wiped the foul dribbles off my chin with the back of my hand. My stomach muscles ached and my throat was stinging so much I'm not sure I could have spoken even if I'd known what to say.

'Toots, I'm not a man who's done anything very dreadful in his life, give or take the occasional lousy 'B' side,' he said in a half-whisper, the words sneaking out between gulps of breath, 'but I did a truly bad thing that night over thirty years ago on this very spot. Because of me you lost your home and the love that had been there for you. I wanted to try and give it back to you. That's what it's all been about, changing your grandmother's will, restoring the house, everything. I did it all for you.'

Vic turned away so I couldn't see his face. He brushed the dirt off a stone bench and slumped down, staring at the teeny skeletons on the floor.

'My only excuse is that you dazzled me, blinded me to the wrong I was doing. Sorry, I know it's all a bit *Death In Venice* though I'd never been into teenage boys in the slightest, I swear it. And anyway, you were nearly sixteen, you'd said. Almost a man. It was you who tempted me in here and I knew what you wanted. But I still never forgave myself.'

I'd gradually slid down the lintel and was sitting on the dirty floor. It was too late to save Hugo Boss; the brambles had done for him and now he had sick in his crotch. It seemed about a hundred years since I'd got up this morning and headed for Camden Town Hall. I must ring this date in next year's diary and simply not get up.

'A while later I heard from my buddy, your grandmother's lawyer, that you seemed to have been more or less banished from Mount Royal, though he didn't know why. But I did of course and I was devastated. Over the next few years, I asked him casually about you often, then he told me you'd disappeared abroad. For ages, I wondered how to put it right. Eventually I guess I tried to bury the whole thing in my memory and got on with turning myself into a national treasure. Then what do you know? By sheer chance, her Ladyship landed in my nursing home. She had the beginnings of Alzheimer's by then and didn't remember me at all. I should have hated her I suppose, but I couldn't manage that. She was so pathetic and I'd done *her* such harm too you see. Anyway, by this time we were living in a Google world and I tracked you down. I woke from a snooze that day beside her bed and there you were. Wow. Middle-aged and a bit of a bruiser now, but I was dazzled once more. All the time we were cleaning up Sibyl's poo, when we had coffee in the lounge, when you gave me that hug goodbye, I was watching for the recognition to dawn in your eyes but it never came. I loved you again from that day.'

I knew I should say something. I'd stopped shivering and was sweating now.

'From then on, I craved your visits like a drug,' said Vic. He was talking faster now, pumping out the sentences as if scared that I might try to stop him.

'At first I told myself not to be a sad old asshole, that my feelings could never be returned. But I sensed an aimlessness in you, a lack of direction maybe. And I began to fantasize that I might be, I don't know, some sort of safe harbour. Despite the age gap, despite the fact that when I bend over now there's a partial eclipse of the sun. The day I moved into this house I was groggy with hope. Nasty shock when the dusky midget appeared but I told myself it was just sex and that he'd pass through your life like a gallstone. So you'll understand why I had a bit of bother getting my Weetabix down this morning after you'd gone off to be hitched. And coming right on top of the tear-jerking discovery of the long-lost kid, well it's all seemed a bit hopeless. I mean what the fuck would you need *me* for? I'd saved Mount Royal for you, this place where I'd dreamed that we might have been together and it had all been a total waste of time. I was just another one of Rory's Boys. Silly old fool. The whisky's been useful so far but I think I might need to track down some absinthe pretty soon.'

There was silence now inside the folly, broken only by the toads still partying in the pond outside. A breeze had got up and it whistled in through the open doorway, stirring up the fetid smells and the images of that other night. The long Givenchy sheath, muddied and torn. The Malacca cane that quivered then fell. The look in her eyes as she stared down at me.

'So I'm the one you heard the trumpets for?' I managed to ask, the puke still burning in my gullet.

'And the walls came a-tumbling down.'

'You're telling me all this now Faisal's gone, now there's a vacancy?'

'Possibly. I don't know,' said Vic. 'I've never been sure whether I'd ever tell you about the past. I've always been careful to hide away photos of me when I was younger, old album sleeves, that sort of thing. I'd even hoped it might never be necessary to confess; that we'd draw closer anyway and everything would be fine. So maybe today's just the catalyst. But I just couldn't keep it inside me for even one more sleepless night, lying in my bed, getting smaller. Not one. And now *que sera, sera.*'

'As your old pal Doris used to sing.'

'Yep.'

I pulled myself to my feet and said I was returning to the house. He asked me to stay and talk but I turned and went out into the Wilderness. I heard him call my name, but I kept on going. When I reached the far end of the finger of water I glanced back towards the folly. It was almost invisible now in the gathering dusk. I wondered if he'd be all right. I could still just see the pinprick of candlelight, then it was suddenly snuffed out. Just as it had been all those years ago.

SEVENTEEN

Whatever the village might once have been, it had forgotten long ago. Perched on a bluff above a winding, unpretentious river, the Chilterns crumpled on the eastern horizon, it ought to have been appealing, the apple of an estate agent's eye. There was a decent Norman church, a sprinkling of thatched cottages, even a Georgian manor house mentioned in Pevsner. But it was blighted by a thirties council estate, bus-shelters doused in graffiti and a playground with peeling swings, where hard-faced young mothers smoked their fags while their kids screamed expletives in competition with the birdsong.

The farm was on the outskirts, but with its back turned against the village, somehow not quite part of it. It looked run-down; shabby barns with corrugated iron roofs streaked with birdshit, the fossils of elderly tractors beached in the fields. The small farmhouse was pebble-dashed in grey; yellowing net curtains at every window to repel the curiosity of the passer-by; an ironic precaution since anyone would have quickened their step at the sight of it. Dolores' vowels might have suggested some Laurie Lee idyll, but the reality of the place where she'd grown up had no such romance.

We sat in the Merc outside the farm gate. This was as far as we were going, she said. She'd no idea if Mr Potts were at home. There wasn't going to be any meeting of her two Dads; she enjoyed a good soap-opera but flatly refused to appear in one. So we'd just driven round and about; I'd been shown her primary school, her secondary school, the local Asda where she'd worked in the holidays, the dog-eared antique shop where she'd lost her virginity to a middle-aged dealer she'd always assumed to be gay. She'd flaunted herself and got more than she'd bargained for; including a pregnancy swiftly followed by a termination. Her parents had known nothing. Her mother would have thrown herself under the combine harvester. Jesus, I'd been a grandfather for about five minutes and known nothing about it.

'There were times I wished Mama had aborted *me*,' said Dolores, peering at the farmhouse from behind a vast pair of shades. 'She wasn't exactly a million laughs. That whole Catholic number, you know? No control over their own lives. Do what the old arsehole in Rome tells you to do. Fuck that.'

'But surely it's thanks to all that stuff that she didn't abort you?' I said it with a grin, to mask the horror that had coursed through me at the thought of it. 'So three Hail Marys for the old arsehole. But I'm sorry you and your mother didn't get along.'

'Actually no, we were quite close in some ways but I was her shame too you see. Only Mr Potts ever knew in fact and she wasn't much bothered about that. It was God knowing that really did her in. You want to go see her now?'

'Sorry?'

'She's in the churchyard,' said Dolores. 'I thought you might like to renew your acquaintance. In fact, I insist that you do.'

I'd not reckoned on this; I'd just suggested a sentimental journey as a possible way of kick-starting the bonding process. She'd agreed but only under pressure. There was still that arm's-length thing going on. I'd no clear idea how she felt towards me. On the night of the big disclosure, she'd said she'd just come to take a look at me. Was that it then? Was that all it would ever be? Maybe it was just her generation and its armour-plated obsession with its own agenda. She'd hardly even raised an eyebrow when she'd heard about the death of Caravaggio; just said 'shit' and begun talking about a copper beech that might need felling. I wondered how you got through to Dolores Potts.

I parked the Merc carelessly close to a gang of feral schoolgirls and followed Dolores through a lychgate and up a sloping path lined with graves. In front of us, the church tower leaned back against a mouse-grey sky. Dolores veered off among the tombstones. Her mother, garlanded with freshly-laid flowers, lay in the shelter of the perimeter wall. On the other side of it, somebody's TV pumped out of an open window. Fern Britton was talking about cystitis.

Cristina Gomez Potts. 1963–2010.

I looked at the headstone and tried, yet again, to bring the face into focus. Dolores had shown me an old photograph but it hadn't helped much. All I recalled were a couple of dates, me half-pissed, another naked body lying on a bed waiting for me to prove myself a proper man. I suppose I'd never been bothered about the faces. Just like I'd never registered Vic's.

'Isn't this nice?' said Dolores sitting on an adjacent tomb and lighting up. 'The family together at last.'

She stared at her mother's grave then back at me. Suddenly

her expression changed from its usual disengaged serenity. She looked desperately uncomfortable.

'This was a mistake,' she announced, leaping up and grinding her fag beneath her red stiletto. 'Come on, let's go.'

Something made me grab her arm as she moved past me. Mascara was trickling down her cheek.

'You fucked up her life,' she shouted. 'She only got forty-seven years of it and you fucked it up for her. She fell in love with you and let you screw her. The good Catholic girl. Didn't you even notice she was a virgin? Then you just disappeared. On to the next one, yeah? But every day for the rest of her life Mama looked at me and saw you. That was why she loved me and why she was so hard on me too.'

'I had no idea...' I said. 'If I'd known... I meant her no harm...'

'People never do, do they?'

'I was a bit screwed up, that's all.'

'And you still are, aren't you? Twenty-six years later, you came on to *me*. Isn't it time you accepted yourself? It's unbelievable in this day and age, it really is. Anyway, you're now one of the most famous shirtlifters in the country, so what's the bloody point? Grow up Daddy before you grow old.'

Dolores turned away from me. She scraped a match across the scabby catafalque of some ancient nobleman and lit up again.

'I just wanted the whole shebang,' I said. 'It's what I'd been brought up to expect. To have anything I wanted; like kids for example. Instead, I lost everything.'

'Oh it's always about you, isn't it?' she snapped. 'Rory Blaine, centre of the fucking universe. So your grandmother dumped you cos you were a poof. I wormed it out of Elspeth. Big deal. Cry me a river. Well you walked away from my mother. You'd been injured and then you caused injury because of it. Even if you didn't mean it, the pain still happened. So you're quits with life, aren't you? Now butch up and get over it.'

Dolores walked back to the grave, knelt down and crossed herself.

'I thought you didn't subscribe to all that,' I said.

'I don't, but she'd like to see me here doing it, so what the hell.'

I wondered if I should kneel down too but just stood there awkwardly. On the other side of the wall, Fern Britton had moved on to teenage truancy. A boy called Shane was explaining why school was a load of bollocks.

'Your photograph's in there among the bones,' said Dolores, 'along with her rosary and a fragment of stone from the cathedral in Sevilla. I put it there myself. Mr Potts doesn't know.'

'Jesus.'

'I guess if Cupid's arrow hits you hard, you're fucked,' she said. 'I wonder what it's like.'

'I'm told you hear trumpets,' I said.

A young curate, scarce out of short trousers but already balding, held open the lychgate to let us pass. He smiled in that automatic way and hoped we'd enjoyed our time with God today.

'Well *did* you enjoy it?' I asked Dolores as we reached the car. 'Getting all that off your capacious chest?'

'Not really.'

'You don't hate me then?'

'Maybe, right after Mama died, but only for about five minutes. And when I came to Mount Royal I soon realized you were just a messed-up bloke like the rest of them. Then I discovered I kind of liked you too. But I wanted you to know about this, which is why I agreed to this little awayday. Anyway, whatever I've said, you're still my Dad. Now let's get the hell out of here before we bump into the other one. '

I glanced back across at the churchyard and in that moment Cristina Gomez's face came to me at last. She'd tripped over a cable in the office and twisted her ankle. I'd scooped her up in my arms like Rhett Butler and carried her to the first aid room. She'd been wincing and laughing at the same time. She'd had a high tinkling laugh. I could see her big dark eyes, the ones she'd given to her daughter, and feel her breath on my cheek.

For a moment, I thought my new-found ability to blub, so far revealed only to Elspeth's lap, was going to prove itself again. Instead I just stared back at the churchyard till Dolores came round and took me in her arms. This time there was no tension in her body as I held her.

'Come on Daddy,' she said, rubbing my back like she was burping a baby. 'Time for drinkies.'

I'd booked lunch at a posh place nearby; a Tudor inn with bulging walls, guarded by regiments of box pyramids and glossy young men who valet-parked your car. Dolores was just as at home as she'd been in the Ritz. I wondered how the girl from the drab farmhouse had transformed herself into what she was now. How long it had taken. What the trigger had been. Or maybe I knew the answer to that last one now.

We needed to talk about trivialities. Vic was recording his duet with Elton soon. Did I think Vic would let her tag along? I said to ask him herself. I hadn't spoken to Vic in the three days since our melodrama in the Wilderness. I had no idea where we went from here. I'd been finding reasons to escape from the house; yesterday I'd gate-crashed Curtis Powell's group outing to the V&A, today I was here with Dolores. It couldn't go on.

Over the pudding, she announced she was going away for a long weekend. An old client had a new estate above Monte Carlo. He wanted her advice and she'd always been interested in Mediterranean planting. More of a challenge than England's rain-soaked earth, she said. Tougher odds. She liked that. She hoped I didn't mind her doing the odd outside commission. I lied and said I didn't.

She asked if I'd heard from Faisal and I told her I hadn't. She looked at me from beneath her long Spanish lashes and toyed with her sorbet.

'Well,' she sighed eventually, 'I think you've had a lucky escape.'

'So you said in your note,' I replied, mildly irritated. 'Maybe everyone has a view? What's Bruce Willis's opinion? Have the Chamber-Laddies taken a vote?'

'He was a decent guy, but not exactly a comfortable presence, was he?'

'Maybe not. But at least, he was a presence. I happened to need that. Or I thought I did.'

'I think you still do,' she said. 'Just choose more carefully next time. You understand feng shui? The way things are positioned in relation to each other? It's quite useful when you're planning a garden. Well I reckon you can apply it to people too. We get too close to some, too distant from others or just see them from the wrong angle. And all the time we could create a much happier space for ourselves if we simply repositioned.'

'Isn't that a bit rich coming from someone whose default position in relation to others is horizontal?'

Dolores threw back her head and laughed louder than people were expected to when paying these prices.

'Yeah but that's the position I've chosen for myself, right now at least. I'll change it when it suits me. Anyway, how dare you presume it's horizontal?'

One of the glossy boys swept the Merc up to the entrance and handed Dolores inside. She asked if his mother knew he was out. He was smitten. We twisted back along the lanes that led to the motorway As I accelerated towards London, Dolores reclined her seat and dozed off.

I'd called Ms Prada's office yesterday. She was no longer in Lanzarote but had extended her itinerary to take in Madeira. Useless. We were nearly at High Wycombe when I swung the car onto the hard shoulder and slammed to a halt. Dolores sat bolt upright and swore. I stared ahead out through the windscreen and told her everything that had happened in the Wilderness three nights and thirty years ago. I left nothing out. When I finished, I turned to look at her. She smiled back at me, shaking her spiky black head.

'Wow, that's the most beautiful story I've ever heard,' she said.

A Highways Agency patrol van pulled up behind us. The driver knocked on the window and asked if we needed any assistance. Couldn't people have a private conversation these days, I asked? He said he'd report me for unauthorized use of the hard shoulder. I told him to bugger off.

'You've done it again, haven't you?' said Dolores.

'Fucking surveillance society.'

'No, I mean you've made somebody else love you,' she said. 'Think very hard before you turn your back this time. You've got form, remember?'

We didn't speak again till the gates of Mount Royal swung open before us. Then she repeated what she'd said earlier.

'Just reposition yourself. That's all you've got to do.'

*

'The boy has come back,' said Lord Billy, peering out the window of the Breakfast Room as he heaped scrambled eggs onto his plate.

I followed his gaze and saw the old Peugeot trundle into the East Court and park bang up against the Merc. Faisal had always done that, even when there was loads of space; an unsubtle dig at what he considered my vulgar materialism. Two suitcases came out of the boot and disappeared into the flat. Shite. And I'd been having such a nice breakfast.

I'm never exactly great first thing but now, three or four times a week, this was where I started the day. Vic had suggested it and, on the days when I wasn't there, he'd make sure he was. He'd said it would engender *ésprit de corps* and demonstrate the management's commitment to customer care. The Breakfast Room was one of the few spaces in Mount Royal you might have called cosy. On bright mornings, the sun poured itself onto your cornflakes, a factor which had led Robin Bradbury-Ross to ban the hanging of any first-rate pictures. So instead of grim Madonnas or martyred saints, the yellow flock walls were cheered by Edwardian water-colours of seaside resorts. Littlehampton looked particularly nice.

Most of the guys appeared for breakfast. There were four well-spaced round tables, so those who didn't want to chat could hide behind their newspaper. Lord Billy often sat alone; he seemed to read Nancy Mitford on a constant loop, splashing coffee on his djellabah and exclaiming how droll it was. Nancy herself had once dubbed him the seventh Mitford Girl; a compliment he treasured above any other.

Marcus Leigh was always there, in blazer and tie at half past eight, his day meticulously mapped out by lunch at his beloved Reform, an exhibition or a matinee or a trip out to Cheltenham to visit his centenarian nanny. He'd lightened up a bit lately, competing with Curtis Powell to see who could finish *The Times* crossword quickest. Curtis was nearly always first for breakfast, sweaty and smug from his jog, still in tracksuit, baseball cap and matching heart-rate monitor; though Beau never appeared, because Angela Lansbury had told him a star never faced the public before ten. Mr Lim would sit quietly behind his pebble-glasses, sipping tea and issuing dire warnings to anyone drinking orange juice, slow suicide for the enamel. The Toffee Twins would be side by side as usual, Jacob fussing to make sure Jasper had a full cup and seconds of sausage and bacon, which Jasper always took without thanking him.

The Archdeacon had just been complaining about a note slipped under his door during the night. It was headed 'Miss Wishart Suggests...' and it turned out they'd all been getting them on a regular basis. The notes were eclectic, from reprimands over unfinished meals and alcohol intake to disapproval over returning in the wee small hours, in which case the culprit would be

advised to have an early night and perhaps even a purgative. The
Archdeacon said his note was of too intimate a nature to disclose,
but that it concerned bed-linen. Miss Wishart was a servant he
said and perhaps I might like to remind her of that? I tried to
imagine myself doing so.

This morning I'd been sitting beside Gentleman Jim. He was
the only one who appealed to my blokeish side. I hated cricket,
but we talked about rugby; I'd offered to take him to see the gay
team. He loved to go hiking in Scotland too, it reminded him of
New Zealand. He'd shyly suggested we might go up there together
sometime and I'd surprised myself by agreeing. I'd been away too
long. He'd been nattering about a possible itinerary when Lord
Billy had looked out the window.

'The boy has come back,' he said again, louder this time,
assuming I hadn't heard.

A hush had fallen in the Breakfast Room, broken only by the
crunching of toast. I went on talking to Gentleman Jim about the
sunset over Loch Maree, till he placed his palm on the back of my
hand and rubbed it briskly, as if I'd just come in from the cold.

'Courage, mate,' he said.

I smiled and got up. As I passed his table, Marcus Leigh
reached out and squeezed my fingers without glancing up from
The Times. In the lobby, a voice called down from the top of the
East Stairs. Two floors above, Beau and his belly were leaning
over the balustrade. He was wearing a bathrobe that was about
three sizes too small.

'Hey babe, I saw the midget arrive,' he shouted. 'Just wanted to
say we all love you. You gotta know that by now.'

I reached the front door of the flat as Faisal was coming back
out to his car. We approached each other, eyes not meeting, like
on that first date outside Covent Garden tube. He was sorry for
being earlier than we'd agreed but he had a lot to get through
today. He'd just get more suitcases from the car and come back in
a minute. I went up and put the kettle on.

He sipped his coffee in a chair as far from mine as possible.
He was flying to the Sudan tonight. He'd arranged extended leave
from the hospital and was going to work with his friend Ruby. I
imagined her, sitting outside a tent with a smirk on her fat face,
saying that she'd told him so.

Things in Slough had gone from bad to worse. His father had

been readmitted to hospital and the truth about Faisal's sexuality had finally exploded into his wider family. His father's brothers had arrived at Khan's Tools & Hardware and demanded that his mother leave with them; she'd resisted at first but they'd more or less dragged her off. His uncles intended to look after the business. It had all been pretty awful.

'So I'm running,' he said. 'I've got a Blue in that, remember? I know it's cowardly, but I don't know what else to do. I seem to be the cause of so much grief I think it's best if I remove myself for a while.'

'Leaving your mother to the bigots?' I said. 'I'll survive without you Faisal, but will she?'

'I don't know,' he said. 'I've been trying to save her from them for years, but they're too powerful for me.'

He got up to get the coffee pot. He tried to tickle Alma's chin but she leapt away. She'd never taken to Faisal.

'I'm really sorry about the other day,' he said over his shoulder. 'I still care very much for you and I always will.'

He came and sat on the Berber rug at my feet and took both my hands in his. 'Rory, I just don't know where I fit,' he said. 'It's not in Khan's Tools & Hardware, I always knew that. It's not in this big house with these rich old men. I always knew that too. But I thought that maybe it could be right here, in this flat with you, hermetically sealed against everything and everybody. But that was cloud-cuckoo land. They were all in here with us, weren't they? So maybe the only place Faisal Khan really belongs is beside a hospital bed with a stethoscope in my hand, a reassuring smile on my face and up to my arse in little black babies. Anyway, that's how it feels right now, so that's where I'm going.'

He stood up and drained his cup. A removal van would be coming in a few days to take his bigger stuff into storage. He looked down at his precious Berber rug, the old coffee stains still visible.

'Shame we couldn't rescue that,' he said. 'Chuck it out if you want.'

We went downstairs to the bedroom. The glitzy clothes I'd bought him were still on the rails. He ran his hand along the suits and jackets then closed the doors.

'I'll not be wanting those,' he said. 'They were just the props for being Rory Blaine's boyfriend, weren't they? Or "paramour", as your devoted Vic once put it. But I guess I was wrong for the part.'

'So it's life with Ruby from now on then?'

'No, it's life with Faisal,' he replied. 'Just me. Just me and the stuff I do best. For a while, anyway.'

'Don't wander out there alone for too long,' I said.

'Well at least you'll not be alone, will you?' he said 'That's partly what makes it possible for me to leave. You'll be okay now, Rory.'

'You going to say goodbye to anybody?' I asked. 'Elspeth, Dolores and Big Frankie even? I know they'd like it.'

'No, but give them all my very best. I really mean that.'

I took him in my arms. It was all so familiar; the smell and feel of him, the reflex bending of my knees. It had lasted just over eighteen months.

Together we filled his cases with more stuff and carried them out into the East Court. He stared across at the house for a moment; figures darted away from the windows of the Breakfast Room.

'Well I guess Lazarus isn't going to rise after all,' he said. 'But try and watch their diets and get them in the pool a couple of times a week, yeah? All their medical notes are in a file in the desk and you'll need to fix up another private GP quickly. Now listen, Marcus Leigh has just been for some tests. It's possible he has the beginnings of Parkinson's. Results next week, but you don't know that unless he chooses to tell you. Just wanted you to be aware, okay? He might be needing a lot of support.'

'He'll get it,' I said.

'You'd not throw him out, would you? Later on, if things get worse? I know that was supposed to be the rule.'

'No, I'd not do that now,' I said.

He promised to email me from the Sudan then handed me his keys to the flat. I refused to take them. There was always a room for him here, I said. But he pushed them into my palm and closed my fingers.

'And hey, thanks for the laughs,' he said. 'I'd not had enough of those till I met you. Everything had always seemed too important. Maybe it still does. But I'll try and do better from now on.'

He got into his car and, without looking at me again, turned towards the arch below the Clock Tower. As I watched it go, the old Peugeot morphed into another car, in the same place but in another time. A Ford Capri, with seats of cracked beige leather, driven by a sweaty man with long hair, a droopy moustache and wide lapels, hired to take me to Euston to catch the train back to Glenlyon. It'd been a fine late summer morning, just like this one. For a second, I closed my eyes against the image and, when I opened them, Faisal was gone.

Suddenly the East Court became Dodge City when the gunfight was over. The citizens popped out again and bustled about their business. Doors were opened and windows flung wide. Elspeth shook out her duster and waved down at me. Big Frankie passed with bin-liners of rubbish and a cheery wink. The Post Office van swung under the Clock Tower and one of the Chamber-Laddies zoomed in late on his rollerblades.

'There's some soggy scrambled eggs still left,' said a voice behind me. 'I hear your breakfast got interrupted.'

It'd been five days since I'd left him in the Wilderness as the dusk came down.

'Thanks. That'd be good,' I said.

Vic turned and preceded me into the house, holding open the East Door and ushering me in with a mock bow.

'All right?' he asked as I passed through.

'Yes thanks, Victor,' I replied. And I knew that I was. Sort of.

Hilarity spilled out of the Breakfast Room. Gentleman Jim had been trying to sing a Scottish song for Curtis Powell and failing to remember the lyrics. When they saw me the laughter was replaced by tight smiles, shyly lobbed in my direction. But I knew every daft word of the song, verses and all. It didn't take long to teach them the chorus and ten minutes later I was leading fifteen elderly homosexuals in an uninhibited rendition of *Donald, Where's Yer Troosers?* Amazing the power of community singing to lift the spirits. It had worked for Baden-Powell and his boys and today it worked for Rory Blaine and his.

'Jeez, toots, you can sing,' said Vic.

*

After breakfast I went to check my emails. There was one from Dolores, away on her jaunt to Monte Carlo. It was the dream project, she said. It could make her reputation. Trouble was they were insisting on it being full-time. So with regret she was handing in her resignation at Mount Royal. She'd be back in a few days but had wanted to let me know at once. She hoped I'd understand. She was sure I'd want the best for her.

EIGHTEEN

The fire started sometime after midnight. It was Big Frankie who'd spotted it. His spanking new telescope had been sweeping the East Front in the hope, he'd confessed later, 'of a glimpse of somethin' tasty'. After Vic's betrayal with Caravaggio and despite his embryonic affection for Gentleman Jim, Frankie now clearly regarded himself as unattached. The new telescope was amazing, he said. Now he could even see the hair up their noses. Whitey papis look out.

Tonight, he'd zeroed in on Lord Billy sitting at his window, blowing the smoke from a cigarillo out into the darkness. Smoking in the apartments was strictly forbidden and Frankie, fiercely loyal, had determined to report it to Elspeth in the morning. Then he'd gone for a quick bedtime chat with the Virgin and when he'd looked again Lord Billy had seemed sort of slumped and with a reddish glow flickering behind him.

Frankie had called the Fire Brigade then pounded on my door. We charged into the house, both of us still half-naked. I smashed the nearest fire alarm and flew up to Lord Billy's apartment. He lolled in his chair, a rug near him well ablaze, the curtains on the four-poster starting to crinkle and smoulder. On the quilt lay a dismantled smoke alarm, its guts spilling out.

I told Frankie to haul him out and sprinted off to bang on more doors. Anxious faces in dressing-gowns appeared; we'd not got round to a fire drill yet. I ordered them to leave everything, get outside and assemble on the grass. Once I'd got round all the bedrooms, I ran outside myself. The Vampire had opened the gates for the Fire Brigade, but where the hell were they? I ordered him to call them again. Lord Billy was sitting on the grass, coughing violently and asking for brandy. I told him he could have his brandy later, but that there would be strychnine in it. I started doing a head count.

'Boss, where's Mr d'Orsay?' yelled Big Frankie.

My eyes raked across the flustered faces. Nobody else had seen him. Christ.

The Vampire raced back, mobile in hand. It was the first time I'd ever seen him move quickly; his piercings were jangling and there was even some colour in his cheeks. There had been a huge fire in Kilburn and a bomb scare in Swiss Cottage. All other fires were being graded according to danger to life. If everybody were out of the building, they'd get to us as soon as they could. I told him to inform them that inside Mount Royal was a much-loved national celebrity and if he fried it wouldn't look good in the papers. Curtis Powell grabbed my sleeve, his eyes awash with panic.

'The pictures and the furniture. We have to get them out,' he said.

'Agreed. But how?'

'I know every item. I can prioritize. We'll start a human chain.'

'Ok but lots of it's heavy. We need more people,' I said.

Elspeth was beside me now, fully dressed, but her hair still in pins.

'I'll get us more people,' she said. 'Frankie, where are the keys to your scooter?'

'But *doux-doux,* you're not ready...'

'The keys, laddie. Now!' she said.

Frankie and I hurried back up the main staircase. At the top, the smoke was drifting from the direction of Lord Billy's apartment. When I opened Vic's door, Alma flew past my ankles and vanished. Inside, the smoke invaded my eyes, my throat, my lungs. These rooms abutted Billy's; somehow it must have seeped through a vent.

Vic was sprawled in the doorway to his bedroom. His breathing was rapid and shallow with a scary wheezing from his chest. He seemed semi-delirious, tried to fight us off and it took a good minute to get him out onto the landing. But now Big Frankie had begun to cough violently, his face soaked with sweat and with water from his streaming eyes. I barked at him to get back out into the air; I didn't need two casualties instead of one. He'd started having hysterics about Vic and was useless anyway. Vic's wheezing had got worse and fluid dribbled from his mouth. I tried to drag him towards the stairs, hoping that his legs might kick in but it was impossible. Fuck knows how, but I got him up into a fireman's lift. Step by careful step, I staggered down the staircase, terrified I'd slip and that, by some grim irony, we'd both suffer the same fate as Caravaggio. Then the fear of the thing brought it about. I lost my footing and Vic went flying forwards. But the Vampire and Gentleman Jim had come in search of us and Vic was netted in their arms, neat as a trapeze act.

By now, old men in dressing gowns were scurrying in and out of the Gilded Hall with small pictures, candelabra, vases, chairs, anything they were able to carry. Curtis Powell ran around directing operations but he was a wee wizened David attempting a Goliath of a job.

Out on the grass, beneath the statue of Father Thyme, Vic lay covered by a blanket, somebody's jacket folded under his head. The ambulance was on its way. He'd started coughing now, so fiercely that I thought his whole frame might break like a ship on the rocks. Nobody could agree if giving him water was a good idea or not. Alma nuzzled against him while Beau mopped his brow and Big Frankie sat at his feet, in no great state himself. Vic's eyes focused in on me. His face was blackened and puffy; the white hair streaked with soot. He tried to speak but couldn't. I gave him my hand and he gripped it fiercely. He tried to speak again. I put my face closer.

'Cold,' he said in a parched whisper.

'Somebody get another blanket. Anything. Now.'

Vic shook his head and pointed at me.

'No. You. Cold,' he said.

I'd forgotten I was still only in my track-suit pants. I'd not realized before that I was shivering, but now I did. Beau gave me his sweater but it didn't seem to make any difference. I suddenly felt a terrible agitation sweep through me. My heart was thumping in my head. The shivering ratched itself up into an all-out trembling I couldn't control.

The Archdeacon came over and knelt beside us. He suggested a little prayer. Big Frankie crossed himself and clasped his hands.

'We don't need that shite Archdeacon,' I said, my voice now shaking like the rest of me. 'Vic's going to the Royal Free and no further. And then he'll be coming home. Do you hear me? Do you?'

Vic moaned and wagged an admonitory finger. He tried to smile at the Archdeacon before going into another wrench of coughing. Beau dabbed the dribble off his chin.

'Don't forget next week,' I said, forcing out a smile. 'The duet with Elton. You'll have to be fit for that. Get the voice sorted. Just think of the sales on your back catalogue. Okay?'

The ambulance screeched through the gates; revolving splinters of red light danced over us. An oxygen mask was clamped like an alien onto Vic's face. My old mate the paramedic murmured that he didn't look too brilliant now, but that the real risk would be in the next twenty-four hours with the chance of pneumonia or even a heart attack. He ordered that Lord Billy and Big Frankie should be taken to the hospital too; everybody else seemed physically okay. Vic was lifted onto a stretcher and levered into the ambulance. I climbed in behind him followed by Alma. Big Frankie sat stroking his forehead. Lord Billy was in a corner, in a vaguely foetal position, fretting about the mother-of-pearl box that contained his pills. I felt my rage boil up against him, the same rage I'd felt the night I'd hit Caravaggio as Vic had lain on the floor. Wanting to hurt anyone who hurt Vic.

The paramedic took off the oxygen mask to put a tube down his throat; to keep the airways clear, he said. But Vic pushed it away and grasped my hand.

'Save the house toots,' he whispered.

'Fuck the house,' I said 'I'm coming with you.'

'No,' he said, getting agitated, 'Save the goddamned house. For everyone's sake.'

'Okay, but I'll be right there in no time.'

The paramedic was anxious to put in the tube. Vic yelped as his singed throat tried to swallow it down; one hand still clenched in mine, the other clutching the cat. The paramedic said they needed to get moving right now. I felt myself start shaking again. The idea that he might not survive suddenly seemed like the worst thing that could ever happen. The event of thirty years ago, that I'd carried in me like a cancer, no longer mattered a damn. I wanted him to be here with me. Without him, Mount Royal would be as desolate as it had been on that day when I'd come back to it. I knew now that nobody had ever cared for me quite like he did and probably never would again. My grandmother had loved me once, Faisal had tried to and I hoped that Dolores might one day, but it was Vic who'd put himself on the line, who'd stayed the course with no reward, who'd thought of me before he thought of himself. My eyes were still red and dripping from the smoke; the perfect camouflage. I put my face right down to his.

'Don't you leave me, you hear me Victor?' I said. 'Don't you dare fucking leave me.'

Big Frankie was still stroking Vic's head. Now the huge hands suddenly drew back. I glanced up into his face. The sadness printed there was only momentary, then he smiled and told me not to worry; he'd take care of Vic till I got there. The paramedics more or less threw Alma and me out of the ambulance and it vanished screaming out of the gates.

It narrowly avoided collision with Big Frankie's lilac scooter, Elspeth in the saddle, her mad hair fanning out from under the helmet. Right behind her came half a dozen cars, soon followed by a squad of designer bicycles and then, minutes later, by a breathless bunch of thirty or forty running men. Some were in sports gear; shorts and singlets: a few were in full leathers, one in some kind of rubber suit. They came in all shapes and sizes; willowy boys, beer-bellied bears, Muscle-Marys built like characters off Play Station. There were even a couple of girls, except they weren't.

'There you go,' said Elspeth proudly. 'I rounded up my laddies from the Heath.'

So the aged human chain evacuating the treasures of Mount Royal was lengthened and rejuvenated. Under the direction of Curtis and myself, the most valuable pieces from the state-rooms were removed; pictures, furniture, tapestries. It wasn't easy; some of the stuff weighed a ton and there were paintings the size of garage doors. And by now, the smoke was pouring down into the Gilded Hall from the first floor. It wasn't nice in there. But they were inexhaustible and, not for the first time, I felt grateful for the pivotal role of the gymnasium in gay culture. The only problem was of momentum slowing down when somebody found himself holding a nice little Monet, unable to pass it on without at least half a minute's appreciation. I cantered back and forth along the length of the chain, encouraging, thanking. *Au contraire*, said a guy in a rubber vest; he'd been absolutely aching to see inside Mount Royal. He gave me his card, confirming my suspicion of a higher than average proportion of antique dealers in the line-up. The lower orders seemed equally humbled by the experience.

'It's part of our gay heritage now, innit, "*Withering Heights*"?' said a gorilla with rings through his nose, as he heaved a Queen Anne armchair to safety. 'Like the Coleherne.'

A slim boy dressed only in shorts had a nasty weal on his upper back.

'Careful son, you've hurt yourself,' I said.

'Nah, it's cool,' he said, 'I was bein' whipped when Elspeth come along on her bike. Crazy granny or what?'

'You call her Elspeth?'

'Oh yeah,' said the kid. 'She's a bit of a party-pooper like, with all her Jesus shit and leaflets about the clap, but I quite look forward to seeing her now. We're all gonna club together and get her something for Christmas. Like a fuckin' hair-do maybe.'

It was nearly two in the morning. The rag-bag battalion from the Heath had taken over the chain, allowing my old guys to take a break. Most were exhausted, just sitting on the grass or making sure others were all right. I went round checking on them, like Henry V at Agincourt.

I apologized to the Archdeacon for biting his head off. He forgave me with that irritating condescension which makes you want to kill all believers in anything. The deep pockets of his dressing-gown were bulging out like flying buttresses; no need to ask what he'd chosen to save from the flames. Wee Jacob Trevelyan was sobbing quietly, clinging to his brother's sleeve.

'Come on, Jacob,' I said, squatting down. 'We might be gay but there's no need to be girly.'

'I'm not gay actually,' he said. 'Jasper is, but I'm not. Well, I'm not anything really. I just go where Jasper wants to go. He's my other half, you see.'

'That's nice, Jacob,' I said.

'You'll not chuck me out now will you?' he asked.

'There might not be anywhere left to chuck you out of Jacob,' I said.

'Oh I'd hate to go now,' said Jacob. 'We'd all hate to go now.'

Curtis Powell stood staring at the house, his face so tight with tiredness the skull was poking through. He could be a pain in the arse, but he'd been brilliant tonight. If anybody else loved the house like I did, the bricks and mortar, the very smell of it, it was probably him.

'Grampa done good, yeah?' asked Beau, patting Curtis on the back.

'Grampa done good,' I agreed.

Beau was relieved he'd not had to climb down a turntable-ladder or anything; he just knew he'd have hurtled off like Jennifer Jones in *The Towering Inferno*. He was sure Vic would be okay; Vic had played the cabaret rooms of Las Vegas, those old lungs were smokeproof by now.

Marcus Leigh was standing apart from the others, leaning

against the statue of Father Thyme. He'd not said anything about his tests, to me at least, but it was pretty obvious something wasn't right. I slipped a matey arm round his shoulders and told him things would be fine. He pulled his dressing-gown more tightly around him and didn't reply.

Then, suddenly, deliverance. The real cavalry arrived. Two fat engines swung through the gates and in no time creamy-coloured hoses like giant tagliatelle ribboned into the Gilded Hall and up the staircase. Everyone was ordered out and the firemen flooded in. The tagliatelle swelled rigid as the water gushed into them. As they penetrated my fragile house, they seemed as scary as the tube that had been put into Vic's throat, but it was out of my hands now.

'It can't burn,' muttered Curtis, his gaze still clamped on the house. 'The lost palace. It mustn't burn.'

'It won't burn, Curtis,' I said with bravado I didn't feel. 'It's not fucking Manderley.'

I told Beau to get contact numbers for all the guys who'd come from the Heath; we'd have to find some way to thank them. Then I asked Elspeth if she was up for another scooter ride and we roared off towards the Royal Free. Having my arms locked tightly round Miss Wishart's waist seemed vaguely indecent, but the wind felt good on my hot dirty face. I threw my head back and closed my eyes; partly from fear, partly from the need to shut out the world, if only for a few seconds. Behind me the survival of Mount Royal was in the gift of strangers; in front of me, Vic was in exactly the same heap of shite.

'Miss Wishart, don't get all excited and think I've found religion,' I yelled as the lilac scooter took a wobbly left into East Heath Road. 'But I don't know the Poor Clares' number so would you pray for Vic now? For some crazy reason, it seems to have something going for it.'

'Do you think I've not been doing it already, Rory Blaine?' she shouted over her shoulder. 'But God will hear. He owes you Mr d'Orsay's life.'

'And why is that?'

'Because apart from the sad accident of that poor Italian boy, you've saved quite a few lives lately. Mine included,' she said. 'Now hang on, I don't like the look of this bend.'

The brutal bulk of the Royal Free loomed before us, its concrete face pocked by squares of yellowy light; harsh but somehow hopeful. I wondered behind which of them Vic now lay and what was waiting for me there. I hoped that Elspeth was right about my having brownie points with her God. I also hoped He'd forget that Vic did not approve of Him, would remember the innocent pleasure the King of Croon had given to millions and overlook the time he'd taken out his willy and waved it at the Singing Nun.

*

And the Lord heard her prayer and it was good. Or at least somebody did, because both Mount Royal and Vic'd'Orsay survived the night of the fire. In each case, the damage wasn't as bad as it looked. The firemen had commented that they'd known how to build them in the old days; the doctors had said much the same about Vic.

The blaze had more or less gutted Lord Billy's apartment but miraculously the wider damage, to Vic's suite and the adjacent corridors, was mostly smoke and soot. First thing next morning, Robin Bradbury-Ross had roared in with his English Heritage storm-troopers in a state of mild hysteria but, having evaluated the mess, he'd calmed down, run his tongue over his lower lip and said how much he looked forward to our working together on the restoration of the ravaged area.

Vic's passageways had been similarly scorched and his chambers filled with smoke but after a few hours in intensive care, they'd transferred him to a private room. But it was facing north and Vic didn't do north, so he kicked up a charming stink till he was moved to a sunnier one. That was when I knew he'd be all right. But his larynx wasn't up to recording the duet with Elton and he'd been replaced at the last minute by Lulu. Elton had sent a huge bunch of lilies and a card that read, 'Sorry luv, that's show-biz!' Vic was well pissed-off.

When they discharged him, he was still a bit weak. His own apartment wasn't yet habitable so I decided he'd move into the spare room in the flat. Everyone came out to welcome him back. There was much hugging and kissing of the air; even Bruce Willis embraced him in a self-conscious, macho way. Marcus Leigh instigated a rendition of 'For He's A Jolly Good Fellow' to which Vic responded with a short and graceful speech of the sort he'd been opening fêtes with for decades; only the phrase 'fuck Lulu' might have been thought ungracious.

Lord Billy seemed to hang back a bit from the crowd. He'd not suffered from the smoke as badly as Vic and, along with Frankie, had been sent home from hospital the day after. The guys had bent over backwards to forgive him, agreeing that it could have happened to anyone. A candle left burning. A faulty toaster maybe. Even, as Beau had suggested, the Archdeacon's DVD player exploding through overuse.

Back at the Royal Free that night, I'd marched into his A&E cubicle ready to bawl him out. He'd been lying there, pale as a wounded swan, pushing back his cuticles. He'd flinched at the sight of me.

'Stop!' he'd pleaded. 'There is nothing more you can say to one which Miss Wishart has not already expressed most intemperately. Quite the most formidable woman I've encountered since Nancy though sadly without either her dress sense or exquisite turn of phrase.'

So I'd contented myself with promising that if he lit a cigarillo inside the walls of Mount Royal ever again, I'd ram them one by one up his scrawny old arse till they came out of his nostrils. He'd still been fretting about his mother of pearl pill-box. I said I'd already let the doctors know he was positive.

'It was a renter in Derby on my way to stay with Debo at Chatsworth,' he'd said. 'Years ago now. Such are the perils of the country-house weekend.'

'Don't worry, Billy,' I'd said. 'We're on your case.'

'I'm not quite sure what that means, my dear,' he'd said, 'but I find it oddly comforting.'

Today he hovered on the fringes of the welcoming party till Vic went and kissed him, asking how he was feeling. Billy then broke down and had to be led into the house by Beau who promised to mix him a Mint Julep as good as any nigger could make.

Big Frankie, untypically, hung back too till Vic sought him out and thanked him for his heroics during the fire. Frankie replied in the faintly robotic way of someone who'd over-rehearsed a speech. He declared that he could never regret having met Vic and that he hoped they would be able to go on being friends.

'Well of course we will,' said Vic, patting him on the cheek.

'Boss, I think Mr d'Orsay should rest now,' Frankie said firmly. He took Vic's hand and joined it with mine, welding them together with his own. Then he took a few steps back, almost bowing as he did so.

Everyone watched as Vic and I walked towards the East Court. Alma, ecstatic at having him back, bolted ahead. My back was dreadful; the day after the fire it had thrown one of its tantrums and refused to go another inch. Lifting Vic on my shoulders hadn't been in its job description. As we hobbled off round the carriage circle, we must have looked like a knackered version of the Start-rite Twins.

*

Elspeth's Lord giveth but also taketh away. Is that the phrase? Think so. Anyway that seems to be the deal, the way He does business. We had been spared death in the fire, but we weren't to be spared it for long.

It was a two-seater plane; the sort they used every day to hop from village to village. She'd been at the controls. Witnesses said it had been climbing into a calm blue sky when the engine noise suddenly changed. It had faltered, floated in the thermals for a moment, then nose-dived a thousand feet into a clump of trees. There had been a short silence before the big bang came and the black smoke began snaking its way up through the lattice of the tree-tops. They said that Ruby and Faisal would have died instantly, but I wondered how they knew that. And at what point exactly? Before the plane hit the trees? As it splintered into a hundred pieces? Or only as they both lay there, broken but maybe just conscious, knowing, if only for a second, what was about to come? I was informed, as delicately as possible, that there wasn't much left of them. Elspeth's Lord had thrown in free cremation on this one.

The call had come at about five in the morning. Faisal's passport, safe back in the camp, had me listed as his next of kin. He'd needed a new one a while back and had asked if I'd minded. He'd thought it right as we were building a life together. I'd said it was cool.

I sat on the edge of the bed for a bit, then trudged upstairs and made some coffee. Vic was softly snoring from the spare room; he and Alma had gone to bed early after his return from the hospital. I took the coffee to my chair in the big window. The lights at the Canary Wharf were winking in the distance, the first reddish-pink flickers of dawn just beginning to rise behind it. The city seemed unusually silent. No planes flew over, no sirens screeched, no stray dogs barked. I sat there soaking up coffee till the birds were all up and the familiar shapes in the gardens started to emerge from the gloom; colour seeping back into the plants and the flowers, the statues on the roof of the Orangery appearing like some semi-spectral chorus-line. I tried to scrub my mind clear of any other image but the one before me, to absorb the play of light and shadow, to calm myself by breathing in its unchanging serenity. But it didn't work. All I could see was the interior of a tiny plane, a piece of scorched and blackened ground and an arching tomb of tropical trees.

I was usually quick to delete redundant numbers from my mobile; I was tidy like that. But by some miracle Khan's Tools & Hardware was still there. I was expecting one of the bigot-uncles but his mother answered. At once she demanded to know if something had happened to Faisal; yesterday had been his usual day for calling her. I heard the panic rising in her throat. And so I found myself telling her that her child was dead. There was a brief silence then a cacophony of dreadful noises the like of which I'd never heard before. It went on and on. I wondered if she'd dropped the phone and forgotten I was there. I hung on in case she spoke again but she didn't. I listened till I couldn't take any more and switched off the phone. When I got up from the chair, I kicked over my coffee mug and sent the contents flying over the Berber rug.

I went back down to my room. I still slept on 'my' side of the bed I'd shared with Faisal; till now something had stopped me rolling over onto what had been his space. But I could still see every contour of his body and conjure up his smell. I felt a sudden sharp longing for that lost landscape, wondering if I'd ever again know the intensity of excitement and satisfaction it had brought me, even if it had never been easy terrain and in the end had proved uninhabitable.

Maybe it was the case, as he'd suggested himself, that he could only really relate to people in hospital beds who thought he was God. Maybe after the intimacy of that, all other human contact came a poor second. I knew he'd tried so hard with me, but it hadn't quite happened. And despite the dutiful devotion to his parents, I doubted it had happened there either. Perhaps fat Ruby was the only one who'd been able to reach him entirely after all. If so, then it was hideously appropriate they'd exploded into infinity side by side. The irony of course was that though, without meaning to, I'd somehow failed him, he'd not entirely failed me. The clam had been shut for so long and he'd managed to prise it open, even just a bit. For that I'd always owe him.

I lay listening to Vic's snoring through the wall. A new and unexpected road had opened to me. A very different road; likely to take me to places I'd never have imagined going, not for a while yet anyway. Less tempestuous places maybe, but maybe where I needed to go. Anyway, there it was. Right now. Waiting. The other day, I'd found Faisal's dog-eared copy of *The Man-Love Manual* abandoned in a drawer. I'd flicked through it to see if it might be any sort of guide in my new situation but there was nothing. I'd binned it, after scribbling down the publisher's email. He needed to be told what a useless pile of shite it had turned out to be. I guess I'll just have to find my own way.

Outside in the East Court, I could hear the day stirring. Big Frankie's front door slammed as he went over to start the breakfasts. Chamber-Laddies trickled under the Clock Tower and swapped endearments. Curtis Powell's trainers scrunched the gravel on their jog towards the Heath.

I desperately wanted to sleep again. I rolled over onto Faisal's side of the bed and dipped in and out of consciousness. For the umpteenth time in the last two hours, I saw the wee plane as it took off from the arid airstrip and climbed into the African sky. But this time it didn't stutter and fall, it kept right on going up into the blue, taking Faisal somewhere he would give the best of himself and be happy in the knowledge of it. I watched it climb higher and higher, get smaller and smaller, till it became just a tiny speck swallowed up by the sun.

Nineteen

'A bit *Brief Encounter* this, isn't it?' she said. But the coffee shop, marooned in a storm of commuters on the concourse of Victoria Station, singularly lacked charm. If Celia Johnson had got grit in her eye here, nobody would've lifted a finger.

'Well it's certainly been brief,' I replied. 'I've only known you're my kid for about two months and now you fuck off.'

She'd not even wanted me to come to the station, but I'd insisted. When they'd announced a half-hour delay on the Gatwick Express, she'd sworn under her breath. I could tell she wanted to get away.

When I'd got the email from Monte Carlo, I'd been stunned, then upset, then resigned. Nevertheless when she'd got back, just after the fire, I'd asked her to think again, told her how much her work was valued, how sad everyone would be to see her go. I'd not even pleaded our personal connection. But she'd claimed that the greater part of her job at Mount Royal, the planning and the planting, was almost done; she'd give me the name of an ace bloke who'd see it all through. Pastures new, she'd laughed; literally and metaphorically.

The guys had clubbed together and given her a bracelet from Asprey's. There had been hugs and kisses on the front steps. Big Frankie had predictably blubbed and Vic had told her she'd always be his rose; despite everything I'd known that he meant it.

'I'm not fucking off, I'm just moving on,' she smiled, one sharp eye on the departure board.

'Do you have the faintest notion what you mean to me?' I asked. There was no time left for inhibitions.

'Probably not,' she said. 'I've never had a child.'

'Neither have I,' I replied. 'It changes everything.'

'You shouldn't let it change anything,' she said, the faintest rasp of testiness in her voice. 'Remember the feng shui thing. You're looking the right way now. Just go for it. Then reposition me a little and we'll all be fine.'

With its tightly crammed tables, the coffee shop wasn't the place for an intimate conversation. On one side sat three schoolboys, each on a mobile talking to somebody else. On the other, a sad-looking woman was reading *Anna Karenina*. Not a good choice for a railway station, you'd have thought. An ugly notion broke into my mind.

'This isn't some sort of twisted revenge is it?' I asked. 'Coming into my life, making me care, then disappearing. Like I did with your mother?'

Dolores ran her hand through her spiky hair and looked at me as if I were mad. Then she laughed and I finally looked into the canyon of disparity between her importance to me and mine to her. It should have stopped me from humbling myself before her, but it didn't.

'Don't go Dolores. People have a habit of doing that to me.'

'There you go again,' she said, the eyes flashing. 'Centre of the universe. Why do you always see it as people leaving you? Mightn't they just be going where they need to go? That's what poor little Faisal was trying to do, wasn't it? Well me too. And anyway, if people do leave you, fuck 'em. You've always got yourself.'

'That's what Vic says,' I replied, then decided to share my terrible secret. 'And I've been seeing a shrink to find out who that is. So far, she's not really told me.'

'Fire the bitch,' said Dolores crisply. 'Anyway I'll tell you who you are. You're the saviour of all those pensioners up there on the hill, you're the son Elspeth never had, you're dear old Vic's dream come true and you're my Dad. Why not just make a start with that and see how you go?'

The slats on the departure board spun round and came to rest as Dolores wanted them to do. The sad woman reading *Anna Karenina* had been finding our conversation much more interesting. As I grabbed the suitcases, I caught her eye.

'She throws herself in front of a train,' I said.

I walked her to the platform.

'I'd planned to take you on a trip you know,' I said. 'Show you the world and all that.'

'Thanks, but I think I should do that for myself,' she replied 'And right now, you need to stay exactly where you are.'

She wrestled a large buff envelope from her shoulder-bag. 'Hey, I meant to give you these; a few preliminary sketches for a memorial to Faisal in the Italian Garden. Vic and the guys asked me if I'd have a think. Nothing fancy. Some nice planting, a bench, a little water feature maybe. Somewhere for the smokers to go for a drag. Have a look; email me your thoughts.'

'I miss him,' I said. 'I'm going to miss you too.'

'Yeah, but we were both false trails,' she replied.

'In some ways maybe, but not entirely,' I said. 'And you come back home whenever you want. Don't forget you're a Blaine now, an Ashridge too.'

'No, I told you before,' she replied, shaking her head. 'I'm just Dolores Potts, the gardener with the funny name.'

'And my daughter.'

'And your daughter,' she said. I couldn't remember her having used that word before. It felt like winning a badge at school or being knighted by the Queen, as I'd dreamed about when Vic had first proposed his crazy idea for Mount Royal. But this was better. This was off the scale.

'I'll text you when I get there,' she said, then *Madonna With A Trowel* picked up her cases and turned away to be vaporized by the crowd. I noticed a few men staring after her, just as I was doing. I wanted to go up to them, tell them who she was and that she was so much more than they would ever see.

I bought *The Times* to read in the taxi home. Among the obituaries was Rory McCulloch, folk-singer and long-ago king of my heart. He'd died of a heart-attack while climbing in the Cairngorms with his lifelong partner Calum. He'd been seventy-one. As the cab crawled up Park Lane, the tears I'd held back at the loss of both Faisal and Dolores, I now shed for him.

*

Elton and David didn't turn up. Fuck 'em, Vic said. They'd probably gone out with Lulu and they'd not be missed anyway. But everybody else came, nearly three hundred of them; as odd a collection as Mount Royal had ever taken under its roof, odder even than Granny's erstwhile gang of unhinged aristos and suburban fascists.

Each of the guys had been allowed ten guests. The people they'd collected in their past lives came to wish them well in their future one. I was introduced to old school chums, bridge partners, accountants, cleaning ladies; occasionally, though not often, a brother, a sister, a godchild even. All these witnesses to whom or what they used to be started to colour in the wispy sketches. As the booze loosened tongues, portraits were painted of dissolute youths and sober achievements, of little peccadilloes and blazing strengths. Harmless confidences were whispered, deep dark secrets tipsily betrayed.

I'd invited the gay establishment too; you never knew when you might need a favour. The intense men and women who ran the charities and pressure groups, the self-righteously 'out' MPs with their overshadowed boyfriends, the actors who'd rejuvenated their careers by barging from the closet better late than never. And every link of the human chain which had helped in the fire had come; some dressed for the occasion, others for the Heath where they'd no doubt round off the evening by force of habit. The Lord Chancellor himself made an appearance; I'd invited the pompous prat as a surprise for Marcus and the smile had been worth it. I'd wondered about asking Ms Prada too till it dawned on me that she must never leave the eau-de-nil room with the droopy azalea. She knew too much.

I was in my full-dress kilt; the Royal Stuart tartan, the black velvet tunic with the jabot of frothing lace, the horsehair sporran, the silver dirk. Robin Bradbury-Ross said I'd made his thong as damp as the cellars at Longleat. Miss Elspeth Wishart was in a nice frock too. This morning at breakfast, Beau had looked at the tweed skirt and mauve cardie and declared that he couldn't go on looking at her without a reduction in his rent. She'd told him to mind his cheek but within an hour she'd been bundled into a taxi heading for Knightsbridge. Tonight, the mad hair had been tamed and highlighted, the eyebrows pruned, the face lightly made-up and the body dressed in a simple but chic black frock with a pearl choker at her neck.

'I feel like a painted hussy,' she said, 'though nobody can accuse me of being after a man in this place.'

It was fine September evening, summer taking one last curtain-call. Mount Royal was floodlit from stem to stern and, as the darkness crept over us, daylight was electronically prolonged across the Italian Garden. A long gazebo covered the terrace under which Big Frankie had organized the food. Out in the Orangery, Beau had set up a sound system and, after supper, took on the job of 'spinning a few platters'. There were many strange dancing partnerships that night; the Archdeacon and the lad from the Heath who liked getting whipped, Marcus Leigh and a Brazilian drag queen, wee Jacob Trevelyan and a big dyke from Rubber Duckies. In the Lionel Ritchie segment, Big Frankie and

Gentleman Jim wrapped themselves round each other like sumo wrestlers. Frankie seemed to be getting over Vic quite nicely now.

When it was nudging midnight, I thought I'd better make a speech. I stopped the music and stood on the top step of the Orangery. Then I realized that what I wanted to say couldn't possibly be spoken; certainly not to this pissed and cheery crowd, not to Elspeth or Vic, maybe not even in the eau-de-nil room. It could only ever be said to myself, alone in the darkness of the night, this extraordinary feeling flooding through me, of never having faced the sunrise with such anticipation. I suddenly remembered the Arab boy from The Catacombs on my forty-fifth birthday. 'It's our time now. You've had yours. Get over it,' he'd spat at me in the drizzling rain. And I'd secretly believed him. But I didn't any more.

'Hello campers, hi-de-hi,' I shouted instead.

'Ho-de-ho,' they yelled back.

So I trotted out a few mundane words appropriate for the occasion and, by telling a lot of filthy jokes that probably weren't, I turned it into a stand-up. Well, I'd never have a bigger audience. I looked out over the ranks of grinning heads, beyond the orange trees in their snow-white tubs, across the gardens and up to the house, pulsing with people and light. It looked both stronger and more beautiful than I'd ever seen it. The motto of Granny's ancestors blazed out from the great stone shield below the pediment.

'Fuck everyone but us,' said the house in Latin.

Not a bad toast really, so I shouted it out to three hundred people and they shouted it back.

At about two in the morning, Beau announced the last dance. Vic took my hand and dragged me into the centre of the Orangery; I'd always been a crap dancer. We'd not said anything to anybody and we'd no intention of doing so. We'd not even said that much to each other. Vic lived in the flat now and that was that. The other day, he'd put a framed photo of himself out on a table; a publicity still taken in his prime, the face as it had been at that time when I'd blotted it out forever. He'd been a handsome bugger once, that bloody smile blazing out. He'd asked me if I was okay with the photo and I'd said that I was. Just yesterday he'd come across my hidden guitar and nagged me till I'd picked it up, red-faced and hesitant, and stumbled into *A Man's A Man For*

A' That'. After a bit, he'd joined in, harmonizing an octave above me. It had sounded pretty good; it really had. Now tonight, as the music started, Vic smiled and slid his arm round my waist.

'Come on, toots,' he said, 'just let me lead you. I'll not hold you too tight. I promise you.'

It was past five when the last guests staggered towards their mini-cabs. I sat beside the Great Fountain with Vic, Elspeth, Big Frankie and a few of my more resilient boys. As the dawn came up, the floodlights faded and died, wrapping us in a sort of morning twilight. Marcus was miffed that the Lord Chancellor had slipped away without saying goodnight and Beau was upset because Angela Lansbury hadn't appeared; she'd been in town and had promised to try. Apart from that, the stragglers all smelt of boozy contentment. Some had taken off their shoes and socks and were dangling their feet in the Great Fountain, dousing themselves in the spray.

Elspeth, mutely proud of her new dress, stayed well back on one of the benches.

'You look great, Miss Wishart,' I said. 'We must buy you a few more like that.'

'You'll do no such thing Rory Blaine,' she replied. 'At my age, one good frock will see me out.'

'Miss Wishart, I've been thinking,' I said, plonking myself down beside her. 'I've not been wearing my Glenlyon uniform for about thirty years now. Do you think I could start calling you Elspeth?'

'Dearie me, I've not been called that by anyone for an awful long time'

'I think perhaps you should be, don't you?'

'Aye, well all right then,' she said hesitantly, as if I'd just suggested we swap underwear. 'But only in private mind, and you will go on thinking of me as Miss Wishart with all the respect that entails.'

Vic and the others were drifting back towards the house. Big Frankie was going to rustle up some coffee and croissants. We said we'd be along in a minute. Elspeth gazed after them.

'You know, Rory Blaine, I used to think that anyone of your persuasion was damaged, like the runt of the litter. But I was wrong about that and I'm sorry.'

'I was wrong too Elspeth,' I replied, the name sitting strangely on my tongue. 'I guess we're only damaged if we allow ourselves to be. Anyway, not many runts in that litter over there.'

'No indeed,' she said, watching the bleary group negotiate the horseshoe staircase up to the terrace. 'A bit rowdy, but not a bad bunch of lads.'

'And just think, you're stuck with them forever. They'll not be leaving you for uni at the end of term.'

'Jings, well, there's a thing.'

Elspeth stood up, dusted down the black dress and studied the Koi carp.

'Her Ladyship would be pleased tonight I'm thinking,' she said.

'With the house maybe,' I replied. 'Hardly with the occupants. The people she hated most.'

'But there was a lot of love in this house once, you told me.'

'Once.'

'Well maybe she'll be glad there is again.'

'You think there is?'

'More as each day passes. Can you not feel it?' said Elspeth. 'Perhaps your grandmother will come to recognize that, wherever she is now.'

'Actually, she's in a cupboard in the flat,' I said.

'You mean the ashes?' said Elspeth, her newly-plucked eyebrows arching in disapproval. 'Shame on you Rory Blaine. Away and get them right this minute.'

And so, as the first pale rays were striking the easterly windows of Mount Royal, I opened Granny's urn and threw handfuls of greyish gravel into the Great Fountain. The spray caught it, toyed with it, then scattered it across the basin, dusting the lily pads and clouding the water. Yet in just a few moments it was clear as crystal again, the fish darting around as if nothing of significance had happened. But it had. That first day I'd met him in the nursing-home, Vic had said that eventually you had to forgive everything.

'There now,' said Elspeth, 'that's better isn't it?'

'Yes,' I replied, 'it is.'

It struck me that I'd not felt angry for weeks now. Not angry at anyone. Not at Faisal or Dolores. Not at Granny. Not even at myself.

I walked Elspeth back to her door. Applause was coming up from the open windows of the kitchens. The King of Croon was treating the breakfasters to a bit of Sondheim. He's been asked to play Desiree Armfeldt's mother in an all-male revival of *A Little Night Music* at the Donmar Warehouse. Legit at last, he'd crowed.

Vic says he doesn't expect me to shag him though he'd not say no to a regular cuddle and perhaps a quick tossing-off on birthdays and Christmases. But no pressure. Only if I can bear it. Anyway, he doesn't feel the urge much now and needs tea and biccies afterwards, like they give to blood donors. Nor does he demand that I never stray. If I want a quick spin on the carousel now and again before it finally flings me into eternal darkness, he says he'll understand. He only asks that I always come back home afterwards. He promises he'll be here till he's carted off in a glass hearse drawn by six plumed horses and I suppose I'll just have to trust him. So that's the plan, for however much time we're going to have together.

The sun was climbing higher now; by the time it sank again the gazebo on the terrace would be folded away, the sound system dismantled, the champagne crates and trestle tables stacked in the caterers' vans. We could shut the front gates, stop being 'Withering Heights' and just get on with it. I went to bed and crashed for a couple of hours. When I got up, I noticed some hairs still dozing on the pillow. I cursed Alma till I remembered that her coat was short and black as coal. The hairs on the pillow were long and golden and glinted prettily in the morning light. Oh fuck.

Ms Prada had left a message on my voicemail. She was back from Madeira now and concerned that I'd cancelled all my future appointments. I called back and left a message on hers. I said that I felt I'd told her all my tales, that I had nothing more to add and that, as Faisal had put it the last time I'd seen him, I thought I'd be okay now. I had come home again and found myself waiting there.